Fugitive Ways

Book Four of The Wielder Series

By David Gosnell

Copyright/License/Notes

Copy editing/proof-reading by Sissy Lynn
Cover design by Damonza, Damonza.com

Find out more at:
thewielder.com or On Facebook at The Wielders Place

Other books in the series:
Betrayal, Book One of the Wielder's Series
The Wielder: Sworn Vengeance
The Wielder: Death Curse
A Mystery and Meal

PREFACE

In the last installment, the story began with Arthur thinking he dodged the death curse laid upon him by Maldgorath, the collector. Arthur had hung up his guns, and taken up with Silithes, his summonling succubus.

Life was good.

But all was not well with the world. The Dzemond, a collective of demon-like races from another dimension developed a gate technology to send "ambassador" teams to Earth. They hoped to build a relationship with an earthen government which will allow for full-scale entry of troops and forces, so they could invade the realm of the Fae. Or so they claim …

The Protectorate, the supernatural governing body of Earth, was focused on bringing down Arthur's brother in revenge, Ahtsag Znuul, whom they felt was the one behind the opening of the dimensional portals. Further exacerbating The Protectorate's zeal to capture or kill Ahtsag Znuul was the disappearance of Karen Redditch. They felt he abducted her and turned her into a blooded servitor – a half Dzemond slave.

In truth, she was with him of her own will, helping to assemble a team of their own, to do what The Protectorate is not – stopping the Dzemond from invading Earth.

Arthur finds out he didn't dodge the curse. It was there all along, trying to kill him and change him into something terrible. As if that wasn't bad enough, Silithes in a fit of indignation allowed herself to face the judgment of the sword, Yayne, and she was made whole, no longer a summonling. Finding herself a true flesh and blood entity and ravenously hungry, she devours an innocent life and goes on the run, a fugitive from justice.

Along the way, Arthur gets pulled into Ahtsag's special forces and learns that Karen was not a blooded servitor, but a full-blooded Dzemond; Baalig specifically. He was also reunited with Silithes, who, according to most that have taken time with her, is "bat-shit crazy" due to sleep deprivation. She turns on Arthur, showing him how powerful she really is.

The story picks up here. Arthur under Silithes' sway, ready to do anything she desires. Like most succubi, she has quite a bit of desire too.

I hope you enjoy this installment, Fugitive Ways.

Chapter 1

She thinks the pleasure will be all hers. She's so wrong. Crawling like a hungry animal, I've arrived at the chair where she sits so invitingly. My gaze moves up to her eyes from the beauty of her womanhood. I know what she likes. I know how she likes it. I kiss the inside of her leg, near her knee.

You don't just dive in there.

Though I really want to. There needs to be some romance, some tension, some buildup to it before going in to take her over the edge. She taught me that.

Silithes. My mistress. My master. My everything.

My trail of kisses follows a meandering path – inside her thigh, on top of her thigh, then back again, leading to her beautiful belly. I start to work my way down when she halts my progress.

"Arthur, stop."

Confusion takes over. I raise my head up. "Did I do something wrong?"

"No. Just stop. It's not what I want now."

She can't mean that. I just haven't started yet. Once I do, she'll be happy. That always makes her happy. I go all in.

Her foot that was over the arm of the chair plants in my chest, stopping me.

"Stop it. Gods, Arthur, when did you become so weak?" she says, punishing me with her accusation.

I look at my mistress, lost for words. I've displeased her. I'm weak and have a useless, fleshy human dick.

"I'm sorry, mistress."

She looks at me critically.

"I don't believe you. I trained you to be better than this."

Training. Yes. I know what she likes. I'll show her.

So I dive back into her soft, sensitive, tasty self with abandon. I'll show her how strong I am.

Or maybe not, as pain shoots up the back of my head as I'm pulled away by the hair.

"Damn it! I said stop. Would you just snap out of it?" she asks.

Confusion fills me.

"Snap out of what, my mistress?"

"You can't be serious. Snap out of it!"

The slap across my face burns. She's really mad at me. I have done something terrible. I bury my head at her feet and beg for forgiveness.

"Sit up!"

I sit up straight.

"Would you just snap out of it?"

The next slap has me seeing stars and my ears ring. I feel my head bounce off the floor. I can't believe the bitch hit me like that.

Crapsticks.

That bitch. The words slip out with the recognition of what's been done to me.

"You damn bitch, you mind-fucked me."

"That's more like it," she purrs back.

I stand up, glaring at her. She's looking confident and relaxed.

"What are you all mad about? I let you go."

"Gee, thanks."

"How did you ever become so weak? I thought I trained you against such things. I guess I'll just have to be more careful with you."

Those statements piss me off. Weak – right? I know what the problem is, so I clue her in:

"Well, Silithes, I think it's that I trusted you. Don't have to worry about that anymore. Want to try me?"

To punctuate, I look her dead in the eyes, daring her to do her worst. We stand there staring at each other when I lose my edge. Not because of Silithes. It's because I'm standing there buck naked. It's hard for me to be intimidating with all my parts hanging out.

"Oh please, Arthur, it's not like I haven't seen it before."

I make a beeline to my undergarments.

"Now, there are matters we have to discuss moving forward, dear," she says. "Things like respect and…"

"Oh, just shut your damn piehole," I spit back at her, interrupting a whole litany of crap I just don't want to hear. "For that matter shut 'em both."

That response gets a momentary look of surprise.

"Here's the thing, before you go all me, me, blah, blah. You need to hear a few things. You never gave me a chance. Not one. You're as bad as Sheyliene – you just ran away and thought the worst. And you believed that damn recording? Knowing who it's from? What the hell? I don't know what kind of mixed-up monsters are running around in that head of yours, but seriously, I'm starting not to care."

Silithes seethes. "You do not talk to me like that. Ever."

"Well, how about this then? Silithes, I've been worried sick about you – no lie. And unlike some people, I just can't turn my emotions on and off. So let me say – just to get it out there… I love you. But right now, I don't like you. Or trust you. At all. So, if you would be so kind, please get the hell out of my room and out of my sight."

The look on her face is shock – for all of half a second before the "yes, you may worship me" face returns.

"Oh, Arthur, that's so cute. You think you can tell me what to do."

"Not telling. Asking. I don't even know you anymore. Have a shred of self-respect and get out. Stand yourself up on those racehorse legs and get stepping."

"If I walk out that door, then I'm walking out forever. You lose me. You lose a succubus," Sil says, daring my request.

So many snarky replies come to mind. Instead, I take a deep breath.

"Just go, please."

She gets up, looking at me with disdain. She walks to the door and stops.

"Last chance. If I go out the door, I go forever."

Silithes being sleep-deprived or not, I'm in no mood to be treated as a toy or a lesser-than.

"Don't let the door hit you."

"Asshole," she hisses, before slamming the door on her way out.

I stand there alone in the realization the Silithes I knew isn't there. Znuul was right – she is batshit crazy. I reel back for a moment and bump against the wall – it's over. Despair turns to anger, and I spin around, punching the wall.

The drywall gives on both sides. Then I realize how lucky I am.

If I hit one of the metal studs, I'd probably have broken my hand.

Chapter 2

Looking at the hole in the wall, I can't help but think that my host is going to be a little upset with me. It was a stupid, juvenile thing to do.

Thank goodness that wall leads to my tiny bathroom/shower area. I imagine my neighbors wouldn't care about that sort of interruption. Fortunately, I'm not without some handyman skills and have patched my share of wallboard. Maybe Znuul won't be as mad when I offer to repair and paint it myself.

I look at the clock on the nightstand that each bunker room has – 3:24 a.m. She couldn't even pick a decent hour.

I go back to looking at my damage. The hole makes me think of my heart. Sure, I'm pissed – but I still care. That has nothing to do with "You lose a succubus." It has everything to do with losing someone I care for. I broke the wall. I broke us up, too. And I'm fixating on drywall because it's the one thing I can fix.

She has to be accountable in this, too. Damn. Nothing good at all came from this encounter or whatever you would call it.

I know someone/something who would be happy at our breakup. Maybe I should congratulate him. I stroll over to where Yayne's box is against the wall and open it.

"Gotta be happy. I know you gotta be happy," I say quietly.

I reach down and pull Yayne from the box and then from the scabbard, his shiny, ever-sharp blade reflecting the light. "Go on… say it. Say 'I told you so.'"

I feel what I think is anxiety; then words ring in my mind, "You are in pain."

"Really? Like I haven't been since you called for whatever it is that you did. Go on, prideful sword; hit me with it," I whisper back, so as not to further disturb any neighbors.

There's a moment of nothingness, which I guess is Yayne thinking. Then words come, "She did release you from servitude."

Now it's my turn for silence. Never in a million years would I expect that response. My mouth starts to move, but nothing comes out because my brain hasn't formed words. I drop Yayne to my side absently.

"Thank you for that," I say quietly.

"It is a difficult time," says the voice in my head.

He's not lying.

I hear my door open and Silithes' voice. "Arthur MacInerny – we're not ending like that."

I turn around rapidly. She takes a step toward me and then stops completely. Her eyes go down to Yayne and back to me. Her face goes blank in terror. Her mouth opens to scream, but nothing comes out. She tries to backpedal, but her feet are moving too fast, and she spills to the ground.

I'm confused and step in to lend her a hand up.

"Nooo!" Silithes screams and scrabbles backward, trapping herself into the corner. She puts her arm up to protect herself followed by a wing.

"To the right," Yayne yells.

I turn in time to be shoved back a good couple of steps by Jxsiga.

"What did you do?" she rails at me, looking down at a now softly glowing Yayne.

"Crap. Nothing," I say, pitching Yayne away so not to seem such a threat.

Jxsiga wastes no more time with me. She's over to Silithes, on her knees, trying to calm her down.

"Hey, baby, it's me. It's okay, nobody's going to hurt you," she says, punctuating it with a stern glance my way. "Come on out; it's me."

Silithes slowly pulls her wing back, and Jxsiga immediately moves inside, wrapping Silithes in a hug and showering her with little kisses, caresses, and "it's all rights."

I can see Silithes is still shaking a bit. Her eye glances at me and quickly looks away. Jxsiga stands and helps Silithes to her feet. Which is an interesting thing, as skinny Jxsiga at five-foot-nothing makes an interesting contrast to a much buxomer and six-foot-something Silithes.

"Come on. I got you," says Jxsiga, leading Silithes away by the hand.

Silithes stops.

"No. I need to stay here. I need to deal with this."

They stand silent, eyes locked for what feels like too long a moment.

Jxsiga is the one to break the moment, turning to me with that baleful glare she does just a little too well and says, "Be nice." She turns back to Silithes, her glare turning to something more adoring. "I'll be in my room if you need me."

Silithes says "Thanks," and follows Jxsiga to the door, closing it after she leaves.

"Sorry about that," she says quietly, while making her way past me to the chair. "Little panic attack there. You see, I've been having these dreams. Two basically. One, we're making love, and I look down and see that I've eaten you all up. That's good for waking up in a sweat."

"Okay," is my safe word, I use it accordingly.

"The other is you, with that damn sword, are out to kill me. You're like some kind of unstoppable terminator monster. When I came in and saw you holding the sword, it was just like out of my dreams." She looks away. "I felt very helpless. Needless to say, I don't sleep much. And when I do, not for long."

Her eyes turn back to me, "I didn't come back here to tell you all that. I, uh… we can't end it like we did."

I don't say a thing. In this case, my poker face is useful – it says "go on."

"Did you mean what you said? Oh gods, of course, you did! You're Arthur Freakin' MacInerny, you don't play those games. I'm sorry. I'm a little off lately."

She looks down, takes a deep breath, and then looks back up. "I'm very glad you still love me. I, yes… I shouldn't have run. I should have come back. I shouldn't have thought the worst. It's just easier to blame you."

"Blame me?"

"I'm not saying it was right. It's just…" She doesn't finish the thought but instead looks away, collecting herself I guess, until I notice that she's very slowly rubbing herself in a most private way.

"Need a moment?"

That statement startles her back to awareness. She pulls her hand away.

"Sorry, the old habits come back with a vengeance. You know how I came about that… quirk, right?"

"It feels good."

That response gets a roll of the eyes.

"Before I was sent to the white for who knows how long, Maldgorath compelled me to self-loathing as torture. There I am in the white, mentally tearing myself apart every second. The only relief was that moment when I wasn't thinking. Eventually, I could just focus on the sensation of the touch and turn my brain off. It stuck."

Damn Maldgorath. All of my summonlings carry deep scars from him, whether they show it more obviously like Sheyliene, or are better at hiding it, like Silithes. I downgrade my posture by sitting down on the edge of the bed and saying, "take your time."

"Thank you. Anyway, I guess it was easier to believe you were thinking all these negative things, of me. Because… because really I was. And I can't do that. I can't let myself do that. I did that for far too long."

Her eyes scan around, and she sees the hole in the wall.

"Mad at me?"

"Yeah. Angry at myself, too. Angry at Yayne. Angry at fate. But the wall was innocent and didn't deserve that."

For the first time since I've seen her, there is a glimmer of a real smile directed at me. But the smile fades away.

"Yes. I understand," she says quietly. "I called you weak. That wasn't fair. Do you want to hear weak? Here I am, living any summonling's dream – to be free and whole again, and all I want is to be in your keep. I'd give all this up in a heartbeat to be back. Isn't that sad? Isn't that weak? You know it's not the pleasure reflection thing, or the insta-feedings I really miss. What I really miss is that feeling when you would walk into the room and were so happy to see me. It's that feeling that I was cherished, not just some concubine to get off with."

She wipes a tear from her eye. "I'll never feel that again. Not the way I did. Our months were the best of my very, very long life. Now just... gone."

All my summonlings are very sensitive to me. She provides me with a reminder of just how much they are.

I realize we're talking – not fighting, not accusing, not posturing. I see the Silithes I know; yeah, she's a bit on the beaten-down side, but it's her. Sil – not whatever face or persona she was putting out there before.

"I'm glad we're finally talking Silithes," I say evenly. "We should pick this up tomorrow after we've had some rest. We both need it."

She shares that foreign look of hers and says, "I understand. Somehow, I don't think I'll be sleeping much. Would you do me a favor? Would you say it again?"

"What?"

"That you love me."

I did put it out there.

"Silithes, I do love you. But we have work to do – on us. You were right. I should have never told The Protectorate anything. And you... you know."

"I do," she tells me quietly, starting to stand.

I stand as well. She steps in toward me, and damn my reflexes, I step back. The look that comes across her face tells me she's hurt.

"Can you trust me? Please."

Those alligator-like eyes of hers are pleading, but there's no telepathic funny business. I check the measures of my mental defenses. This is one of those moments where the decision you make has longstanding repercussions.

"I'll try."

She closes the gap between us without a word and wraps me in a hug, laying her head on my shoulder. I meet that hug. It lingers. It's nice. We release it, and she takes my face into her hands and kisses me softly.

It's nice. It's real.

She takes a step back and says, "Please. I need you to trust me again."

Before I can say a word, she undoes the tie-down on her robe and then removes it entirely.

"Silithes," I say, shaking my head.

She turns around and climbs into my bed. Then she rolls over and holds out her arms.

"Make love to me, Arthur. Please."

Chapter 3

Beijing, China

Cheng Ming sits at the head of the table, surrounded by aides and looks at Zang Jun with a critical eye.

"So you have no idea what this is about – why they would call an emergency meeting with such short notice and why they would insist the president himself attend?"

Zang knows. But he's not telling. In his mind, Cheng is messing everything up. He knows that for a fact because Jneailith told him so. Instead of telling the truth, that he shared with the ambassadors his government's plans for delay and confiscation of their property, he tells Cheng what he was instructed to.

"All I know is they received information that displeased them. From where or what that information is, they would not say. But they insisted on this meeting so as I told you already, they could determine if moving ahead is still possible."

Cheng scrutinizes Zang. He has known Zang for some time. There's something different, a confidence in him.

"So what are your thoughts?" he asks Zang.

Zang takes the measure of Executive Director Ming, a man he has both feared and looked up to. He seems so small and out of touch with his own machinations.

"You mean what do I guess the problem is? Let us be clear, all I can do is guess. But my guess would be somehow they have caught wind of your plan for their cargo."

"Impossible," responds Cheng.

"A guess only. But is it that impossible? Please tell me you have not involved the dock authority? Corruption at the docks is a fact. Leaks at the military are possible, too, even if they have no idea what they are intercepting. Someone sharing a vessel name could be more than enough."

"Yes," says Cheng, "your logic is impeccable."

Cheng will not admit he has indeed involved the dock authorities. The aides say nothing.

The speakerphone intrudes. "The ambassadors have arrived."

"Send them in," Cheng replies. "They are five minutes late," he tells the room after making sure the speakerphone was off.

Moments pass, and Ambassadors E'Fenk and Jneailith enter the room flanked by armed military guards. The guards take their place at the door. The ambassadors approach the table. Their demeanor is stern. Both of them scan the table.

"Any without the highest of clearances should leave now, we will not broker our words or feelings," commands Jneailith.

"Where is the president? We were very clear in his need to attend this meeting," follows E'Fenk.

"You are dealing with me," says Cheng. "The president cannot be bothered with such things. His schedule cannot simply be changed at the whims of others."

"Then we are done," says E'Fenk. "Make good use of the building. We cannot be bothered with liars and schemers."

Jneailith says nothing but shares a hateful smile as they both turn to leave. Approaching the door, the military guards step inward after a signal from Cheng.

"Stand aside," says E'Fenk.

"You are going nowhere. Who do you think you are, commanding the president of the People's Republic of China and his appointed representatives?"

Jneailith turns from the guards to look at Cheng, "So this is the end of diplomacy?"

E'Fenk says, "Enough, stand aside," and attempts to brush the guards aside. His wrist is grabbed by a guard, twisted, and put to a knee in the blink of an eye. The other guard attempts to menace Jneailith, who smiles and looks down at E'Fenk, his arm barred. She looks at the guard holding him.

E'Fenk stands, despite the guard attempting to punish his arm and wrist. He turns his wrist and arm through the guard's best efforts until he is facing him, finally ripping his arm completely from the guard's grasp. E'Fenk grabs the guard's upper arm, but doesn't return the favor; instead, he flings the guard over the conference table, over Cheng Ming and into a large landscape painting on the wall.

The second guard goes for his gun, but Jneailith is on him before he can pull it. Her hand covers his face and slams his head into the thick, ornate door jamb. Then, she flings him by the face to the floor.

Cheng reaches to sound the alarm on the speakerphone but is stopped by E'Fenk's eerily calm words: "Consider your actions, diplomat. We wouldn't want a repeat of Novgorod here in Beijing, would we?"

Jneailith, whose back is still to the room, smiles; the humans are so predictable.

"You think to bring treachery to the Dzemond Collective? We are done. Good luck in future endeavors," he says turning.

Zang Jun jumps up from his chair and yells, "Wait!" Not because he's in panic, but because that is his part in the script. "We are all diplomats here. Surely we can work through our differences?" Zang looks disapprovingly at Cheng then back to E'Fenk, "My superior has had a lapse in judgment with the guards. Please, do not think his actions indicative of the good people of The Republic of China."

Jneailith turns to the room, suppressing her smile at Zang's improvisation.

"Tell us what this is about," Zang says.

Cheng is silent but does signal the guard that was flung across the room to stand down. The guard face down on the floor is motionless.

E'Fenk's eyes are boring into Cheng, telepathically pushing intimidation and thoughts of failure. He turns those eyes to Zang, releasing the telepathy.

"We demanded an audience with the president, as sometimes they are unaware of the treachery of their underlings. It makes sense that the executive-director would not want him here. If you can get him here, we will talk. Otherwise, our dealings have concluded. We are trying to maintain good faith, unlike that one," E'Fenk says, pointing at Cheng.

"I don't have the authority to call the president," says Zang, holding out his hands in apology.

Cheng stands and pulls the speakerphone to himself, then picks up the handset. After punching a few buttons, he says, "You are required in the talks. Matters have gone poorly. Yes. The sooner, the better; they are insistent. Yes." He hangs up the handset and looks at E'Fenk and Jneailith. "He will be here shortly."

The room is dead silent for minutes. E'Fenk and Jneailith stand at attention on either side of the room, hands clasped behind their backs unmoving as statues. Finally, the door opens, and the president enters, flanked by bodyguards.

He turns to E'Fenk, "It is good to meet with you again."

"We will see about that. Please be seated, and we will begin. We have grievances."

The president considers their statement for a moment, then smiles and takes a seat.

"What is all this about?"

E'Fenk removes his jacket and begins unbuttoning his shirt, to curious looks from the room. "This is time for truth," he says, then mutters some words under his breath. His skin begins turning pale, wings and tail explode forth. He bends over, allowing the transformation to his true form to run its course.

Jneailith follows in her re-transformation.

All eyes are wide.

"This is how our people are," says E'Fenk. "The Dzemond is made of other races that are far from our beauty and some closer to it. This is our truth. Now, we must speak of yours. Our intelligence sources – yes, we have a vast network of informers on our payroll – inform us of two disturbing facts. First, the construction of our facility is being deliberately delayed. Second, plans exist for the theft of our cargo aboard the Alexi Maru. What is your knowledge of these things, Mr. President?"

The president looks at E'Fenk, then swivels his chair around to look at his diplomatic team.

"The president knows nothing," says Cheng. "The delay and the consideration of securing your cargo are my doings."

"Shut up, Cheng Ming," says the president. "I take responsibility in these matters. It was the suggestion of my executive director but done by my authority. Matters and plans such as these do not happen without my knowledge."

"Then you admit this treachery?" asks Jneailith.

"Hardly treachery, nothing has been stolen, and stalling is always a common tactic in negotiations. Like your stalling in providing us the weapons and technology promised."

"Well, finally we are speaking plainly," says E'Fenk. "I thought Zang Jun was the only one with heart enough to tell us what we didn't want to hear."

That statement gets the president's attention.

"We had pressured him to get the construction moving at a brisker pace, he told us it will move as fast as The People's Republic of China says it will. We were not very happy with that answer," Jneailith says.

"But we respected it because it was truthful," finishes E'Fenk.

"If you both are going to talk, please stand together, so I do not have to look from one side of the room to the other, please," says the president. "I hope you can respect our concern. There are those within the government who are skeptical of your promises. The forces and weapons you promise us could be used against us."

"Yes, they could," says Jneailith unabashedly.

"Let me reiterate," says E'Fenk. "Our designs are not on this planet or even this realm of interdimensional space. Our goal is the full-fledged invasion and domination of T'uel Faeden, what you would call the realm of the Fae. They have locked their realm so that this is the only entry point."

"And believe me," adds Jneailith, "we have looked."

"They have committed atrocious acts against the Dzemond Collective and will pay. Further, their realm is a bounty of coveted resources that can be found no place else. We will not be denied revenge or the bounties of conquest," says E'Fenk calmly. "This… Earth is of no consequence other than being the only staging area we have for T'uel Faeden's invasion and conquest. The Dzemond are trusting and giving, but once betrayed, once harmed…"

"We show no compassion," finishes Jneailith.

"Threats?" the president asks.

"Facts," Jneailith and E'Fenk say in unison.

"How do we move past our differences?" proclaims Zang, playing his role to a tee. "I have said this before, are we not diplomats? What is it that each side requires? Now that we have no more plans or pretense to hide behind, do we move ahead, or do we part ways?"

All eyes are on Zang.

The president turns back to the ambassadors.

"That is the question. For our part, we ask for nothing new, just the technology, weapons, and assistance in securing China's rule of Earth."

The ambassadors look at each other.

"This is no small matter. Our homeworld is obviously aware of your poor faith and dishonorable actions," Jneailith says, "It may be beyond us. Would you excuse us while we confer privately, Mr. President?"

"Of course."

"Thank you," says E'Fenk.

He takes Jneailith to a corner of the room, and they begin speaking in whispered voices, further muffled by the cover of wings. The wings fold in, and they turn to the room.

"Let us talk," says E'Fenk. "But know that we follow the strict orders of our emperor. His word is our law. As yours is here, Mr. President."

They approach the table and sit down on the same side, causing one of the shell-shocked staffers to scoot away.

"What is it you need to put our dealings back in a place of openness and integrity again, Mr. President?" asks E'Fenk directly.

The president considers these winged, horned demon-like creatures.

"Perhaps we should reconvene tomorrow so everyone might better consider their needs," says Cheng.

E'Fenk casts his gaze on Cheng and then returns his eyes to the president, a smile coming to his face. "We'll go first, then as we know what our needs are. First, we need a scapegoat for the actions of your government to present to our leaders – someone to blame. Both explanation and solution, if you will. Without that, I fear homeworld would not abide a continuance of the relationship after the intelligence they uncovered. Second, we need to be able to trust you."

The president nods his head in consideration. "You have a suggestion for this explanation and solution?"

"Executive director, Cheng Ming of course," says Jneailith. "All breaches of good faith have been at his recommendation to you. He is a deceitful, disingenuous little man that covets power."

"I protest! I serve the people! These things are not to be trusted. They will bring doom to us all!"

"He must be let go," says E'Fenk. "He has no vision. He has no integrity. And he doesn't dare to speak the hard words. So, Mr. President, what are your needs?"

"You cannot…"

"You will be quiet," the president yells at Cheng. "We need the weapons and technology you promised in advance of your people's staging for the other realm's invasion. We need what we have discussed."

It's E'Fenk's turn to nod in consideration.

"We will require a portal to be opened to our homeworld. We have a smaller gate and team to operate it. One that was used to bring us through. We can arrange for a small amount of Dzemond weaponry and armor to come through. Please know we are limited by the size of the gate and time. Time does not flow the same in our realm as yours. There are issues in timing the opening of the gate."

"How many weapons and armor?"

"As many as can be carried by two coming through simultaneously. But once you have deciphered the technology, duplicating them will be easy enough."

The president turns to Cheng, "I'm sorry. Hopefully, you understand. It is for the greater good." He gestures to a bodyguard who whispers into his cuff. The doors burst open, and military guards carry off a protesting Cheng Ming.

"It seems you are in need of an executive director," purrs Jneailith. "May I suggest Zang Jun? I think he has proven himself above all others, wouldn't you agree?"

Chapter 4

The wave of spiritual cleansing washes over me – the last part of my morning curse medication routine. Having showered and cast healing upon myself before, that only leaves my morning talk/prayer with Dorothy, my guardian angel, my wife who passed on.

"Hey, it's me," I say, almost whispering so as not to wake Sil in the bedroom. I've even stuffed last night's t-shirt in the hole to keep the noise down. "Going to be short today, so not to wake somebody up. You know who. You are not forgotten. I still love you."

I realize last night that Sil's "make love to me" was not as much a plea for me to get her off as much as it was a plea for trust. After all, if I was willing to put myself in the place where I would be most vulnerable to her, I had better trust her. Seems like I do.

It was a sweet reunion, hardly what you'd call hot makeup sex. Honestly, I think that's what we both needed – something loving, something meaningful. The only thing that could have been better would be that I could have brought her to climax, too.

The Cubati have what Sil calls the succubus self-defense reflex – a powerful neuromantic pulse that they involuntarily emit when they climax. That pulse strongly encourages whoever their partner is at the time to do the same. As she says, it's hard to take advantage of someone at the moment if you're having a moment, too.

There was none of that; no neuromantic nonsense at all. She didn't even try to keep me in the game. I asked.

She just said, "That was beautiful. I'm tired, honey."

Then she rolls over and falls asleep. I guess not sleeping for a few weeks can do that.

At the time, I didn't think much of it. Now having time to reflect, it leaves me a feeling a little strange. When she was my summonling, it was mutually assured ecstasy. If she came, I did. Thanks to reflectivity, when I did – she did. And if we did together, oh baby.

Her humbling statement of me having a "useless, fleshy, regular, human cock" rings as potentially true. But, even if that is the case, at worst it means a cessation of the physical part of our relationship. Deep down, I know we're okay. That's the most important thing – by far.

I get myself dressed and leave the bathroom. There she is, still asleep, breathing heavy and with a huge stream of drool coming from her mouth forming a little puddle on the bed. Not her most succubussy moment. I still smile.

I make for the door to get some coffee, figuring I'll let her get another hour in – the big briefing is in about two hours. I turn the knob and jump at the words, "Where are you going?"

I turn and see Sil sitting up in the bed, looking wide-eyed at me.

"Getting coffee. Meeting's in two hours. I thought I'd let you rest for another hour."

She relaxes. "Yes, the meeting. She rubs her hands on her face and discovers the drool with a disgusted look. Her eyes turn down to the bed, and no doubt she sees the puddle.

"Please tell me you didn't see that, Arthur."

I don't have to say a word.

"Great... Get me a coffee, too? You know how I like it. I should help Edgar set up the room."

I do know how she likes her coffee.

"One coffee coming up," I say, carefully opening the door so not to share the vision of a naked Sil with everyone.

Not that she'd worry about it.

Breakfast looks yummy. Znuul has manned the griddle and appears to be making mounds of pancakes. I'm guessing Kitten did the eggs and sausages. Most everyone except Arix, Clyde Smith, and Jason Schaumberger are eating outside.

"Oh, good. You survived," says Arix snidely. "How is our fine succubus? Oh, that's right... she's not ours anymore."

Jason looks at Arix like he must be out of his mind. After all, where they come from, what summonling would dare speak to its master so? But, as I'm sure Arix would tell me, given the opportunity, we're not at his homeworld.

"She's good," I say, making my way to the large decanter of coffee.

I pour my cup and am preparing Sil's when I'm interrupted by the voice of the lady herself – Jxsiga.

"Is she all right?"

I don't bother stopping or turning around.

"She's good. Got some sleep."

"Great. She really needed it."

I stir the half-and-half and sugar, not really having much to say to her.

"Well, obviously you were nice. Thank you. You know she loves you," she says.

I pick up the cups and turn around, rather unsure of what angle she is playing. There she is, looking very corporate in a business pantsuit.

"So how much have you two talked?" she asks me. There doesn't appear to be any of the intimidation that she's so good at throwing around.

"Some. If you're wondering about any details regarding you – not yet."

"Oh," she says, looking a little surprised. "Well, I'm glad she decided not to make you her slave. If that counts for anything."

"She had me and let me go. Rather humbling."

She responds with a curious look and says, "Well, at least she let you go. You know she wasn't exactly in the best frame of mind."

Not really wanting to continue the conversation, I say "coffee to deliver," and hold up the cups to emphasize the point.

"You should let her sleep."

She gets Arthur's dead-eyed stare of displeasure.

"I see… carry on," she says, stepping out of my way.

I make my break, but don't get far. Vets is standing in the middle of the huge living area. She intercepts me and stands there looking at me. Analyzing me is more like it.

"Are you… you, my wielder?"

"I am, Vets. Let's get the team together after the briefing. Can you organize that?"

"It shall be done, my Wielder," she says, bowing her head and beating her fist on her chest.

"I've learned all I care to know," proclaims Arix, obviously listening in.

Vets and I consider one another silently.

"I understand," she says. "The sorcerer is not required, I will assemble the others."

I give her a smile and a "thanks."

I bring the coffees to my room. Once inside, I hear the shower stop. I put Sil's coffee on the nightstand and take a seat in the chair to wait.

I don't have to wait for long. Out she comes, fully in human form, with a towel wrapped around her. It covers the upper assets. Asking for more of a regular towel is a bit much to ask. She flashes me a smile and then sees the coffee.

"Oh good. Thank you."

She takes the cup in both hands and takes a huge unladylike slurp, followed by a bigger gulp.

"I swear, I've been living off this stuff," she says as she puts the cup back down and turns in my direction. She takes a couple of steps toward me and settles on the corner of the bed.

"We have some uncomfortable things to talk about," she says, turning away.

It becomes very quiet. Then I see her eyes are closed, and yes, she must be a bit nervous. Knowing a bit more of the why behind that particularly unique habit, I give her a moment, and then I say as gently as I can, "Must be pretty uncomfortable."

She startles a little and begins to apologize, which I promptly cut off.

"If it helps, I can do that for you," I say, hoping to lighten her mood.

"That would be wonderful, but then, we probably wouldn't end up talking about the things we have to," she says with a mischievous smile. "We'd probably miss the briefing, too."

She makes a good point.

"So, what's so terrible, Sil?"

"Not terrible, just awkward. Actually, it's kind of nice. It's about Jxsiga… and me."

Well, there it is. I take a deep breath to still the jealous thoughts, followed by some coffee.

"Well, obviously you two hit it off."

Sil gets up from the bed, walks over to me sitting in the chair, uncrosses my leg, and sits herself down in between my knees on the floor.

"We bonded, Arthur."

"I'd say," is the only light remark that comes to mind.

"Arthur, I'm serious. We did the soul touch. Well, really it was more like a wallow. She's going to be a part of my life forever. I know how you are about the monogamy thing. I can't… at least not now. It wouldn't be right. I can't turn my back on her. I'm not choosing her over you; I just can't turn her away like that."

Soul touch. Yes, I remember that. I remember Sil's life flying before my eyes. I remember that feeling. Bonded. I get it.

Damn.

"Arthur, once you get to know her, you'll really like her. You two have so much in common. She's really beautiful on the inside. And outside, too."

I'm not even sure what my poker face is saying right now. I'm not even sure what I'm thinking.

"Why would you do that? The soul thing? That's so intimate. I'm confused."

"It's a Sisterhood thing we do with ones we have not met. It's not supposed to go as far as a touch – just a glimpse, to make sure that we are of the order and still abiding the ways. It keeps other succubi from posing as Sisters. After all, once we're at soul level, there's very little they can do to protect themselves without our training."

"It's that dangerous?"

"It's the Sisterhood's most advanced and feared training. Once on the inside, we can totally subvert the soul we touch. The Dzemond prize self before all things. The touch can be used to make the target prize us before anything else. They have no idea of anything except that we are their everything. And, no, I did not do that to you before you start wondering."

She knows me so well.

"It's a strange situation, Sil."

"Well, it's going to get a lot stranger," she replies before I can finish my thought. "I made Jex a promise to get to know Fxsigym better. We kind of have a date tonight."

"Well, he seems like a nice enough guy, Sil," I say, figuring there's no harm in getting to know someone.

"Arthur..." she says, putting her arms on my legs and looking at me like she anticipates an explosion. "We will be getting to know one another… carnally. In our way. For whatever reason, it's very important to her. That makes it important to me. Arthur, I already said yes. You don't want me to break my word, do you?"

She knows me. She knows how important my word of honor is to me. But still, I am in no way good with this situation. My face shows it. I lean back and cover my face with my hands and groan.

"I know," she says. "At the time, I didn't think we had a real chance. Well, maybe I wasn't thinking at all. But I am now. Is this a deal breaker? Because I have to warn you – it's going to get even stranger than that eventually."

That statement breaks through the spinning of my mind.

"You can't take care of all my needs, not anymore. My special diet, remember? There will be others I'll need to use for that. I'm not like Jex; I will not half starve myself and just subsist on the blue crap. Not when there's so many who would be eager to share in what I offer."

Damn. She's right. Or is she? I have five summonlings attached to me, which does give me a certain spiritual mass and density. I speak my mind as best I can.

"I can try, right? I mean, I'm not a garden variety human being; I can take it."

She sighs and lays her head on my lap.

"Jex said her Frank insisted, too. Listen, there are two things. First is, I can't have you spending every day exhausted. Second, just... no. When we make love, we make love. I'm not going there with you. The feeding is not romantic for me. It's work-like sort of."

The dreams. It's got to be. I can see how they might make her hesitant. I break eye contact and resume spinning on my thoughts.

"Let's just get through tonight, okay," she says quietly, her hands now kneading my thighs.

The spinning stops. Tonight. The incubus. Her.

"Sil, is this what you want? I mean, I understand keeping your word. Well played with that. I mean... damn, this is awkward."

"This is not a game, Arthur, so we get that straight," she says sternly, the loving, understanding look being replaced with something a bit more on the indignant side. And as for what I want," her expression lightens, "I think I do. It has been a long, long time since I've been with one of my kind. Well, male anyway. There are things we do for each other that other races just can't."

That is a kick in the balls. I can't bring her to climax, and she's going to go at it with a supercharged incubus sex machine that can probably do it with a touch and a whisper. I have to look away from her. Not that it's her I can't stand to look at. Right now, I'm not sure I want her looking into my eyes. No telling what she'll see.

Got to get it together.

Her hand on my chin guides me gently back to her gaze. "I told you it would be awkward. No more running away, right? See, I learn."

"Not sure I'm equipped to deal with all this."

I feel a bit sad at my own truth. To turn her away now, just because... I can't even bring myself to acknowledge it all again.

"Can you try? Please? You and I are about more than just a good time, aren't we?"

I close my eyes to shut out her pleading green eyes.

"Yes. We are."

She's set everything out – addressed it straight on. No running. No hiding. And damn sure no sugarcoating it. I remind myself it's not like the culture she came from has any real monogamy. I stop myself before I go spinning again. The answers are simple: stick with her or bail out and hope to stay friends.

I open my eyes to see she got up and is putting on her robe.

"You know I'll try. I can't make any promises beyond that. I missed you something terrible, Silly. I'm not going to let go at the first bump in the road."

"I'm going to have to kill that fairy," she says, tying off her robe.

"Rather you didn't. Besides, I'd just have to bring her back."

She rolls her eyes and shares the sneer with me. I chuckle.

We come together and share a long hug. It's nice.

"I have to get dressed and help Edgar get the room set; he's been fussing over this meeting for a while."

"Yeah," seems like the right thing to say.

She leaves, and I plop back down in the chair. I remind myself that, despite the content of the news she shared, she took it head-on. Treated me like a real adult.

I'm just not sure how much I feel like one.

Chapter 5

I had to take some time to digest what Sil laid on me. Well, really, I'm still chewing on it. After what feels like too long, I settle on two things.

First, she cares. Cares about me, cares about Jxsiga, too – obviously. I know it wasn't easy for her to put all that out there. But she did and did so honestly.

Second, maybe I shouldn't hold her to a standard I can't hold for myself. I am unwilling to let go of Dorothy. That makes me a cheater. I'm either cheating on Dorothy physically with Sil, or cheating on Sil emotionally with Dorothy.

That is one bitter pill to swallow. Maybe that's why I'm still chewing on it.

I do know it's all too easy for me to overthink things and sabotage myself. So I stand and decide it's best to take in some company and attend the briefing fully in the moment.

Besides, breakfast is the most important meal of the day.

Stepping out of my room, I see that guests have spread out both inside and outside. I also see we have some new faces – three ladies that Znuul, Karen, and Carmella are chatting up. I also note that the red light is flashing.

That means more coming. I see Znuul excuse himself. I make tracks for the fruit and sausage. I'm piling my plate with morning fuel when I feel a tug on my shirt. I look down and see Pffiferil.

"Big girl told me about the meetin' after the meetin'," he says quietly. "I seen the wench, befores she disappeared into the office room. She didn't seem as pissy as yesterday. Ye two make up? Are ye all right?"

Pffif looks a little worse for wear and still smells of liquor. I scan the room for Mark and see him outside with family at one of the picnic tables, his head down on his arms.

"Yeah, Pffif, I am, and I think we did. So, is tequila still awful?"

"Aye, master Arthur. It still be. Had three pours to make sure. Then I needed another three of the rye whiskey just to clear me palate." He looks at me with bleary red eyes.

I make my way over to the sofas, where Clyde Smith, Arix, and Jason are seated. I indicate to Pffif he should follow.

"So, quick trip to the white in order, Mr. Pffiferil?"

"Blessed be!" he says, "Now yer readin' me mind."

I stuff a cube of pineapple in my mouth and run my finger along his sigil. "Return."

Pffiferil ripples away, his clothes falling to the floor.

"Atrocious," says Arix, looking at me shaking his head. "He never learns."

"Au contraire," says Clyde. "He's learned Arthur is his hangover cure."

Clyde is so right.

I finish my plate, then run my finger along his sigil and say, "Come."

A ripple in the air and there stands my buddy in his long red coat, hat, and pointy shoes.

"Thank ye, Master Arthur. I be as right as the sunny day now. Meetin'll go much better."

He scoops up his clothes and makes toward his room.

I'm about to get up when Karred and Carmella join us with the three new arrivals. Two of them are dressed in bohemian/gypsy traditional clothing of a colorful billowing cotton dress, with a shoulderless top. The other is wearing black leather pants and one of those ruffled black renaissance shirts you usually see rocker guys wear.

"Arthur, Clyde, Jason, I'd like to introduce you to the Rosza sisters," says Karred. They are here representing one of the largest neutral covens in Eastern Europe."

"Greetings to you," says the larger one. "I am Dorryta. This is my sister Treszka and my sister Annuska, who fancies herself a rock-star poet."

"I do not fancy it," clarifies Annuska, "I am published."

We exchange greetings.

"Who is that?" asks Treszka of Arix, as Karred chose not to introduce him. I guess he's on her most unpopular list, too.

"I am Arixtumin, A'rl Skaar sorcerer and former high teacher of the Dzemond College of the Arts Arcane."

"He's one of my summonlings," I add, which rankles Arix a bit.

"Yes. A lowly slave to a human."

"Poor Arix," says Carmella.

Karred's eye goes to the front door.

"Carmella, would you continue the introductions? It appears we have another arrival."

Carmella agrees and escorts the sisters out back, where Greg, Bobby, and family are sitting along with Kitten, Vets, Sheyliene, and Hjuul.

I sit back down to address my coffee and take in our newest guest, a rugged-looking man with a closely cropped beard. He seems a bit uneasy with Znuul and Karred. Znuul is trying to work his best smile on the guy.

Clyde waves to the gentlemen.

"That's Jack Maxtor," Clyde says. "North American Were-Pack."

Witches, demons, werewolves, and wizards. What a collection we are.

Znuul and Karred bring him over, and he seems nice enough until he looks outside.

"What is that doing here?" asks Jack, pointing at Lukas.

Then it all comes back to me; Lukas is Skr. Skr is wanted by the Were-Alliance for the kidnapping and rape of one of theirs way back in the day. The nice meet and greet just took a turn for the worse. Jack produces a huge knife from inside his blazer and starts off to the rear porch.

A quick step and a hand on the shoulder from Znuul stop him. Jack wheels around on Znuul with the knife and takes a swipe that Znuul evades.

Silence. Jack is looking at everyone like they're a potential enemy. I can't read Znuul's demeanor from his back. Karred's expression is all surprise.

"We don't fear demons and their beasts. I knew this was a bad idea when I was told to attend," Jack spits out at Znuul.

There's a slight sag in Znuul's shoulders I interpret as exasperation.

"Kill him already," comes the Russian-accented voice of Ahzna Luunz.

That statement gets everyone's attention, especially Jack's. He throws off his jacket, bends down and changes.

It's not like a movie transformation – it's sudden. There's none of the pain or grimacing that comes with the transformations I've seen from others around me.

Jack lets out a warning growl, casting his knife aside.

Carmella comes through the sliding door to the porch like she's on fire.

"Were! What is the meaning of this?"

Jack, now more werewolf than man, turns to her and replies with a series of growls and chuffs.

"I don't care who's here," she says back, like a mother scolding her child, "this is not only a place of diplomacy, but you are a guest in someone's house. Did they not teach you the accepted rules of hospitality?"

Carmella turns to Karen and Znuul, "I am very sorry for this outburst. I assure you it's not of the ordinary."

"Rrrurrr?" Jack replies.

Not ordinary indeed, I think to myself.

"He not only pulled a knife out but attempted to harm my fiancé with it," Karred says, "after we gave the warmest welcome."

Carmella's mouth opens, and she looks at Jack totally aghast.

"Attempting to harm the host... His life is forfeit," says Ahzna, "May I have the pleasure?"

I see both of Znuul's hands reach up to his face, and he is rubbing his temples. Even from behind, I can tell he's getting a bit fed up.

"No," he says, turning his head to Ahzna.

Jack shakes and transforms, in that alarmingly fast way he does, into something that I would say is one-third human. In almost the same motion, he turns to Ahzna.

"Try it, demon!"

Ahzna is not impressed. She just gives him a demure smile and looks back over to Znuul.

"Well, I for one thank you, our host, for your tolerance at this unacceptable behavior," Carmella says, "Were, are you young? I cannot imagine Barrett sending someone without some seasoning on a diplomatic mission."

"No, druidess, I am quite old and…"

"Then you should know better. You embarrass your pack and all were-kind with this violent outburst. Apologize and make yourself presentable."

Jack twitches.

"But, Skr… he killed my great uncle. There must be blood revenge."

"Not here," says Znuul definitively.

"Be a good doggie and go to your master's heel," says Ahzna.

Jack lets out an angry growl and wheels around on Ahzna reverting to a full-on death machine wolf-man hybrid. He lunges at her with all appearances of intending to tear her neck open with his claws.

Most would back off and try to avoid such a thing. Not our little Ms. Russia. She moves in just as quickly, blocking the swing at his bicep, then catches him with a blur of an uppercut. There's a muffled cracking sound. Jack's forward momentum stops, and he flops over backward, feet over his head, falling to the floor and turning human.

Carmella rushes to Jack.

Znuul says, "Damn."

I think everyone else is just stunned.

Ahzna looks around and says, "I have witnesses; it attacked me. And he is not human. Your direction was I cannot hurt any person, meaning human."

"Arthur… here please," says Carmella. "We need healing, his jaw is broken, and I fear his neck, too."

Carmella is a good healer in her own right, especially for the furry woodland creatures – which I would guess Jack somewhat qualifies as. All the same, I rush over, clear my head, and begin reciting the strongest healing spell I know. In between her chanting and my spell, Jack's eyes open up, and he groans.

"Stay down," I whisper to him.

"Listen to your healer," Carmella adds.

"Skr…" he groans.

"Skr is not going anywhere, and you," she says, pointing a finger into his shoulder, "need to remember why it is you are here and have some manners. If these weren't decent beings, they would have been well within their rights to end your life. And I think you realize now, how easy that would be."

Jack does not care for the lesson Carmella just forced upon him but accepts it all the same.

"Yes, I lost my composure. I loved my great uncle dearly… But, I will behave diplomatically. However, that thing is still going to know of me."

"Him knowing of you is fine. Pulling out a knife, attacking our host and others is not," Carmella says sternly.

We stand, and I see that all eyes are upon us – well, really, on Jack.

Jack looks at Ahzna, "Nice, whatever that hidden weapon was you hit me with."

"Pathetic," Ahzna says, before turning for the food warmers.

In all this commotion, I hadn't noticed the blinking red light.

"Z – The light," I say to let him know.

He turns to me and starts to say "thanks," but is stopped by another commotion taking place outside.

Apparently, the witches have a beef with Jxsiga and Paul.

"Darling, would you mind tending to that, while I get the door?" I hear Znuul ask Karred softly. "I think I need to recharge my patience."

Chapter 6

The newest visitor was Sheriff Robert. I escorted him in along with Znuul. Way too much drama going on. I never have found out what the witch's bitching was about. I'm not going to worry about it either.

I plan to head to the office and get a good seat for the show. Simple enough, and after all, it's supposed to start up in another fifteen. I call out for Hjuul, and after a bit, he trots to my side.

We step into the office to see banks of fold-up chairs have been set up with little notepads on all of them. Percy and Edgar are conferring over a tablet computer. Edgar is first to notice me.

"Good morning, Arthur, and you, too, Hjuul."

"Hey, Mr. Arthur," adds Percy.

All the screens turn on and show a computer desktop.

"That get it?" comes Sil's voice.

"Yes ma'am, Miss Silithes," Percy replies.

Sil stands up from behind the desk, straightens her tight one-piece, curve-hugging knee-high, sleeveless dress. It's one of the illusion dresses that accent curves – like she needs that. She has her hair in a neat bun with a couple of chopsticks holding it in place – and black librarian glasses.

Her vision is beyond perfect. She does not need specs. Though she so owns the sexy secretary thing.

"Would you bring that box over there to me and open it up?" she asks.

Might as well be useful.

After I'm through with Sil's chore. Edgar suggests, "Grab a good chair, Arthur. The room will be filling up soon," pointing to one up at the front.

I will. But my idea of a good chair is more to the back, so I can watch everyone in the room as well as the presentation.

Edgar responds to my moving to the back of the room with, "Don't fear, Arthur; there won't be a test." I move the notepad and scribble my name at the top to mark it as mine.

All the screens have the same graphic up on them. It reads "Invasion Briefing."

That's an attention grabber.

What else grabs my attention is Paul, sticking his head in the room and pointing at me like, "there you are."

He walks over, gives Hjuul a moment of regard, then sits down next to me.

"Been looking for you. I suppose Silithes brought you up to speed with tonight's arrangements. I hope that's not going to be a problem for you. I really enjoyed hanging out with you last night."

I glance at Sil, who is still diligently entering notes from the little boxes that come from the big box I just brought to her. I know she probably hears every word.

"Yeah, Paul... Not happy about it. So, is that how your kind get to know one another – really?"

"No. I mean, eventually, it leads to that. Everything always leads to that or... Listen, I'm not sure why Jex is so adamant that we break down all the barriers tonight. I'd kind of like to be courted first."

I'm pretty sure he was trying to be humorous. That still doesn't mean I have to find it funny. I don't even try to hide my lack of appreciation, not that I'm any good at hiding my thoughts.

"Right," says Paul, taking a cue from my silence. "Well, for whatever reason, it's important to Jexi, so that makes it important to me, too. Not my idea, Arthur. But, as they say on the poker circuit, I'm all in."

Best to keep my mouth shut. That's the smart play. Sil is listening in. Paul is at least making an effort. Of course, the smart play isn't always my forte.

"Well, glad to know you're committed to the cause there, Paul. You just make sure to take good care of her and do all those things a simple human being can't."

"Yeah... right. Can't help you're just a human and I'm Cubati. Tell you what, I bet I can talk Jexi into getting to know you a little better."

"And you would be okay with that? Oh, wait ... just a human. Yeah, that's no competition."

His eyes widened; it was like a light bulb went off inside his head.

"Well, here's the thing," he says, "I would be okay with it if she'd let her damn hair down and enjoy herself. She's actually more likely to just go through the motions and be a good hostess. She's just become very selective of who she allows herself to let go and enjoy the moment with. But she's entitled to her ways."

"Hostess?" I say, more asking because those must be some kind of freaky parties. "And just so I'm clear, what you're saying is she'd probably be okay having sex with me, she just wouldn't enjoy it."

"Right – you got it. And another thing, before I forget. You and I are not in competition. In competition, there's a loser. Nobody has to lose, I'm not hoping to win her hand in marriage."

"Easy for you to say, but thanks for saying it all the same. Listen, Paul, this is way out of my comfort zone. This may just be another day in the office for you, but not for me. I'm trying to deal with it, and that's all I can promise. I am entitled to my ways, too."

Paul rises, understanding I've heard all I care to about this topic.

"Yeah, Arthur. I hope we get past this… sometime."

He gives me a nod and turns to leave. I reach down to Hjuul to scratch his neck. I look up at Sil, and she looks back at me with a wink and a halfish smile. Turning, she joins Edgar and Percy to talk about some presentation nuance.

∴

The room fills slowly, with each group staking out their own little territory. Sil, Jxsiga, and Paul sit on one side of the room. The witches sit across on the other side. Jack puts himself at the front in what I am guessing is some Alpha claiming territory thing. Lukas, Bobby, and all, give him a wide berth. Me, I'm surrounded by my summonling crew.

"Do you think they'll have popcorn?" asks Sheyliene.

"It's not that kind of a show," Arix says.

Everybody now in, Znuul closes the office door and walks to the front of the office.

"I'm not one for platitudes. Everyone here knows me or has at least met me. Everyone here has met Edgar Tinkerman. For those who may be out of the loop, Edgar no longer is involved with the guild he founded or The Protectorate. I am convinced that The Protectorate is trying to suppress the information we are sharing with you today. Edgar – go."

Edgar stands and addresses the room.

"Well, I guess I should get to the point. But regardless, many of you here knew of me as the head of the Techno-Mage Guild affiliated with The Protectorate. Prior to that, I was a mage of the inner ring with the Magerium. I have been involved in the fight to protect our realm for well in excess of one hundred sixty years. Even against some in this very room – which by the way I can tell you from firsthand experience, do not pick a fight with the twins."

He nods to Jxsiga and Paul.

Annuska pipes up, "The incubus knows better than to trifle with gypsy witches."

Paul says nothing. The room goes quiet.

"A lesson we should all learn from," Edgar says, "You have all been provided with a notepad and pen for questions. I would prefer we hold onto said questions until the end of this presentation. You will be given a copy of the full presentation when we conclude. First, a bit of background. Long, long ago, the Dzemond discovered and invaded the realm known as T'uel Faeden. The Fae were able to drive them out and lock their particular realm away where it can only be accessed from one other dimension in the multiverse – our fair Earthen realm. But the Fae weren't done. They created a magical lock to our realm that requires a human lifeblood sacrifice for any of another realm to enter ours, other than those from T'uel Faeden. That sacrifice has to be given in free will."

A chart fills the screen showing a series of interconnected circles, one labeled Earth and the others labeled Helterezen and T'uel Faeden. They intersect with Earth, but not each other.

"Just so I'm clear," says Sheriff Robert, "someone had to give up their lives for all of you to even be here?"

"Some of us are human, too, simpleton," Annuska says.

"Cost seven to get me across," says Znuul. "And that was when magic was strong."

"Influencing the ability to open such gates is the prevailing overall psychic energy that mankind emits. Some call this the balance. When the balance is more suited to the energy of the realm incoming, the opening of the gates is easier and can stay open longer, accommodate heavier traffic, etc. Needless to say, with the recent worldwide atrocities over whose god is the true god, our fair balance is not in the best stead."

Edgar signals to Percy and the screens cut to a photo of where we killed Maldgorath in Houston, the warehouse for M-Biologicals.

"Fortunately, due to the combined efforts of many in this room, the instigator of that unrest was put down for good here in Houston, Texas, USA. In addition to one very nasty enemy removed from our midst, we gained access to his company's network and inventory. What we found was disturbing."

The screen changes to a stainless steel glyph on a desk.

"This is a Dzemond glyph used with the blood gates. There are eighteen that are used to dial in a realm. Our cleanup teams found four. Percy Baumgarter, the man pushing the buttons over there, discovered this schematic in their network."

The screen changes to a blueprint of sorts that is very hard to discern. It looks like a birdcage.

"Further research and a little hacking into other companies discovered these plans."

Another schematic pops up.

Then another that is more recognizable – an arch with the Dzemond glyphs.

"This is our rendering of the whole contraption."

The image changes to a coffin-like thing, connected to a box, control panel, and the gate.

"Modern technology is not working in our favor," Edgar says, gesturing to Percy as the coffin-like thing comes up in greater detail. "This is where a blood donor is attached to the device. The schematics indicate both input mechanisms and output mechanisms. The output pumps the donor's blood into nozzles on the gate, creating the thin wall of blood required. The input puts blood, plasma, or saline back into the donor. The first implication is simple: Nobody has to die anymore. Bribes are now a viable means of creating a freewill acceptance for the sacrifice of their blood. But this is where it becomes disturbing. The technology is scalar.

The image changes to a single pod and small gate in the corner. More pods appear, and the gate gets larger with each one.

"There is the very real potential for the creation of an army-sized portal. In fact, they were working on it," Edgar says.

He lets the room take that in before saying, "Carmella, there are those of your guild who are quite sensitive to such things. How many potential breaches of our world have been reported?"

Carmella stands and faces the room, "We have reported a total of four to The Protectorate. One of which is corroborated by her appearance," she says, pointing at Ahzna.

"Goddamn," says Bobby.

Znuul stands and walks up next to Edgar. "We believe two came through each opening. A pair of ambassadors. Either Cubati, like our friends there, or Tseretsen, like Mr. Newfield."

"Or both," adds Silithes. "A Tseretsen/Cubati team make for formidable negotiators."

"True," replies Znuul. "Ahzna, get your armor on. We need to show and tell. Anything else, Mr. Tinkerman?"

"Unfortunately, no. I wish I could tell you where they are now."

Znuul turns back to the room, "So you can see, you were not asked here idly. We need to…"

"I see this is a matter for The Protectorate," says Annuska over the top of Znuul. "Our coven has been neutral for hundreds of years, respected by Protectorate and Gratia Potentia alike. What you ask of us is unreasonable, especially given that you include the likes of Fxsigym and Jxsiga in your ranks."

That statement gets Jack standing.

"Yes, there are issues. If you wish to count on the power of the Were Alliance, the first thing we will ask is you either give us Skr, or his head."

"No," says Znuul rather finally. "Both of you are missing the point. My homeworld, our homeworld," Znuul says, looking to Lukas and Paul then back to Jack and the sisters, "if allowed to bring forces here in scale, will bring this fine place we call home to its knees and usher mankind into the cruelest of slavery. They will not respect any neutrality."

Carmella, ever the diplomat, stands and says, "Obviously some healing needs to happen here. But we cannot lose sight of the real issue, our Earth stands to be raped and pillaged by Dzemond invaders. After this meeting, I insist all of you talk to one another. Jack, you especially – the story I heard is not like the story the pack tells. And you, Paul, make some time to address your wrongdoings and what you have learned from them."

"We do not need to hear such things," says Annuska.

"Shut your mouth," says Dorryta, "You do not speak for the coven alone. And I, for one, wish to hear such things."

Annuska looks both shocked and embarrassed. She does as she's told.

The office doors open again and there stands the beast of Novgorod. Ahzna has forsaken any attempt at a human appearance. She's covered in some kind of shiny black coating, over everything except her face. It's heavier at the vital areas and carries a subtle patterning. She walks over standing next to Znuul and Edgar.

"So, do you want I show them what this can do?" she says in her Russian-tinged accent.

"Not here," says Znuul to her. "But we'll give a brief demonstration of some basic capabilities for those who are not familiar with our nanite-based technologies. You see, the Dzemond are more than just strength and magic, they are a highly technologically advanced race also. Ahzna, please put the suit into strength mode; then give me your arm."

She hands her arm over, and Znuul takes her by the wrist and starts to bend it in a harmful way.

"You will note, that the nanites have built up at this area to buttress against me overpowering her wrist," he says, pointing to a ridge that has appeared at her hand and wrist. He guides her around so the room may note, then releases the hold.

"Now, please note that the accumulation of nanites has receded."

"The suit is driven by an AI, subjugated to the wearer through a neural link. It is stronger than steel and capable of assembling into some complex and simple weapons. By complex, I mean energy weapons, like what you saw in Novgorod."

The top of Ahzna's forearms expands, revealing the weapons she used in her fight with Znuul and others.

"Let's all step outside, and Ahzna will demonstrate."

"I am not a trained hound for your amusement," says Ahzna to Znuul.

"No," says Karred, "you are his will-bound slave. You can either get moving and do as he says or let everyone watch as he dictates his will upon you."

She gets to stepping, after throwing a seriously venomous look Karred's way.

We all get up and follow Ahzna outdoors. I take place at the rear again, then jump as my rear end is pinched. Sil walks by like nothing ever happened but does turn around to give me a smile and a wink after catching up with Paul and Jxsiga.

"So what do I destroy?" asks Ahzna.

"Just aim for the ground," replies Znuul.

She holds her arm out. I see the raised area on her forearm glow and hear a "voomph."

The ground explodes about twelve feet in front of her, leaving a small crater.

The box-like structure on her forearm recedes.

"Ahzna, show them the hand-to-hand weapons," Znuul says.

She gives him a nonplussed look, then makes a fist, spikes protrude from the knuckles. She brings her elbow up, and a blade appears off it.

"Ahzna, go over some of the more common weapons we are likely to encounter during a conflict with Dzemond shock troops."

"Plasma sword is a common issue; zero-point grenades create gravity singularities; sonic disruption devices cause both pain and intestinal failure in some lesser species; energy pulse weapons similar to what you just witnessed from my suit are common, only more powerful; and gravity guns are a staple of the Baalig forces because of their ability to convert local resources to ammunition."

"Explain the gravity rifle, please. I am not familiar with the concept," Edgar requests.

"Of course you are not," says Ahzna. "The rifle takes a relatively small projectile and increases its gravimetric density through energy transfer. Then it is projected by a controlled, stronger burst of anti-gravity at supersonic speeds. It is not a fast-shooting weapon like the energy weapons, but is self-charging, able to create stores of projectiles from local materials and provides excellent stopping power."

"Imagine if you will a marble with the gravimetric density of a twenty-pound lead ball, moving at high-powered bullet speeds," says Znuul. "It takes approximately two seconds to charge a round."

"Closer to a second now," offers Ahzna.

"Holy shit," Sheriff Robert says.

"Nothing holy about it," Jack the werewolf adds.

"Okay everybody," comes Silithes' voice from behind us. She's standing atop one of the picnic tables, looking happy to be the center of attention. "Show and tell is now over. We need to break out into groups. Group one will discuss current assets and limitations we have. Group two is brainstorming how we can increase our assets. Group three is brainstorming problems we will face. After you've participated in all groups, we have a sign-out for secure phones and a ghosted bulletin board. Group one meets in the office, two in the living area, and three out here. Percy over by the door has a bag with ones, twos, and threes marked on chips. That will establish what group you're in. All random."

"What if we have someone in our group we cannot work with?" asks Jack.

"Yes," adds Annuska.

"We are counting on everyone here realizing the issue is greater than personal differences," says Sil matter-of-factly to Jack. "If you feel you do not have the professionalism to participate, then please don't. It's that simple."

"We're all here for love of Mother Earth, our home," adds Carmella, "Let us not forget that, please. After all this is done, I will take time with each party to help the healing begin."

"Somebody put a sock in Miss Love and Togetherness' mouth, please," says Annuska much to the dismay of both of her sisters. "And whose brilliant idea was it to let this bimbo speak?"

"That would be mine," says Edgar. "I thought it appropriate as she came up with the idea of the groups to begin with."

"You should think with your larger head, old man," she spews back at him, resulting in cringes by her sisters.

I have to laugh. Edgar does not fancy women; that's not his thing.

Chapter 7

Everyone opted to act professionally. Sil set each group's transition on a forty-five-minute timer with a fifteen-minute refreshment break between each. There was good information shared and taken down by a dedicated monitor compiling the input – namely Edgar, Znuul, and Karred for each breakout session accordingly.

Healing of past wounds was approached as Carmella had suggested. The sisters, except Annuska, all hugged Paul goodbye. Jack actually shook Lukas' hand as he parted with Bobby.

Bobby, Lukas and family, Jack, Carmella, Johnny, and the sisters left almost immediately.

All in all, a rather productive day I think.

Now I find myself in the garage surrounded by my summonlings, less Arix. After all, he knows everything he needs to. With all eyes upon me, I address the burning question.

"Sil and I are good. There's no threat or whatever anymore."

The door to the garage opens and in walks Sil, "Hey, everybody," she exclaims. "It's good to see all of you again. Listen, I wasn't exactly in the right frame of mind before, I… I wasn't seeing things clearly. But I am now and want all of you to know I would never harm Arthur."

She wraps her arm around my waist and kisses my cheek, too.

I guess our "never a public display of affection" thing is out the window now.

"Well, a good thing that is for ye," says Pffif with no nonsense whatsoever.

"I suppose it is, Pffiferil," Sil says seriously. "After all, now when I die, it's a true death. And you know, I could never raise my hand against any of you. You're like family."

Shey was first to break ranks with a hug and a, "you are, too!"

Sil is now off my hip because Sheyliene is on hers.

"So, must be pretty nice bein' all yerself again, eh wench," Pffiferil says.

"Actually it's kind of scary. I've been a summonling so long, I'm not sure that I care for facing a true death. That and it was so nice being close to Arthur. All of you know what I mean – not just… that. My needs were more than met. I… I actually wish I was back in with you all," she says, looking over to me.

"So if ye feel that way, why ye leavin' dead men at our door and threatin' our good master Arthur."

She lets go of Sheyliene and bends down to a knee, to look Pffif in the eye.

"I also carry some very deep scars from our past master. I wasn't thinking right. But I'm better now. All of you know about scars. None of us will ever be as we were before."

"Wells, as long as you aren't the hell-bitch ye used to be before he punished ye, I'm thinkin' it okay. Had us 'fraid you was back – in the bad way."

I see her stand but can't make out her face.

"Yes, Mr. Pffiferil, I can understand where you are coming from. I still love you; you drunkard of a leprechaun."

"See," exclaims Sheyliene, "She still has love in her heart – for all of us!"

"And maybe a few more, too," I add, before I think better of it.

But Sil doesn't shy from the statement, or even cast a look of displeasure as she turns around.

"Yes, I've found some others," she says, "But I learned from Jerry, Marge, and all of you that the heart can grow. Just because I find feelings for others doesn't mean I have to feel less for any of you."

"You mean that succu-bitch that chewed me up in the airplane, don't you? You are not allowed to see her. She's a bad influence. She does not have love in her heart," Sheyliene says with a stern look and fists on her hips.

"But she does have love in her heart, my little Sheyliene," purrs Sil back to her.

"And I'm thinkin' a fire down below judgin' on the sounds coming from yer rooms all yesterday."

"Yes, we both have a bit of the fire, Mister Pffiferil. But you already knew that," Sil says, sliding her arm back around my waist.

"I still don't approve," Sheyliene says.

"Well, Sil is free to do as she pleases and you are free to disapprove," I say, hoping to mollify the situation.

"I am pleased we do not have to battle," says Vets from her at-attention pose. "You are formidable."

"Me too, Vetsy. You are formidable also, you know."

That compliment is as least as well met as putting extra food on Vets' plate, based on the very short nod she gave in response. Any reaction is a huge reaction from the big girl.

The door to the garage flings open, followed by an exuberant Jxsiga.

"Silithes, we need to borrow you for a moment. Someone's done something very nice, and I know you'd want to say thank you."

"Oh," is Sil's curious response. She looks around at the gang, then to me, "Well, we all like nice things and giving thanks is always polite." She turns back around to the gang. "I meant every word. Gotta go."

She turns to leave, and Sheyliene lets her thoughts be known.

"That succu-slut is going to turn your heart black again. She eats people!"

Sil stops and gives Sheyliene a bit of the pouty lower lip.

Jxsiga, to my relief, doesn't take the bait and fan the flames of Sheyliene's resentment. She does say, "Sorry for the interruption," before escorting Silithes out and calmly closing the door.

Sheyliene is furious, her fists clenched into little balls of fury.

"Someday I am going to smash that tiny little bitch's teeth down her throat and hang her from a tree by her spine!"

Nobody is quite sure how to respond, other than look at each other.

She turns around to us, "She's going to steal Silly away from Arthur using succubus tricks and turn Silly back into a soulless lust monster just like she is! Arthur's just human and can't do all those… diiirty things they do."

She just stops and stands there blinking for a moment, then fires right back up.

"Who's with me? Let's kill the demon scum right now before she corrupts Silly!"

"No" is my simple answer to that rally. "Nobody is killing anybody. Especially when we are guests in another's house."

"What he be sayin', ye daft pixie."

"It would be unwise," says Vets to all our surprise.

Silence. Sheyliene appears to be crushed we aren't a full-blown lynch mob.

"Arthur can't do what they can do. It's not fair."

That sort of hits me in the gut. Tonight Sil returns to her kind, or at least the male of her kind. I remember Paul telling me it's not a competition. Easy for him to say. He doesn't have a useless, fleshy… no, not going there again.

By this time I see, I'm getting curious looks from the gang, most likely due to my reaction to Shey's comment.

"Yeah guys, it's not fair. But, life's not always fair either. You just have to play the hand you're dealt sometimes," I say.

"Aye, true words there, Master Arthur," says Pffif.

Hjuul presses against my leg, letting me know he's there, too. I reach down and give him a good rub. "Come on guy," I tell him, "Let's go see what's so nice for Sil, eh?"

I get a chuff from my hellhound in agreement.

"Thanks, all of you. All of this craziness will work itself out," I say before Hjuul and I head back inside.

Once inside, I see Sil and Paul walking away hand in hand down the hall off the kitchen that leads to Znuul's room. Znuul, Karred, Kitten, and Jxsiga are talking. Jxsiga hugs Znuul, then turns to hug Karred, who meets the hug but I can tell does not have her heart in it.

Karred sees me coming, and the look she gives tells me something's up. I smile at her and keep moving.

"So, what's the good news," I say to break the ice.

"Ahtsag and Karred were kind enough to lend the master suite to Silithes and Fex for their get-together tonight," says a bubbly Jxsiga.

"Well, it is the most soundproofed room in the place and off the beaten path," says Znuul. "And thank you again for the heads-up, Lady Jxsiga. The other guests will appreciate not having to listen to all… that."

"Just courtesy, and please call me Jex."

"Oh, yeah. That noise." I say absently.

"Yes, that noise," says Jxsiga. "Paul told me how thin the walls are on the small rooms. How embarrassing… I thought Sil and I were kind of quiet."

"Well, thanks again for the heads-up," says Znuul, putting his hand on my shoulder. "I know for a fact this one does not want to hear any of it."

That is so true.

"Thank you again," Jxsiga says to them an endearing look in her eye, "And you, little Kitten, enjoy having them in your room tonight."

Kitten latches onto Znuul's side and says, "I will. Thank you."

Jxsiga turns to me with a polite bowing of her head and says, "Arthur."

Then she leaves us.

"Figured it was for the best, Arthur. Besides you know… Cubati," says Znuul.

Like that's a real explanation of all this nonsense.

"It's nothing serious, Arthur," Znuul continues, "Just fun and games. You have to take it in reference to where we came from. I think whoever invented the term casual sex had to be Cubati, or under their influence."

"I want fun and games," adds Kitten, squeezing Znuul just a little more.

"That's all you ever want, you little nympho," Karred says.

Like a shot, Kitten is on Karred's waist.

"I like what I like."

Karred's somewhat dour face lightens at Kitten's hug, and she says, "me too."

"Another disaster averted," says Znuul, walking off to the kitchen.

I give Karred and Kitten the best smile I can muster, which probably isn't much of a smile.

"See you at dinner."

I give Hjuul a pat and turn to make tracks to my room. I'm stopped short by Karred, who ushers me over to the front door. We step outside.

"I'm so sorry. Ahtsag had already promised the room, and when he said it's the least we can do for Karred's best friend, I was trapped. I just don't understand this nonsense. If she cares for you like she says she does, she wouldn't be throwing herself at that... incubus."

"It's all right, Karred. I knew this was going to happen tonight."

Karred is taken aback. "And you are good with it?"

"Not really... but trying. Would be a shame to patch it up, just to break it up again."

"Well, I don't understand any of it. I may have this new body, but inside I'm still very human. I don't care how good it's supposed to be for them, at some point your heart comes before your twat. If anyone should be using our room with her — it's you."

Not knowing what to say to that I just smile and say, "Yeah, maybe."

I'm wrapped in a hug and told, "I am so sorry. At least you won't have to hear any of it."

"True, let's go back in."

Upon entering, the smell of the barbecue being reheated greets me and reminds me that dinner is rapidly approaching. Ahzna has come back out. Edgar's sitting at the kitchen's peninsula next to Percy and Jxsiga. My group is in the living room watching something on the television with Jason and Clyde.

No sign of Silithes.

I'm guessing the date has officially begun.

Chapter 8

I chose to be fashionably late to dinner and forced myself to eat something. I ate with my gang as Jxsiga appears to be attached to Znuul and Karred.

And I've really about had enough of "The Lady."

Now done with dinner, part of me wants to slick back my hair, put on some thick eyeliner, a black turtleneck shirt, and declare to the room, "I will be outside wrestling with the depths of my burning emotions. Do not disturb me."

But I don't own a turtleneck, and I have no idea how to apply eyeliner. So, I opt for taking my disposable dinnerware to the kitchen garbage and sneaking out to the back porch to enjoy the night and some solitude. Before I can slip away, I see Vets joins me in the kitchen.

"What do you require, my Wielder?"

"Just some peace and quiet for now, Vets. Can you pass it along to the group to not bother me, unless they really need to? Discreetly, please."

"Your will be done, my Wielder. Meditation is a good choice. Problems are best addressed with a clear mind."

I tell her "thanks," and we leave the kitchen. In the hallway from the kitchen, we hear a muffled something coming from behind the huge red doors that lead to Znuul's and Karred's chambers.

"Strange," Vets says to me, "it sounds like the incubus is the one chained to a breeding block. The Cubati are strange creatures indeed."

Her ears are much better than mine. I really don't care to discuss it, so I nod in agreement and start to go outside, stopping. "Hey Vets, before you pass the word around, would you mind bringing me my tablet and notepad?"

∴

The night is quiet, broken only by the occasional laughter from inside. I've taken one of the sun chaises and set it next to a picnic table, so I'd have a place to set the tablet as I write notes. While I may appear sullen and withdrawn, I am at least productive.

Oh, who am I kidding? I am sullen and withdrawn, but I am working the problem of where our Dzemond invaders may be. My initial thinking has me looking into areas of poverty as those people might respond best to bribes of wealth.

Damn, that's a longer list than I would have thought.

I hear the sliding door to the bunker open and shut. I guess someone had to come to check on me. I don't bother turning to look, instead focusing on my notations about Congo.

"You look troubled," says Jxsiga, now standing next to me, "You should wrap those troubles in dreams."

I look up from my pad to see her standing there in a yellow sundress. She takes the pleats at her knees and waves them back and forth in a half-hearted can-can like display and gives me a coy look.

Great.

"Yes, troubled by these damn Dzemond invaders."

"Ahh, yes," she says, now walking around behind me, "Do you mean the ambassador teams or the succubus invading your personal space?" She comes around to my other side and climbs up the picnic bench, sitting on the table portion looking down on me with an inquisitive look on her face.

"Might not want to sit there, I could see up your dress if you're not careful."

Last time we spoke at length, on the airplane, she was very clear that she did not want me peering up her dress.

"I'll be careful," she says, making sure to tuck her dress between her legs. "Besides, all you'll see are panties," she says with a little tease to her voice.

Wonderful. Looks like I get to find out how succubus-resistant I've really become.

"Bet you can't guess what kind of panties I wear," she says, the little tease becoming a full-on flirt.

Knowing succubi as I do, I assume it's a trick question – she's probably not wearing any and using the quiz as an opportunity to flash me the goods.

"I'd rather not. Besides, you're probably not wearing any at all."

Flirtatious turns irritated.

"I'm not your enemy, Arthur. And I always wear undergarments when I'm out. Cotton because they're comfy. Fex calls them granny panties, but they are in fact, sport cut."

"And I care because?"

No flirty response to that one. We fix eyes for a moment.

"I told you. I'm not the enemy. I'm just trying to break the ice between us."

"Insisting Sil bed down with your brother was a nice start. And just for my curiosity, that doesn't bother you one bit? God knows what they're doing to each other in there."

She takes a deep breath collecting herself. I could care less if I'm getting on her nerves. She wasn't invited to bust up my alone time.

"First, I have a pretty good idea of what they're doing to each other in there. Second, I don't know if bother is the right word. I don't think jealous is either."

She gives me a look like she's collecting her thoughts, starts to say something then stops.

"Bothered? Maybe a little insecure. Silithes is so strong and curvy and soft. Look at me. What was that you called me – freaky muscled? That's sexy... So yeah, I'm a little insecure that I won't match up to your sex-goddess girlfriend."

Not what I expected to hear. I expected something more like "it's just physical" or "our kind is so much more liberated than yours" or even, "come on, we're Cubati," like that should explain everything.

She smiles at the tell my face is sure to be putting out there.

"At least you're in the same league. I'm just human."

"So was my Frank. What I would give to have him back," she says with wistful eyes. "But I understand, I think. I can imagine Frank would have been intimidated by Fex, too. He tried so hard to be good with it all. Eventually, I just gave up on feeding off others altogether a while after Frankie, Jr. was born. I just trained myself to live off the blue – and a little of Frank once a week, because he insisted. There's nothing he wouldn't have done for me. Funny thing is he didn't need to do anything, he was perfect just as he was."

I forgot all about Frank and Frankie. I forgot all about her terrible loss. The lingering pain shows fresh in her face – I know that feeling, all too well. So I say nothing. Because there's really nothing to say; it's an intensely personal thing.

After a few moments of silence, she says, "Thanks for understanding. I didn't mean to get all dark and gloomy."

"Dark and gloomy are old friends of mine. Don't apologize. In fact, I think I was hanging out with them before you got here. But still, why insist on those two getting together at all? I'm just at a loss of any explanation other than trying to steal her away."

"I don't have to steal her away. She's already given herself to me. And I gave myself to her."

"That's not answering my question."

She smiles.

"I suppose not. Truth is, those two would get together on their own eventually, biology and curiosity almost dictate it. There'd be little flirtations. That would lead to little touches, to little kisses, to full-on satisfaction. Then, they'd feel guilty. How do we tell her? How do we tell him? I'm sparing them that conflict. It's already out there. There's nothing to hide or feel guilty about. After tonight, they are lovers."

Yet another surprising answer.

"She loves you tremendously, Arthur, though for a while she was a little too messed up to admit that to herself. That fucker Maldgorath really did a number on her. Thanks for ridding us of him."

"Had a lot of help."

We let that moment hang a while.

"Sooo…" she says, changing her tone from the serious to the seriously inviting. "Why don't we get to know one another, too? I am a succubus after all. How bad could it be?"

Back there again. It always goes back there. I look at her giving me her best lusty come hither, which is another new face from her for me – and one she does damn well. I think what Paul said about how she can go through the motions. My answer is made.

"Sorry, no."

"I could make it so good for you."

"Yeah, you could," I say back. "But you'd probably just be going through the motions. I mean it would probably be great for me, but for you, it'd just be some stupid human humping on you that you have to entertain. In my mind, it's best when it means something to both parties."

Her look shows surprise. I'm anticipating the whole "you cannot reject me" thing. She looks away from me.

"Wow," she says offhandedly, then looks back. "That is very considerate, Arthur. I'm not used to someone actually thinking about my experience after the offer is made. Usually, it's just… got to get me some of the succubus," her voice slipping into the Mobile, Alabama, southern drawl. "All the same, I do the motions, really, really well."

I have no doubts, especially with the look she shares following the statement. All the same – I'm still not going there. My chuckle lets her know the message was received.

"You're a strange one, Arthur MacInerny. But I like strange."

We linger on that statement for a moment, and she breaks the silence with a question.

"Do you think my Frank and Frankie are in your heaven? I mean, you don't think they're being punished because of me? Frankie couldn't help who his mother is, and Frank was in love. Your wife is an angel. Is there any way she can find out about them – if they're okay?"

"I wish it worked that way. I'm pretty sure I can babble my brains out, and she'll hear it. But me hearing her – it's not that direct. I could ask Yayne; he kind of straddles both our world and the beyond. But he usually just tells me to talk to her myself. No telling how he'd react to a request from you."

"Yeah," she says offhandedly. "I'd just like to think they're in a better place than where I'll end up. We go to the well of black. It's like a soul-eat-soul place. Only the strong persist and have a chance for reincarnation. It's supposed to be vicious, primal, and painful. Maybe that's what you call hell. For us, it's the opportunity for the self to prove itself, consume the weak, and persist."

"And this is what your religion aspires to?"

"The alternative is to have the light wash you away into nothingness. Your realm's interpretation of the light is little different. I kind of like it. Moreso now that I've heard of your Dorothy. We need to get off this topic, but promise me you'll talk to your guardian angel and the sword about my Frankies."

"I promise. And if it means anything, Dorothy has probably already heard us."

She plays with the pleats of her dress in that little can-can like thing she did when she first arrived. "We should go back in. They're playing Pictionary. Besides, I want to mess with Clyde. It'll be fun. I'll throw myself at him, and we can watch him squirm. He would never, you know. He has to be in control of all things at all times."

"And if he calls you on it?"

"Then he gets to enjoy me going through all the wonderful motions."

Chapter 9

We go back inside and join the party. Jxsiga starts in on Clyde Smith immediately, insisting she sit next to him, calling him "cutey" among other things and constantly touching him.

I think Clyde is ready to run away. Part of me wants to laugh, part of me feels it's a cruel joke. Clyde thinks it's time to get up and get a drink. So he excuses himself and breaks away.

"Me too," says Jxsiga, scurrying after him.

I have learned that "The Lady" can be relentless. But she's not pushing it too hard, just riding that fine line to keep Clyde uncomfortable. After all, should she push it too far, then she's got to follow through. At that point, I think the joke's on her.

Or at least Clyde would be on her.

That entertainment aside, I find it strange that I'm surrounded by these characters, playing a version of a game that's a staple of young couples around the world. I'm amazed Znuul is playing along. I think Clyde is happy to play if it means he gets away from Jxsiga's constant suggestions. Clyde's associate, Jason, actually seems to be enjoying himself, even though he's still relatively fresh "off the boat" — that is, he is newly inhabiting this body in our realm.

Clyde returns right when it's time for Sheyliene's and Pffif's turn to play. Sheyliene insists on being the drawer and even tells us that she's doing an "all play" because she has a good one. After a round of robust discussion, punctuated by Shey's "All play is still a card," we agree to let her go on.

She begins to sketch a very crude tree, followed by a stick figure with a cape or something, and some kind of rope thing that it is hanging from. She turns around and the minute starts.

Crapsticks.

Pffif looks at me, understanding what our darling pixie just drew. He's shaking his head "no" as in he doesn't want to be the one to say what it is. I know, too. I don't want to be the one to say what it is — after all, Jxsiga is my picture partner because we came in late.

People guess tree. Some guess lynching. Jason says hanging angels from trees. Arix asks, "Are those horns on that dreadfully primitive drawing?"

Sheyliene points at him enthusiastically.

"Hang a devil from a tree?" asks Kitten.

Sheyliene points at her enthusiastically.

The minute timer dings, and Sheyliene is very let down.

"Mr. Pffiferil, you knew what it was – why didn't you say it? We would have got points."

"Pixie, you ain't right."

"Well, tell us what it is, Sheyliene," says Znuul.

I cringe.

"Okay," she says in her overly chipper way. "It's that bitch Jxsiga hanging from a tree by her spine after I kicked her teeth down her throat and beat her to death."

Crapsticks. Crap thorny sticks.

Jxsiga looks from Shey to me, with one of her patented serious-as-a-heart-attack looks.

"You knew what that was, Arthur. We could have had the points."

"Oh my, I should be paying for entertainment like this," says Arix.

"I actually agree with you, Arix," says Znuul, leaving me feeling like I'm on a stage macabre.

"Well, I want to set things right," says Jxsiga, standing. "Everyone, I wronged Sheyliene. It was before I knew her wielder and before I had the privilege of being Silithes' lover. I want to apologize to you, Sheyliene, in front of all here. Please, I am sorry for eating you on that airplane. Will you accept my most heartfelt apology?"

"Not a fucking chance, demon whore, soul-eating bitch," Sheyliene responds before anyone can even take a breath. "The only thing you're going to get from me, succu-slut, is a beating, followed by me ripping out your spine and hanging you from a tree by it."

They stand there, staring each other down.

Jxsiga sits back down.

"Yeah, I thought so," spits out Sheyliene.

Jxsiga shoots me a look I can't read. Do something about her? She's going to do something?

"This is much more entertaining than the human games," Ahzna adds. She's been sitting off to the side, refusing to be involved. "Fairy thing, you should try to kill the succubus now, so we can lick your delicious green blood off the floor."

Not one face in the room agrees with that goading.

"My dear host Ahtsag Znuul," Jxsiga proclaims, "I am afraid I must present an honorable challenge, within the rules of hospitality to the pixie Sheyliene. I fear our differences can only be solved in combat. Would you allow such in your house?"

"You bet he will," exclaims Sheyliene, "Bring it, bitch!"

Jxsiga's eyes haven't left Znuul's since making the proclamation, which I guess is supposed to be considerate or something like that.

"Not in my house please; take it outside," says Znuul. "And I presume you have ground rules to this challenge?"

Jxsiga's smile is wide in response to Znuul. I suppose neither of them are strangers to the whole challenge under hospitality thing.

"Of course, my host, the first ground rule is that no lethal force will be used," says Jxsiga to Znuul. "Guests may have conflicts but should be expected to live under a host's hospitality. Second, no weapons. Third, the contest ensues until one is unable to continue or submits to the other."

"I would rather you two just get along," says Karred.

"They'll take it outside; we won't have to be bothered dear," Znuul says.

"I'm in," exclaims Sheyliene.

I'm not sure I want her in. Jxsiga is way too calm about this. I'm guessing she has an angle. When she turns to look at me and smiles, I know she does.

"Sheyliene, can't we find a way to deal with this that doesn't involve violence?" I ask, already knowing the answer.

"Hell no. The Succu-bitch has to pay!"

"So all is sanctioned by our host, and you agree to the rules of combat," Jxsiga says, smiling widely.

"I'm going to kick your teeth down your throat, tear your face off, and wear it like a mask," screams Sheyliene, fists balled and so ready.

"Jxsiga, I have to warn you," says Znuul, "Sheyliene here is quite an accomplished warrior. Fast. Well trained. And as determined as you will ever find. This will not be an easy domination. In fact, if we were wagering – I'd put my wager on her. Do you really want this?"

Jxsiga's grin is ear to ear until she speaks. "I see no other way to solve our differences."

"Well, Zebediah," says Clyde, using Znuul's human name. "If you are taking wagers, I'll wager on behalf of Jxsiga. We all know what she means by submission. The pixie will submit and beg for more."

"Bullshit," cries out Sheyliene.

"What do you wager, Clyde?" Znuul asks, pushing things in a way I wish he wouldn't.

"Dinner," Clyde says. "Anywhere and no restrictions. Wine, appetizers, desserts – the whole thing."

"I agree to that wager," says Znuul to Clyde, punctuated by pointing at him.

Jxsiga suddenly jumps on Clyde and tries to kiss him, which he turns his head away from, like a child trying to avoid the cooties.

"You believe in me, Clyde. I want you so badly," she dramatically calls out to the room.

Poor Clyde. She's not going to stop.

"Bitch! I'm right here, and you have to face me now," says Sheyliene.

Jxsiga unstraddles Clyde and looks at me.

"Compel her not to use lethal force, Arthur. I don't think she can stop herself."

That's actually smart, because Sheyliene is not known for her self-control. So I touch my will and say, "Sheyliene, you will not use lethal force in your fight with Jxsiga."

"You are lucky he did that, succu-bitch, because I would find a tree and…"

"Hang me by my spine; I know. I hear you, Sheyliene," Jxsiga says, standing and turning to the outside.

I know, my fairy, and part of the arrangement is no weapons. So I say, "Sheyliene, no weapons, lose them."

I get an aggravated look; then she pulls the knives from her shit-kicker boots and the throwing spikes and knife from under her plaid skirt and a ninja star from the back of her bra.

Damn.

"Let's get it on," Shey yells.

Jxsiga stands and says, "Follow me then."

They both head outside to battle.

"All of you can keep drawing your pictures," says Ahzna. "I'm going to watch some real entertainment."

Greg starts to get up, too, but a sideways look from Karred stops that.

Part of me wants to go out there as well. I guess I'm worried for Shey. But that wouldn't be fair. After all, The Lady doesn't have someone to heal her wounds.

Chapter 10

Maybe I should have gone outside to watch the fight. The group consensus is that Pictionary was fun, but it's time for something a little more adult. So, poker. Znuul sets up a banquet table, Kitten gets the chips, and I am reintroduced to Texas Hold'em.

Five hands into the game and I finally get something worth a darn – a pair of jacks. I bet cautiously at open, hoping not to let on. The flop rolls out and yes – another jack! The betting gets around to me, and I raise cautiously. Znuul folds.

"I'm out; he's got something."

Clyde follows affirming Znuul's observation. Pffif, too, with an apology. Greg lasts one more card. Karred, bless her heart, was the only one to stay in.

By the time the river card fell, I had a full house – jacks and fives.

Betting is robust. Karred even acknowledges, "He sure looks like he has something."

Curses, poker face.

Like all things, the time of reckoning has come. I lay my cards down. "Full house: jacks and fives."

"Told you he had something," says Znuul with a wink to me.

"That is a good hand," says Karred, revealing her pair of fives. There's also a pair of fives on the table – four of a kind. I've been snookered. My chip-wealth is seriously damaged.

"Wow. I did not see that coming," I say to Karred in congratulations.

"None of us did," says a smiling Znuul, "but we saw you coming, so thanks for that."

"Aye, that was a hand of woe, she was holdin'," Pffif adds.

My scanning eyes pick up the shadow of someone outside approaching the patio area. The fight must be over.

"Excuse me for the next few hands; looks like the brawl is over. I need to check on Shey," I say getting up.

"I'd leave the table for a few hands, too, after taking that beating," Greg says with a laugh.

He makes a point.

The silhouette outside becomes Ahzna as she steps into the light of the porch's light. She walks over to the sliding door nearest the kitchen and lets herself in, making a beeline for the kitchen.

I walk over to the peninsula separating the kitchen from the cavernous living area.

"So, who won?"

She's pulling out plasticware with shredded beef and says, "The succubus prevailed. By my estimation, she could have won the match very early on, but for whatever reason did not push her advantage. It cost her much in pain after your fairy regrouped. I can see why my captor would have wagered upon the fairy."

All without as much as looking at me.

"So, where are they?"

"No doubt, still lying in the grass. I do not understand," she says, actually looking at me now with confusion on her face. "In combat, to the victor belong the spoils. The fairy submitted, but the succubus continued to pleasure her. It should have been that the succubus grabbed the fairy up by the hair and made it pleasure her in front of us all to accent her shame in the loss."

Crap a brick.

"So you're saying that you left them out there, diddling one another?"

"What is this diddling?"

"Sex."

Ahzna looks at me like I'm a fool, then she says, "The succubus was dominating your fairy with pleasure when I left them, well beyond any point of submission. If that is how failure is rewarded in this realm, I may have to challenge the incubus and throw the fight."

Great. Sheyliene may be all quivery now, but I know my fairy. She's going to resent Jxsiga even more for being manipulated in that way.

"Hey, do you want to take my place?" I ask. "We're playing poker now, and I think I'm going to have to tend to Sheyliene."

Ahzna's attention goes back to sandwiches.

"What is this poker?" she asks, her back turned to me. "I do not play demeaning slave games."

"It's a gambling game using cards."

She turns around.

"Gambling? You mean a game of wagers where you take your opponent's wealth?"

"Exactly."

"I will learn of this," she says, turning back to the completion of her number whatever meal. Damn, she can eat and then some.

I leave her to her food, and turn back to let the table know I'm out.

"Hey guys, EB is taking my place. I'm going to need to attend to Sheyliene – looks like she lost the battle of champions."

"Magnificent!" says Clyde, looking at Znuul. "There are so many places I would like to dine. This will take some consideration."

"Red and I look forward to dining with you wherever that may be," says Znuul.

"Who's EB?" Greg asks.

I try not to crack a smile.

"Why that would be the evil bitch herself, Ahzna Luunz."

"What?" comes Ahzna's questioning voice from behind me.

"Oh nothing, EB," Greg says. "Pull up a chair, and we'll teach you the game."

"What is this EB?" Ahzna asks.

The table erupts in chuckles. I make my way outside before I have to contend with what I started. Opening the door, I'm greeted by the nice night air. Knowing I saw Ahzna come from the side area, I sit at the picnic table closest to that side.

It's a beautiful night – clear, cool, and starry. My solitude has been restored, and I enjoy the wide-open space. It appears that the throwdown has been good for me. I haven't thought about Sil and super-incubus at all.

Until now. Hours. They've been going at it for hours. Hours upon hours. That's not something that happens when you're just going through the motions. That's what happens when you don't want to stop.

Ugh.

My mental spinning stops before it can really gear up at the sounds of footfalls. I look up and see what must be Jxsiga, given the silhouette – the wings give it away; Shey's are more butterfly-like.

Slowly, Jxsiga makes her way to me, and when the light reveals her, I'm a bit shocked. One eye is moused, the other bruised. There are remnants of her blue blood crusted under her nose and chin. Her lips are swollen also.

She walks gingerly up to me sitting atop the picnic table.

"She can fight," Jxsiga says.

"Could have told you that."

"Some things you have to experience on your own," she says, plopping herself down on the bench seat of the picnic table.

"Was a good fight, though. I haven't scrapped like that in a long, long time."

"Better than the Russian gang thing?"

She looks up at me, no nonsense at all in her gaze. "That was a planned tactical slaughter. But she does make them look like wussies. That fairy can fight. I had to resort to succubus tactics."

"So I heard."

"She's about as willful a creature as I've met. Took some time to get that first 'oh yes' from her. But after that, they flowed like sweet maple syrup. She was all mine."

Obviously, Jxsiga did not chow down on her spirit. I'd know when Shey returned to the white. So, what the heck?

"Oh hell, Arthur," she says, obviously reading my confusion. "The whole idea of this fight was to give her a pound of flesh. She needed to lay hands on me to feel some vengeance. What I did on the airplane was rather heinous. But damn, fairy blood does give you a rush. Listen, Silithes likes her – a lot. I had to try to make some amends."

She motions me to follow her as she gets up and moves toward the sliding doors nearest the rooms of the bunker holding onto her side. I move ahead and slide the door open for her.

It never hurts to be polite.

"Thank you," she says, gently rubbing her side. "She broke some ribs. I need to get some healing potion into me. It's going to be unpleasant resetting these."

She steps inside to some applause, and I see in the light of the bunker how terribly bruised her left arm is. I slide the door closed and return to my perch atop the picnic table to wait.

And I don't have to wait long. After a short while, I see the limping outline of my pixie fairy. She sees me sitting at the table and gives a wave. Slowly she makes her way to the porch, and when she is finally graced by the porch lights… I'm in shock.

She looks worse than Rocky in the twelfth round. It's probably her green blood that makes it look so ghoulish. She plops herself down on the bench where Jxsiga did.

"She torqued my knee – and tried to break my ankle. But I broke her ribs good," she says, beaming a smile at me. A smile with missing teeth.

"You're not mad at me for losing, are you?"

"Of course not, Shey. What do you say we get some healing on you?"

For the swollen eyes, I can't really tell what kind of look she's giving me, but I think it's appreciative.

"I think we're past that point, Arthur. Just send me away. Damn… I kissed the mouth that ate me, bones and all."

I try not to respond to that statement and instead reach to her glyph on my arm and say "return."

All that's left to do now is pick up her stuff and call her back.

Chapter 11

With Shey's shit-kicker boots and clothes in hand, I make my way to her room, stopping at the table to see how the game goes.

Ahzna's still in it, my paltry stack of chips now more.

"Good to see you're still in the game, EB," I say.

I get a wicked look. Apparently, I am beneath words.

"Yeah, EB's catching on pretty quick," says Greg, apparently unconcerned for her wrath.

"Enough of this," she says, looking at Jason. "Wager or fold."

I snicker and leave to Shey's room. I lay the boots next to the bed and set the clothes on the small dresser each room has. Then I sit down in the chair and run my finger along her glyph and say "Come."

The air shimmers, and there she is, in her light almost gossamer-looking battle dress, looking at me with those pupilless golden orbs of eyes. She smiles, revealing all her teeth back where they belong and says, "Hooray! I'm back again. I feel so much better now."

I can imagine she does.

She blinks at me a few times, a sure sign of the wheels turning.

"You're sitting down. Does that mean you need to have a talk with me? I didn't kill her —you made it so I couldn't."

I have to chuckle. She'll run headlong into a fight against insurmountable odds, but a "talk" is enough to send a chill up her spine.

"I'm just sitting because it's been a long day, Shey, that's all. No need for a talk, unless you just want to talk."

"I like that kind of talk."

She jumps on the bed, laying on her stomach, her chin resting on her hands while looking at me.

Something's off. Then I realize what it is — she should be throwing a fit and going for the knives.

"You seem remarkably… okay given you just got your butt kicked and… uh, submitted."

"It was a fair fight. Yeah, it's strange how it ended. I think I might have preferred being knocked out. Maybe not. She did make me feel all nice and gooey."

She rolls over on her back and leans her head off the bed, looking at me upside down.

"But that's just how they subdue their food. I don't know. It's confusing. Should I be angry? I'm not sure how to feel about it. She did say some very nice things. But she messed my face up, too. And sometimes they just say things to make you all pacified and stuff so they can suck your soul out."

"It is a conundrum, Shey. I can't tell you how to feel."

"You're my wielder; you can make me do anything."

"But I don't and won't – except maybe to protect you or us."

"I know," she says, rolling back on her belly and looking at me right-side up. "That's why we love you so much. So should I hate her and keep planning to hang her from a tree by her spine?"

Personally, I do not know how one just stops hating, or loving, on a dime. But Shey is different. I recall some of Sil's and my conversations about her. One comment Sil made rings with clarity to me: "For as long as she was in Maldgorath's hold, and with what he did to all of his pixies' minds, it's unbelievable she functions at any level."

I've never asked for details after hearing what that bastard made her do to her own sister. If that was just the tip of the iceberg, I have no desire to know what's under the surface.

"Shey, I think I'm the wrong person to ask that question – she's not high on my list of folks to take out to a nice dinner. The answer has to come from you. It's what you feel. Now, I will say that holding onto grudges can wear you down over time. I mean, you let go of your hate for Znuul, and I think that helped you. Just do what feels right for you."

My answer gets met with a wall of blinks and finally an exasperated, "I don't know."

"Well, if you're not sure, then you probably don't need to hang her from a tree by her spine, right? I mean, that's a you-have-to-be-pretty-darned-sure kind of thing, isn't it?"

"Yeah, I suppose. It's just strange. Like one second we're trying to rip each other's faces off, but then I think she's trying to choke me out because she takes my back and, like, has it where I can't free my legs. But I know how to defend a choke. Then I feel that tail of hers slither up my leg, into my underwear and..."

"Shey, way too much information..."

She blinks at me a few times, I think trying to figure out a way to respond to that without coming off poorly.

"They can do things with their tails, Arthur. Things…"

I have no response, other than to try not to paint a mental picture.

"She made me say I submit to you, Lady Jxsiga. I actually said those words. Then she asked me if I wanted her to stop."

"Let me guess what you said…"

Shey rolls over on her back again but doesn't dangle her head upside down off the bed.

"Yeah, I caved in, Arthur, but you know what it's like. I'm really conflicted. Can I be mad at her for making me feel that way? I mean, I said I submit. But I don't quit. Is it me? I mean I understand I denied General Znuul and Maldgorath. Is it me? Why would I submit – to her?"

She's getting pretty wound up, and generally speaking, that's not a good thing.

"Shey, take a deep breath," I say evenly. "It was just a backyard fight. Life or death was not on the line. You two just needed to work something out. Maybe you did. She beat the crap out of you. And trust me, you beat the crap out of her, too. I saw that."

"Yeah, the bitch can take a shot."

Shey rolls back over and looks at me. "This is confusing. Sometimes I'm not sure how I'm supposed to be. How am I supposed to be?"

"Just be as you want to be, Shey."

We let a little quiet settle between us, but of course with Shey, it can only be a little.

"Is it true? What Silly said, that you wouldn't have kicked me to the side, just because you two were… well, you know."

Well, a total shift in conversation. And I sure as heck don't know how to answer that question.

So I use my safe word – "Okay."

She takes that as I'd expect, full steam ahead.

"I was angry and couldn't imagine you'd want anyone else after having her. You know, Silly – she's so… succubussy. Jxsiga was something, but Silly is like, oh man. You know when I went back to help her, we talked a lot. And she shared herself, too. But like I said, we talked, and she said you love me and would have never cast me away."

Shey rolls back and forth on the bed, then stops and looks me dead in the eyes with an expecting smile.

"Would you take me back, Arthur?"

"I never sent you away, Shey."

She cocks her head and gives me that look that lets me know I am without any clue.

"I meant into your bed, Arthuuur."

Crapsticks. This is messed up.

How can I say yes to her, and be faithful to Silithes? And what about Dorothy – there's that, too. Am I already an unfaithful cheating bastard? Then the realization kicks in. If I say no to Shey, then more than likely the crap will really hit the fan.

"You're freaking out," she says, rolling off the bed and landing on her feet. Three strides and she's planted herself across my lap.

"I know you're worried about hurting Winx's feelings. I am, too. He'd be crushed if I left him to go back to you."

Shey in my lap is not necessarily a flirtatious thing. She just likes to be close sometimes, well – a lot. I have so many memories of lying in our backyard hammock with her curled up next to me. Dory bringing us ice tea. And yeah, me bringing them ice tea, too. Shey likes to cuddle. And thank goodness she came up with the answer because I am lost on that one.

"It would be bad if his feelings got hurt."

"Yeah, but you know, if he knew I was your summonling, he'd call me evil and run away. That would break my heart."

"Shey, you don't know he'd do that."

"No, but I know if I broke up with him, it would break his heart."

"So maybe you should give it a chance."

"Yeah," she says, "But you know you were the best ever. My wielder... Even better than my last wielder, though he was very, very strong. I never felt like some meat-hole blood-Slurpee with you. I felt like I was treasured. You were even better than Silly and lady bitch face together."

Well, I guess I have some insight into how she really feels about Jxsiga.

"You know, Shey, the better thing is a control mechanism. Making your wielder happy makes you happy. You hurt your wielder; you hurt a lot more. It's a sick thing. It's control."

"It's still badass. Do you remember our first time, Arthur? I'll never, ever forget it."

I do remember our first time. I remember how Shey was shaken to the core. I remember her sweet mutterings. And yeah, it was pretty good for me, too.

"So would you take me back?" she asks, those golden orbs of eyes staring into mine.

"I can't say no to you, Shey, but you know how I feel about Silithes. It would be strange."

She kisses my cheek and tells me, "You are so strange sometimes."

That's nice.

"So should I end it with Winx?" she asks, about stopping my heart. How the heck do I answer that? My turn for a deep breath.

"Shey, if it really is true love, then he'll see past the whole summonling thing. And if not, then you know. But if it is true love, why would you want to end it?"

That answer gets me a massive hug around the neck and kiss on the cheek.

"You are so wise! I love you so much, Arthur MacInerny. You want me to be happy, even if it means with someone else. That's true love. I am so blessed."

"I wish it was that way, Shey," I say, knowing that at the end of the day, she's my slave.

She hugs me again and rolls off my lap. "But it is that way," she says. "Even if it doesn't work out with Winx – you'll be there for me. I know it. I know it's true."

She's hopping up and down clapping, so very excited. It's hard not to be excited with her being so excited.

That is, until she stops hopping and opens her mouth again.

"Don't forget, I can help you. Can I help you right now? That would be great!"

I'm really not either ready for or wanting "help" by her definition at this moment.

"I'm all right, Shey. No need for help at the moment."

"But it would be good."

"Not the right night," I say.

"Oh yeah, Silly's with that boy succubus," she says with a serious look.

"Incubus," I correct.

"Yeah, I know that," she says, sounding irritated at my correction. Then her tone changes back to her usual sing-song. "But you want to be all broody and moody. I guess I understand. After all, I thought I was going to hate you forever. I thought I was going to hate the Jexubus forever, too. Sometimes we have to work at being upset. It's hard work. I'd make you all happy and mess it up. But you have to remember that it's not really fun being moody all the time. They call it happy for a reason you know."

"Thanks for understanding, Shey."

"You're not an easy one to understand, Arthur. And I have practice at trying to understand you," she says, waggling her finger at me.

"Thank goodness you do, Shey," I say, beaming a smile at her.

"That's right," she says returning the smile. "Well, I probably need to tell the Jexubus that the feud is off. It'd probably be nice to help her with her ribs, too. I smashed 'em real good."

"Well, I see you made up your mind about her."

"I can't tell you not to hold onto to your angries, if I'm holding on to mine. Besides, succubusses can be fun when they're not eating your soul, stealing your boyfriend, or mind controlling you to suck toes and stuff, I think."

I am not going to correct her incorrect plural of succubus or ask about toes. I'm pretty sure that was a "not me" she did at Sil's command ponderous ages ago. Instead, my safe-word is called for.

"Okay."

She gives me a "Yay!" and steps over to take me by the hands and pulls me up. "Hugs," she says, following with a nice hug as opposed to one of the spine-crushing ones.

Pixie fairies are stronger than they look.

A bit of lingering on the hug is nice.

"Now for kisses," she says in a voice that makes me think she's up to something. "Just lips, the good kisses are cheating," she says, looking at me with those Pixie eyes of hers.

"As long as we're not cheating," I say back to her, then I am pulled down looked at very lovingly, and kissed.

And kissed. And kissed some more. Lingering kisses, short kisses. My upper lip, my lower lip, both my lips, my cheek, her finishing up on my neck and that spot right below my ear that drives me nuts.

"Are you sure that's not cheating, Sheyliene?"

"Uh-huh," she says, arms still around me looking at me like she just got away with something. "No tongues. But it does look like you could use some help now." She grabs my behind pulling me into her for emphasis.

No doubt to the evidence.

"Think I need to hold onto my angries just a little longer, Shey."

She lets go of me and gives me the pouty lip.

"You are strange. But I love you. Try not to be angry too long. It's not healthy."

She waves goodbye and, like that, is out the door.

I take a couple of blinks. Hey, if it helps her think, maybe it'll help me, too. I look around the room and see a problem. Yayne, laying on the floor – left where I flung him last night. I take a moment before heading to pick him up.

"Well, guess I'm the one due for an earful, this time," I say, before grasping the hilt and bracing myself.

Silence.

"So we're not talking again?"

"Considering words," says the sword's voice in my mind.

"Take your time," I reply quietly as I sit down and place Yayne across my legs.

"You have reunited with the succubus. Yet you are still troubled. It surprises you that it, she, would seek comfort in her own kind?"

"Well, when you put it that way."

"Now, I must register complaints."

"I shouldn't have thrown you away like that. I just didn't want things to escalate," I say, attempting to anticipate the problem.

"Throwing me away is excusable. Leaving me on the floor all day and night is not. In the future, consider me. Now, most importantly, next time you decide to share carnal pleasure with her, can you please make sure I am in my box or another room? Or in my box in another room… on the other side of whatever building you are in."

Well, we are certainly talking again.

"Sorry, Yayne. It was a strange time. I wasn't thinking. I wasn't planning on that happening either."

"Nor were you planning on her stealing your mind and making you her slave. Or falling back in with those of her kind. Or the fairy offering to leave her true love for you? That is selfless. She is nice. Her soul is of the light, and she appears to want to help you."

I don't think Yayne knows what Shey means by "help."

"She is nice. And what she means by help may not be what you think."

"How so?"

I take a moment to think about how to phrase it, so as not to be crude.

"Her definition of help is a special massage resulting in my ejaculation."

I can't hear the groan, but mentally I feel something akin to it. It makes me snicker.

"Then she wishes to be your handmaiden?"

My snicker turns to a groan at the pun. Is this humor? From a holy sword?

"I think so, Yayne. To her, that's not cheating on her boyfriend."

I sense confusion.

"Yeah, me too, Yayne. She marches to the beat of her own drummer."

"Three warriors have wielded me. You are by and far the most… different. Please reassure me again we are bound together to smite evil from this world."

"Yes, Yayne – we are. The thing is, evil isn't always as simply defined as by what something is. Sometimes bad things turn good. Sometimes good things turn bad. Lately, it seems a lot of good things turn bad."

"Things were much clearer with my other wielders."

I suppose so. But there is still clarity to our mission. A clarity that should have been shared during today's briefing. He'd get it. He'd be all in.

"Yayne, I have to confess I slighted you again. I just realized it. I need to bring you up to speed with a meeting we had today – why I'm here. The Dzemond have figured a way past the blocks to our realm. It sounds like they're sending scouting parties. Worse yet, if they can talk people into supporting them, then they may be able to send an invasion here. We are needed, Yayne, and all of these strange folk around us are on the same page – protecting this world and mankind."

"We will battle for the fate of Earth and mankind?"

"Nothing less, Yayne. Just keep in mind that you're with me; so it might be strange. We may have strange company. But our cause and partners are righteous nonetheless."

"I sense the truth of your words. Please put me at rest properly and do not forget me again. We have work to do."

"Yes, we do," I say, taking Yayne by the hilt and beginning to stand.

"Wait," comes his voice. "Something I must say. The, your… Silithes… did not feast upon you, and I was watching for that. She seemed moved at your reunion, though you were the only one who… She shed a small tear. I feel she very much cares for you. I must say this, as to me it is truth. I cannot disapprove of your relationship. I just don't need to witness such things between an eater of souls and you. It's hard to see any beauty beyond the expectation of you being devoured."

"I'll keep you in mind, Yayne. I'm sorry. I have not been the best of partners."

I stand and bring him to his case and sheath. First, I take his cleaning cloth and make sure the blade is pristine. Then I return him to the care of the sheath. I'm about to put him away when I remember something. Holding onto the hilt, I state my question.

"Yayne, one of the other strange characters I'm with – another succubus, by the name of Jxsiga."

"The small one you discarded me for?"

"Yes, the small one. She married a human. Had a child with him. Lost them both to a drunk driver. She wants to be sure they're okay, like, they're with God.

She's worried her son will be condemned to her place because she's, well, what she is. Any way to find out if they're in the good place?"

There's a pause that feels like consideration.

"I can pray for an answer. I straddle the realms but am really of neither. I cannot know unless told. My existence is not as yours and not as theirs. You say she married a human. Do you feel she loved him?"

"Sure of it, Yayne."

"Then I will pray for an answer. Maybe we will know. You should also. After all, you have the guardian angel. She is with you right now."

My heart races. "You can see her? Sense her?"

"Yes. That I can do."

"Thanks, Yayne. I will see you tomorrow."

I put him in his case and latch it up.

"Hey, Dory. I understand you're here. I wish I could hug you. See you. Interact with you – wow that's me being romantic, eh? Interact? Nice, only I'd say something like that."

I bury my face in my hands and work my fingers through my hair.

"I guess you heard everything – saw everything. I'm not sure how to deal with all this. Can you just come back and then I'll know what to do?"

I actually laugh a little at how pathetic that sounds; how pathetic I sound.

"Time for me to get some sleep, Dory. I should sleep really well knowing you're watching over me."

Chapter 12

The sound of the door opening wakes me. I sit up.

"It's just me," comes Silithes' voice.

I lay my head back down on the pillow, not wanting to hear about how good it was and that she has to leave me now.

I see she's come to the other side of the bed, by the alarm clock's light. I see her slough off her robe. She flips the covers up.

"Make some room," she says as she inserts herself under my covers.

I oblige.

Her naked, human form wriggles into place next to me into a nice spoon. The barely perceptible tingle is nice – as it always is.

"I'm all sexed out; I hope you understand," she says very quietly. "Okay if we just cuddle and sleep?"

I lop my arm around her, not in advance but just because that seems the best way to say "yeah." She takes my hand and puts it on her breast, squeezing it slightly.

"All sexed out, huh?" I say.

"You have no idea."

"You bond with him, too?"

I can feel her tension at that statement across her body pressed into mine. "No. Nothing like that. You really don't want details, do you?"

I don't. So I just say "nuh."

Her hand tightens around mine on her breast.

"Good night, Arthur. I hope my being here isn't something lost on you. Sweet dreams."

Chapter 13

There's always one thing consistent waking up next to Sil – the soldier is always at attention. It's that high-watt nervous system of theirs – always projecting that barely perceptible tingle that says "nice" and "now."

I'm not going to wake her. Regardless of how happy the happy fun time was with Paul, she came back to me. That point is not lost. The reality of it still kind of hurts, though. I slowly begin to roll out of bed in the opposite direction, so as not to disturb her.

"Where are you going?" she asks, turning with me.

"Was just going to clean up and start the day. Figured you needed your rest."

"Roll yourself back here."

As the whole don't-wake-Sil thing is shot to heck, I roll.

Just like that, I'm straddled, and the soldier at attention is slowly engulfed. Man, she knows her craft. She raises up and begins slowly moving those hips. She is a wonderful sight astride me. Her smile tells me I'm appreciated, too.

We both jerk at the knock on the door.

"Not now; come back later," I yell.

But the door opens anyway.

Jxsiga's face peeks around it. "There you are," she says to Sil. "I've been looking for you." She slips into the room, closing the door discreetly behind her. She turns around and stops, taking in the sight of us.

"Oh, my. Don't you two look comfy," she says, the words dripping with sensuality. She walks over to us, then faces Sil. I see her hand take Sil's breast. She leans in. It must be a kiss.

And one heckuva kiss based on the reaction of some very specialized muscles I'm privileged to be deeply ensconced in.

"Hey, baby. We have a change in plans," I hear Jxsiga say. "Fex got a call that his substitute in tonight's darts league came down with the flu. We have to go. He's having a fit."

Jxsiga turns around and looks at me with an all-too-seductive look. "And look at you. Oh my."

She reaches down to touch me, but I stop that before it happens.

"We're having a private moment here – do you mind?" is all I can think to say.

Jxsiga smiles and turns back to Sil.

"He's so willful. Look at him turning me away. Let me see you two move."

"You're freaking him out, Jex," Sil says, sounding not too sexy, "I think it's time you go... please."

Jxsiga obliges and starts to go, but turns around looking at both of us with a look that hints that she's turned on.

"You two don't take too long now. Fex is having a breakdown. We need to go."

She closes the door.

I look up at Sil and am wondering what the heck.

"Something you need to tell me, Sil?"

"You know I have to start my new life," she says. "It's not like I can go back to New Orleans with you. I've got to start finding feeding partners. They have things they're doing."

"And you were going to tell me about this... when?"

She runs her hands through her hair.

"It's been such a rush of things. I'm not sure. I was going to, I know..."

I push my hips back and put my hand on her belly to disengage us. I'm not happy.

"You're running away with her and her brother and telling me is a secondary thought?"

She looks at me like I hurt her. But, damn, I'm feeling hurt, too.

"Arthur," she says, "you're almost immortal. Me, too, if I take care of my needs. This is just a short time to get my life and needs in order. We have forever."

I take that in. Sure, she has needs. Real ones. But they don't kick in hard for a while.

"I get it, Sil. But what I don't get is, what's the rush? I mean, yeah, we're going to live a long time. Jxsiga and Paul, too. Why are you in such a hurry to leave me? I love you. Do me a favor and just tell me honestly what the hell is going on? You have forever to start what you need to."

Sil's face goes blank. She plops herself down on her butt, between my legs.

"Yeah. What's the rush, right?"

We take each other in silently.

"Why can't you take some more time with me, Sil? I mean, if you're just trying to let me down easy – don't. If you'd rather be with your own kind, I can understand. Just tell me what the heck is going on. I'm not that fragile – come on, you know that. Truth is what's called for here."

"I think I'm just caught up in this whirlwind of... whatever this is."

I don't have anything to say. We just look at each other. Her face becomes serious.

"I'm staying – at least until the hungries get too irritating. I love you, too. But I told you, things would be strange. And whether you believe it or not – they're strange for me as well. Wonderful, but strange."

Wow. She's staying. I prop myself up and look her in the eyes. I see nothing but concern.

"Yeah, strange, Sil. I might not share in all of the wonderful point of view, but that's me. I'm glad you'd take time with me. I know things aren't like what they were and can't be again. But being able to take time with you is important to me – and you know I don't just mean frisky time."

She smiles ear to ear.

"But frisky time is good. Do you want to finish?"

I'm not feeling it.

"Yeah," she says reading my face, "we'll pick that up later. I'm going to go tell Jex. Paul is something fanatical about his friends and game leagues. He's kind of OCD about it from what I hear. I bet he really is freaking out."

She scoots off the bed and puts on her robe.

"Make sure to do your healing stuff and don't forget to talk to Dorothy. I'm going to get this handled with Jex and Paul. I am not rushing off. Not at all."

She leaves with purpose, and I'm lying in bed feeling a bit shell-shocked. But at least I know what to do. After all, Sil gave me specific directions.

Chapter 14

I follow through with my morning routine as quickly as I can. But there's one change – there's no morning chat with Yayne. Instead, I unlock the case, grasp his hilt, and say, "You're with me today. Much to share."

No response other than a feeling I take as affirmation. I strap him across my back and tighten it up. I bet I look ready for battle, in my nice oxford shirt and khakis. I lean my head back slightly to make contact with the hilt.

"And just like that, we can talk."

"You mean, you can hear me."

"Same difference," I say, heading out to greet the world.

In the huge living area, breakfast is being taken. I see luggage about, so I figure our ranks are clearing. I know for sure of two that are going. I look toward the front door and see Znuul, Karred, Edgar, Sil, and the twins talking. Paul catches my eye for a second and turns away.

Whatever. All the same, I should be polite and say my goodbyes.

Znuul is the first to notice me and raises an eyebrow – having Yayne strapped on can do that.

"They're still my guests, Arthur," he says in his characteristically large way. The smile lets me know he's not really feeling threatened.

Paul, on the other hand, does appear threatened. He stops talking with Edgar and stiffens to more of an on alert. That doesn't bother me.

Now when Sil looks over at me and takes a step back with wide eyes, I become bothered.

"Just taking Yayne out for the day," I say as nonthreateningly as I can, "No need for alarm. He's part of the team, too."

"Well, that speaks volumes for your bond with the sword," Karred says with a smile.

Not smiling is Jxsiga. But I'm growing accustomed.

"Please put that sword down and come with me. You and I have things to discuss privately before we go," she says in the business-like tone she does so well. She takes off walking, her purple hard-shell roller luggage in hand.

"We don't have time for this," Paul says to her back, about as close to cross as I've heard him.

"Yes, we do," she says, not even turning around to look at him. But she does turn around to look at me. "Don't just stand there; Fex will blow a gasket."

I unstrap Yayne, taking him by the hilt and say, "Just a moment. I'll be right back."

"Well, I'm taking my luggage to the car," Paul declares to all who would hear.

Yes, he's being a bit anxious. Darts must be important.

I walk over to the room Jxsiga is standing in front of. She sees me coming and goes in. I set Yayne against the doorjamb and enter. She's throwing her pretty purple suitcase on the bed.

"This hurry up and go now thing is about on my last nerve," she says, turning around to me and taking a calming breath. "I'm not the enemy, Arthur. You are the lover of my lover. I am the lover of your lover. In the middle is Silithes. We need to coexist for her sake."

"Hey, I left the sword outside."

"Cute, Arthur. This is serious," she says, turning back around and begins to unzip her luggage. "Listen, I know how tough it can be, from the succubus point of view, being in love with a human. I got a really good flavor for what it's like from the human point of view, too – and that was without other Cubati sticking their noses into it."

"It's not the noses as much that's uncomfortable for me, Jxsiga. I think it's the other body parts."

I see her slowly shake her head at my comment. She produces a box and turns around. It could be a make-up box but seems a little large for that.

"Like I said, I am not the enemy. This is for you, Arthur, though Silithes will be the one enjoying it."

She hands me the box.

I'm thinking it holds some kind of device that uses batteries.

"Open it," she says.

I man up, unlatch the box and open it. No sex-toys in there, just a whole host of tiny plastic stoppered ampoules containing a bright blue fluid – mage recovery potions.

"They are preportioned. My own personal carry pack. If she uses one a day, that's twenty-three days. Every other day – you get the gist. My gift to you, Arthur, is time. I'm not trying to steal her away – I just want to be a part of her life. Oh, sorry, I am part of her life. Forever."

That is a heck of a gift. I'm kind of speechless.

She chuckles at me and turns around to zip her luggage back up.

"So can we try to coexist for her sake?"

She flips her luggage to the ground and extends the handle and turns back to me?

"We… uh, I can try."

"It's not easy, I know… and Frank was much more open-minded than you. He knew what I was before he married me and put a child in my belly. Can I give you some advice?"

There's no intimidation. None of the telepathic stuff, she's just looking at me rather intently.

"Advice is always good."

"Try to pretend she's from a culture that looks at the physical act of coupling as nothing more than manipulation, pacification, or just carnal release. Imagine – and I know this is hard – that she's a whole other species, with a whole different set of senses, perspectives, and needs than you."

I'm starting to get a little pissed. What the hell. Like I don't know that. I start to say something in my defense but don't get the chance.

"In your favor, Arthur, you have her heart. And that puts her at a disadvantage because our culture doesn't train us how to deal with love and care of others. She has to deal with all your human cultural nuances. She has to deal with a whole other species as an equal – which is much different than dealing with another species as a lesser. Are you getting where I am coming from? It's not easy – for either of you."

I stand there with my eyes locked on her eyes. I'm not pissed anymore, just feeling stupid for having to have the obvious explained to me.

"Okay."

She smiles. "Good. So you can grasp higher concepts. Just relax, Arthur, you're in a relationship with a succubus. She can't hold you to her standards, and you can't hold her to yours. Welcome to compromise. It's well worth it, though. This message comes from one who worked through it and cherished the relationship and family she built. I'm not the enemy. I'm the lover of your lover… and would like to try to be your friend."

"Yeah, friends are good, Jxsiga," I say, still feeling a bit on my heels.

"It's Jex for my friends, Arthur. Please remember that," she says.

"Not Jexi?"

"Don't be a dick. Fex can call me that because he can call me anything. Speaking of him, he's bound to be freaking out. I need to go. We have plenty of time, but it's not part of the plan. So he's all…"

"Freaking out," I say, anticipating the statement.

"Yeah," she says, taking her hand off the pretty purple hard-shell luggage. "Now hug."

She comes forward, not really giving me an option except to push her away and say something like, "Ewww! Cooties!"

Or take the hug. It's really no big deal – it's just a hug.

And a nice one all the same.

"I really need to go," she says. "We do need to talk more. Maybe we can do that when Silithes comes to stay with us for a while to get her affairs in order."

The realization of that inevitability washes over me.

She laughs, obviously reading me.

"Come on," she says, wrapping her arm around my waist. "Go with it," she says looking up at me. "We need to show a unified front for their sakes. It would be good for you to say a proper goodbye to Fex, too."

"He prefers Paul," I say, putting my arm around her waist and walking to the door.

"And I prefer Fxsigym."

We leave the room looking buddy-buddy. I make sure to stop for second and grab Yayne. Holding him by the hilt in direct contact I'm open to his commentary.

Silence.

We walk up to the group by the door, and Jxsiga breaks away, launching into Paul with a hug.

"Would you calm down," she says.

Sil throws me a sly look.

Goodbyes to all are made, and handshakes/hugs exchanged. I figure I maybe should listen to what I was told and step forward to Paul with my hand out.

"Good to meet you. Kind of strange how it turned out," I say.

"Yeah," he says, taking my hand but still seeming distracted. "Don't mean to be rude, but I have people depending on me and have to go. I do hope you'll come to visit, though. I just need to get going."

"No problem, Paul."

They head outside, and Sil stops me. "Arthur, I am going to give them both a proper kiss goodbye. You probably don't want to watch that."

I look at her and, knowing what I was told, just use the safe word.

"Okay."

She's right, I really don't want to see that.

Chapter 15

I figure I'll grab a bite while Sil shares her goodbyes outside.

Greg, Clyde, Jason, Shey, and Vets are sitting at the banquet table that was a poker table. Ahzna is taking her meal at the sofa area. She's wearing one of those athletic-cut bikini things that I first saw her in. I guess today is going to be spent sunning – or playing beach volleyball.

I walk by toward the kitchen to grab my food and catch a sideways look from her.

"Morning, EB," I say happily walking on, knowing full well that's not going to make her happy.

In her usual way, though, she says nothing. Good for me.

Looking at the pared-down breakfast offering, I still have the feeling that Znuul enjoys feeding his guests: biscuits, gravy, sausage patties, leftover pulled pork, fruit, and pancakes. I know Kitten does most of this, but I've also seen Znuul flipping the pancakes, and I think he enjoys it.

I look across the peninsula bar that separates the kitchen from the cavernous living area and note my crew taking it in with Greg, Clyde, and that Jason guy that used to be a Dzemond girl. It's nice.

My mind goes to EB, or more specifically to her summonlings. They're in the white, that mind-numbing brutal world of nothingness. Best I can tell, she has a Vetisghar also, along with some kind of flying monkey and a creepy-ass giant spider.

I do not care for spiders at all, but all the same, if it's anything like Hjuul, it doesn't need to go silently mad in a nothing prison.

I take my plastic plate of breakfast and coffee and make it a point to join Ahzna at the upholstered area. I figure I'm the one to break the ice. Besides there's something that's been bothering me.

"You know, EB, keeping your summonlings in the white is pretty abusive. I mean, it's well beyond any kind of solitary confinement."

Her eyes train on me, though her expression is inscrutable.

"They do not matter. They are slaves," she says back in that Russian-tinged accent. "If the holding is hard on them, then fine. They should know to make themselves useful so we might keep them with us more often. But you, you are weak; you actually are concerned for summonlings? They have given up their right to be."

Well, I'm not getting far in this argument today, but for nothing more than the sake of being stubborn-headed, I choose to pursue my failing argument.

"They'll serve you better if you treat them better."

"They wish to kill me. All summonlings wish to kill their masters. This is known."

I have to smile after swallowing my bit of sausage biscuit, I got her there.

"Mine don't. Except for Arix maybe, and I don't think he even wants to kill me."

The glare of doom. That's all I get from her until she reaches down for food. The glare returns.

"Perhaps your summonlings are addled or defective in some way, I cannot say. But as a rule, the wielder should never trust her summoned. Or he... assuming he is capable of a base intellect."

Touche.

"Come on, Ahzna. Treat it like an experiment. Give 'em a month free. If they don't seem appreciative enough, then send 'em back."

The glare of doom has become an inquisitive look.

"What is in this for you? Why do you concern yourself with the slaves of another? Do you propose a wager – do you hope to gain something from me?"

I get it. The concept of doing something for someone else's benefit, without an end game for yourself, is completely foreign to her. Heck, for their culture. So I smile big, take a gulp of coffee, and prepare to expand her thinking.

"Not at all. It's just good to do nice things for others. I want nothing from you."

I continue to receive the inquisitive look for a few moments. Then her face breaks out in a wide grin. She leans back into the sofa, crosses her arms under her chest, and stretches out with a smile.

"I see now," she says in a knowing voice. "Those that are not sure of themselves must have affirmations of their worth from others. So weak, Arthur MacInerny. You seek the affirmation of those that gave their very souls away. Do I need to say it... pathetic?"

Well, there's nothing like a good debate, and obviously, Ahzna's a bit more than just muscle. I figure that whole thing of apples and trees, remembering she's of direct lineage of Znuul. So, game on.

"Yeah pathetic, guess so, EB," I say just to rankle her a little.

An opponent off center is a good thing, even in debate. Especially in debate…

"But what's really pathetic, caring for others or punishing others because you, in fact, aren't much better than they are? I mean, if anyone's compensating here, wouldn't it be you?"

My retort gets a smile from her, but not a genuine one. More like one that says "your turn is coming." I kind of like that; debate is fun.

"So, you want them away from the holding. I see that. What is it worth to you?"

A simple question changes the whole complexion of the exchange. We are no longer debating. This is now a negotiation. I've got nothing to negotiate with.

"What do you want?"

"Nothing you can give me," is the answer I fully expected.

"Well then, Ahzna, we are at an impasse."

I'm ready to go away – after eating my breakfast. I'm not going anywhere until then.

"Do you wish to fight me for their right to enjoy this world?" She leans in. "Hand-to-hand combat. Should you defeat me, they have right to roam free. Should I defeat you, then, humiliation."

"What exactly is humiliation, Ahzna?" I ask, not sure I even want to know.

"You pleasure me with your mouth in front of all in this house and all that are yours until I tell you to stop. Perhaps I also put my fingers in places, though I am guessing you would enjoy that."

Well, sounds like Znuul's family has a thing for public humiliation based on his stories and what EB wants me to agree to. But, I'm not agreeing. Hand-to-hand with her is a losing proposition. I'm neither strong enough or fast enough to pull it off.

A man has to know his limitations.

I'm about to say such when Vets' voice behind me speaks first.

"That is an unfair proposition. My Wielder, I mean no affront. She sets odds in her favor and hopes your emotions push you to a poor decision."

"I must agree with Lady Vets," comes Znuul's voice. "I won't allow for a Baalig humiliation of my friend."

Ahzna, looking so happy with herself, says back to him, "Perhaps then you'll humiliate me. In front of everyone, my master."

I get the feeling, she'd like that. Sick.

"Not going to happen, Ahzna," says Znuul.

"It would be unfair. After all, Baalig muscles are as corded steel. He would stand no chance," Ahzna says.

The look Ahzna shoots me tells me she certainly believes that. Having seen some of Znuul's feats of strength, I think sparing myself the pain is a good thing.

"Yes, Baalig muscles are as corded steel," repeats Vets. I look up at her, and she is looking right into Ahzna's eyes – a sign of disrespect. Vets walks around the sofa to stand next to me.

"It is good when the lessers realize their place, is it not Ahtsag Znuul?" Ahzna asks with a smug look on her face.

Znuul's look to me tells me he's getting a bit exasperated with his charge.

"Now perhaps a fair challenge is something to be considered," Vets says, taking all of our attention. "A fair challenge would be for a lesser such as myself to bring you to a knee. Certainly, I cannot hope to harm one whose muscles are as corded steel. But talent in the fighting arts could bring a superior being to a knee."

Vets' proposition intrigues Ahzna; it's obvious. She sits up and moves in.

"And if you lose, Vetisghar, your master pays in humiliation."

"No," says Znuul.

"If I lose, then I fetch your water for a week's time. It seems important to you that I do," responds Vets.

"And if you win?" asks Znuul.

"Then my master's will is done. Her summonlings leave the white," Vets says to Znuul. "Of course, to face muscles such as corded steel without a weapon? Muscles like corded steel, great one."

There's some communication going on between Znuul and Vets. I can tell. What it is, I have no idea.

"Master," purrs Ahzna, "You'll have to grant me permission to bring harm to this lesser."

I am prepared to fight the Baalig with muscles like corded steel," Vets says, looking Znuul dead in the eyes. "My master can heal me easily when we are done, or return me from holding. I do not fear death or harm. They are only muscles of corded steel."

"Yes, they are muscles of corded steel," he says back to Vets parroting her response. "Are you sure you wish to do this? She can end you with one blow."

"She must land that blow," says Vets.

"Are you good with this, Arthur?" Znuul asks.

I'm not. But Vets is looking at me like to say anything but "yes" is an indictment of her skill. I can't let her think I don't believe in her. Besides, it's only a week of fetching water at the worst.

Well, worst after whatever happens to her.

"If that's what you wish, Vets," I say. "I believe in you."

Ahzna's laughter reverberates throughout the cavernous living room. "Now, master, speak the words so I might have permission to cause her great harm."

Chapter 16

"This goes outside," Znuul says, after granting Ahzna the permission she needs. "I'll not have my house destroyed.

"It won't last that long," says Ahzna, "but let's go outside; it's a nice day."

She gets up and goes outside with most everyone following.

Except for Vets and me.

"You don't have to do this," I say to her.

She turns her ring and whispers "T'Shighar," and transforms into her normal Vetisghar self. "I wish to do this. For you, my Wielder. I have a plan, but if I cannot deliver the first proper strike, I will most likely be fetching her water."

She turns and leaves me for the back porch in her typically stoic way.

I'm about to leave when the front door opens. It's Sil. I guess she's done with her kisses goodbye. I stand in place, and she walks over. I see her eyes looking at the growing spectacle outside.

"I missed something," she says.

"Yeah, Vets and Ahzna are going to throw down."

Sil's eyes go wide open..

"You can't allow that. She's just a Vetisghar. Ahzna's like some battle-guard Baalig."

I shrug at Sil and share my conundrum. "If I don't let her, then she doesn't think I believe in her."

"Damn," Sil says, and makes for the patio, taking me by the hand.

Once outside, I see Vets stretching a little and Ahzna standing across from her, arms crossed under her ample chest. But it's Znuul's voice that gets my attention.

"Please compel Lady Vets not to kill Ahzna, if you don't mind, Arthur. I am will-linked to her after all. I can't allow this to continue otherwise."

"Me either," says Karred.

"Really? This is a Vetisghar," says Ahzna, looking insulted.

I understand, so I touch my will and speak the words, "Vets, you will not kill Ahzna, knowingly or otherwise."

Vets nods to me, then turns to her opponent.

Ahzna smiles and holds her arms out wide. "Come take the first blow, Vetisghar. Your best please, though you may not wish to use a closed fist. It would be so sad for you to break your hand before the contest really starts."

Vets' face gives a little bit, and her eyes bend my way. Knowing big girl as I do, I take it as a smile.

Ahzna stands there with her arms out smiling at Vets. Vets is looking at her all over, focusing on her midsection. Vets pulls her right hand back in preparation for a palm-heel strike.

"So, my first blow is free?" Vets asks.

"The sooner you strike me, the sooner I can crush you," says Ahzna, hoping to move Vets from her considerations.

Vets squares up close in front of Ahzna, looking at her midsection intently. She takes a powerful stance and squares up, pulling her right hand back for a palm strike.

Then her left hand flies up, her thumbnail striking into Ahzna's Adam's apple.

"Gaagh!" is the sound in response from Ahzna. Her face is one of surprise. Vets ducks down immediately and the clubbing blow, thrown by Ahzna in return, misses. Vets throws a small blow to Ahzna's side, and Ahzna's hand goes downward. Like a viper, Vets jabs her forefinger and middle finger into Ahzna's eye, causing her to step back.

Vets attempts to buckle Ahzna's knee with a kick but gets nothing but a wild backhand strike in return. Vets bends backward, then twists into a roll avoiding the blow, and pops back up. Ahzna's face turns to hate, and she turns to Vets.

Vets propels herself to Ahzna in a well-telegraphed superman punch. But the punch wasn't what it seemed as it was the thumb of Vets' left hand that jabbed into Ahzna's other eye.

Ahzna screams, and her flinging arms catch Vets, propelling her across the patio and into a picnic table. Vets comes up quickly and launches herself back into the fight.

I hear Znuul's voice quietly over my shoulder, "Not too many Baalig muscles where she chooses to strike."

I have to smile. Vets did have a plan.

Vets' kick lands in Ahzna's gut. Ahzna screams, not as much from the pain, I guess, but being blind and not knowing where her opponent is coming from. Vets rolls and pops up on the side Ahzna was striking.

Using her palm, she blasts Ahzna's ear, causing a dull popping sound. That strike actually falters the Baalig warrior.

Then again, if my inner ear were burst, I'd probably falter a bit, too.

"Nice," I hear Znuul say.

Then Vets throws herself into the back of Ahzna's knees, causing Ahzna to fall to the ground.

I'm in elation because Vets did it – she brought Ahzna to her knees. Then I realize that Ahzna is smiling. Smiling because she has her hands on Vets. Vets is trying to get away but to no avail. I see Vets' face grimace in pain.

"Damn," says Znuul.

Ahzna, having a grip on Vets, flips around and powers her head to the ground. She holds Vets to the ground by her head, then drops an elbow.

The "pop" of Vet's skull breaking fills the air. Vets stiffens and her limbs tremble. Ahzna rolls off her, smiling.

"The price of victory," Ahzna says, her voice croaking from the throat strike.

Recognizing the devastation done to my Vets, I begin a healing prayer. When the incantation is finished, I release the healing and Vets' trembling stops. Vets groans and begins to roll over.

Ahzna sits on her knees smiling. Even though she lost, I can see she still won in her mind.

"I'll get a healing potion, for the loser," says Znuul, turning to go back inside.

Vets stands up and walks over to me.

"I did this for you, my Wielder," she says softly, her eyes looking downward in subservience.

"Lucky," croaks Ahzna, knees still on the ground.

Ahzna's comment gets a huge reaction from big girl – she actually cracks a small smile.

"You did great, Vetsy," Sil says.

Shey and Pffif share in the sentiment.

Znuul strides back through us all with a vial of red liquid in hand. He puts his hand on Ahzna's head, and she leans back. A couple drops go directly in her eyes. The rest gets poured into her mouth.

"Wait a few moments, then transform to your natural form. That should get you right," he says to her good ear.

She does wait a bit then undergoes her retransformation. Now we have a purple-skinned Baalig demon/Dzemond in an athletic bikini amongst us. She opens her eyes, and they are good again – if you call red, rattlesnake eyes good.

"Now, congratulate your opponent for a smartly fought bout," he says.

"That's not our way," she says, standing up.

"Is it our way to allow your opponent to take the first blow wherever they wish?" Znuul asks in a patronizing tone. "Really, that is beyond arrogance. We crush our enemies using any advantage is how I remember the College of War's teachings: not give them the advantage."

"Fine then," Ahzna says, looking over to Vets. "Well fought, Vetisghar; intelligently done."

Ahzna holds out her hand.

"Thank you," says Vets, who steps over and takes her hand.

That civil moment ends with the sounds of crunching bones and Vets' face contorting in pain. Ahzna pulls Vets into her and grabs the back of her head with her free hand. Then Ahzna drives her forehead into Vets with one of her horns embedding into Vets' skull. Ahzna pulls her head up violently causing the horn to tear out of Vets' skull in a gory splash of red. She releases Vets who stands wobbly for a brief moment before collapsing to the ground.

It happened so fast.

"Ahzna," Znuul shouts, "this is unacceptable!"

She turns to Znuul, a wicked smile on her face, "I still have permission to harm her." With that said she brings her foot down on Vets' shin with a resounding crack of the bone.

Vets begins to liquefy and turn to steam like all summonlings do when they are killed. The brain trauma must have been too much.

I'm going to say something, but am beaten to the punch by Sil.

"You worthless bitch!"

"Yeah, what she said," comes Shey's addition.

Ahzna looks me in the eyes, as I'm Vets' wielder. "Perhaps you wish to try for retribution?"

Not going to take that bait. But someone else does.

"Sorry Z, I'm afraid I have to kick that bitch's ass," Greg says. "Right now."

Znuul steps in between them, though that's not likely to hinder Greg if he's determined.

"She's will-linked to me, my friend. Remember how I was to Grey. If you kill her, you kill me, too."

Greg takes that in and looks away, pissed off.

"I'm still going to kick her ass. There's no excuse for that. She's a damn bully," he proclaims.

"Yes, she is," says Znuul flatly.

"Little human, you are less than a Vetisghar even. I've eaten the flesh of your kind. Quite delicious," Ahzna says.

Man, she has no idea the trouble she's making for herself.

"Cut her loose on me," says Greg, with shoulders squared, ready to go.

"Yes," agrees Ahzna, looking for another kill.

Znuul looks from Ahzna then to Greg. Then back again.

Karred's voice breaks the silent tension.

"Greg, if you kill her, you will be killing your friend and my fiancé, too."

"He is human. He will be killing no one," Ahzna says, with tail twitching.

She has no idea who she is up against. Greg is the Sword of Balance, the protector of our realm given by the spirit of the Earth itself. She will not see him coming; his gift is speed.

Znuul says the words, "Ahzna, you may fight Greg Inosanto, but you may not kill him."

The way the words are said leads me to believe they are will-touched, meaning she can't kill him.

"And you also understand, Mr. Inosanto," Znuul says to Greg.

Greg looks at Znuul in all seriousness.

"Yes. But EB is going to get a smackdown. Oh, wait, Vets needs to see this, Arthur."

He is so right. I run my finger along Vets' sigil and say "come." The space ripples and there's my big girl, armor and all.

The death's head mask turns to Ahzna. But instead of going for the sword, she says, "You have no honor. And you still lost to a Vetisghar."

Her response makes me proud. Apparently, it really ticked off EB, who says nothing but lets her red eyes do the talking.

"We thought you might want to see Greg abuse her," says Sil. "I know I'm looking forward to it."

I imagine a smile under the helm. It's probably just my imagination.

"Warrior's advice for you, Gregory Inosanto," Vets says in her way. "Do not let her take hold of you. You cannot break her grasp, and she will certainly break you."

Attention focused on Vets, Ahzna springs forward to end the fight early. She lands and throws what would have been a body punch to end the match, but he wasn't there to hit.

Instead, following a blur of movement, he's standing behind her. He brings the heel of his boot down on the tip of her tail in another blurring move.

Ahzna knows where he is now and chokes back, crying out in pain. She wheels around, her tail bleeding out her blue blood and puts her arms up in a defensive posture.

Greg explodes into Ahzna faster than the eye can track. Ahzna goes flying back doubled over, landing on the grass.

She picks herself up and casts a look at Greg who's standing on the porch. With a sneer, she moves toward him.

"One blow is all I need, human," she says, taking on Greg with her eyes.

"Whatever," is all he has to say to her and then he blurs again.

Her right knee buckles inward rather violently, and she topples over. Greg is now standing well out of her striking range. She picks herself up, favoring the leg that was just blown out from under her, and shoots Greg a hateful glare.

He disappears again, appearing where she was trying to stand, both palms out from the strike he just landed. Ahzna is flying backward, folded over, and smashes into the grill, the iron doors clanging and dislodging.

"Best to surrender to the weak, inferior human, Ahzna Luunz," says Znuul with a seriousness that borders mocking.

Her response is to roll up to her knees, bare her teeth, and let out a feral scream of frustration.

"Never surrender," she hisses and starts to pull herself up to stand, eyes on Greg.

"Good," says Greg, not a sign of emotion on his face. "I didn't want a submission victory."

Ahzna's head snaps and her body goes lax as she falls to the ground. Greg is shaking his hand from what must have been a palm-heel strike.

Znuul falters a moment.

"Gregory," Karred shouts, "Please!"

I'm looking at Znuul, who is reorienting himself.

"We're done," says Greg. "She doesn't take a shot as well as you do, Big Z."

"Few do," Znuul says back to him, then over to me. "Let's drag her off the patio. Then you need to cast some healing on her, Arthur."

I remember when I cast healing on Znuul, after we took Maldgorath's head, he barfed his guts out. I guess he's assuming the same for her. Not all react to the divine healing love in the same way.

He drags her limp body out past the slab of the porch and looks at me to do my thing.

So I do. I recite the incantation for the strongest healing spell I know. The words recited, I feel the warm essence humming through my being, so I release the healing to its intended target.

"Be healed, Ahzna Luunz."

She releases a gasp and begins trying to bring herself up in a most disoriented fashion. She doesn't quite make it up all the way, but breakfast does. I'm watching the ground steam and understand why Z didn't want her barfing on the porch; that's some mighty powerful stomach acids.

Znuul laughs. Greg is chuckling. I'd like to think Vets has a smile under that helm. She takes it off and, nope, no smile. Sil shoots me a wink.

Ahzna pulls herself up to her knees.

"Banner day, Ahzna Luunz. Failed in combat against a human and a Vetisghar," Znuul says with a mocking tone. "I guess you realize you're lucky he didn't make it to Novgorod before us."

Ahzna doesn't bother to respond verbally, but the way she tucks her wings in and twitches her tail speaks volumes.

"Great one," says Vets, taking our attention from the demoness in the beach volleyball outfit trying to gain her composure. "You should re-command your slave not to harm others. Gregory Inosanto and I are in danger of her. You have seen she acts without remorse or honor."

"Yes indeed, Lady Vets. Ahzna Luunz, you will harm no one without my express consent," Znuul says.

Ahzna, her back still to us, is shaking her head – most likely in exasperation. She picks herself up, turns around, and takes a limping step forward. Her red eyes cast around to all of us – is that embarrassment?

"Release your summonlings," Vets says with authority. "This was the wager. I did bring you to your knee. Make good on your loss."

Ahzna's eyes briefly go to Vets; then she turns to Znuul. He doesn't say anything. He really doesn't have to. His demeanor and the crossing of his arms over his chest do it for him.

One by one she calls them quietly. "D'heir," she says, and the damn spider appears. "Hargul," and the imp appears. Finally, she says "Vetisghar," and he appears, immediately dropping to a knee.

"Waaa-hoo! We're here with you," exclaims the imp, now flapping up to hover at eye height for Ahzna.

Pffif groans. "Please be sayin' that Mr. Hargul there ain't a rhyming imp? Ain't nothing more annoying than a damn rhyming imp."

"Pffif's statement catches the flying monkey-reptile thing's attention, and it turns to look at him.

"Hargul only rhymes when he wishes to. But that's all the time, so very true."

Yes, I can see where Mr. Hargul is going to get on the nerves pretty quickly.

Shey thinks it's hilarious; "Haha! He rhymed back at you!"

Ahzna has chosen to make a strategic limping exit to the indoors, and her entourage follows on her heels once realizing it.

"Well, that's enough excitement for a day," says Karred. "She's going to need another healing potion later." With that said, she heads indoors.

Greg and Znuul follow, leaving me outside with my group and Sil.

Vets, helm under arm, still takes to a knee in front of me and bows her head.

"Your will has been done, my Wielder. I am honored to have served you."

"Uh, yeah. Thank you, Vets. You really did well," I stammer, despite the fact I should have seen it coming.

"You were amazing," says Sil, going down to a knee herself to hug Vets around her neck.

"Aye, big girl," Pffif says, patting her armored shoulder.

"You stomped that stupid, ugly, troll-smelling, fucking evil bitch's ass into a blood puddle," adds the foul-mouthed fairy in her form of praise.

Arix is giving light applause even.

And I know Hjuul is proud; I can tell by the wagging of his tail.

Vets looks up at me, smiling. Yes, full on smiling. I smile, too.

"I think someone earned a hug from her wielder," says Sil with a seriously naughty look. "And probably a little more, too."

"What does she mean by more?" Vets asks me, now looking quite concerned Sil may be talking about "the breeding" again.

I have to laugh. Things may have changed, but they're still so the same.

Chapter 17

Outside of Al Tabqah, Syria

"I will be so happy to be free of these zealot humans," Hthifis says to Czerbial. "They cannot even trust themselves around female beauty. Can you believe they make me cover my face and wear this tent?"

"I'm not sure what displeases you more, the fact that they make you wear the burqa or the fact they insist on speaking to me only," Czerbial replies with a chuckle.

"Definitely that they insist you speak," she snaps back. "I am the senior on this assignment."

"Yes, you are," he says. "You did bring the weapons? I have a feeling that when I tell them our news, we will have to fight our way out."

"I will not let them harm you," says the driver.

"I am trusting that you will not," says Hthifis. "As our appointed Hjuulak, you are expected to destroy those who would harm us, Gartm. You were bred for this, no?"

"Yes, commander," Gartm, the driver replies, "I will slay all that oppose you, at your command."

Hthifis smiles as does Czerbial. The Hjuulak were bred to be loyal, and Gartm is no exception.

"So to my earlier question, did you bring the weaponry, senior ambassador?" asks Czerbial.

"Of course I did," she snaps back. "And they are in a very uncomfortable place that cannot be patted down but can be released quickly."

"You, my dear, are a consummate professional," Czerbial replies.

"Which weapon will I receive?" asks Gartm.

"You will take and use the humans' weapons against them. The sonic disruption and pulse weapons will be ours," says Hthifis curtly.

"Yes, of course," says Gartm.

"And, Czerbial, just so we are clear, I will be speaking today. It's time they realize a female's role is what she chooses to make it."

He nods in agreement, but his face belies concern.

She smiles at him, "Yes. I plan to be a complete terror. And if that worm thinks to bring us harm, I will kill him myself – most unpleasantly."

The vehicle moves through a series of checkpoints, and they are directed to what may have been a grocery store or other kind of large retail business. The car stops, and they get out following the heavily armed men. Czerbial smiles. Nobody can see Hthifis' scowl under the burqa and veil.

Once inside, they are patted down, though they spend much more time and attention on Hthifis, much to her chagrin.

Gartm, noting her displeasure, looks over protectively. Her eyes tell him assistance is not needed.

"Follow us," says the lead armed militant. "We will take you to Abu Adan Al Qa'im."

They follow to a stairwell and climb to the next floor. A short trip down the hall, past numbers of armed men, and they arrive at an office area where they are greeted by Abu Adan Al Qa'im.

"Greetings, ambassadors. It is good to see you. I trust you come with good news. We have made much progress, and more cities are coming to God."

He pauses and looks at Hthifis. "Please leave us; this discussion is for men."

Hthifis responds by pulling off her veil and pulling back her head covering. "No. It's time for you to understand that I am the lead ambassador. I have grown tired of humoring your little male ego. Beautiful, aren't I? I hope you can control yourself."

With that said, she sloughs the burqa over her head, revealing herself. Her light ambassador's armor clings like a second skin over her torso, protecting vital areas. Under that is a short black skirt and sandals.

"Cover yourself, cur," Abu Adan Al Qa'im calls out.

"Silence yourself, human," Hthifis spits back. "Your days of false authority are over. Our emperor heard your demands and replies as such: no. We will not adopt your pathetic excuse of a religion. You insult us with your demands. Perhaps if your religion can prove itself against the others of this realm, we may consider hearing you. Otherwise, you have offended the Dzemond Collective. And you have offended me as well. We are done with one another."

Czerbial is braced for the response. Gartm, isn't moving at all – except for his eyes, which are taking in potential threats.

Abu Adan Al Qa'im laughs.

"Quite a message," he says, looking at Czerbial. "Perhaps you will be kind enough to return a message from Allah and his warriors."

The gun in his hand appears from almost nowhere, and he opens fire on Hthifis, the room filling with the sound of gunfire and her shrieks as she covers herself and falls to the ground.

"Tell this to your emperor and your Collective! The People's Islamic State does not barter with unbelievers," Abu Adan Al Qa'im says proudly to Czerbial. His pride turns to astonishment when his eyes catch sight of Hthifis turning to her true self.

Gartm lunges into the armed guards tackling them to the ground.

Hthifis stand and pitches a rectangular object to Czerbial, then locks eyes with her would-be murderer.

"Allah must not be with you now," she says, leveling a curved device at him. It whines a "wee-ump," and Abu Adan Al Qa'in's midsection explodes and his torso collapses on the desk, his legs falling back in the other direction. She grasps his hair and pulls his head up to look into his dying eyes.

"Who's superior now, pathetic human male?"

For good measure, she bounces his head on the desk.

Czerbial follows suit and changes to his true form. Gartm has also stripped off the ring that allows him to appear human and is reverting to his more beastly nature.

The door flies open behind them followed by militants with automatic arms. Shocked at the sight of the creatures before them, they hesitate. Gartm, now resembling more werewolf than man, leaps across the room tackling them both to the ground, claws ripping and teeth tearing into them.

Czerbial jumps over and slams the door shut.

"We need to get outside and to wing," he shouts.

The sound of automatic gunfire erupts, and the ambassadors fall to the ground as the drywall is ripped to shreds. Abu Adan Al Qa'im's torso dances from the bullets.

"Subdue them," Hthifis shouts to Czerbial.

He responds by activating the device in his hand. It morphs from a basic rectangle to a banana-shaped instrument with a conical head. He takes a moment to program it for automatic use – widespread pattern, maximum intensity at a fifteen-second interval with a ten-second delay.

"Gartm! Move to the back of the room – this could affect you!" he shouts.

Gartm belly-crawls along the floor to the back of the room.

Czerbial commands his armor to put up a shield for his head and lunges for the door. He opens it, only to be greeted by gunfire. His armor being thin, he still feels the stings of the blows, though they don't penetrate.

It's not pleasant, but he manages to slip the device out into the hall.

A short moment passes, and a modulating "oooooom" sound comes from the device followed by the cries of the guards outside. The sound continues as does the lament of those outside.

"Hjuulak, kill all in your path. Once we have escaped, you may, too. Do you understand?"

"Yes, I will clear the way," says Gartm, who collects all the weapons he can carry and bolts outside. The sound of his gunfire comes shortly after.

"We make for the outside and take to wing," says Hthifis.

"We should look for a window, it would be better than fighting our way to the street," Czerbial replies coolly.

"Agreed, we go now while they are still puking and crapping themselves," she says back.

Czerbial is first to the door and collects the sonic disruption pistol. Hthifis is hot on his heels and enters the hall.

"There – the window," she says, pointing to the end of the hall past the retching, writhing, and moaning militants.

They start to make their run to the window but are greeted by a pair of militants that avoided the sonic bowel disruption. They take some fire, and Hthifis returns fire her weapon, making the "wee-ump" sound. The shot sprays one of them into the doorjamb they popped out from and makes the other jump back in the room opposite.

Hthifis turns the pulse pistol toward the room the others ducked into and levels the walls with pulse after pulse. Czerbial covers their flanks with pulses from the sonic gun. Hthifis raps his shoulder, and they both run for the window, Hthifis crashing through first.

The soldiers on the ground aren't sure what to think about the two winged creatures flying away quickly, but they manage to shoot at them all the same.

Chapter 18

It's been three weeks at the bunker. Normally, I'd be pretty itchy being locked in like that. But the truth is, I haven't been locked in. We're free to come and go as we please.

And I've been with Silithes.

Not that the whole time has been juicy, messy fun. Sure there's been some of it. Okay – a lot, but we spend more time just being together. Talking. Sharing. Being together. Besides, it's not like she could come back to New Orleans with us, being on The Protectorate's "most wanted" list.

Today's like most days. We start the day with some happy fun time. Then she goes to assist Edgar and Percy with the work they are doing after a bit of freshening up. And of course, she has to spend time on the phone with Jxsiga – every day. Sometimes for hours.

Me? I work out with Vets and try to get to know Ahzna's summonlings. After all, it only makes sense to get to know them after freeing them from the hold of the white.

D'hier, the spider, is mostly unfathomable to me – and freaking creepy. Znuul has explained that they can communicate with non-spider types through an intricate sign language. I've seen some of that language. I'm pretty sure us human types could sum it up his words for me with a single middle finger.

Today, I've decided I'm going to take another run at "Vetisghar" – Ahzna's unnamed servant. He's taken to being quite the attendant of the place. He's basically taken over for Kitten in cleaning the bunker, and right now, he's scrubbing the baseboards.

I've never seen Kitten do that. But then, as I understand it, a "house Vetisghar" lives only as it is useful to its owners. Otherwise, it's sold or harvested for its meat.

Sick, like so much of Dzemond culture.

So, despite his prior rebuffs of "my master dislikes you" and "I will be punished for speaking with you," I try to engage this guy again.

"Leave me alone," he says, "You make only problems for me."

I can't leave it at that.

"Oh come on. It's not like she really even pays attention to you or what you're doing. I just want to get to know you."

He looks at me with a blank expression.

"Hey, you belonged to some Garrigan before, right? So did my guys. Was your previous master more rotten than EB? Those Garrigans..."

Just like that, I touch a nerve. His ears flatten back, and his eyes narrow on me.

"Service for Queen Midizria was the highlight of my whole existence. I was given purpose, value, and a name. The queen herself acknowledged my good work on behalf of the city."

His ears unflatten, and his expression softens.

"I felt her gratitude. She even said she appreciated me. She was so beautiful and gracious. I do not know what I did wrong to be punished in such a way as to be given to... Ahzna Luunz."

I nod in agreement, not willing to share my thought that maybe it was just that he wasn't as important to his former master as he thought. That would be a horrendous thing to say – even if true. Instead, I go with the positive.

"What was your name?"

His chest swells out with pride, and he stands up straighter on his knees.

"My name was Waste Technician 143."

Not much of a name. Poker face sells me out again.

"It is a good name! It speaks to my role and place. I wore that name proudly, She gave it to me personally and wished me well in my function. She wished me well! Beautiful Queen Midizria herself!"

I guess when you've spent a life not worthy of any individuality, being Waste Technician 143 is a big deal, and the truth is, being acknowledged and appreciated is a big deal to anyone. Certainly, it is to him. Damn, if he doesn't make it sound like having his soul stolen wasn't the best thing ever. From what Vets described to me about how they raise the warrior class, there may be something to that.

"Well, that sounds pretty great when you put it like that. Mind if I call you WT, for short?"

His eyes narrow and his brow furrows.

"Do not give me a name. My master will punish me. She will give me the everlasting hatred. The gifting of a name must be from her and her alone."

"Fair enough, WT," I say, flaunting her control of him. "We humans like to have a name for everyone we deal with. I'll explain the intricacies to her. But from now on, you're 'WT' to me."

"Oh nooooo."

"Listen, it can't be that bad. She'll come around – you'll see."

He shakes his head, not approving of my decision.

"Listen, WT, even if we do nothing she's going to be an evil bitch toward you. Maybe, just maybe, we might be able to move her to be more reasonable toward you. If we do nothing, we can expect nothing – right? I mean, look, we got you out of the white."

"And into her resentment."

Well, I guess he told me. Resented by your wielder is probably not pleasant based on what my crew has shared with me.

"I'll fix this."

He shakes his head at me like I'm an idiot and goes back to cleaning the baseboards.

"Good morning, my Wielder," says Vets, my Vetisghar warrior, walking through the living room with purpose to the kitchen to get her morning meal. Vets catches the eye of WT, who stops with the cleaning to watch her.

"Warrior class," he mutters.

"She sure is."

Given no reply, I move to the peninsula bar that separates the kitchen from the living room area to spend a little more time with big girl. She's, of course, going for the eggs and meat.

"Make some up for me, too," I ask.

"I would be honored, though I am not a talented preparer of foods."

"Good enough for you, good enough for me, Vets."

I get what I think is almost a smile, and she says, "I will strive for adequacy in this food preparation, my Wielder."

"I know it will be fine."

Heck, how do you screw up eggs, ham, and sausage?

I enjoy watching her preparations when my attention is broken by the porch door opening.

"Vetisghar! Water! Now," Ahzna commands.

WT wastes no time getting up and rushing to the kitchen. He brushes by Vets to get a glass for her. Apparently, that was the wrong thing to do.

Vets grabs his arm spinning him away. There is one quick strike to the midsection that doubles him over. Then she throws him over the peninsula bar, crashing to the floor, causing me to duck to the side.

Just that fast. And without a thought of it, she's back to the eggs and meat.

"Was that necessary, Vets?" All he did was brush against her.

She trains her eyes on me with all seriousness.

"I know what males want."

Crapsticks. Again. But then, if I was subject to what she was, I might be a bit twitchy, too. Apparently "The breeding" involves being beaten, tied down, and raped.

WT gets up in a panic.

"I must get her water!"

"I'll get it for you," I say, hoping to set him at ease. "Vets, would you pour me a tall glass of ice water for Ms. Ahzna?"

Vets raises an eyebrow. She turns and just like that, it is in my hand. I take the glass of ice water and look at the very pensive WT.

"I got it, WT. I'll bring it to her for you."

He has no words. Apparently, he's not used to people doing favors for him.

I slide the door open and make my way to the lounge chair holding EB. Once there, I announce myself.

"Your water, EB."

Eyes pop open, and she turns to regard me.

"On the table, human. I must say, this is a bonus. I ask my slave to bring me this. Instead, I get to see you act as one."

"I do that every now and then. Hey, I was hoping we might talk about WT."

She stops in mid-drink and cocks her head.

"What is WT?"

"Your Vetisghar. He works so hard. I just thought that maybe…"

"No. He has not earned his name by me. He is nothing. He is a summonling. You will not call him by anything but…"

"WT," I say, interrupting her this time. "Listen, it's a human thing. We even name our dogs and cats. No offense to you, but I can't just call him 'Vetisghar.' You do what you want, but everybody gets a name here."

My only response is a very unnerving look that tells me that if she could hurt me, she would and badly.

I hear the porch door slide open a bit more and turn to see my Sil standing there.

"Arthur, big news in the war room," she says with no nonsense. "You need to come now."

"Thanks for the talk, EB," I say, before turning to join Sil. I don't get two steps before Ahzna lets me know what she's thinking.

"I am bidden to tell the truth, Arthur MacInerny. So know this… You call me EB, evil bitch. I will show you what evil bitch means someday."

That's enough to get me to turn around.

"When I am free, and I will be free, once my now-master tastes of my talents. I will destroy your life. I will start with her," she says, pointing to Silithes. "I will tear her wings from her back and break her pretty neck. Then I will seek out and kill all you hold dear. Only then will I consider killing you and most likely that will be done in increments."

I'm stunned.

"Yeah right, bitch. Dream on," Silithes says. "Arthur, we need to go – this is urgent."

The two exchange seriously evil looks at each other.

"Let's go," I say to Sil, walking past her staring contest with Ahzna. Luckily, she follows me, and we walk toward the office.

"She's all talk, Arthur – don't give it another thought."

I have to stop because there's something Sil hasn't considered. It's bothering me something fierce.

"Sil, she's bound to speak only the truth. She's not just all talk."

Chapter 19

The screens in the office area are abuzz with news coverage. I see flashing headlines like "Demons of the Middle East," and "P.I.S. claims victory."

"Good for you to join us," comes Edgar's cheery voice from behind what used to be Znuul's desk. "I think you've got the gist of things. Apparently, some of Helterezen's ambassadors have shown their faces."

"Percy, play back the Al-Jazeera English coverage," says Znuul with his back to me, fixated on the screens along with Greg.

"Got it, Big Z. Arthur, center screen," Percy says.

I turn my attention to the center screen over Edgar's desk. There are three men in battle garb and what looks like a werewolf's head on a spike. They are speaking in Arabic, but it's subtitled.

"Demons have come to test our faith and failed. Behold the head of our enemy – the enemy of Allah and the enemy of all true believers. The other demons fled us in fear!"

At that comment, a box appears with what must be cell phone video of two winged beings flying away.

"We call all true believers to our cause. Our victory proves we are the chosen of Allah! Come to us. Join our holy cause against these demons and all the infidel nonbelievers."

"Cubati ambassadors," says Silithes. "Typical. And an interesting gambit going after religious zealots. You'd think they'd see it was doomed to fail."

"Wasn't their call," says Znuul, turning around. "They were working on orders, no doubt from the emperor himself. He has a thing for subversion. Percy, do we have any higher resolution images of the ambassadors?"

"Suspecting something? Do share," says Edgar, leaning in.

"Something I thought I saw, Edgar. But the images aren't clear."

Greg looks at him as if to say, "Well, don't keep us in suspense."

"Screen 4 Z, it's the native phone file from the internet," chimes in Percy.

We all turn to that screen and watch as two Cubati fly away from a building.

"Freeze that. Go back half a second and blow it up as best you can," directs Znuul.

"What are you looking for, dear?" asks Karred.

We wait a moment while Percy does his magic. The screen next to it now has a zoomed image.

"That," says Znuul, pointing to the arms of what appears to be the female ambassador.

"And that is?" I have to ask.

Znuul turns to me, grinning that grin of his.

"That, Arthur, is part of the conflict of my command – what your friend Kaanim said. He was trying to tell us he's already under control. I think that's a command bracer. Hard to tell, but it makes sense to me. The conflict comes when I get my armor back. Tricky-tricky Phagorite. He didn't want to say anything they could make him repeat. And trust me, they would."

Then it comes back to me – Znuul's armor. Kaanim, when he abducted me, told me Znuul would want it. Or was he trying to tell me that Znuul needs to get his armor? Tricky Phagorite/master vampire indeed. But after hearing how they treat his kind, I can understand why he's not looking forward to Helterezen's dominance of the Earthen realm.

Who'd want to be freeze-dried and put in storage?

"Ahtsag, if you are thinking what I think you are thinking, you know you can't even get close to it," Edgar says in all seriousness.

Znuul turns his smile to Edgar.

"No. I can't. But he can," he says, turning his grin my way. "He has a key."

"What key is that, Z?" I ask.

"That would be his sword you are talking about," Edgar says, leaning in over the desk to Znuul.

"It would."

"Please. You two feel free to clue me in anytime since Yayne appears to be the key to getting your armor."

"His armor is held in the Vatican's special collection," says Edgar, turning to me. "It has angelic protection; your sword allows you to pass. While Ahtsag's nature... does not."

"What it means, Arthur," Znuul says, walking over to drape his huge arm around my shoulder, "is that you and I are going on a road trip."

Chapter 20

Apparently, our outing is going to be a duo mission. Just Z and I. He was rather adamant about it despite both Silithes and Karred insisting our "better halves" should accompany us.

All of that was stilled with several statements of "No" by Znuul, followed by an authoritative "This is not a European vacation."

Edgar's snickering and winks at me throughout the discussion helped break the tension – for me anyway. Karred was not pleased, but relented. Silithes never uncrossed her arms.

I broke the news to the team: they will stay here in sunny North Dakota, while I go and fetch Znuul his armor. After promising I'd summon them if needed, all was good.

Nothing is left now but the packing. Znuul wants this show on the road ASAP. How he can get us flight arrangements in a day or so, given our most-wanted status is a mystery? I suppose that's Edgar's and Percy's doing.

I look over to the corner at Yayne's case. He needs to be brought up to speed, especially considering he's "the key." I start over that way and am stopped by the door opening without a knock. Sil sweeps in. I can tell she's a little bothered about these last-second arrangements. She looks at me, makes an effort to put a smile on her face I know she's not feeling, and sits down on the corner of the bed next to my gradually filling duffel bag.

"I thought we'd have more time," she says after a few moments of silence. "The weeks have flown by."

So true.

"We need to talk. A serious talk. I'm not staying here. It's time for me to join Jex and Paul."

Well, damn, that is serious. I understand, too; our road trip most likely won't be a day or so. I turn to her and see she registers my comprehension of the situation.

"Let me talk with Yayne first."

"No. We come first." She pauses a moment, looks at Yayne's case, and turns back to me, relenting the point, "But if you must, find me outside."

She gets up and stops to give me a kiss on the cheek. I know she gets Yayne must be treated with consideration.

She opens the door, stops, and proclaims, "Big work ahead, Yayne, but it should be easy work."

With that said, she goes, leaving the door open.

I have to smile, Silithes stealing my thunder.

I grab the case and flip it on the bed. After unlatching it, I take him by the hilt.

"I presume you heard the news?"

"Yes," comes the voice in my mind.

"Retrieval mission, we need to secure Znuul's armor."

"Why do we need to arm the demon?"

"Well, not arming as much as securing a device to let him control another demon."

"And this is necessary to protect the Earth?"

"Well, if we don't control that guy, the bad guys do – so yeah."

"So we will slay the evil holders of this armor?"

I cringe a bit.

"Well, no. It's stored at the Vatican under angelic guard. We will be slaying no one. Just getting in and seeing if we can persuade them to let us have it."

"And if these good people say no..."

"Then out of luck, I guess. I won't raise my hand against them. Or you."

The feeling I get is one of acknowledgment. Kind of like a psychic "Okay." That's followed by, "Go to your demoness. She seems to have important matters to discuss."

He's right.

I say my "Thanks," put him away properly, and get going to the rear porch, where I see Silithes patiently sitting on one of the picnic tables. We exchange eye contact and smiles as I make my way out to straddle the bench seat underneath her.

"All yours, Sil."

"If only you were..."

I have to chuckle at that, only because she's right. So much of my heart still belongs to my passed-on wife, Dorothy – the angel on my shoulder. There's no sense in even denying it – it's the truth.

"So you're going to move in with the twins, eh? Isn't that kind of risky with The Protectorate looking for you? I mean, birds of a feather..."

"Maybe," she says back. "I can change my appearance. I know what you mean, but where else am I going to go? But I didn't want to talk about my safety; I wanted to talk about the strangeness. And there are some strange things we are going to have to deal with – especially you."

"Go on."

"My needs to begin with. I'm not going to live half-starved and subsisting on the blue stuff like Jxsiga does. Arthur, there will be those I use to take care of my needs because I won't use you that way."

That registers. I'm sure my face does, too.

"Then there's the other thing," she says with a sly smile. "We, Jxsiga and I, tend to be rather... affectionate. I have no plans of turning down any affection given with a pure heart … And her heart is pure."

I have to look away because I know my face will show my thoughts.

"That goes for Paul, too."

Shit. Just shit. I put my face in my hands as I try to collect myself.

"I told you it would get strange, Arthur."

She didn't lie. But then, Silithes has been pretty good about being straight with me since we took back up.

"Yeah, Sil, yeah."

She laughs and then runs her fingers through my hair. "You ready for it to get really strange? I mean, blowing your mind, your-world-will-never-be-the-same kind of strange?"

"No, but I'm not one to duck fate."

"You and I are going to have a baby."

"Crapsticks!"

I bolt up off the bench and look at her, completely in amazement.

Her eyes are playful. Her smile is, too.

"I don't mean right now, Arthur. I mean we will. I have five eggs left. You're getting at least one of them – probably most. I bet we'd make cute halfsies."

My heart rate starts to settle down, but still, Sil telling me that we WILL make babies is a bit unsettling. Unlike us humans, Dzemond females control the when of birth. I'm pretty sure she can coax my part from me anytime she wishes. I don't get a word out.

"Arthur, I am very committed to our family. You know I consider, Helen, Jerry Junior, all mine, too – same with the great-grands. I plan to contribute to our family tree. That, and I think it gives our bond more depth."

She turns away from me, looking out across the horizon. I allow the silence. I need a moment, too.

"We haven't soul-touched since I've become... real... this. We need to refresh our bond. You need to feel me, how I am now. You need to know I feel, not just hear it."

I have to smile. The truth with Silithes is sometimes found in the in-betweens.

"And you need to feel me, how I am now – right?"

She turns back to me, a smile on her face.

"I can't get anything past you, can I? You were always able to read me when I was your... summonling. You know I miss being yours? Right? The vivid feeling of love, the pleasure reflection."

I have to laugh. The pleasure reflection, it sure must have been intense for her as it was so mind-bending for me. It's even more so for me now that the governors are off from her being a summonling.

"Does it always come down to the pleasure, Sil?"

I get a very disapproving look that tells me all I need to know.

"So, you want to soul-touch again, Sil?"

"Do you trust me?"

I've since learned the touch is actually the Sisterhood's most feared weapon. But I also know she's never used it that way against me. If anything, it's been a beautiful thing – a true union.

"Of course I do. I think it'll be good."

She smiles, letting me know that she feels the same way.

"Let's get this moving on."

She gets up and takes my hand.

I follow.

∴

The funny thing about the soul touch is, even though it's triggered by a most carnal act when it's run its course, the last thing you feel is turned on.

More like overwhelmed.

This time was like our first time, all over again. Her life, feelings, fears, and dreams all passed before my life at light speed.

I'm laying here Silithes atop me, but that is the last thing on either of our minds. Silithes lets out a deep breath and slides off to my side. Neither of us says anything, not really having to.

Silithes' alligator-like green eyes go wide in acknowledgment of our experience, and she runs her hand through her dark bed-head hair to collect herself.

"Well..." she says.

"That was like the first time," I say, finishing for her.

That elicits a little laugh, and her hand goes from her hair to over my chest.

"We're going to be finishing each other's sentences for a while again," she says, snuggling in close, making sure not to poke with me with her small horns. My arm reflexively goes around her pulling her in even closer.

"Yeah, I guess it makes sense it'd be like the first time."

"Since I'm basically the new me," Sil says, finishing my thought.

We share a smile and some very deep eye contact, knowing our bond has been strengthened – that and we will be finishing each other's thoughts for the next week.

Or not, I have to go secure some armor.

And she's going to join up with Jxsiga.

Crapsticks. Jxsiga...

"You're thinking about her... Jex."

She's right. I try not to be jealous, or whatever it is that I am. But...

"You know it's more than just a physical thing, right? You had to feel that when we touched. I know you won't believe this, but you two are alike in so many ways, Arthur. Not the least of which is your hearts belong to the dead."

I know she didn't say that to be hurtful – she's right. I've never let go of Dorothy. I have no plans to.

"Yeah, Sil. But alike? Not seeing it."

"You just have to get past the whole face of dominance she puts out there. It's kind of like the face of the temptress I used for so long. After a while, it becomes a habit you know. Once you get to know her, you'll see. She's not really like that at all. She has a very goofy side."

We enjoy a quiet moment of consideration between ourselves – there's really no reason for words. Up to a point.

"You're right, Sil. It's going to be strange."

"Told you."

Chapter 21

Sil, Karred, Znuul, and I are the passengers. Kitten is driving us to the airfield. I'm equipped with a new ID, and some special makeup to foil the facial scanners – a couple of nice moles, a wart, unibrow, and a mustache.

Percy assures me they'll never know it's me. I still think he went a little overboard on the ugly.

Kitten pulls us over to the side of the road, which surprises me.

"Okay, master, here we are," she says in her perky way.

"Thank you, Kitten," he says, opening the back door. Kitten wastes no time putting the car in park and bolting outside herself.

"I guess I should go out, too," Karred says while scooting herself outside.

Sil, in the front passenger seat, turns back to me.

"Aww... they're so cute, aren't they?"

Znuul's big head, now in his natural Baalig form, enters through the driver's side door complete with that car-dealer grin of his.

"See you on the plane, Artie. Enjoy customs."

I have to admit to some confusion, but then, I know better than to question the big purple one. If he says he'll see me on the plane, then he will. Besides, he's sure to set off all sorts of flags, human-looking or not, being as large as he is.

Karred and Kitten return, and we are back on track for the airfield.

Karred shakes my knee to get my attention.

"I expect you to keep him out of trouble, just so you know."

"That's too much to ask of anyone," Sil comes back hiccup-quick.

"He still needs to try. You will, won't you?"

I take in the playful look on Karred's face and know that underneath she still wants me to try to keep him under wraps – but won't hold it against me if I can't."

"I will, Karen... damn. Karred."

That's good for a laugh all the way around. I don't even think she's used to her "new" name.

We get to the airfield and say our goodbyes at the dawn of the morning. Sil makes sure I know to call. I say I will – on our secure lines. Customs goes without event, mostly because there isn't really customs at this mostly agricultural airfield.

I get in the Gulfstream and am greeted by the pilot, who invites me to take a seat. I look about the cabin, noting a ripple in the space of the rear. It has to be a camouflaged Znuul. I point over to the ripple, and the spell drops revealing Znuul.

"I told you he'd spot me," Znuul says to the pilot who doesn't seem bothered at all by an enormous demonic-looking being in the back of his plane.

"Yes, you did. I'll get us ready for takeoff, Mr. Znuul," is his reply as he closes and seals the cabin door. "Mr. Arthur, we won't have attendants on this flight; there are beverages and sandwiches in the refrigerators."

With that said, he heads to the cockpit, and Znuul moves to take a couple of seats at the front.

"Road trip, Arthur," he says, nodding and smiling. "Just you and me."

"Yeps, just you and me, big guy."

"I have to admit, I'm hoping we can talk about some things. Like... you know, this whole monogamy thing. It's pretty important to Karred. I figure you're the expert."

"That's actually pretty simple, Z. If you love somebody enough, you don't need another."

He nods at me, taking in the statement. "But what does that have to do with sharing pleasures? I mean my heart, if you will, is certainly affixed to Karred. But I still like to have my cock stroked and..."

"Just stop. Z... We humans tend to equate those acts with the heart. It's not a separate thing. I mean, when we declare love, we make that person our everything."

"Well, it makes no sense to me. And you, how are you going to have a monogamous relationship with a succubus? They are considered to be... I don't have to explain how they view the act of sexual congress, do I? I mean..."

"No, you do not have to explain that to me."

The airplane speeds up, and takeoff is imminent. My attention is distracted.

"See, we have a quite a bit to talk about. I need to know about this whole monogamy thing, which is already dubious for me, given how Karred and Kitten carry on. And you need to come to grips with sharing your girlfriend with goodness knows how many others."

I feel the airplane leave the ground.

"Hey," Znuul says, reaching over and grabbing my leg. "I have a great idea. Let's go to Amsterdam and pick up a few red-light girls. Three for me, one for you — come on, we'll get you into the Cubati mindset."

"How about not, Z. I don't think Karred would be too happy with either of us if we did that. Besides, you need to practice up on the one and only thing, right?"

That gets me one of Znuul's more sinister smiles. He leans into me as the airplane ascends to cruising altitude.

"Not as much as you need to practice the fine art of casual pleasures. Amsterdam..."

It's my turn to lean in, though my smile has no sinister overtones.

"No. You definitely need practice more than me."

Chapter 22

The tap on me knee wakens me. Not that my losing argument with Znuul was anything but interesting, it's just I've taken to the habit of using melatonin to reset my sleep clock when doing large international jumps.

That, and Sil wasn't really in the mood for sleep before I left.

"Landing soon," Znuul says, handing me an energy drink.

"Thanks."

It says a great deal about the changes in my life that waking up to that demonic face doesn't have me screaming in blind panic. I regard the energy drink, looking forward to the boost but dreading the syrupy, over-sugary taste.

Coffee is more my speed.

"When we land, I'll camouflage, open the door, and fly out. You close it – quickly. I'll meet you at the Europcar rental. They're supposed to have an SUV or something for us. You should be able to grab a shuttle."

"Europcar – right," I parrot back, popping the top on my disgusting liquid energy.

The pilot's voice comes over the intercom, advising us to make sure our seat belts are on as approach is imminent, followed by the sound of the landing gear deploying.

"I can hardly wait to get out of this tin can," Znuul says, looking out the window at our approach.

I smile, remembering when Grey Lightbringer told me he used a small closet as a means of discipline with Znuul. Mr. Destroyer of Hope and Devourer of Souls has a touch of claustrophobia.

But then if I was locked in a demon trap for something like five thousand years, I might not care for confined areas either.

I feel the rear wheels grace the ground followed by a whisper of the front ones. We begin to decelerate. Znuul unbuckles in a flash.

"Come on, Arthur."

I unbuckle as well and follow Znuul to the front of the craft, where he appears to be speaking with the pilot.

Hunched over in the cabin, Znuul moves to the door, turning to me before opening it.

"There won't be a cabin pressure issue; step around me over here. Once I'm out, close it fast. Hit the cabin lights, Rick."

Znuul mutters some guttural words and becomes transparent. The lights go out. Znuul opens the door and says, "Have fun in customs."

Even though I can't see it, I know he's got the bogus grin going.

Znuul dissolves into the dark, and I wrestle the door closed with all my strength.

"Enjoy customs, my ass."

Chapter 23

Silence can be maddening. Particularly silence from a customs agent. So far, the only thing out of his mouth has been "papers, please." I try to keep a pleasant demeanor. He's looked me over and keeps checking a computer screen.

He pushes my papers back to me, looks at me inscrutably and says, "What is your purpose for coming to France from Canada?"

As Yayne is part of my luggage, trying to dodge that is a guaranteed losing proposition, so I go straight on.

"Personal, mostly. Shopping. I collect things. Medieval things. That and I've never been to Paris before."

"So that is why you bring a weapon with you. Do you plan to sell this weapon? Have you brought any other currency or valuable items?"

"Sell it? Never," I say with as much indignity as I can muster without appearing bogus. "That sword is one of a kind. It's the hallmark of my collection. I like to show it off to other collectors and sellers. It's instant credibility. And no, the sword is all I brought of value."

He looks back to his screen and then scrutinizes me.

"Enjoy your visit, sir."

"Thank you, sir."

I pass through and go immediately to my luggage. And Znuul's... I thought to pack light with one duffel and Yayne's box. Luckily Z thought the same way, one duffel, and a huge garment bag. I'm not carrying this stuff to wherever this Europcar rental is – at least not on my back. I grab a luggage cart and load up. After asking for some direction to the car rental location, I'm on my way.

After a short while of pushing the luggage cart along Avenue De l'Europe, I sense I am in the right place, not because I know where I am as much, but by the sound of Znuul's very deep voice yelling at someone in French.

I follow the booming voice around a corner to see my now in-human form friend having a heated debate with the attendant. Znuul gestures to the car, followed by pointing to himself, and I now get the gist of the problem: The car is too small for his taste.

Znuul sees me and holds up his hands in exasperation.

"Arthur! Look at this; I ordered a large SUV. This is neither. How am I supposed to fit in this?"

It's certainly an SUV-style vehicle but is on the smaller end of the spectrum. I push the cart up and give the now pair of attendants a smile.

The first one looks at me, I guess hoping for some understanding, and says, "It is most certainly a Sports Utility Vehicle and is the largest we have now."

"Anything larger? Minivan... a bus?" I ask in the most conciliatory tone I can, given Znuul is now obviously exchanging words in French with the other man who I guess is the manager.

"We are sold out. Had we known, we could have better suited.... his needs."

"Z! It's an SUV. We need to go."

I have all of his attention; apparently, I am a traitor.

"This is unacceptable," he booms.

"So is your behavior. Have you tried to sit in it at least?"

Finally, there's a pause in the commotion as Znuul looks from me to the car.

"No, he has not," says the attendant.

"I am of mind that you can take your business elsewhere," says the manager. "Were it not for your sensible American friend."

"Is it really worth all this drama, delay, and attention?" I ask.

There comes a deep growl from somewhere inside Znuul, startling the auto rental duo. I kind of share the feeling, the growl wasn't exactly human sounding. He looks at me, nods, and puts the car-dealer smile on. He turns quickly to the manager and attendant.

"My sensible Canadian friend is right. We'll take it."

"Ah, Canadian, that makes more sense," says the manager.

As my passport and identity are indeed Canadian, I cannot defend the stars and stripes; damn the ugly American stereotypes.

"May I help with your bags, sir?"

"Thank you, yes."

He flips the rear hatch up, and I notice the locker trunk that Znuul brought with him from who knows where – it wasn't on the plane. Apparently, Z made provisions, which would also explain his change of wardrobe to a nice tailored blazer and slacks.

The attendant reaches down casually for the locker, and the look of surprise on his face tells me whatever is in that locker isn't fluffy down pillows.

"My friend is rather strong. Why don't we let him get that?"

"It just surprised me. He handled it as it were nothing."

With a deep breath, he takes the locker by both handles and awkwardly loads it into the back.

"We have it, see."

I hope he didn't blow out his back.

Znuul strides out of the office, artificial smile in place, and looks us both up and down.

"All packed up – good. I'm driving. If I have to be cooped up in this thing, I will at least be in control."

I hear the driver's seat sliding all the way back, and Znuul grumbles under his breath. I get in to watch him fumbling with the seat controls and steering wheel.

"It'll get us there."

Znuul doesn't respond to my comment other than to look at me with contempt, then start the car.

"I suppose it will."

We start our journey, leaving Le Bourget Airport in relative silence. After a while, it's silence I must break.

"Have to ask, why Paris? Couldn't we have flown directly to Rome?"

Znuul's smile returns.

"It's closer to Amsterdam."

Chapter 24

I'm jarred awake by the large hand shaking my shoulder and an "Arthur, wake up. You know where we are?"

I look at Znuul through bleary, just-woken eyes.

"I just woke up."

"Look around."

I do and must admit it feels familiar. In fact, it feels like driving back to the Chateau.

"Dordogne?"

"Yes, sir."

There's a giddiness about Znuul at the moment. It's not an affectation or a "face" as Silithes calls them. I won't point it out because then he'd be self-conscious of it. And I kind of like seeing him like that. It's not his natural condition.

"We're going to the Chateau then?"

"Well, we're really going to Christophe's. But we'll be stopping there along the way. I haven't been there since I was..."

So much for giddiness.

"Yeah. It'll do us both good to pay respects to Grey."

A smile returns to his face, but one I think is more of appreciation.

"Hey, since we'll be in the neighborhood, I know of a pleasure house. Old man banned me from it after a little incident, but those girls have long since left I'm sure. Who needs Amsterdam, right?"

"So our not-so-little discussion of monogamy didn't sink in at all?"

"You lost that argument, Arthur. Monogamy is driven by male-dominated reproductive biology in humans. Where the male sprays his seed, babies follow – remember? Not so for the Dzemond."

I do remember. And his logic was pretty impeccable. He even quoted biblical references – including "the king shall not have too many wives." Man, he ran that "too many" right down my throat. In the end, he wrapped it up all around differing biology and "male controlled" breeding culture.

"I don't think Karred is going to be thinking about biology or theology if we go raid the whorehouse, Z."

"Love is love. Pleasure is pleasure. Wonderful when the two mix, but they don't have to."

"How much pleasure would it take to make hurting her feelings acceptable?"

Znuul furrows his brow. He looks over at me and says nothing.

"It's not just about you, or biology, it's about the one you love. About putting their feelings first."

I get looked at again, then his gaze returns to the road.

"You win the argument, Arthur. I concede all points. Even from last night."

Now it's my turn to look at him in disbelief. I could say something like "daaaaamn!" but that seems a tad immature.

"What, no gloating?"

"Doesn't seem appropriate, given the topic. Just glad you see the point."

He grabs my knee again, with a huge smile. "You're such a goody-goody, Arthur. Please don't go changing."

∴

We turn into the very long drive to what was the Chateau. It used to be you could see it across the vineyards. Now, there's a shattered building atop a field of wild vines. The ever-so-vibrant home to so many I held close is hardly even a skeleton of former greatness.

Znuul and I have been in relative silence since the monogamy discussion, more or less taking in the scenery. But I can't be silent in the face of this travesty.

"Damn, Znuul. Just damn."

He stops the almost SUV and steps outside.

"Yes, Arthur, most damnable."

I hear the hatch open in the back and get out. By the time I get around to the back, he has flipped open the locker and is taking off his blazer.

"Shocking to see it from here. It's the first time for me, too, since the day it happened," Znuul says somberly. "Karred is the executor of his trust, but needless to say, she hasn't been actively involved other than giving the green light to the lawyers for basic operations here."

Znuul pulls out a custom double shoulder holster out of the locker and begins strapping it on.

"I had toys delivered, in case."

"So I see," I reply, "You didn't happen to remember your good friend Arthur, did you?"

112

"Of course I did."

His attention again goes to where the Chateau was. It's hard not to take in the sight. After a moment he pulls out a pair of silenced double-eagles. He loads and holsters them appropriately. His attention goes back to the box.

"These are for you; hope I got it right."

He hands me a single-shoulder holster, followed by a large-caliber revolver. Upon examination, I see he's handed me a Smith & Wesson Governor. That's followed by .45 caliber quick-loaders custom to the gun. Yeah, he did good.

"I don't expect issues here. If anything, it will be the grounds crew," Znuul says. "But you never know when those pesky Protectorate types might show up."

"Not sure how I feel about shooting up Protectorate types."

"Aim for their legs," he says, handing me a pair of nine-milimeter automatics and a leg holster. "Unless it's the ground crews – we really don't want to shoot them."

I chuckle at Znuul's situational ethics while I strap on my weaponry. I have to admit, being armed does make me feel better in a strange way.

We put our blazers back on and stand there looking over the desolate scene. I put my hand on Znuul's back and give him what I hope is construed as a comforting pat.

"We should get over there, Arthur, so we can get to Christophe's before dark."

"Looking for something?"

"Yes and no," Znuul says, reaching into his blazer pocket. He pulls out two small corked glass vials on silver chains. "One for Red, one for me. Plan to fill them with ashes from home. Something to keep with us."

"Other than memories. I understand."

"Thanks. We... I... miss him terribly. He showed me so much. About people, about myself, about truth. The world is a darker place without Monsieur Lightbringer."

"I agree, Monsieur Znuul. Let's get rolling."

Further words aren't needed. He closes the hatchback, and I move to the passenger side. He gets in and starts the car. A brief fumbling with his phone follows, and some rock-and-roll song blares over the speakers.

"AC/DC – Bullet to bite on," Znuul says with a grin. "I know you're an old country guy – just deal with it."

Znuul cranks up the speakers a bit too loud for my taste and puts the car in drive. We go down the all-too-long drive that I remember so very vividly. Now it's overgrown and the vineyards tangled. The ruins come clearer into focus. I listen to the words of the song, screeching about dealing with loss, and I wonder where my bullet is.

The magnitude of destruction is only rivaled by the magnitude of my feelings of loss.

Znuul pulls us in front of what was the Chateau and waits for the song to finish. We say nothing. He turns off the car.

"I'll grab the ashes. The old man also had a secret lab in the basement. I'm sure it's been routed, but in the case it hasn't, I'll check. Why don't you see if your son's stone survived the bombing? I'll find you... after all, it's pretty much open area here."

"Yeah, Z."

We get out, and he tromps into the Chateau. I work my way around, worried that flooring could give out and I'd break a leg or worse, falling into wherever. Znuul goes about his business, and I move toward the backyards, where my son's headstone was.

The yards used to be so well manicured. Now they have literally taken on a life of their own. I try to reconcile my memories of grounds with the still partially scorched, destroyed landscape that's before me. I remember taking Silithes to Jerry and Marge's stone and walk in that direction.

I follow my memories to the end of the yard to where Jerry and Marge's stone should be. It's still there, though overgrown. A tear starts to well. I quickly nip that in the bud.

My moment is interrupted by the sound of a motor revving in the distance. I look up and see an ATV screaming up from the walnut groves. Znuul did say that basic operations were maintained, and I guess security would be one of those basic operations. I don't run. I don't move. I just watch the ATV zooming to me.

After what feels like forever, the ATV arrives, and the man on it gets off, pulling out an over-under double-barrel shotgun. Znuul is nowhere to be seen. He must be in the basement.

Chapter 25

"Que faites-vous ici," the man shouts at me.

I figure he has to be asking who the hell I think I am to be here. "Je parle un peu français," I respond, hoping he might speak English.

"Who are you, and why are you trespassing here?"

Lucky me.

"Arthur MacInerny," I say, not bothering with my passport alias. "I lived here for almost two years. I'm paying my respects."

"Don't know you, young man," he says, the gun now pointed at my chest. "Best you move on."

"I... my son's headstone is right here."

I remember I really don't look like someone who had a son and qualifies for a senior discount at Denny's.

Mr. Groundskeeper lets me know the shotgun is ready.

"Your son's headstone, you say?"

I point to the stone and see Znuul burst up dramatically from the basement of the ruins far behind Mr. Groundskeeper.

"I do see... here."

"Sure you don't mean your Grandfather's?"

By this point, Znuul has been striding with purpose toward us. I guess my eyes give him away because Mr. Groundskeeper turns his attention, but not the gun, away.

"Oh hell," he spits out after setting eyes on Znuul. "Did you bring that thing back here?"

"No, actually kind of the other way around."

"Gerald! Mon bon ami!" Znuul bellows out, not missing a step.

"I may not be able to hurt you, beast, but I can certainly hurt your friend. Stop where you are, or I'll give him both barrels!"

Crapsticks. Znuul doesn't stop, but he does slow.

"Gerald," Znuul yells, holding out his hands in a sign of acceptance. "Your gun would hurt me, just not harm me. Arthur there is innocent. Please, let's not do this."

"Back to the scene of the crime, eh, demon?"

"Hey, Gerald," I say. "He had nothing to do with all this. Didn't you know that?"

Gerald now is looking between us, with more than a little paranoia. That doesn't make me feel great considering a paranoid man with an over-under is even more likely to use that weapon.

"Put the shooter down, Gerald," Znuul says, "All you'll do is harm an innocent man."

"Damn," Gerald says, dropping the shotgun down to a less-imposing posture.

Znuul continues toward us and puts a hand on Gerald's shoulder.

"I would never harm Grey, and I'd prefer not to harm you. I had nothing to do with any of this."

"Then who did?"

Znuul smiles and shakes his head.

"You don't do the internet, do you?"

I laugh.

"It was a Dzemond, the same one that attacked Rome. He and I killed that piece of shit. I did a video," Znuul says.

"Oh," Gerald responds absently. "They said you were responsible for this."

"And you believed them?"

Znuul is smiling at Gerald. Thank goodness there doesn't appear to be any ill will. He again grasps Gerald's shoulder and shakes him a bit.

"Reginald was the traitor within. He sold the old man out for a few million euro and a house in Barbados."

That's news to me.

"No... After all Monsieur Grey did for him and his family?"

"Yes."

"I assume you have caught up with him and..."

"I paid him a visit, yes. Shortly after that visit, he put a gun in his mouth. Maybe it was something I said."

"Something you said... surely that must have been it," Gerald deadpans. "I was given a phone number to call should you return. They said all criminals return to the scene of the crime. Should I call them?"

"No," I answer. "You should not."

"What he said," offers Znuul. "How is the family?"

"Good."

Gerald looks around the landscape, then looks Znuul and I over again.

"Take your time. I must get back to the Grove."

He turns back to the ATV, then stops after a few steps. "Reginald? Really?"

"I am no liar, Gerald. Reginald took the payday and sold us all out."

Gerald shakes his head, more in recognition than anything. "Shame." Then he turns back to the ATV, putting the shotgun in its place and taking his seat.

"You did good, digging those kids out in Russia," he says to Znuul. "Good to meet you, too, young man."

He starts the ATV and goes on his way.

"A man of few words," I say in observation.

"Indeed. Glad he didn't shoot you. So did the stone survive?"

I step over to it and point it out under the overgrowth.

"The secret lab?"

"Cleaned out. But we got our ashes. Let's get moving to Christophe's. I don't like how this place makes me feel anymore."

I agree.

∴

We stop at a small shop on the way to Libourne. Apparently, Znuul feels it necessary to have gifts in hand for our visit to the LeBlanc's. It does not leave me comfortable that the older lady, who is apparently the proprietor, recognizes Znuul, though I'm pretty sure she doesn't really know who he is. Two bottles of wine, some cheeses, butter, and two loaves of bread later, we are back on the road.

After a short drive, we pull into the LeBlanc's – a place I've never been, despite the fact he was my primary teacher in the healing arts. I can respect privacy.

"Look, Chris, finally got a real car," Znuul says, pulling up the drive to what appears to be a country cottage. "Good man kept the old beater, though."

Sure enough, there's a well-used Renault sedan in front of the house in addition to a very nice Mercedes to the side.

Znuul wastes no time, turning the car off and bellowing out, "Christophe Leblanc! I come bearing gifts."

I follow out of the car, looking forward to seeing my friend and teacher.

The front door bursts open with Chris following, looking very animated and just a bit concerned.

I realize why, when Gunter Hoffman strolls through the door behind him, Patricius in hand and fully armor clad.

Chapter 26

"Ahtsag Znuul, foul demon, prepare to return to the hell from which you came," Gunter bellows.

Christophe attempts to position himself between them, arms out.

"I will not allow this. This is my home. I will not have bloodshed here!"

"Only the demon will bleed, his head lopped neatly from his shoulders, Master LeBlanc. You, as one of the light, must understand the necessity of this action."

Ahtsag looks at me with a somewhat dismayed, but otherwise nonplussed demeanor, and turns back to Gunter.

"Gunter Hoffman, my old friend, may I propose a brief cease in our hostility? Say a forty-eight-hour parley? I have information of interest to the order. Besides, you took your best shot in Nebraska."

He could have left that last part out.

"Gunter," I shout. "Hear him out. He has good information."

Gunter's eyes turn to me. Cold eyes, scary eyes.

"You consort with the enemy and lay with foul creatures. No information is worth giving up your soul." Gunter's eyes turn back to Znuul. "Creature of darkness, prepare to die."

Christophe gets brushed aside, and Patricius begins to glow brightly.

"Fine," Znuul mutters, barely loud enough for me to hear – much less Gunter at least ten-plus paces away.

Gunter wades in, the sword at ready and eyes locked on Znuul, who reaches into his blazer and pulls out the desert eagles. Znuul's arms weave, guns in hands. Gunter reacts to every move, pushing inward.

Finally, there's a gunshot. Or was it two simultaneously? I see one bullet wink off Patricius and Gunter hobbles.

"I have four more rounds in each gun," Znuul boasts. "Your sword can only be in one place at one time."

"Foul one, you know not what you face," Gunter says, taking one hand off Patricius and setting it on himself. "Holy father! I lay my hands upon this man. Help me heal his wounds!"

I know now that Gunter is fully healed, the laying of hands performed. I look to Christophe who shares my apprehension. But Christophe's attention is broken by his wife, Lucille, breaking into the fray.

"How dare you two bring your differences to our home! I'll not have this taking place here. If you two want to hurt and kill each other, take it away from our home!"

Gunter looks at her as if she's lost her mind.

"Lucille, this is demonkind. I must smite it."

Znuul drops the desert eagles to his side and looks at Gunter in disbelief.

Gunter moves ahead, and Znuul engages again in the strange dance of desert eagles: guns pointing and twisting, while he twirls and moves in response to Gunter's advances.

The guns fire in unison again with thumps from their silenced barrels.

Again, one shot winks off Patricius, and the other finds its way into Gunter's arm.

Gunter growls.

"Can't use the laying of hands again until sunrise; Gunter, can you?" Znuul says in a mocking tone. "Be ready, Paladin, the demon comes for you now."

Znuul again begins the twisting turning dervish-like spinning of himself and the weapons. Gunter tries to keep up. But Patricius being a two-handed sword – that poses problems for him.

Lucille shouts in protest.

Znuul responds by stopping; then he turns on that bogus smile.

"Gunter Hoffman, I have a suggestion. Say a forty-eight-hour parley? I have information that may be of interest to the order. What do you say, a brief cessation to hostility? This is a limited-time offer, of course. What do you say? After forty-eight hours, you can try to kill me as you please."

"Twenty-four hours, demon."

Znuul responds by going into the dance again, now spinning around Gunter with guns moving in all directions.

"Fine! Forty-eight hours. But not a second more."

Christophe is in motion immediately running to Gunter. He calls out to me. "Arthur, lend me your strength and prayers so we may heal him."

Chapter 27

"I will make sure Abu Agas receives this information personally," Christophe says looking from the tablet Znuul gave him to Znuul himself. The tablet has Edgar's whole presentation of the Dzemond invasion threat on it. Znuul did a good job during the presentation himself, though Edgar I felt gave it a little more emotion and urgency.

Not to say the information wasn't urgent in and of itself.

"This is information that The Protectorate itself should have," Gunter says, setting his tablet on the kitchen table we all sit around.

"True that is," says Znuul. "So given that, why is The Protectorate not doing anything about it? They prefer to focus on me and other issues of little importance. Why is that? Why is it Edgar and I are the only ones concerned? Oh, yes The Protectorate is more focused on Edgar, too."

Gunter doesn't answer verbally, he just shoves the tablet away and makes a disgusted face.

"Tell me, at least, you will share this with Frederick," Znuul says, tearing off a piece of the bread we brought and slathering it with warm butter.

"You have my word, demon. I will share this."

"Finally, we agree on something, Gunter."

Christophe and I erupt in laughter. Lucille is not laughing.

"So, Ahtsag," she says over us. "Just so I am clear, hell is coming to our world."

Znuul composes himself for a second and takes a drink of his wine.

"It appears my world is coming to yours. I mean to stop it. Is that hell coming here? Not literally, but close enough. We cannot allow it."

Lucille clutches herself and looks away.

"We won't let it come to that," says Christophe, reaching to comfort her.

"This does represent problems," Gunter acknowledges. He looks at Znuul, "I will make sure the order uses this information."

"Good," Znuul says.

His response pleases me, because "You better" or "I told you to" has no place in this discussion.

"So what brings you and Arthur here, outside of sharing this fine information?" Gunter asks with gusto.

I can't believe he's so openly fishing, but that's Gunter.

"I wanted to go to Amsterdam," Znuul says. "Get some red-light girls and smoke potent weed. Maybe not in that order."

Gunter looks at me with a cocked eyebrow.

I laugh. Znuul did not lie, but he did deceive. Albeit, rather poorly.

The word "Papa" takes my attention, and I see that Christophe's two smallest children, Caterine and Robert, are hanging outside the door to a hallway and looking in on us.

Christophe gives them the nod, and they come running in, crying out "Ahtsag!"

They swarm by big friend who is all smiles, greeting them in French. Even though my French is sketchy at best, I pick up something to the extent of "Up!"

Lucille looks at Christophe with a question in her eyes.

"If Grey were here, we would not hesitate," he says.

"Oui, but he is not here."

"I do nothing without your permission, good Lucille," Znuul says, while being tugged on by enthusiastic children.

Christophe says, "Hey," and the children immediately calm and pay attention to their father. Christophe and Lucille lock eyes for a moment. There is the look of relenting on her face, and she turns back to Znuul.

"If you drop them, I will kill you."

"I have never dropped them before, and I will not start now."

The kids figuring that approval was given, grab Znuul by the hands to drag him outside. He rolls his eyes and relents, allowing them to pull him from his chair. He speaks to them in French again. They respond with disappointed sounds.

Christophe says, "in English for my friends, and practice – please."

The kids look at us and say, "We're going to go flying after dark!"

I have to smile, I can imagine that taking Znuul rides would be fun for the kiddos. Apparently, Gunter disagrees.

"Master LeBlanc, this is disgraceful. You would risk your own children with this beast? What if he decides to fly off with them and…"

Znuul's hand slams on the table. Poor Lucille looks shell-shocked.

"I have known these children since their birth! Christophe and Lucille are my friends!"

Znuul looks away from Gunter to collect himself.

Gunter wastes no time in response, "I have had enough of this parley, and I do not break bread with demons. I cannot know what games are being played here, but

I do know that this creature is prophesied to bring about the downfall of man. I have had enough. I will see you again. We will finish this."

Gunter stands and starts for the door.

Prophecy?

"Gunter Hoffman," Znuul says loudly enough to stop the large German. "I have one reminder, two observations, and a suggestion for you before you leave."

Gunter turns around.

"The reminder is what the old man thought of prophecy as a whole, that they are open to interpretation – not the least of which is by the person that received the prophecy. We have heard nothing first hand."

"Grey had issues with literal interpretations of any prophecy," adds Christophe.

"Thank you, Chris. The observations are simple, I have defeated you twice – once with a can of flour and just now with human weapons. And both times, I showed you mercy. Now for the suggestion: The next time you decide to come for me, make sure I don't see you coming. Because if I do, I may take it personally. If I do, you will not survive."

Gunter doesn't waver from Znuul's gaze. He stands there, staring down Znuul, then turns and bolts out the door.

"I would very much appreciate it if you wouldn't take it personally," Christophe says. "He means well for mankind. He's just…"

"A zealot," Znuul says. "I won't make such promises, he comes for me again, and death awaits him. The Protectorate think I fear them because I hide. I hide for their sakes."

This get-together has taken a turn for the even grimmer, given Gunter's intolerance and what looks like Znuul's "had enough" attitude. I can tell Lucille is uneasy and Christophe feels the same as I. Znuul is bristling. Sometimes we have to make sacrifices for the better of our community; I know what I must do.

"Well, for my sake would you pour me a glass of that wine, big guy?"

Znuul's demeanor goes from brooding to surprised.

"You who does not partake is going to partake with us?" asks Znuul, reaching for the bottle of wine.

"For the record, I do partake, just very infrequently. And this is a special occasion, us all being together, despite someone's zealotry. Besides, when in France – right?"

"When in France," Christophe says, holding his glass out to me.

Znuul pours my glass and lets the table know the bottle is gone after finishing it in his glass.

I hold my glass up. "A toast. To friends, family, and good days ahead."

"Here here," everyone chimes in, the sounds of clicking glasses filling the air.

"And good times they will be," Znuul says, "filled with the sounds of children's laughter as I fly them around the cottage."

The mood is much better. The wine's not half-bad either.

Then the door opens, and Gunter comes striding back in, a large cooler in one hand.

"I brought beer to celebrate my victory. It appears we must celebrate yours."

The entire table goes silent.

He sets the cooler down, pulls out a beer and looks at Znuul, who regards him in return. Gunter tosses the bottle to Znuul, who catches it and reads the label.

"Krombacher Dark, nice."

Gunter pulls out another, pops the cap, and approaches the table.

"I was disrespectful. Regardless of what my training and beliefs dictate, one does not return a favor with an insult. The order taught me not to trust a demon. My mother taught me manners," he says sitting down, "Christophe, would you break me off a slice of the bread. For the record, that favor was the sharing of the information on the tablet."

There is the silence of disbelief around the table. Christophe tears off a piece of bread, spreads some of the butter on it, and hands it to Gunter, who wastes no time taking a bite and washing it down with the beer.

Even Znuul is without words.

"Open your beer so I may toast your victory, Ahtsag Znuul. You waste time; I will be on my second soon."

Znuul pops the top of the beer with his fingers and holds the beer out for a toast. Gunter clinks his bottle against it, then gets up and moves the cooler closer to the table. He sits back down and gets beer number two.

"So," says Znuul, breaking the silence. "Who are you and what did you do with Gunter Hoffman?"

"Strange times, yes?"

"Getting stranger by the moment," adds Christophe.

Gunter opens his beer and takes a swig. He looks at all of us with a half-smile on his face.

"Indeed. A succubus passes the judgment of the sword. A demon shows mercy to a Paladin – twice. And then it shares information in hopes of stopping more of his kind from polluting our home."

"And a paladin breaking bread with a demon," adds Znuul, taking a long drink of his beer.

"Times are too strange for this simple warrior to comprehend. And you just admitted you are demonkind."

Gunter laughs.

Lucille and I are waiting for the next shoe to drop and the fireworks to start. Christophe is all smiles, taking in this sight. He lets us know why.

"Gentlemen, this is proof that the divine works in mysterious, incomprehensible ways. Let us enjoy this camaraderie and know that we are being smiled upon."

"That does not mean that we are friends," Gunter says, holding his bottle out to Znuul.

"Of course not," Znuul says, clinking his bottle to Gunter's.

∴

The next while was rather pleasant. Gunter and Znuul exchanged quips about shared missions. There was the tale about when Znuul and Greg faced one another, no idea of who each other really were with only rules to "capture" and under no circumstances kill. They also talked about some of Grey's more clandestine activities – apparently, he was a bit of the ladies' man.

But pleasant is destined to end. There are too many elephants in the room to ignore.

Gunter, never bashful, is the first to dive in.

"So, the beast of Novgorod… A female of your kind, is this true? Is it true you beat it down and claimed it for breeding stock? There is talk you raped it, and it carries your offspring already."

Christophe's expression doesn't change. Lucille, on the other hand, looks aghast.

Znuul smiles, turns and winks to Lucille.

"That information will cost you another Krombacher, good Paladin."

Gunter wastes no time fishing another out and tossing it to Znuul. Znuul flicks the lid off.

"Very female and yes, Baalig. I didn't really beat her down. She was in terrible shape, having run into several of the Grace's upper echelon. As for breeding stock, I cannot deny that potential exists, but I have no interest. And no, I did not rape her. Even if I did, Dzemond females control when they get pregnant."

"Does it still live?" asks Christophe.

"Yes. Bound to my will in much the same way I was to Grey."

"She's a concubine then," adds Gunter, raising his bottle to Znuul with a smirk. "Your appetites are no secret."

"She is not."

"That means there is someone else taking care of your appetites?" asks Christophe quietly. Which brings me to ask of our dear friend Karen. There is a nasty rumor that…"

"She is your blooded servitor," Gunter finishes for him. "A slave to you in body and soul until death – a hybrid creature of neither world. Most foul."

Znuul says nothing, but downs the other half of his beer and sets it on the table.

"You know the price for information."

"Enough of this," Gunter shouts, standing up and spilling his chair out behind him. "She is our friend! This is no game!"

"It is not. So, please set our worried souls at ease," Christophe says quietly, yet firmly.

"She is not my blooded servitor. Yes, she has been in my company – by her choice. Her will is totally her own. She is fine. She is assisting me in… retraining the one we spoke of earlier. Now, where's my beer?"

Gunter is considering the request for another beer. I think Znuul has swerved the issue of what really happened – and that Karen is now Karred. He who does not lie, but does deceive indeed.

"So she is good?" asks Lucille.

"She is better than good."

I have to smile at Znuul's well-measured responses. Unfortunately, I think my smile on the inside became one on the outside, too, as I see Christophe raising his eyebrows at me. Raising eyebrows turns to a pointing finger.

"He knows something."

Znuul rolls his eyes, then cocks his head at me in disbelief.

"What? What is he not telling us?" Christophe says to me.

I turn back to Znuul, who hasn't moved – or blinked for that matter.

"Everything he told you is true."

But there's more to it." Christophe turns to Znuul with his own gaze.

Znuul stops staring at me and turns to Christophe.

"I cannot take Arthur anywhere."

I stand up, look Gunter in the eye and step around him. I'm sure he's boring holes in my back. I reach into his cooler, pull out a beer, and hold it out to Znuul.

"Spill. All of it. These are her friends. They're going to know eventually."

Znuul takes the beer, giving me the stinkeye. His gaze shifts to everyone in the room with much less stink.

"Your words The Protectorate will know nothing of what we discuss."

"My word," says Christophe without hesitation.

Gunter pulls a gulp of beer. "She is not a blooded servitor, and her will is her own. Then this must be truly heinous news. Karen is more than a mage in the fight; she is my friend. You say she is well?"

"Very much, Gunter, but The Protectorate is not. If you cannot keep this in confidence, please leave us so I can share her news with Chris." He looks over at Christophe. "I was going to share with you all along. Gunter was unexpected."

"She is my friend. I will keep this in confidence for her sake," Gunter says, pulling his chair up and back to the table.

I realize the nature of Znuul's issue with Gunter. Karen is Gunter's friend. Karred, though, must be smited.

"Gunter, try to keep an open mind," I say, patting him on the shoulder.

∴

All in all, they took the news pretty well. Christophe after further assurance that Karen is still Karen, only with a new name and body, pretty much rolled with it. After hearing, they were going to get married in the church of "her god," he was pretty much all in. The whole "miracle" aspect of it didn't hurt either.

Gunter took it pretty well, too, for Gunter. His response after cursing Znuul for desecrating her humanity was to get hammered drunk. I think when Znuul explained it was really her idea to try for a blending so they could raise a family, he just mentally threw his arms up in the air. That was after physically throwing his arms up in the air.

The children were flown around the yard over and over, which allowed Christophe the opportunity to take me aside. I was both grilled about and chastised for my relationship with Ms. Silithes. He summed up his feelings with, "Why can't you just find a nice human girl?"

Chapter 28

The LeBlanc household is abuzz as the kids are getting ready for school, while Znuul and I are getting ready to head to Rome. Lucille gives us both hugs as she shuttles the kids out the door.

We won't be far behind them – the idea is to get out before Gunter rises. Given all the beer and wine he put away, we have a good, long head start.

I savor the last of my coffee on his front porch, looking over at Znuul and Christophe having an earnest discussion in the wake of Lucille and the kids' exit, near our mostly SUV. No telling the topic – it could be Karred, it could be the information we shared, it could be anything. But what I know for sure is, it's between friends.

"Arthur! Time to go."

I start walking, meeting Christophe halfway. I hand him the coffee mug and look him in the eyes. "It looks like bad getting worse – the invasion thing."

Christophe smiles one of those smiles he does that makes you feel like everything will be all right.

"Yes, though our large German friend might think Karen's circumstance was the worst of the news. I don't know what you two are up to, but I am fairly sure you didn't come all the way to see us for an evening. Be safe, Arthur. Please try to keep him out of trouble."

He pats me on the shoulder and heads back inside. I head for the passenger door of the vehicle.

"Fourteen hours to Rome, Arthur," Znuul says. "Not including stops. And I know a nice place near Fréjus we can stop at for a bite and a drop. It's almost halfway. The old man and I stopped there once."

"Oh, sounds quaint."

Znuul laughs. "Yes. I wish to reacquaint myself."

Chapter 29

"Is this our exit," I ask

"Not sure yet," Znuul responds.

"I thought you knew this place really well."

"It's been a while. It was very colorful. Oh, look, we're heading the right way."

I see a sign indicating the direction of the port.

"What do you mean by colorful?" I ask, suspecting that colorful means the color of naked flesh.

"Ambiance and colorful characters, some food, and drink, too. It was interesting. Grey liked it."

I figure if it's somewhere Grey took him, then it's probably safe – though I have found out that he was a bit of the ladies' man. But something has been bugging me that we didn't get to address last night in between Karred, Silithes, and the flying of children: this prophecy of Znuul as a world-crusher.

"Hey, we kind of glossed over this prophecy thing. Grey never mentioned it. You haven't either. Spill."

"It's not hidden. It's on the protecta-net, hyperlinked on the page about me. You didn't click it?"

I didn't. Damn page was long enough.

"Spill it."

Znuul chuckles. "Fair enough. When we get stopped. It requires dramatic presentation. Now, you know never to take a prophecy at face value, right? The old man and I saw eye to eye on it from day four."

"Day four?"

"Yeah, it took four days for news of the prophecy to get to us. No internet, fax, or cell phones back when."

∴

We pull into a gravel lot across from a fairly grungy-looking bar in the bay area. I'm not feeling culinary adventure here, more like cheap beer and shady deals.

"All right – first the backstory," Znuul says, snapping my attention from the place in front of us. His hands are ready to talk as much as his mouth is. "Allegedly, the moment when I was released, Madame Hanna Papdoulas, the then-leader of the seers guild, burst out in a fit, proclaimed this prophecy, followed by her death of a massive stroke. So, all we have are what the people around her claim as her words. We don't have her opinion, detail of her vision, or anything like that."

"That's kind of scary. At the moment of your release?"

"That's what they say. And, yes, scary."

His hands and eyes move to accentuate the scary, and I realize that for him, this is probably the equivalent of a camptime story told to kids.

It better not end with a hook hanging from the door.

"Okay, so I will tell you word for word what we were told of the prophecy and what is on that page you couldn't be bothered to click. This is where the dramatic presentation is important."

"The caged beast is freed!" he says loudly in his version of an old woman's voice with his hands waving wildly.

"The beast is bound again. The beast is freed again. Hell on Earth! The blood of innocents flows! The demon king rises. The fall of man! The sword reborn. The demon king is no more." He pauses. "So, what did you think?"

"You're the demon king that brings about the fall of man?"

"One interpretation. Let's say that Zebelbuub, emperor of Helterezen, my former lord and master, is successful in deploying these invasion gates and eventually bringing down the whole life's blood lock on this realm. Wouldn't he then be the demon king?"

"Crapsticks." My head wraps around what he's saying. It's not black and white.

"Then, there's the thing that, just because it's prophecy, doesn't mean that it has to come to pass. It's a glimpse into a future timeline. Timelines can be screwed with. Remember the movies about the cyborgs that go back in time to do that?"

"I'll be back?"

Znuul nods in the affirmative.

"The old man believed most are prone to accepting prophecy at face value and, therefore, making it self-fulfilling. I've known this for a fact, before coming here. That and they tend to be vague to the point where you can see whatever you want in them."

Znuul gets out of the car. I follow.

"Let's get that rumbling belly of yours taken care of. They have perfectly adequate ham and cheese and maybe more."

"Z…"

"Oh yeah… and beer."

Chapter 30

One long day on the road found us in Rome at a very small, yet very nice and modern, hotel. I took time with Sil on our double-secret phones. Karred and she were enjoying the company of the twins. I shared Znuul's constant references to Amsterdam which met with amusement and the suggestion, "you might learn something new."

Wasn't sure how to take that; so I did in the best humor possible.

It took no time to fall asleep, and seemingly it took no time for the sun to rise

Having enjoyed the shower, I prepare for my morning routine. First is the prayer of spiritual cleansing. Next is the healing spell. Then I go for Yayne. Box opened, I grasp the hilt and say "Welcome to Rome."

Nothing. But that's not too surprising. What to say? Yayne is a sword of very few words.

"Have you been here before?"

"Many times."

"Been to this place we're going? Anything I need to know?"

"Yes – once. Much. It is highly guarded. You cannot leave with anything unless you have express permission. Do not attempt to steal away with anything. Only death will await you."

That's kind of what I figured.

"Good advice. Thank goodness I'm not a thief at heart."

Nothing. No response. Sometimes I think Yayne is just a bit too serious.

"You want to be in case or out of the case? We have the whole day."

Nothing. So the case it is. He's safer that way – at least people will be less likely to mess with him. Those people being the cleaning staff.

So Yayne gets put away, and I look out the window, realizing where I am. It's surreal. I stand there looking out over the reconstruction of the holy city. Friggin' Maldgorath – it makes me smile that I was the one that took his head.

But that smile goes away remembering I took his death curse, too.

Still, the view is nice. The knock on the door takes my attention. When I look through the viewhole and see only chest, I know who it is. So I let him in.

"Beautiful morning in Rome, isn't it? Ready for breakfast?" Znuul says, coming into my room. The room feels just a little smaller now. But he has that way.

"I am. We should probably talk tonight's strategy, too. That is, I assume we aren't going in broad daylight?"

"You are correct, sir. That's why I like working with you. We think alike."

"No, we don't. Amsterdam, remember?"

He nods at me knowingly. "True. But tactically, we see eye to eye. That's close enough."

∴

I have two choices. He would pick me up like a child and fly me from the hotel to the vault entrance, or I would make my way to the wall – then he'd pick me up like a child and fly me to the vault entrance.

I go with option "b." With Yayne hung from my back and as clandestine as I can, I make my way to the outer wall where directed. Once arriving, I only have to wait a short while before I see the large ripple in the air that camouflaged Znuul. He lands in front of me. Despite knowing who it is and what he wants – it's still somewhat disturbing.

The camo drops, and there he is: guns strapped on and wearing a huge Black Sabbath tee, ripped in the back for his wings. It's funny, as big as the desert eagles are, I'm more intimidated by the huge knife strapped to his leg and what appears to be a war-hammer on his back. Mr. Z is dressed for business.

I just hope that it's business we can avoid.

"So you can camo me, too?" I ask as I ball up the raincoat I was using to obscure Yayne and set it next to the wall.

"As soon as I have you in my arms, for sure. Do me a favor, and just go limp. I know how to compensate for gravity and ragdoll physics. If you tighten up, I'd have to compensate for you. That I can't predict as well."

There's nothing to do but grumble, and go limp when he scoops me up.

He lifts me up under the crotch, grabbing his arm across my shoulder, and up we go. I close my eyes. If I didn't, I might go less than limp. I remember teaching my son Jerry to drive and know my instinct to push the passenger side brake is strong. I feel that we land, open my eyes, and become less than a sack of potatoes.

"Wait for my call," he tells me and then makes for the stairs leading down.

I look around. There are signs of reconstruction. But the desecration of this place can't be denied. Maldgorath's summonlings did a number here – like an army swept through. The truth is that's exactly what happened.

"Arthur!" comes Znuul's voice from down the stairs. I make tracks, trying not to trip in the darkness. Once at the bottom, I can't see a thing. It's pitch black. My hand is taken, and something is put in them.

"IR goggles. Guards were wearing them."

I feel around them, and put them on in the way I think they should be. Znuul flips a switch on the side of them, and the world illuminates in green. I see three guards on the ground, unconscious, two with goggles like mine.

"You didn't kill them, did you?"

A large slap on my back follows. "Naturally unconscious from a concussive blow, unnaturally asleep until the morning."

Well, good enough. I look around and see two large metal doors. Ominous metal doors. The kind that say they're there just as much to keep things in as out.

"That's the library?"

"It is."

"I don't see anything keeping you out, big Z. Come with?"

"Take the goggles off and see things through my sight."

I've done this before, taking a peek at the nature of Karred's soul, so I pull the goggles down. His huge hand grasps the back of my bare neck, and there's the feeling of disorientation I remember from last time. I see the gateway in a black-and-white way. Around that entry are two spectral forms, billowing, prepared, and certainly focused on Znuul.

I feel the hand leave my neck and the connection breaks.

"I don't mess with the noncorporeal unless there's no other alternative. I have meat to hurt; they don't, though there are ways to harm them. It's just not a winning proposition."

I put the goggles back on and see Z, his eyes fixed on the entry. He takes a step back.

That speaks volumes to me.

"Guess we go in."

We, being Yayne and me.

"Take this first," he says, reaching back over his shoulder and handing me the war-hammer.

"Why?"

"Well, swords aren't good against stone golems. This is a better weapon. That and I'm sure you don't want to raise that fine sword against anything here. You hear that, Mr. Sword. I was considerate of you."

I chuckle that Znuul calls out Yayne; then I heft the hammer. I'd be needing two hands with this thing. I string the large leather loop over my shoulder, making sure it doesn't hit the tablet I brought.

He hands me a pair of gloves.

"In case you can get my sword, too. You don't want to touch it. It's very old school – a living sentient blade created by necromancy. It's a hungry one, too. The armor is AI-based, and its energy stores are most likely expended. If you can get the sword, I'd like that. But know the armor is what we need – that's where the control module will be."

"So the armor isn't alive, but the sword is?"

"Can't get anything past you. The sword is beyond evil. Not saying you don't have the will to handle it – but why put yourself through that? It will test you. The gloves will let you avoid that."

I now have zero motivation for dealing with this sword, but I take the gloves all the same, just in case.

"Oh, I'll need the phone I gave you, too. Just in case you don't make it back out."

That's nice – but I get it. I fish out the phone and hand it to him.

"I'll be back for that."

Taking a deep breath, I turn to the large doors and walk to them. I reach out and open the door, the light from inside blinding my night vision goggles, so I pull them down. There's a very large hall with torches lit for the first quarter of it. I see light at the end of this tunnel. Stone gargoyles line each side of the hall.

Guess it's time to get moving.

Chapter 31

I walk down this long, dimly lit hallway, noting all the gargoyles in the wall niches. There must be at least fifteen on either side. If these are golem constructs, this is one helluva a choke point.

No sense worrying. I just get to stepping, finally reaching the antechamber. Like the hallway, it's lit by a series of gas lamps with large reflective mirrors behind them. The lighting is good, though it lends an antiquish feel to the place.

And the place is large. There are rows and rows of shelving going up at least twelve feet, spaced where one could easily walk between them. Stone Gargoyles sit at the top of each one.

There is an inviting desk right in front of me, spanning at least ten feet, where one might study at more ease.

Before I can call out "hello!" a man rounds the corner of one of the columns of shelves. He's dressed in robes, but they don't feel like clerical robes – they are much too ornate. He has numerous rings on his fingers and a large talisman hanging from his neck.

"May I help you?" he asks.

"Yes, I was hoping to see the armor of Ahtsag Znuul."

"Why, may I ask, that specific item?" He looks me over. "And why would one who carries a sword of the order, be carrying a war-hammer also? Why would you need such a thing?"

He obviously knows The Order of Light's way.

"It's a blessed Viking hammer."

I can tell he doesn't buy it. He takes the talisman from around his neck in his hand.

"So, you wish me to take you to the armor of the demon Ahtsag Znuul? What is your business with it?"

"I hope to take it with me so it might be used against a greater threat."

"That armor will not leave this keep. Under no circumstances. So tell me, supposed warrior of the order, what is your name?"

"Arthur MacInerny. And yours, good sir?"

There's a pause in the conversation, not one of the good ones. It's the kind of pause that makes you think someone is considering your fate.

"The Wielder. Yes. We of the Magerium are aware of you. You are not of the order, entirely. A friend of the beast Ahtsag Znuul. You seek to return his armor to him."

Busted. So busted… But I won't raise my hand against anyone here. So I go with the truth, reaching back for my tablet to show him what's going on.

"Let me show you what we're facing here."

He steps back.

"Answer me! Do you seek to return this armor to Ahtsag Znuul?"

We're in a holy place. I'm not going to lie.

"Yes, let me show you…"

"Kill him! Rend the flesh from his bones!"

The gargoyles on the top of the shelves shudder to life and jump down to the floor.

I look at the robed man and say, "Why?"

He laughs at me.

"Alistair will be pleased that this pawn is off the board – your death is coming for you, traitor to mankind."

Chapter 32

I tear off running, watching multitudes of these gargoyles drop to the ground. A couple of things become crystal clear. First, this mage asshole is not part of the Vatican. He's one of Alistair's. Second, a crapload of 250-pound pieces of stone are coming to seal my fate.

I peel the hammer from my back, taking it in two hands. A stone gargoyle plops down at the end of the corridor between the shelves I am running down, with a stonish thunk. It turns to me and starts tearing my way on all fours, not like a four-legged creature but more like a gorilla. I swing the hammer back and meet it hard, in an underhanded polo-like swing, causing it to shatter. I look behind me and see at least four of those things starting down a corridor after me.

I follow the swing's momentum, turning to spin and bring the hammer downward on another coming out of the hallway formed by the shelves.

I bolt ahead, running into another that rakes its stone claws outward, scraping me as I reflexively jump to the side. It steps forward, and I bring the hammer swinging from the side slamming into it, destroying one clawed hand, chipping its head and knocking it over with a clunk.

I try to keep the hammer ready to go. I must be ready to go because they are coming from all directions and in great numbers. I slam one to my left and bolt down a corridor of shelves. Having a moment, I take my finger along Vets' sigil and then Hjuul's.

"Get me some space!" I yell at them.

They wade into the fray.

Not for long, though, as I feel them overwhelmed and destroyed by hopping, clawing, living stone.

I run like hell for a few moments, then stop and call Arixtumin out.

"Gargoyle golems!" I yell at him. He manages to get one wall of force spell off, clearing my way ahead, before the golems swarm him from behind, and around the corner.

I run like hell again, swinging the hammer wildly and knocking parts of any golems off that would get close. At the back of the room, with a half a moment of breathing room, I run my finger along Shey's sigil.

She ripples into reality and looks at me with a question mark.

"Get into the air and stop these damned things," I yell at her.

She wastes no time.

I call Arixtumin back, who is immediately attacked by a stone gargoyle and driven to the ground.

His call is followed by Vets and then Hjuul again as both jump back into the fray.

I see a gang of stone gargoyles coming around the corner of the case before us. A plan formulates.

"Ignore those! Get the others to follow you!" I yell to Vets and Hjuul, who do as told.

The golems I that were paying attention to Vets and Hjuul are now fixed on me and come at me in that gorilla-run they have. So I tear down the aisle as fast as I can, the golems in the chase.

I get to the end of the aisle skid to a stop and grab the end of the shelves.

And I push and shake, like my life depends on it; because it does. The shelves begin to topple, and I put my full effort into. The shelf falls, causing a domino effect on all the shelves in front of it, and catching the golems moving toward me.

"No! This is my library! You cannot do this," comes a voice from the front of the library.

Rounding the corner, I see the mage apparently having heated words with someone at the front of the room, out of my sight. I pull my Governor and put a round into his leg that winks off.

Damn shields.

That gets him to turn around, and I recognize that he's working on a spell-cast for me. I go to evasive maneuvers, ducking into shelves only to find gargoyles waiting for me there. So I reverse gears, run a few steps, and slide back into another shelving corridor.

A lightning bolt careens down the hall, barely missing me.

I call Arixtumin again.

He is obviously nervous from being swarmed, and he looks at me with all seriousness.

"Golems must be controlled. The mage. He has something."

My response is simple: "Take him out."

I don't want to die at the claws of stone golems – and he's not Vatican.

Arix takes off in his direction, and I mine, hammer slamming anything that grabs at me.

Arixtumin yells out, "Pixie! Shoot the mage, shoot him to death – he holds the key."

I flow out into the middle of the hall, to see fairy arrows winking off the wardings of this mage. He sees me and smiles.

"Arbrexuit," is the word that comes from Arix's mouth, and there is a sound of shattering glass. I see Shey's magical arrows pierce the wizard once, twice; and he turns to run, going out of sight.

Sheyliene buzzes down, bow at the ready. "He's down! Hey..."

Then I see something I didn't expect, a brown-skinned gargoyle flying past Sheyliene toward the downed mage. It bumps her, and she does a mid-air 360.

The stone golems stop in place.

It becomes very quiet, that is, until I hear the voice cry out, "My Collections! My beautiful library, what have you done?"

Chapter 33

Sheyliene lands on the ground with her bow pointed ahead, but her face shows confusion.

"You're a gregowaile, dragon servant."

I hear the voice that wailed lament say, "Dragon friend? And you're a pixie. Here?"

I run ahead taking advantage of the lull in the action and the stillness of the gargoyles to see what's going on. In this case, the apparent mutual confusion works to our advantage. Once near Shey, I see the source of the confusion – there stands a gargoyle. Not one of these stone constructs, but apparently the model for them. He's holding the mage's talisman and is taking me in as much as I am taking him in.

"Why would you –" he starts to say before the mage yells, "He's in league with Ahtsag Znuul; he'll kill us – horribly. Look what he's –"

"Sesoon" is the word muttered by Arix, and the mage falls to the floor, his eyes rolling. Arix always was impressive in how fast he could throw a stun spell.

"Demon souled! How did a Dzemond get in here?"

Mr. Gargoyle holds out the talisman as if it's a shield. "If you try to kill me, I will command all these to rip you to pieces. Then, I'll break the talisman, and the order cannot be taken back."

Well, that's negotiating from strength. I hold my hands out in the universal "let's all calm down" gesture.

"Mr. Sir. Uh… I didn't start this fight. I did come here to try to acquire Ahtsag Znuul's armor – but not by force. In fact, if it were refused to me, I would leave in peace. I carry a holy sword of the Order of Light, Yayne. He'd never forgive me if I hurt someone under angelic protection. I may already be in for it. But I'm pretty sure that…"

"Sesoon."

The mage clutches at his head.

I turn to Arix, "Did you have to do that?"

"He began a hand-casting."

Okay, so he did have to do that.

Mr. Gargoyle is a bit twitchy. Arix has his attention, and when Hjuul limps up, Mr. Gargoyle's eyes go straight to mine. I get the message: He will enact the nuclear solution.

I turn to Hjuul and whisper a healing prayer toward my limping Hell Hound.

"That was a holy spell of healing; I know of that incantation," the defensive gargoyle says.

"Sesoon," Arix says again, causing the gargoyle to jump. He looks between Arix and me not sure what to do. So he holds out the talisman.

"I trained under Christopher LeBlanc of the Healing Hands guild. And... do you have a hand block and bag of silence? That can't be good for him, being stunned over and over. He has some wounds that require attending to also. He's bleeding pretty bad."

"Demons here... how?"

I set the hammer down but where I can grab it. I pull off my blazer, roll up a sleeve, and show him the sigils."

The gargoyle takes a step back. "In a league with a soul-slaver and Ahtsag Znuul? Leave now, while you can."

I like that. A good offense is often a good defense. I meet his gargoyle eyes and nod in acknowledgment.

"I killed the Garrigan who tried to use me as his pawn. Ahtsag, well, that takes some explanation."

"The Garrigan was Maldgorath the Collector. And I assure you our master cleaved his head from his shoulders most efficiently," adds Arix followed by "Sesoon."

That wizard is getting his brains scrambled.

"Maldgorath? I have heard that name. He stole a dragon young."

The clinking of armor takes our attention as Vets approaches, leg dragging. She gets a healing spell as well. She straightens up after it lands and pulls off her helm.

"Vetisghar," the gargoyle says.

"I have a name, given me by my master... Vets."

"I meant no offense," it replies. "Your race once held promise. Before... before the Dzemond."

"Hand block and bag? Surely a place like this has them. I need that man immobilized before I can start with the healing."

"You would heal your foe?" The gargoyle cocks his head at me, "I have your word, on the honor of your sword, you will not attack me?"

"Yes."

The gargoyle hops around and engages his wings and flies off to a small off room nearby.

"Sesoon," mutters Arix.

I think he's enjoying the stunning way too much.

"We should just kill him," Arix says. "It would be easier and tidier."

"No."

Arix shrugs indifferently. I see Mr. Gargoyle returning with the apparatus. He pitches it to us, not fully trusting us, despite our oath. I quickly flip over the mage and block his hands behind his back.

"Chair," I call out. Vets quickly responds, grabbing one of the knocked-over wood chairs at the reading tables. We set the mage in the chair, arms behind him, and I cover his head with the bag of silence. Shey did a good job avoiding vital points. But he's still bleeding heavily, especially from the leg. I begin the chant for the strongest healing spell I know, feeling the energy coursing through me. Energy now staged, I release it into the mage with a simple, "Be healed."

I follow that by chain-casting my lightest healing spell three times.

That should definitely stop his bleeding and deal with the concussions Arix landed. I can't leave someone for dead in this place. I reach my arm back over to grasp Yayne and realize that a golem got my back pretty good. I take him by the hilt and say, "No casualties. And I did not pick that fight."

"No you did not," comes Yayne's voice in my mind.

"So, you will explain all this to me? Why my library was… Is that smoke I smell? Is something on fire?" Mr. Librarian Gargoyle goes into a panic. "Fire!"

I look to Arix. "Extinguish any fires that don't belong, please." I figure the please wouldn't hurt. "And hurry, precious things in here."

"Cursed and evil items mostly," Mr. Librarian Gargoyle says.

Arix takes off, and I am left with our new acquaintance. The mage tries to get up, and I step over and shove him down. After that, I look at the gargoyle, still clutching the talisman.

"Well, I tried to talk with this guy. He apparently preferred not to talk. I was in defense, just trying to survive. I did what I had to do. Really, I didn't come here to make trouble. Just make a request. I never got the chance. By the way, what's your name? Mine's Arthur."

"My name is Gauranthixmetaheminrfrbil. Most just call me Bill."

"That's a beautiful draconic name," adds Sheyliene.

"Thank you, young pixie fae." He scans the surroundings, I think feeling a little less at risk. "This is a mess. Everything is out of order."

He starts to hyperventilate a little.

"We can help clean up," I offer.

"This is days' or weeks' worth of work."

I let a moment of silence hang, which Bill breaks.

"So why would I let you leave with the armor of Ahtsag Znuul? It has not spoken in ages; the spirit in it is dead. But even if you were able to resurrect it, why? It was most foul."

"Well, first it's not a spirit – it's an AI, artificial intelligence. And the reason it isn't speaking is that the battery has depleted."

"Ah, magical batteries. Yes. I know of these. I was given this some time ago. It creates an orb of light with no incantation. They say it will work until the magical battery runs out."

He pulls out one of those keychain LED lights and turns it on with a large grin.

"How long have you been here, Bill?"

"About eight hundred years. The other five of my kind were killed defending various churches. We were delivered here by the dragon Aspirgiliusfrmtygymistgorlixiousfrylum."

"That's a very beautiful name," adds Shey.

"A most beautiful dragon, pixie fairy. He was my lord and brought me here to protect these fledgling churches of promise." He turns back to me. "So if I were to grant you this armor, would the beast Ahtsag Znuul be able to reanimate it."

"We hope so."

"Then I must decline your leaving with the armor. This one is well-known by the dragons. He is not entirely of this world or any world. Do you understand? He is an abomination of abominations. He eats life and hope and dreams."

"Can we sit down and talk? There is much happening. I need to explain myself and him better to you. If you feel the same after we're done, I'll respect your position here as keeper of this place."

"Librarian, please. And yes, talking is civilized. Let us talk."

I reach back for the tablet with Edgar's presentation and realize it must have fallen early on in the scramble.

"Shey, find that tablet for me, would you. It's important."

"Sure!"

Bow gets compacted and put away, and she goes off on the hunt.

Bill and I make our way to a table. I flip up a chair for him.

I sit down across from him and try to appear nonthreatening.

"The first thing you need to understand is this world is in great peril. The next, as strange as it sounds, is Ahtsag Znuul wishes to protect it. The third is that the armor holds the key to being able to nullify the vampire threat."

"You have my attention, Arthur, wielder of souls. Tell me more."

Shey found my tablet with Edgar's presentation. The screen was a bit cracked, but it still worked. After all my stilted explanations, having the tablet to set it out was just perfect. That and apparently Bill, the librarian, has never seen anything like my magical tablet.

I realized soon after that, he was just as much as part of the collection as its keeper. They've kept him in the dark. There is no electricity in this place. No plumbing. It's totally sealed off.

Some aspects of that are just gross. Chamber pots? Ewww.

But Bill understood what I was telling and showing him. That's why he guides me to a separate vault off the main library. I behold the sword and armor of Ahtsag Znuul. The armor is in its block with handle shape. The sword, well, it's a sword in a scabbard.

"So, you need the armor, and it wishes the sword, too?" Bill asks me.

"Yeah."

"And this will help defend the world from the Dzemond?"

"Yeah."

"Take what you need."

"Thanks, Bill," I say, moving over and taking the armor. I have no ambition for returning the sword to him after hearing what Znuul himself told me of it and having that embellished by Bill. The sword sounds evil. It can hang out here a while longer.

"You do not wish for the sword?"

"The armor is what we need, Bill. The sword is just wicked from what I can tell. Let's just leave it here for now. If it really becomes needed, we can discuss that then, okay?"

Based on the smile my gargolyian friend gives me, I think my answer was a good one.

We walk to the front of the keep, the long hall full of stone gargoyles.

Now it's my time to have some trepidation. That hall is death. If he engaged those stone-cold killers on me, it would be over – quick. I look down at him.

"You wouldn't… I mean, I'm pretty vulnerable in there."

"No, you may pass. The fact you didn't take the sword spoke to me of your intentions. As to the demon Znuul, who knows his motivations. But I feel you are sincere. Now, I do have a question – will you send me these moving stories you told me of? Like the presentation on your magic pad?"

I have to laugh. They have kept him so in the dark about the outside world.

"I will do what I can. But you have gatekeepers, my friend. There's this whole other thing called indoor plumbing which is rather nice, too. Someday I'd like to be able to share the outside with you. Not just movies on a tablet computer."

"I have such a mess. Can you stay and help me put this back in order? The golems are helpful, but you must direct every detail."

Bill is very flustered at the mess we left. His eyes dart around, and he's just plain anxious.

"Vets! Shey! Front and center," I yell out. They respond quickly.

"You two are staying behind to help out with the rebuilding of this place. Follow our friend Bill's lead."

"Sure!" says Shey. Vets thumps her chest and bows her head to me.

"You're in good hands, Bill," As an afterthought, I remember Arix.

I shout out, "Arix, do what Bill requires – please."

Chapter 34

I make it out of the hall, and as I push the large doors to the entry open, I feel a great deal of relief. I look out into the darkness and realize I left my night vision goggles on the inside.

"You there?"

"Lounging on the stairs," Znuul's deep voice replies. "Where are the goggles I bought you?"

"Lost 'em when I went for the hammer."

"Ooo… you had fun."

Remembering the layout somewhat, I take about four steps out. "Your definition of fun is a bit strange. Come get this armor and guide me out."

"Not getting that close to the door; keep walking. I'll tell you when to stop, probably."

Nice. I walk ahead cautiously carrying the some thirty-pound armor block, my sword, and a hammer. A hand on my shoulder stops me, and I feel him take the armor from me.

"Aww, do you want me to carry you out of here?"

"Bite me, flying monkey."

"Well, as much fun as it might be watching you creep the stairs, it'll be faster if I take you out and then to wing. I'll drop you outside where I picked you up, and we can meet up at the hotel."

I consider creeping the stairs, strongly.

"All right, make it quick."

I feel an arm go under my crotch, and I'm quickly picked up. He mutters some guttural words, and I have to assume we're camouflaged. I feel us bound up the stairs, take a few steps, and ascend to the sky.

Like last time, I basically close my eyes and go limp. As I feel us descend, I open my eyes and see we are outside the walls again. When we land, he releases me, and I feel the tingle of the camo drop.

"I'll take the hammer back."

As I don't feel like carrying it back to our hotel, I say "sure" and hand it over.

My raincoat is still crumpled in a ball at the base of the wall, and I put it on to obscure Yayne. "Meet you there."

Znuul smiles, camouflages, and takes to wing.
Time to get walking.

∴

Once back at the hotel, I knock on Znuul's door before going to my own room. It's right next to mine, and I figure he got back well in advance of me. The door opens, and I'm greeted. I see the block against the wall with a cord running to a wall outlet.

"I got it jump-started and directed the AI to the plug. Not quite life force, but it can filter it. You did good, Artie, but … where's my sword?"

My turn to smile at him. "Good politics to leave it. Besides, anything so vile I have to wear protection to touch it, ain't my thing."

He nods at me with a knowing look.

"I can get it some other time."

"So, does it still fit?"

"Funny. As a matter of fact, it does. Thanks for asking. You hungry? I'm starving."

"You're always hungry. So, you contact Kaanim yet?"

He shakes his head. "No."

"Not on an empty stomach. Let's call for room service."

Chapter 35

Ahtsag Znuul bid Arthur a good night after a small meal. Well, small for him – more than enough for Arthur. Ahtsag had promised Arthur a debriefing after he spoke with the Phagorite, and that seemed good enough for Arthur.

He recognized Arthur was tired and needed rest. Arthur recognized it, too.

Znuul sat down in the large plush sitting chair in the room. Not so large to him. He looks at the armor, remembering the AI, its personality, and how they worked as partners – brutal and unrelenting partners.

He walks to the block and telepathically directs it to prepare for him. Pads extend where he can step on them. He does and says "now." The armor responds by slowly coating him in its nanite substance. He feels the penetration of the suit to his spine, creating the direct neural link.

The familiar voice of his suit fills his mind.

"Shall I disengage from this power source?"

"Temporarily, leave the tendrils at the ready. We will relocate to the chair, where I can be more comfortable."

"We would not want Lord General Ahtsag Znuul less than comfortable, would we?"

The comment makes Znuul smile.

"My quip pleases you?"

"There's been some changes in my perception of what pleases me."

"Yes, it has been some time. I will analyze the changes in your neural patterns, Lord Devourer, and make adjustments to better anticipate your needs. Who shall we be destroying today?"

Znuul's smile widens. The AI feels so familiar to him. He's sure it must be likewise.

"No destruction. Just bothering Phagorite 47; reasserting ourselves."

"Phagorite 47, yes. Uppity one he was, but effective."

"Open communications to it, now."

Znuul waits and the AI announces, "Neural command structure established. Commune at will."

"Phagorite 47," Znuul says aloud, as it takes less concentration than segregating specific thoughts to broadcast.

He can almost feel the sigh through the connection.

"Well, someone has their armor back. I am ready for your command, dread Lord Ahtsag Znuul."

"How many others have control of you?"

"Only two, so far."

"Where?"

"I do not know exactly. I would surmise in the Middle East up until the well-publicized…"

Znuul's thought snaps to the suit's AI, and he commands the pain protocol to level seven. He senses the agony he's inflicting and imagines the Phagorite writhing on the floor. He commands the suit's AI to cease the pain.

"Where is the other?" he asks aloud.

"I do not know. Was that necessary?"

Znuul senses the feeling of panic coursing through the Phagorite at the realization he just questioned the necessary nature of the pain inflicted upon him. That usually means he's just asking for a whole lot more.

Znuul lets the quiet work for him, sensing the panic and swirling fears of Phagorite 47.

"You will say nothing of our contact," Znuul says.

"Of course."

"I will contact you later, as the need arises. You will say nothing. Confirm that you comply."

"I have no choice but to comply, most dreaded Lord Ahtsag Znuul. I await your command."

The comment of "most dreaded" rubs against Znuul. He thinks of who Grey Lightbringer brought him about to be. He thinks about the friends he made at the Chateau, in his dealings with The Protectorate, not to mention Arthur next door.

"Phagorite 47," he says aloud.

"Master."

"You call yourself Kaanim?"

Silence.

"Oh please, Phagorite 47, this is not unpublished information."

"I am as you will me to be, dread lord."

"And as the others will to you to be."

"Yes."

"Let's see if you can earn that name – what do you say?"

There is a pause. "As you wish, dread Lord Ahtsag Znuul."

"Fair enough, Kaanim; await my direction," he says aloud. Then, through the neural link, he tells the armor AI to shut down the connection. Znuul smiles and leans back in his chair, knowing he just called Kaanim by name, essentially validating his delusion of self-worth.

He knows the Phagorite is smart. And old. Phagorites don't get old without being smart. Znuul chuckles to himself about how Bobby tricked him as he did. He also realizes that Kaanim is one self-serving creation of the Dzemond.

"My analysis is complete. Your neural patterns have changed most substantively. Do you wish me to discard the old patterns? I cannot accurately predict your behavior with them."

"No," says Znuul, "I'd like to review them before you discard them."

Chapter 36

The knocking on my door wakes me. I look at the clock and see it reads 4:37 a.m. Damn drunks that can't find their own room. Knocking turns to more of a pounding. Crapsticks, I get up and shuffle to the door. I look through the viewer and see nothing but chest.

That has to be Z, so I open the door. It is.

"Get your things together. We are going," he says.

"Good morning to you. It's four-freaking-thirty, you know."

"Of course, I know that. I don't require sleep the way a human does. We go now. Meet me downstairs, and do not delay."

He turns and leaves. I think our exchange was just a little strange, so I stick my head out into the hall and call out as quietly as I can.

"We have company incoming?"

Znuul stops and turns around.

"Don't question me, human. Just move as you're told. We go now."

He turns back around, and I reconsider shouting some choice words at him. No sense waking everyone in the place. He sure is in one damn bad mood. Oh well, I know my brother in vengeance. If he says we need to roll, then we do. So I close the door and get it together.

Luckily, I packed light. After my morning cleansing and a shower, I hit the elevator to find Z standing in the lobby, looking stoic with his hands clasped behind his back.

"Ready to roll, Z. Assuming we're grabbing breakfast on the way to where we're going."

He lets out a disgusted breath.

"You can't even find it in yourself to call me by my proper name? I am only worthy of one letter of my name?" Perhaps I should call you A."

"Better than A-hole I guess."

No reaction. Nothing. I thought it was kind of clever and on the spot. Heck, it's the kind of humor I thought he liked. Znuul just strides forward, toward the mostly SUV that the valet has brought around.

The valet hands him the keys, and he throws them to me.

"You drive. I don't serve you."

Not sure what to think of that statement. I throw my things into the back of the vehicle and take the wrong side of the road driver's seat.

"Where to?"

"Bologna airport. Put this in the GPS."

He hands me a strip of paper with an address, not bothering to look at me.

"Ok, maybe we can get a sandwich there."

No response. Not even a groan.

∴

About an hour and a half out from Rome, I can't stand the quiet anymore. Znuul is usually a chatterbox about one thing or another, just generally engaging whoever is around. Today – he's silent.

"So you got the armor to work. You spoke with Kaanim?"

"Phagorite 47, yes. He deludes himself worthy of a name."

"And?"

I am greeted by the coldest stare I've been graced to feel in a while. I look back to the road.

"It will do as it is instructed. As it was designed to do."

Without question, something ain't right with Z. I can feel it in his responses, his eyes.

"Hey, Z, uh Ahtsag Znuul, why don't you take off that armor for a while? I'm thinking that maybe it's having an effect on you."

He turns to me and takes my leg in his hand, squeezing harder than I'd like – a lot harder than I like.

"The armor does not have the facility to affect one such as me. I control it. It does not control me. Know your place, human, or I will show it to you."

He releases my leg, and I feel good it's still attached.

Not sure what to say, I just keep my mouth shut and keep driving.

Chapter 37

We pull into Guglielmo Marconi Airport and move to the commuter section. Once there, we get out, unload our stuff, and turn our car in. Znuul is still strange, distant.

Our things unloaded and heading for customs, I have to be a bit worried. Znuul did have a crap-ton of weapons.

He passes through without issue, and so do I.

We walk out to the tarmac only to be greeted by Frederick Reigner and a host of Paladins, including Gunter Herrman, all in formation in front of our plane.

"Ahtsag Znuul. Greetings to you. You have taken something from the vaults of the Vatican," Frederick shouts.

Znuul smiles. It's not the kind of smile I want to see. It's the smile that says, "I'm going to kill you all and bathe in your blood."

I step in front of Znuul and try to diffuse the situation.

"Hey, guys, good to see you…"

My statement is interrupted by Znuul, sweeping me to the side.

"I did not give my armor to anyone. It was stolen from me and is rightfully mine. Come take it if you can."

Frederick looks at Znuul quizzically, then says, "Gunter?"

"Ahtsag Znuul," the big German bellows, "May we propose a brief cease in our hostility? Say a forty-eight-hour parley? We have information of interest to you and your efforts."

Frederick holds out the tablet we gave Gunter.

Znuul's smile disappears.

"You use my own words."

Gunter smiles back at him. "You speak with Frederick. We need to speak with Arthur. Information will be exchanged, and we both move on."

Znuul seems to consider this for a moment. I think he wants to throw down.

"Fine. Parley is accepted. Let us talk, Frederick."

They walk away to the side, and Gunter waves me over.

"Well, what is it?" I ask.

"The incubus Fxsigym petitions on behalf of your succubus, most seriously. It may be that the Order of the Light is the deciding vote for her pardon. We must speak with Yayne as he put judgment upon it."

"It?"

Gunter actually smiles. "Her, yes. All the same, we require the testimony of your sword. This situation is most unusual."

They bring Yayne's case to me, having been vetted through customs. I have no choice but to open it. I take my sword by the hilt and bring it against my shoulder.

"Yayne, tell them what they need to know of Silithes," I say aloud. "But please do not break my word of other matters. Please consider the integrity of my word in these things."

"I shall" he says telepathically.

I hand Yayne off to Gunter who lays it upon the ground and sets Patricius upon it. Whatever is going to happen is now happening.

I stand there helpless to influence what is happening with Yayne, or what is transpiring with Znuul. So I try to relax.

"Ahtsag is acting strange," Gunter says. "I would have expected him to laugh that I used his own words. I had hoped a little mirth might remove some of the tension."

He's right. Znuul is not acting like himself.

"I think the armor has had some effect on him. Honestly, I think I'd rather go with you guys."

"Maybe not; there is the issue of the stolen armor you must atone for."

"Not stolen, Gunter – given. Freely and without duress. And, by the way, someone needs to better poor Bill's living conditions. Chamber pots, really?"

Gunter looks at me curiously.

"You mean the gargoyle with the name no one can pronounce?"

"Yes, sir – Bill."

"I can raise the issue. It's not really the Order's business."

To my side, I see two of the other Paladins pick up our swords. They walk over and present them to us, properly, over the arm with hilt to us. I take Yayne, and Gunter takes Patricius.

"All questions addressed?" I ask my sword.

"Yes, honestly," is the voice in my mind.

"Thank you."

I turn to Gunter, who doesn't have to speak aloud to his sword. I can tell some serious debriefing is taking place. Gunter sheaths Patricius.

"Well? What's the word?"

"Much to consider, Arthur," is his non-answer to me. "What the incubus asks for we are inherently opposed to."

"Fair enough. So, got room for one more?"

"Yes. But you need to stay with the demon. If he is returning to the creature of old, someone needs to be close to put him down. Keep Yayne close and the order updated."

I walk over to Yayne's box and pull out the scabbard. I sheathe him and loosely sling him over my shoulder. If not anything, I justify this action with the fact it's got to be better in the cabin than the cargo hold. Znuul and Frederick are returning.

Frederick looks over his men, nodding in approval.

"Did we get what we need from the sword?"

"We did," Gunter replies.

Frederick says nothing, but his eyes do. I'm not the only one feeling uncomfortable, though Frederick is putting a good face on it. He turns to Znuul.

"Board your plane. I trust, should you have anything for us to act on, you will find a way to share it."

"Of course," he replies, after a dramatic pause. Znuul's eyes turn to me. "Parley includes you, too," noting the sword slung casually over my shoulder.

"Just thought it nice to share the cabin with him instead of being in the cargo hold, since he's out anyway."

"It would do you little good in such close quarters. Now, come."

He turns and makes toward the plane.

Frederick calls out, "He will be a moment, I would have words with him."

Znuul doesn't bother with a response.

Frederick doesn't have to say anything. I can tell by the look in his eyes.

"Yeah, I know. He's not acting himself."

"Or he is starting to act himself again. That is the concern."

"Arthur and I have discussed the matter," Gunter says.

"I'll try to get the damned armor off him. I think that's part of the problem."

Frederick nods to me and finally smiles. He moves forward and hugs me.

"God be with you," he says lightly.

"And you, too, sir."

I start to make my way to the plane and stop at the ladder. How am I going to get that armor off him? What if that doesn't make a hill of beans of difference? Confrontation is probably the last way to approach things. Somehow, I have to make it his idea to take off the damned armor.

"Dory, any thoughts on the matter?" I say aloud, more to comfort myself than anything. Of course, there's no response – or response that I can discern anyway. Enthusiasm. Yes, I must be positive and enthusiastic.

I put a huge smile on my face and bound up the ladder, thinking what would put a smile on big Z's face. I have to push the positive.

Once in the cabin, I say "hey" and put Yayne in a seat about three rows away – just to be on the nonthreatening side. Or really, so I don't come across as feeling threatened.

As I turn around, I see the pilot shutting the door.

"We'll get underway immediately, sir."

"I'm imagining Znuul told the pilot to get it going rather directly. Hopefully, he didn't call him "Human Pilot."

I sit down in front of Znuul, beaming a smile. Znuul pays me no heed, reading a newspaper. I fasten my seatbelt because that's what you're supposed to do. I feel the airplane starting to move.

"So where are we going?" I ask as chipperly as I can.

"Dubai," he says not looking up.

"They probably have our flight plan."

That gets him to put to newspaper down. "I have considered that. We will be evasive."

The look he gives me tells me I must be dimwitted. I smile.

"We might want to mix it up."

"I know what I'm doing."

"Of course you do. But hear me out. This is the perfect time to take a detour. It'll be fun."

"Speak plainly."

"Amsterdam. We take a detour, pick up some red-light girls. Three for you, one for me – remember?"

His eyes are boring holes in me. It is downright uncomfortable, but I don't let up.

"We could even call Pffif over – he loves pipeweed. Whadda ya say, big guy?"

"I have no need for human prostitutes. I have two willing Baalig females awaiting my return.

I nod knowingly back to him. Karred would kick his big purple ass if he did lay his hands on Ahzna.

"I'm just curious, though, you were so eager about it before?"

He's getting ready to reply. I lower the timbre of my voice and cut him off.

"What changed?"

I lean in, but takeoff somewhat reduces that dramatic effect.

"Well?"

First, he looks pissed, well more pissed. Then he looks confused as maybe he's thinking about it. I can only hope.

He unbuckles his seatbelt and stands up as best he can in the ascending plane.

"I changed."

The quiet, "slicka" sound of the armor comes from him, and after a moment it is in its ready-to-travel box form. He reaches down and puts it in the aisle. Then he looks at me again this time without the attitude. The plane buffets a bit, and he catches his balance.

"Well, didn't see that happening." He sits down. "How's the leg?"

"Good, I heal fast."

"That is good." He runs his hands through his long black hair. "I was just curious. I didn't think I'd go reprogram myself. I just wanted to feel it."

He sounds distant.

"Two willing Baalig females?"

That gets a little smile. "That's true. Now, one of them would probably chain-cast a world of hurt on me if I touched the other."

"Let me guess… the red one?"

"Not getting anything past you, am I?" The smile was weak but sincere. "I think I'm going to have to sleep this off. I'm not meaning to be rude, I'm…"

I've only seen Z this shaken up once before, after he kicked my ass in Grey's office. He looks at me with tired, questioning eyes.

"Nothing used to matter to me. I mean, I didn't really feel anything. No fear, joy, no belonging – just malice and hunger." His eyes leave mine and dart about the floor searching for something that's not there.

"Maybe you shouldn't put that back on."

"I wiped the mental engrams."

"So no more bad memories, then?"

"They weren't memories per se; they were more like patterns of thinking. I let the AI keep its memories. I'm used to its brand of snark."

"You have snarky armor? Go figure."

"Good AI likes to remind you the I is for intelligence. I do need to sleep this off. Sorry. If you need conversation, the pilots are there and so is your sword."

He scoots over, lays his head against the wall, and closes his eyes.

Out like a light. That's a nice skill.

Chapter 38

Znuul was up when we landed and in a much better frame of mind. He hit the phone immediately to Karred, followed by putting that damn armor on. Customs went quickly. Once out, Znuul had lined up transportation to some very swank, pyramid-shaped hotel. I didn't care for the effeminate affection he used checking us in or the "Oh, no, one room is enough, isn't that right, Pooky-bear?"

Yes, the old, or new, Ahtsag Znuul has returned, and he's going to get us killed or worse. The lifestyle he is mimicking is very frowned upon in these parts. Very. It could get us killed.

He expresses understanding our room would not be ready for another three hours and has our bags checked into holding.

"Come on, Pooky-bear, we're going shopping."

Great, Pooky-bear is going shopping, carrying a big-ass sword in a box. I don't say anything; I just follow. Nothing I say can help. We get outside, and we wait. Znuul advises the valet, "No, young man, we are expecting a special ride." Several cabs come and go, Znuul finally spies something away from the hotel.

"Toodles, young man. We are off. Come, come, Pooky."

As soon as we're out of earshot of anyone, I mutter, "Pooky-bear… my skinny white ass."

He laughs and says, "Hey, there's our ride."

It's a nondescript panel van with Arabic writing I can't decipher on the side. Znuul knocks on the window and starts speaking in Arabic, the only word I understand being, "Smith."

After nods in the positive from Znuul, he walks back around. "Let's get in the back, Pooky."

"I want a divorce. You are the worst wife ever," I say.

We get in the back of the van, and it's obvious: Znuul knows our luggage is bugged. He's hired a courier to get us where we need to go – the Dubai bunker. But, why Dubai?

There's no seatbelt – there are no seats. But what we have is what we need, a fairly invisible means to an end. I sit on one of the long crates in the back and Znuul on the floor.

"You know, Arthur, you're really homophobic?"

"Yeah, and you couldn't resist pushing it, could you?"

There's no answer except that over-the-top, can't-be-real smile he does. Yes, the armor is on, and today it's the Znuul I know.

"Well, it's still better than how you were acting."

The smile is wiped away immediately. Not exactly what I intended, but you get what you get some time.

"I'm not one to apologize, Arthur. But, I was not…"

His eyes fix on me. He takes a deep breath.

"No worries. We all make mistakes," I say to let him off the hook. Apparently, apologies are an epically bad thing for my large friend.

"Thank you. And as for the homophobic thing, you know your girlfriend is a succubus, right?"

"Yeah."

"You know what's better for her than having sex with you?" his eyes go wide, and he is grinning in a way I wish he wouldn't.

The words, "fleshy human cock," run through my mind. Damnit.

"Z, pushing all the wrong buttons right now."

His face becomes one more of understanding. He nods.

"I didn't mean any deficiencies on your part, Arthur. Just, she's succubi, and they are a squirrelly breed. Let me tell you the punch line."

I really don't want to hear it. But, maybe I do. He knows more about their kind than I ever will.

"Go ahead… lay it on me."

"The only thing better than having sex with you is having sex with you… and him at the same time. Whoever he may be."

I have to laugh. First, it's funny. Second, it's probably true.

"Thanks for the reminder."

"What's a good wife for, right?"

Chapter 39

We got to the bunker, and Znuul took possession of one of the crates. The driver gave me the crazy eyes when he saw Znuul just heft it out of the back. He was tipped liberally, and Z had some private Arabic words with him; I would guess it went something like, "don't say anything, ever."

He grabs up the wooden crate, and we walk to the big red door, Z opens the door and looks around. He steps back outside and looks around.

"Yes?"

"I was expecting a delivery."

He hoists the crate back up with one hand, and we head into the bunker. Same as all the other bunkers. He flips on the lights, puts a hand against the wall, and the runes for guarding against magical intrusion flare blue.

I can't escape these places. One day, I'll just have to buy one and retire there.

"Why Dubai, Z – sorry, why Dubai, most powerful Ahtsag Znuul?"

He turns on me, raising an eyebrow.

"It's about time you gave me the respect I deserve. The answer is Syria. The Ambassadors were courting The People's Islamic State. I need to pay them a visit. This is the best place to deposit you."

"You think the army of I.I.S. will tell you shit?"

He points at me with a huge grin, making his way to the kitchen, no doubt for a freezer-chilled bottle of Stoli. "Worst abbreviation, ever – right? But yeah, hopefully, they'll tell me something. If not, then… I'll leave in peace."

"Unless they try something."

I know how he thinks.

"Indeed," he says, rounding the corner, a good quarter of the bottle of Stoli gone already. "I leave in peace or leave them in pieces."

He flops down on one of the huge plus-size sofas he keeps in the living room area and takes another large pull of the Stoli.

"I'm so glad I didn't kill you."

Crap.

"Hey, I was thinking all kinds of dark stuff. But, I didn't do any of it. Grey wins. Memory engrams lose." He holds the bottle in a toast. "Grab yourself one; you're fun when you're drinking."

"Gonna pass."

I wait a moment, prop Yayne in the corner, and sit down in the big chair that he usually sits in.

"So how close was I to biting it?"

"Not as close as those Paladins. I can't believe Gunter used my own words. Seems funny now; I see it was meant as a joke. Not a bad one either… that Gunter."

I'm kind of speechless at his rambling. But better this than a "Kneel before Ahtsag Znuul!"

"What did they want you for, Arthur?"

"Needed to talk to Yayne, something about Paul pushing for Sil's amnesty from The Protectorate."

He nods at me, all-knowing-like. "Nice."

Both of us are startled by the knocking on the door. Loud knocking. Urgent knocking.

Znuul is not amused, but not angry either. Thank you, Mr. Stoli.

"You didn't turn on the security, did you?"

He holds up the bottle. "This seemed more important. I have armor on – I'll answer the door."

So he gets up and walks to the door. He doesn't bother looking through the peephole; he just flings the door open.

"May I help you?" he asks, Znuul's voice booming.

I can't see around Znuul to know who or how many there are. What I hear is the response.

"If you are Zebediah Newell, then yes. I have a delivery for you."

"Oh, yes. I am. Please come in."

Znuul's voice is not booming anymore.

I see a man, obviously of Middle Eastern descent, enter carrying a crate on wheels behind him. He does not appear put off at all, either by Znuul's initial demonstration of volume or his size.

"Did the sender request such a personal delivery?" asks Znuul.

"No. But considering I am the sender and the maker of these weapons. I wished to set eyes upon one who might use these implements of death."

"So you are Sharjeel Megwhar?"

"I am," he says, bowing.

"The weapons are made to my specifications?"

"Of course, that is why I am here. You obviously have experience in the forging of weapons. That and the strange script you wished engraved upon them. It is in the demon language – or what The Protectorate would call the Dzemond arcane lettering."

The fact this guy is aware of The Protectorate red-flags me immediately. I stand from my chair. With a better view, I see the large crate with wheels and latches. He notes me and nods.

"Some cool stuff I found on the internet. Did you etch it correctly?" Znuul asks.

"If it is for decoration, then what does it matter? If I may ask, where did you find this… stuff."

"With what I paid you, does it matter? Show me the weapons."

Znuul takes a double gulp from the bottle.

Sharjeel unlatches the box and flips the lid open. There are two swords there, large… huge. One is curved at the end with double prongs off the curve. The other is a straight blade.

"One to capture the prey, the other to finish," Sharjeel says. "Both with keen edges, killing weapons individually. Each to your specification of thickness, taper, and balance. And, of course, the lettering etched into the very blades. If I may ask, what is the script for?"

"It looks cool," Znuul says, raising the bottle to the man.

"These weapons weigh more than a normal man might wield. Might I see you test them?"

Znuul looks at this sword maker quite seriously by my judgment.

Znuul sets the bottle down on the concrete floor. He takes each sword out, holding them out apparently testing their balance.

"Perfect. I expected no less," Znuul says. Then he turns, and the huge swords begin whipping in dervish-like fashion – around, in, out, finally ending in a defensive over-under posture. Znuul loosens up, the huge blades twirling in his wrists. "Did you get the magnet and the harness, too?"

"Of course. I am a professional."

Znuul walks over to the crate, sets the swords down on it, and pulls out another box. From that box, he pulls out a large circular slab. He picks up a sword, and the metallic slab clicks to it.

"Perfect." He pulls the sword from what seems to be a big-ass magnet.

He looks at Sharjeel and says, "You wish a bonus for work well done?"

"No, I wish to see what kind of man could wield swords such as these. I wonder if such a man is a man at all? There is press coverage of a creature by the name of Ahtsag Znuul. This creature took my attention and returned me to my faith after so many years."

"What faith is that?" he asks, easily twirling the other huge blade.

"Why the faith of Allah. I believe the demon's words on the YouTube were something to the extent of, if you are going to believe in good, do good – believe in evil, do evil. But don't think doing either in the name of the other is anything less than being corrupted. I realized my faith is mine. That what I choose to believe in does not have to be dictated by others' interpretations I do not agree with."

"Missed that on YouTube. Think I heard about that guy in Russia recently. What does that have to do with me?"

"I found my way back to the path, mostly. I still make weapons that could be used for evil purposes. Tell me, Mr. Zebediah Newell. Mr. Z, Newell, have I made implements of evil?"

Crapsticks. He knows.

"Can't say. These? No. At worst they're just implements of death; should they be needed that way. Otherwise, they'll look really cool in my office." Znuul sets the other blade in the crate and returns the magnet to its box, tossing it into the crate. "You probably wouldn't want to meet that Znuul thing anyway, being one of Allah's."

"No, but perhaps he may wish to meet me and my god."

"Sounds nice," says Znuul, wrapping an arm around the guy and leading him out. "Your work seems great. Thanks for coming by."

They stop at the door, and a few moments of silence pass between them.

"May they decorate your office well, Mr. Newell."

Znuul says, "Thank you," and closes the door.

"He knows," I call out.

"He suspects, strongly. You going to summon the troops?"

"Not for another two days. They're helping the librarian rebuild."

"Sucks for you. I'm heading to Syria, and you need to keep quiet here. No phone, no nothing. They suspect we're here. So, pull the battery and the chip. They'll be scanning cell-com for words linked to us, voice patterns, and who knows what. Silithes can handle a day or two without your call."

If he only knew – a little alone time is not a bad thing for me, at all.

"Arthur, seriously, a day to get to the war zone. Two days to track down who I need to speak to. Maybe time to track down anything they share with me, assuming they do. Plan on four to five days on your own."

He takes another slug off the bottle, and I can see he's serious.

"This isn't a something-the-armor-told-me-to-do-it kind of thing, is it?"

"Planned all along. But know this, if these… people… decide to harm me, unprovoked, I will set upon them with a fury they are not ready for."

"Please tell me you're not going in there picking a fight."

Another chug of the bottle follows.

"No, I will be the model of restraint and decorum as father would have me be. But if they turn on me, I will send a message to The Protectorate and the world at their expense. Ahtsag Znuul is not to be trifled with. I grow tired of being nice with no nice in return. Arthur, I am…"

That moment hangs. Hangs way too long.

"I am the most dreaded Destroyer of Hope and Devourer of Souls. It always comes back to that. I try, but, at my core, there is much darkness. There is no escaping what I am."

More silence hangs, and he slurps the Stoli again, leaving the bottle done. I'm not afraid. This is just Znuul speaking his feelings. We're all entitled to that.

"You know, I'm reminded of a certain fiancée of yours. She told me something once, and I'm paraphrasing: that what she is doesn't define who she is. Don't let what you are define you. You define you, Ahtsag Znuul."

"Well, aren't you a do-gooding little ray of sunshine?" he says, with a smile taking over his face. He stalks over, puts that huge arm around my shoulder in a man-hug, and gives a fairly gentle slap on the back – for him. "My Karred's words. Grey would be proud of you for that one."

He toasts me with the bottle, another belt diminishing it. He looks away from my eyes; why, I have no idea.

"Let's hope they don't do anything foolish. Because if they do, I will enjoy being able to assert myself for a change. I don't lie, Arthur," his eyes returning to mine. "If they come for me, I will kill them all and relish the experience. So we're clear, as I do not lie; I won't be picking a fight or pushing for one. But if they cross the line, there is no return. The Protectorate needs to know that I'm not ducking for fear of them."

"Yeah, Z, I get it."

"Five to seven days, Arthur. Then we get you back home."

Chapter 40

Shenyang, Liaoning Province, China

Blood splatters on the plastic sheet set up as a barrier. The ambassadors see the silhouette of the group that just came through the gate and smile that someone on the other end was thinking so efficiently as to push so many through at the same time.

Jvarg stands, looking at the support incanters who have passed out on the floor – like they always do.

"Welcome to the Earthen realm," Jvarg proclaims. Then he moves to the plastic barrier and pulls it down, revealing a Bularj holding two smaller Genois engineers and an A'rl Skaar sorceress harnessed to its back.

E'Fenk smiles and says. "Come forward, all so we might see you better."

The Bularj moves ahead covered in blood, as are those he carries. Its deep voice says, "This blood is tasty. I want more."

"Then you are to be disappointed," Jneailith says. "You serve these creatures until our dominance is established."

The Bularj drops the Genois from its arms. "Free this creature from my back," it shouts, referring to the A'rl Skaar sorceress on its back.

"Yes! Please release me from this humiliating position," the sorceress exclaims.

Attendants surge forward and release her from the bindings. She shakes the human blood from herself.

The Genois immediately start communicating in their strange binary language of rapid-fire clicks.

"You will speak so we understand you," says E'Fenk.

The two look at each other and share a quick click of an exchange. The larger one looks at E'Fenk and says, "It is not our fault you cannot comprehend our language. The fault is yours."

E'Fenk looks to Jneailith.

"Fair enough," says Jneailith. "E'Fenk, please let Emperor Zebelbuub know that it is our fault we cannot comprehend their language, and because of that, they choose to disobey us."

"Oh, yes. I will. Adding in my report that, of course, they understand us totally."

The Genois look at each other with some urgency.

The larger one steps forward.

"Perhaps we have mistaken the fault – it is obviously our own."

E'Fenk nods at the strange gray creature with a bulbous head and two sets of arms.

"Yes, it is… now did you bring the weapons and schematics as requested?"

"Yes. Old, non-nanite weaponry, consisting of one gravity gun and two energy pulse weapons. We have schematics and basic theorem behind the weapons we believe translated so these humans' so-called technology might read it. I would be surprised if it took less than decades to decode and comprehend our less-than-advanced technology."

"The showers are over there," says E'Fenk. "Enjoy them – water is clean and plentiful here, for now. Clean yourselves and then join us. The Earthen politicians must see us as we are. Think of it as honesty."

"Then why are you in their form?" asks the Bularj.

"Because they already know what we are, and it is uncomfortable converting back and forth to human form," Jneailith says.

"Do as you are told," says E'Fenk.

The newly arrived contingent head for the showers.

"They question us," says Jneailith to E'Fenk.

"Silence. Those new to a realm always try to assert themselves. You should know this already."

"Of course," she says, her hand stroking his back gently. "Sometimes I need the guidance of a more experienced hand."

"No, you don't, sweet one. But nice try."

Jneailith smiles at E'Fenk. "Surely you can't blame me for trying."

E'Fenk looks at her imperiously. "No blame; just remember our mission. I would hate to have to feed you to the emperor. That would make me sad. So very sad."

∴

Dr. Jvarg and his assistants disconnect the politicians from the gate apparatus and bring them glasses of juice. Once everyone is assembled, they are brought to a receiving area, where E'Fenk, Jneailith, and the sorceress Kirtijix, await them.

"The other travelers are still cleaning themselves and your gifts," Jneailith purrs, gliding toward them. "May I present the most wise and powerful sorceress Kirtijix? Please pardon her attire, she is fresh from the shower and thought it most important and respectful to be here promptly."

Kirtijix smiles, knowing that she has been given political credit.

"Kirtijix," E'Fenk says, "This is General Cho and General Yang. Also, allow me to introduce ambassador Zang Jun. This fine gentleman is Bai Yi, of the Academy of Science, and his second, Zhou Lu. They will be in charge of interpreting and producing our technologies."

They all stare at Kirtijix, with her pale white skin, elongated limbs, and upside-down tear-drop-shaped head with a slit above her eyes.

"I am honored to meet you all. Please excuse my clothing," she says, holding her arms out in a presentation of the bathrobe she wears. "I have not had time to unpack my things. I thought it more important to meet you than to put on airs."

"So you will be assisting us with the technology?" asks Bai Yi.

"That is not my specialty. I am more of the arts arcane. The engineers would be of greater assistance to you. My role is to help in attuning the gates for longer and greater openings. Calculations and mathematics get you close, but feel is needed for true optimization."

"What is that slit above your eyes?" asks General Yang.

She responds by opening her glowing third purple eye, to their awe.

"This is my third eye that allows me to view the spectral and energy spectrums. I am pleased you appreciate its beauty."

General Cho turns to E'Fenk, "Where are the weapons promised to us?"

"Being cleaned of blood sir, please allow us to present them to you in a pristine state. My understanding is that our engineers have brought technical specifications for your team as well. You will have one gravity rifle and two energy weapons of differing strength – as promised along with schematics."

"Most excellent."

∴

The ambassadors and the sorceress arrive at their hotel in human form and get Kirtijix her key. The engineers and the Bularj left with Bai Yi to give a more robust introduction to their gifts. All are in a good mood as things could not have gone better.

They take the elevator in relative silence, as most likely it is under surveillance.

Once up to their floor, Jneailith nods for Kirtijix to follow them to their room. Now inside she says, "silence please."

Kirtijix nods and mutters some words in their guttural dialect. "We may speak freely now."

"Most excellent," says E'Fenk.

"We appreciate your sensitivity to the politics before us; your play was flawless," Jneailith says.

"You set the direction, lead ambassadors. I only followed."

"Continue this performance, and you will gain rank," says E'Fenk.

Kirtijix turns her head to the left, exposing her neck – a sign of subservience.

"Let us return this fine service," says Jneailith, "What pleasures may we offer you?"

"Are you of the order, madam Jneailith?"

"No, I am not."

"Then there would be no intellectual enhancement. As you know, our race is not inclined to the carnal pleasures as yours is."

"Perhaps a neural rub of the spine? While not erotic, it is considered most relaxing and pleasant by your kind."

Kirtijix smiles. "I think not. I am here to serve the mission, and you are the leads. I should not be served, but serving."

E'Fenk laughs. "You mean you should not allow yourself to be so easily manipulated by a pair of well-practiced Cubati, good sorceress?"

Kirtijix doesn't blanch.

"Yes."

"Good." E'Fenk says. "I am glad we understand one another so well, and we speak without pretense."

"So there is nothing we can do for you?" Jneailith asks, pushing the point.

"Well, is it true that the one who killed Maldgorath still lives?"

"Oh, yes. Do you want him?"

Kirtijix smiles at Jneailith.

"Not exactly, I want Arixtumin. He is bound to this human. I was apprenticed to Arixtumin in the academy, and he was beyond dreadful. Should we catch his wielder, I would wish to be the one to deliver the death strike, preferably while Arixtumin watches powerlessly."

"I always heard he was… pompous," says E'Fenk.

"That is an understatement."

Chapter 41

Qa'im, Iraq

Znuul lands on the roof of the main building of the phosphate plant. Still under camouflage, he's careful of his steps and surveys his surroundings.

"No sign of potential aggressors," comes the AI's voice into his mind.

Znuul says nothing, merely nodding an acknowledgment which is more than enough for the AI. He glides over to a ventilation unit, using it to hide his presence, and drops the camouflage spell.

After a moment of concentration, he speaks the guttural words for a shielding spell, then the words for another.

"So considerate to include me in the shielding, eminence," the AI says. "Few consider that the armor should be the last resort."

"Set view to my flanks, protect and advise of threat. Do not bother me with idle chatter," Znuul responds via the mental link.

"Understood," the suit replies. "But one question before we enter battle."

Znuul pauses, then gives a mental affirmation to the AI.

"Will we be consuming lives today? I do enjoy how that makes you feel and how it builds our reserves."

"Hopefully not," he responds, meeting with confusion from the AI. "I enjoy it also, but the devouring is not conducive to creating good company."

"I have much to learn."

"Yes. Now… we are on tactical. Silence."

There is no reply. The AI knows what to do.

Znuul recasts the camouflage spell and moves ahead carefully, being remarkably quiet for a being of his size. He carefully addresses the door, noting it is locked. He twists the knob with force, and it comes off in his camouflaged hand. That failing, he reaches into the open cavity from the knob and pulls. Enough metal exposed, he takes grip and pulls the door open.

Once inside the building, he makes his way down the stairs and to the door leading into the main facility. His vision shifts to the life energy spectrum, and he sees the way to the door is clear. He enters the facility, scanning his surroundings. He counts twelve soldiers on the upper level. One is walking his way. He jumps over the railing and, with an expanse of wing, lands lightly on the ground and makes his way to cover as the camouflaging is not invisibility, just a blending of the background.

He scans around, noting a concentration of people in the midst of this building. He allows his vision to transform back to the normal spectrum as running into inanimate objects would defeat the purpose of his camouflage. He moves toward that concentration, noting that they appear to be in a manager's office.

Perfect. He had tracked the field commander, Abu Adan Deir Ezzor, to this location, formerly used by the man who held the position before him. He knows this man is the number two or three in the People's Islamic State organization. He shifts again to the spectral view, noting all the people in that room seem to be surrounding one man.

The one man he needs to speak with.

Znuul moves across the floor and takes a position, putting himself in front of that office door. He drops his camouflage and yells out, "Abu Adan Deir Ezzor! Ahtsag Znuul wishes to speak with you. Come forward in peace, and let us discuss our mutual enemies."

∴

Everyone in the office jumps at the deep voice that carries through the walls. Abu Adan Deir Ezzor looks around to the people in the room with him. "The demons return. Prepare our soldiers to converge upon this one, like the last. We shall overwhelm it and show its evil head as we have before."

The men around him begin giving instructions through their radio-devices.

"Abu Adan Deir Ezzor, I still await your company," booms the voice from outside.

He looks to the people around him. "Are we ready to respond to this demon?"

The ones with radio devices, stammer various forms of "Yes." Those without radios bring their weapons to bear, making sure that any safeties are off.

Abu Adan Deir Ezzor strides to the door of his office, with all the confidence of a man that knows he has just deployed a significant army against one foe. He opens the door and sees the one calling him, sitting on his knees with hands on his thighs and clad totally in black. He sits in a nonthreatening posture. The large horns and wings belie any real humanness.

"You come groveling before us, after the others who failed before you," Abu says, "Allah shuns you; so do we. Speak your words and leave us, unclean beast."

"I am not affiliated with any of the others. They are not my associates. I hunt them as they present a threat to this realm. You saw through their false promises. I applaud you. Help me hunt them."

"More lies, demon. Why would one demon hunt another?"

"Why would one human kill and persecute another?"

Silence follows.

"I propose a discussion. You tell me what you know of these ambassadors. I know your organization has intelligence: where they stayed, where they ate, patterns of action, and communication. I will use this information to find them, stop them, and if you wish, bring them to you so you may claim credit for their demise."

"So many promises, demon. I have but one question: Are you a true believer?"

He sees the demon Ahtsag Znuul cock his head to his question.

"I have many beliefs to which I hold true. Your question is really, do I hold to your faith? That answer is no. But I don't begrudge you your beliefs."

"Then you cannot be trusted, demon."

"What if I was Shi'ite? Would you like me better then?"

"Kill this demon and bring me his head!"

∴

The AI warns of a cluster of combatants behind him, on the upper scaffold walkway surrounding the plant. Znuul disregards the warning until Adan Deir Ezzor screams for his head. Znuul swings one hand backward, calling up a arcane shielding and brings up his other as the soldiers surrounding Adan Deir Ezzor bring their weapons to bear.

Znuul's will pushes into the shielding, so well-trained that it is little more than an extension of himself. It absorbs the punishment of the guns as he pulls himself inside the walls of protection. The bullets stick to the shielding, accumulating as mushroomed heads in a wall of nothingness.

"Larger weapon incoming from the rear contingent," the AI advises.

Znuul hears the rocket-propelled grenade launch and pushes the shielding off his left hand, to the rear toward the incoming missile. It meets the projectile about thirty feet from his rear, and the explosion backsplashes over the men on the scaffolding.

Znuul stands, his attention now forward, seeing that Adan Deir Ezzor is being directed inside to the office. Znuul turns the shielding toward the left part of that contingent and pushes it forward into them, crushing them into the wall of the office.

Znuul hears the doors fling open before the AI can warn him of the soldiers flooding into the building. A bullet winks off the warding of his body and armor. He turns to that soldier, concentrating, then sending energy through his eyes to assault the shooter, who falls.

He reaches back and pulls off the swords from his back with large clicks of the magnet as they disengage. He concentrates and wards himself again, renewing his shields and smiling as those shields extend to his swords via the embedded script. He turns to the incoming mob and runs toward them. He takes to wing at the last second, lifting up from them. Bullets fire and miss terribly. Znuul, now directly above them, folds in his wings and drops into their midst.

He brings the huge swords to action.

The first swipe with his righthand sword cleaves soldiers on his right from shoulder to waist. The next swipe with the left sword takes the head of another, and the top of another's skull in the finishing arch. Znuul flexes his wings to create room and then starts swinging around as if a mad dervish, the result being large pieces of the soldiers being cleaved off. Guns fire but the swords are like an insane weed-whacker, and the soldiers are the weeds, falling in chunks of limbs and parts.

Znuul's tail lashes out also, with soldiers finding instant death from the venom in the stinger inside.

This contingent no longer a threat, Znuul turns to the group behind him set to cover the office. The AI announces the wards have broken, and his armor is taking light damage.

Znuul turns around slowly to the group behind him, now reloading their guns. He takes a moment to recast his warding, then holds out his right hand with the sword and calls the shielding. He stalks ahead toward them. They shoot in futility at him, their bullets meeting the shielding. Having closed the distance, he throws the shield, knocking two of them into the wall.

One powerful slice cleaves a soldier, leaving a weaving torso as his shoulders and head fall to the ground. The strike from his righthand sword cleaves off the shoulder and arm of another.

Znuul smiles as a soldier drops his weapon and runs. Another drops to his knees, groveling. The sword comes down brutally splitting his head.

"You shot me first, worm. No hope for you," Znuul mutters.

He hears the office door slam shut and feels automatic gunfire wink off his wards from a soldier on the catwalk who found some courage. Znuul turns and waits for the shooter to present himself, the energy built to project from his eyes at the ready.

∴

The captain slams the door shut and turns to the group surrounding Abu Adan Deir Ezzor. "Get the commander out of here. Rear exit, now! We will lure the beast to the streets and use large weapons fire."

Abu Adan Deir Ezzor, looks at his fourth, rushing to push whatever he can in front of the door. He shrugs off an attempt to pull him out with them.

"Our soldiers?"

"Dead, horribly. Go! You two stay with me. We will try to hold it back."

Abu Adan Deir Ezzor heeds the advice and takes the escort out the back of the office. Sounds of screams echo through the phosphate plant. As they rush outside, he barks orders through the radio: "Bring the trucks with the fifty calibers. We will mow this thing into pieces."

The group rushes him out through a short area of the plant, his second, Adnan, shouting into his own walkie-talkie. Once outside, Adnan points toward a building, and they rush in its direction.

As they run, he tells Abu, "We have a helicopter to pick us up on the roof of the refining building. It is on the way."

As they run, he sees the Toyotas with rear-mounted machine guns tearing toward the main processing plant that they just left. They stop briefly and see the demon burst through the door, out into the street with two huge swords in hand.

Abu meets its eyes and freezes momentarily, fear starting to overwhelm him. The moment is broken as Adnan pulls him away.

"Come now! The guns will stop it. You must go!"

Adnan follows, and they round the corner of the building across from the main processing plant. Abu feels the pressure of the fear lift, but the reality of the situation hits him: this thing is coming for him, and it has cost him many men already.

He hears the fifty caliber machine guns fire. He stops and smiles.

"Don't stop," Abu's second shouts. "We must get you to safety first. You did not see what I did in the plant."

Znuul bursts through the doors of the plant and immediately sees the fleeing group. He figures the one in the middle must be Abu Adan Deir Ezzor. When the man turns to him, he knows it is. He begins a fear-cast, but his line of sight is interrupted when another drags him away around the corner of the building across the dirt road.

"Aggressors with larger weapons incoming," the AI announces.

Znuul slaps the swords to the magnet on his back and crouches down. He pulls up his shielding, forming a triangle in front of him.

"Yes, those are fifty caliber guns and would cause some harm to you, my fine armor."

The trucks slam to a stop as the gunners swivel the guns toward him and open fire. The hateful gunfire slams shell after shell into the casted shield. Znuul pulls into his personal reserves, keeping the shields up. The guns fire and fire, then stop.

Znuul stands, maintaining the shields, then shoves them forward into the trucks, causing little damage but enough commotion. At the same time, he takes to wing, vaulting into the air. Once well up in the air, he sees the helicopter coming. He also sees the three Toyotas beneath him. The Toyota that wasn't a recipient of a shield bump trains the gun on him. Znuul dives for the right-most truck, the fire missing.

He lands in the bed of the Toyota next to the gunner. The fire from the nonshielded truck follows him, tearing up the driver's compartment and bouncing off the small shield on the machine gun. They stop quickly once they realize they've killed their own.

Znuul snaps a sword off the magnet and cleaves the gunner in half. Then he's to the air again. He wastes no time plummeting down on to the next truck. The gunner's head rolls off at a swipe of the huge sword. He drops the sword, takes the gun, turns it on the remaining truck. He breaks out in a huge grin. Znuul squeezes the trigger, spewing death into the other truck.

∴

They bolt up the stairs, noting that the gunfire has stopped. There is one short radio communication to the effect of "Aieeee!"

Adnan calls out, asking for status.

The silence tells him it's not good.

"Did we kill it?" Abu asks as they approach the door to the roof.

"I have no communication from the trucks."

The look Abu Adan Deir Ezzor gives him conveys disbelief.

"Outside," proclaims Adnan. The lead soldiers burst through the door, and the group follows. They take a defensive formation and see the helicopter coming to set down.

"Go," screams Adnan over the din. "We will ensure your escape."

"You come, too," yells Abu.

They start to make their way to the helicopter but stop when they see the large, black, winged figure with one of the caliber chain-fed guns from one of the trucks in its hands. It sets down on the rooftop and rips into the helicopter, shredding the prop and mount.

Adnan, seeing the carnage, grabs Abu and drags him backward. The soldiers with them start firing at the winged abomination. Adnan and Abu duck back into the stairwell. The sounds of gunfire and devastation come from behind them.

"This demon is not like the others," Adnan says to Abu, who appears in shock. "We must flee. This one is not as easily overrun."

Abu snaps back to the moment, nods to his second, and runs down the stairs, the sounds of gunfire punctuate the violent shaking of the building from the helicopter's destruction.

As they run down the stairs, Adnan barks orders into his walkie-talkie, trying to rally troops to their location. They are almost on the ground floor when they hear the roof door slam open followed by the deep bellowing of, "Abu Adan Deir Ezzor!"

Panic sets in, and Adnan takes Abu by the arm. "We must flee this place. Go to the exit and wait for me." He pulls out a grenade and quickly begins setting a trap at the door. Trap finished, he runs to Abu and locks eyes with him. They communicate silently, Abu knows that Adnan is going to lead the way. Adnan pulls his service revolver, takes a deep breath, and bursts the door open. He looks around then beckons Abu outside.

"We must move; it comes. Quickly, we must find a vehicle."

Abu steps outside, following his second's direction. Adnan looks him in the eyes, then turns to indicate the direction they should run. Abu stops, noting some kind of movement behind Adnan – a formless shimmering of sorts. Adnan picks up on Abu's facial expression and starts to turn around.

But he can't because the large hands of Ahtsag Znuul wrap around his chest, camouflage dropping. Abu sees him pick up Adnan, the dark fingers sinking into his ribcage. Adnan is trying to scream, but no words come out. There is no blood coming from where the creature's fingers have entered his chest.

Abu starts to turn to run back inside, but one great stride and a kick closes the door. Abu looks at the monster which is holding his gasping second. It smiles at

Abu, then leans in closer to Adnan's ear and whispers just loud enough for Abu to hear.

"Yes, fight it. Fight harder. Aww, not hard enough."

Abu looks in horror as Adnan literally wastes away in front of him, steam coming from him as the life drains from his body. Now a dry, shriveled husk, Znuul releases him, and he falls to the ground, skin breaking off in large chalky pieces.

Abu screams and unloads his gun into Znuul at point-blank range.

Znuul smiles back at him.

"Do you know what they called me, Abu Adan Deir Ezzor?"

"Foul demon, I deny you!"

"They called me the Destroyer of Hope and Devourer of Souls. Well… you just saw the devouring. No virgins and milk for him, eh? He's just… food for the beast."

Abu ejects the magazine from his gun and goes for another. He quickly inserts it, despite trembling hands.

"I deny you," he shouts and lifts the gun toward his head.

Znuul stops the effort to escape via suicide, his large hand engulfing Abu's. A sudden twist is followed by the pop of bones breaking and the gun clattering to the ground. Znuul leans into the pained Abu Adan Deir Ezzor.

"Suicide is a mortal sin. You know that. There's no martyrdom for being a coward. How did that verse go? *And do not kill yourselves; surely God is most merciful to you.* But as you may have guessed, I am not merciful. I came to you in peace, seeking a common enemy."

He releases Abu's broken hand. Abu looks up to this monster with defiance in his eyes despite his pain.

"One cannot trust the words of a demon. Allah shall strike you down."

"Maybe so. But he better move fast, if he's going to save you."

Silence hangs between them.

"Very little hope for you, but, there is some. Tell me everything your intelligence has gleaned about the Dzemond ambassadors, and I may be inclined to let you go."

"You lie."

"No, I do not. Deceive, certainly. Lie? No. Tell me, are you a true believer?"

"I am," Abu says, posturing up as he finds strength in that statement.

"Good. Now ask yourself, are these demons worth losing your seat in heaven? If I devour your soul, well… we've covered that with him, didn't we? You attacked me. Your life is forfeit. Unless I choose to let you go. This is the law of retribution. So, keep your soul? Or does the beast feed upon you and move on to the next in command?"

"I cannot remember everything, all the details," Abu says shakily.

"Good enough. Let's step back inside and talk of this. I believe I hear more trucks coming. Best we stay out of sight. You wouldn't want more of your army to die unnecessarily, would you?"

Chapter 42

It was too much to expect that Znuul's intelligence-gathering mission would be only that. After four days of almost solitude, the media is shouting the news: "Demons Attack Again!"

Well, really it was just Znuul. I'm watching the grisly footage of bodies and blood, all the while reading the subtitles. Apparently, he attacked ruthlessly, without provocation, and totally by surprise, according to whoever was talking to the media.

The image changes to a long-bearded man, who is apparently a field commander for the People's Islamic State: Abu Adan Deir Ezzor. He's very impassioned in his speaking, though I don't understand a word of it.

Thank goodness for captioning.

"The demon threat is real. We, the true believers, are the only ones who have been able to repel this threat. This demon, Ahtsag Znuul, attacks us without provocation. Many were lost in the battle, but we prevailed, thanks to Allah, blessed be his name. The demon fled us. We call all true believers to join us to fight against these monsters and nonbeliever infidels. There can only be true safety within the People's Islamic State."

I watched this circus repeat for about three cycles and had to turn it off. Man, did Z pitch them up a public relations softball. Maybe it's my more jaded nature, but I'm not ready to get all up in arms that Z went off the reservation yet. The biggest thing making me raise an eyebrow is they claim they ran him off.

It really doesn't look like he ran off.

I'll hear his side first. Though … damn. He left a bunch of bodies in his wake along with a helicopter and a bunch of those hopped-up Toyota trucks. He did say if they picked a fight, he was going to make a statement.

I reach down and give Hjuul a scratch on his huge head. He wouldn't be much help fixing the damage done down in the Vatican Library. So, he's been with me. It's been a while since it's been just us knocking about.

"Well, Z really stirred the pot, eh?"

Hjuul responds with a light chuff.

"It's time to call the group back, big boy."

He bounds his hulking self onto one of the large sofas in the main living area. I go freshen up my coffee, then join him and roll up my sleeves. At least when Arix returns, we can get Hjuul back to a more regular, wolf size; we're running low on the dog chow Znuul stocked from last time we were here. I'm sure it's a bit on the stale side, but Hjuul would never let you know that.

First up is Sheyliene. I draw my finger along her sigil saying, "Return." Then I run my finger along it again saying, "Come." The air ripples, and there she forms, wearing her light gossamer-like Fae battle dress. It really doesn't look like a battle dress, but with all the weapons and stuff she pulls out of it, no question that's what it is.

She doesn't look happy.

"Fucking Protectorate assholes! Dirty scum-sucking, troll-licking, bottom of a death-cap mushroom-sharing backstabbers! They chained up Gauranthixmetaheminrfrbil! That Gregowaile wouldn't hurt a firefly. Unless his dragon masters told him to – then he'd be all claws teeth and grrrr."

I take a moment to process her outburst.

"So The Protectorate came and interrogated you all?"

"Yeah. They were all like, where is Arthur? Where is Znuul? What are they plotting next? I will destroy you! That half-pint mage that's always hanging on Alistair's coattails thinks he's a real badass."

"He didn't hurt you or Vets, did he?"

"You didn't ask about Arix." She giggles. "They tried. Well, they kind of slapped us around a little, maybe broke a bone or two. But when they tried to do really bad magic, Arix stopped them. He can cast a dispel really fast. I didn't think The Protectorate allowed the use of black magic. Maybe that little half-pint doesn't care."

"Hold that thought, Sheyliene." I immediately re-call Vets and Arix to holding. Then I summon Vets. She ripples to existence in front of me, fully armored. Her fist bumps against her chest and takes to a knee.

"We told them nothing, my Wielder."

"Yeah, Vets was incredible," Sheyliene adds. "They broke her leg, and all she did was growl at them. I cussed up a storm when they put the thumb-screw on me."

"What did they do to Arix?"

"They tried to do a bunch. But he was all warded and would do this translocation thing when they tried to grab him. He didn't do any offensive magic. I think you have to tell him it's okay to do that still. But he kept them from putting a mindworm in Vets' ear and casting all sorts of other stuff. I always knew he thought he was a badass, but he really made those Magerium types look pretty amateur."

"The sorcerer's use of defensive magic was appreciated. Though he should have shielded me before they took a blunt instrument to my leg."

I nod in empathy to her. I call Arix.

He looks around. "Ah, which of Ahtsag Znuul's warehouse homes are we in?"

"Dubai. Heard you did well covering for the girls. Thanks."

"I am not a girl," proclaims Vet. "A girl is a small human child. I am a Vetisghar warrior."

We all regard Vets in her armor with the death's head mask. Nope, she's not really what you'd call a little girl.

"Good for them you couldn't cast offensive magic or you'd have owned them," Shey adds.

"Oh, I could cast offensive magic. That would just further complicate matters with The Protectorate, little pixie. That and I do believe Arthur would punish me if I killed anyone."

Arix is many things, but not stupid. Except for that whole giving up his soul for a promise that couldn't be kept.

"Thanks, Arix, the consideration is appreciated. So I take it we didn't get to help out Bill much?"

All three heads nod "no" in unison.

"The mage stationed there must have called for backup immediately. They arrived rather promptly. We had maybe a day of work in the library," Arix says for the group.

"Sorry guys. I had no way of knowing. Arix, if you would wolf-size Mr. Hjuul and help Vets with her appearance also, that would be great. The only other news is it appears our host decided to make a statement at the expense of the People's Islamic State: many bodies and much carnage."

Sheyliene says nothing but doesn't have to the way her eyes narrow.

"Oh my, I was wondering when he might assert himself," Arix says, as if Znuul was a player in a pee-wee football league. "Did he cast a pestilence? I taught him that necromantic summoning in the Academy of the Arcane. Of course, that was well before he became what he is now. What he can do with it now is impressive I hear."

"Haven't heard anything about strange diseases, Arix. There's just a lot of people dead and at least one that he ate the life out of. News coverage is on in the office, Arix. Help yourself after you help Hjuul and Vets. Everyone grab a room; you know the drill. We aren't strangers to this hotel."

"Come, Vets, let us make you presentable," Arix says. Vets gets up from her knee to follow, helm coming off along the way.

"You have the usual room?" Shey asks.

"Yep."

"He ate somebody's soul?"

"Looks like it."

Her face lets me know she's not happy. She pads off to one of the rooms near mine, turning to wave before going in.

I look over at a still massive Hjuul as he lounges on the sofa, quite comfy.

"Your turn is coming."

He rolls over partially. I don't think he's too concerned, based on how his big tail is thumping.

I get up to refresh my coffee and step out to the backyard for air. Once there, I reflect on my situation. No question, I'm in hot water with The Protectorate. Based on our run-in with the Order of Light at the airport, I can hope that maybe it's not boiling hot. Those guys are usually the first to bring the issue of smiting evil to the table. Maybe if I just keep my head down, I won't get sucked into a political or professional reprimand.

Yeah, right.

The red perimeter light goes on. It must be Znuul returning. I trot back inside, flip on the TV, and hit the security camera channel. This place isn't like the other bunkers with a long drive and lots of warning. By the time I see the small pickup truck stop, it means he's already here.

But it's not Znuul getting out of the truck. It's Sharjeel Megwhar. Given the fact he just checked his weapon and tucked it behind his pants, it appears he means business.

Chapter 43

"Armed company coming."

Hjuul scrabbles off the couch, looking at me as if to say, "What do I do, boss?"

As he's still basically his normal hulking hell-hound self, I just say "Hide and, if shots are fired, come running."

He takes off down the hall past the kitchen leading to Znuul's master chambers. I dart to my room and stop, realizing we didn't bring arms with us other than Yayne – damn customs. The doorbell rings. I turn back around and run back to the screen, focusing on the camera at the doorway. Looking at him, he seems a little pensive. There's just enough fidget there to sense his nerves. I hear Sheyliene's door open.

The doorbell rings again. Arix steps out looking human as does Vets. He looks at the TV screen, at the door, then me. His hands twist and arc. I sense the crystalline feeling of being enveloped in a warding. I nod to him.

Time to man up. I go to the door just in time to hear the doorbell ring again. Taking a deep breath, I open it.

"Hello."

"Good day. Is Mr. Newell in?"

"Afraid not."

"When might I expect his return?"

"No idea."

"I don't believe you."

Well so much for cordial conversation. I keep my eye out for the move to the gun.

I wasn't looking for the stiff-arm into my chest. At the same time he shoves me back inside, he pulls what is certainly a .45 auto. He falls into a shooter's stance, gun trained on my chest.

"Where is he?"

"Can't say exactly."

Sharjeel's eyes move, and I know why – Arix, Vets, and Sheyliene.

"But you can tell the little girl with the pretty bow to stop pointing it at me."

"Bite me, camel jockey," Sheyliene says.

"Why don't we all relax a bit? Especially you, Shey."

"Ahtsag Znuul. I know it is you. Come out and face me," Sharjeel shouts.

Arix chuckles. It's one of those "you poor bastard" chuckles.

"You think this funny, old man?"

"I find it humorous you would knowingly burst into the lair of the Destroyer of Hope and Devourer of Souls carrying only a simple firearm. What? Were you hoping that you might kill him? You would be lucky to only hurt his feelings."

"Where is he?"

My eyes haven't left Sharjeel, and they don't have to. I know the condescending look on Arix's face.

"How should I know? I just got here," Arix deadpans.

"You should put the gun down, and we should talk like civilized people," I add.

"You will tell him I came to speak with him and that I will return."

"Sure. You're welcome to wait for him if you like. Just holster the pistol."

"I think not," he says, starting to back out.

"Hjuul…" I call out.

His eyes go wide. I think he just saw his first hell-hound.

"Sharjeel, come back in. We can't let you go now. Trust me, Hjuul likes to play fetch. You just don't want to be what he's fetching."

I make a motion with my finger to Hjuul to move to the center of the room. Sharjeel hasn't moved the weapon from me. His eyes are darting around in panic.

"Oh enough already," Arix says followed by "Sesoon."

At the moment the stun spell hits him, the gun goes off, the bullet deflecting from the ward. I feel the ward fail.

A blur of pixie fairy flashes by me, tackling the stunned Sharjeel to the ground and disarming him. Vets is over in a rush as well, to help restrain our attacker.

I turn around to Arix, "Really? You're just going to let him shoot me?"

"The ward held like I knew it would. Even you have to admit it was getting tedious."

I hear the sounds of Sharjeel coming out of the stun spell and turn back around to see that Vets has him on his belly, straddled, one arm in a hammerlock and her forearm pushing his head into the concrete floor.

"Tell your master I do not make weapons of evil. Go ahead and kill me. I will curse these weapons and you all."

That hits home. I don't need another curse.

He starts saying things in Arabic, or whatever language it is that I don't understand. When the "Allah" comes up, I figure it's got to be a prayer. I let him go with that. Prayer is a good thing. After a few moments, it turns back to English.

"Well, what are you waiting for?"

"You to finish praying. Interrupting a man in conversation with God is rude. If we let you up, will you behave?"

"You wish to save me for your master?"

"He's not my master. And truthfully, he's got a lot of answering to do about that whole mess he just left in Syria."

Vets is looking at me for direction. Sharjeel isn't saying a word.

"Pat him down and let him up."

Shey and Vets get busy on my direction. Vets produces a knife, and Shey produces a gun from an ankle holster. Vets hoists him up rather unpleasantly, maintaining the hammer-lock and her arm now under his chin and around his throat.

"Let him go."

He dusts himself off and looks at me, not fully trusting any of us.

"The beast there," he points to Hjuul. "It belongs to the demon?"

"Naaaw, that's my puppy dog." I turn around to Hjuul with a big smile. "Come here! Yeah, who's my good boy?"

He comes and gets his affection, tail thumping heartily. Hjuul enjoys his hugs and scritches.

"Are you also a demon?"

"No. It's kind of complicated. Why don't you come on in, take a seat, and I'll explain it all to you. But, needless to say, I can't let you leave until the big guy gets here. Care for something to drink? We have water, tea, coffee, and vodka."

"Tea, yes. Tea is good."

"Arix, would you brew us up some tea?"

Arix sighs heavily and puts on a pained smile.

"Of course. I exist but to serve you, my master."

Chapter 44

Hatay Province, Turkey

The persons along the street in front of the hotel instinctively stop and move away from the not-quite-easy-to-see disturbance which appears to land there. When the camouflage disappears, and everyone sees Ahtsag Znuul stand from a crouch, panic ensues.

He takes in the sight and moves toward the hotel. He looks at the revolving door and thinks better of entering the tiny confined area, instead using the valet door to enter the hotel. Once inside, the occupants also start to panic – the lobby becomes pandemonium.

He steps up to the line for check-in/checkout. The line thins out fast.

"I'm not trying to butt in line. Take care of your business, please," he says in his best and most polite Kurdish.

For whatever reason, everyone decides that moving away is the better idea.

Znuul approaches the front desk. The two attendants are frozen.

"Good day," he says as happily as he can, putting on his best car-dealer smile. "I'm here to inquire about a couple that stayed with you several weeks ago. Might I speak with your manager?"

The attendants look at each other somewhat befuddled. The lady attendant picks up the phone and punches in a number.

"We have a guest that needs your attention." She puts down the phone. "The manager will be with you shortly."

"Thank you," Znuul responds politely.

After a short while, a door opens from the rear, and the manager almost comes in. That is, he stops dead in his tracks at the sight of Znuul – the guest needing his attention.

Znuul flashes the smile at him and beckons him to approach.

The manager, after some consideration, walks up to the counter.

"How may I help you?"

"Yes, thank you. Two persons took residence here off and on, under the names of Mr. and Mrs. Smith of Leeds, United Kingdom. I will require all guest and financial records."

The manager gulps.

"We do not share financial or guest information. Our guest's privacy is paramount to us."

Both Znuul's and the manager's attention is broken by the sound of a man's voice yelling out, "Your hands in the air and down on your knees now!"

Znuul doesn't turn but tries to discern what's going on in the textured, mirrored backdrop of the front desk. He sees one man with a shotgun and others filing in behind him. Znuul raises his arms and slowly begins to turn around.

"Who is in charge? We need to speak before this escalates." Znuul scans the group. It must be the guy with the shotgun who came in first. So he locks in on him, "Come over here; we should talk."

Znuul walks away from the front desk toward a corner, signaling the man to join him. The man comes forward shotgun at the ready, perspiration beading on his forehead.

"Best you lower that so we might speak in a civilized way," Znuul says in a whisper, locking eyes with the man. "I don't turn the other cheek. If that goes off… it will not be good for you."

The man lowers the gun.

"I am going to need you to get on your knees and put your hands behind your back."

Znuul smiles at the man and beckons him closer with a curling finger. Once the man is close to him, Znuul bends down to his ear.

"If an army with weapons so much more than yours couldn't stop me, what makes you think I'll yield to you? Do you remember what happened in Novgorod? Your men are so anxious… They best not let loose with aggression. Now, I can see that, unlike the others, you and your men appear to be good folk. You wish to protect. You wish to serve. Let me propose something."

The man looks up into the red snake-like eyes of Ahtsag Znuul.

"What do you propose?"

"Simple. I will turn my swords over to you in a symbolic gesture of respect to your authority. You will do nothing. It saves you face and allows me to gather the information I came here for, without having to harm anyone."

The man looks confused.

"Just step away and demand them from me. Shout, whatever. Establish your authority. People will feel at ease. I'll take care of my business, and no one gets harmed."

"Yes, nobody harmed is a good thing."

He walks back a few steps and looks at his men. Then he turns back to Znuul.

"You will relinquish your weapons!"

Znuul reaches back and pulls off a sword with a "snick" of the magnet holding it there. Then he does the same with the other. He sets them together and presents them hilt first to the leader of the law enforcement group. The leader nods to another who holsters his pistol and comes to take the very large swords.

Znuul turns as he hands the swords over to him, "Be careful. I keep them very sharp." Znuul turns back to the leader. "I'll be a minute or two."

Znuul strides back to the service counter and gives the manager another way-too-happy smile.

"Where were we? I need financial records of Mr. and Mrs. Smith who stayed with you."

A small pocket opens in the armor, and he hands the manager a slip of paper listing names and dates of stay.

"As I said, it is against hotel policy to…"

Znuul hops over the service counter and lets himself into the back office area. The manager scrambles behind him.

"Only hotel personnel are allowed back here!"

Znuul turns, his smile fading.

"Oh, I think I broke your rule. Now, let's be plain. I will have this information. Either you will supply it to me, or I will take your server and all of your information. It's unfortunate I must be this way, but you could not imagine the trouble those two are trying to make. It's end-of-world stuff."

"End of the world?" the manager asks.

"Yes. And speaking for myself, I would prefer it not to end. Now, either give me what I want or try to run this hotel without your server. I will not apologize for my behavior. It is necessary."

∴

The sergeant and his crew have been holding their position. The sergeant has fielded more than a few questions asking, "Is it safe?"

He tells them that he feels the situation is under control. Still, people scurry away – except for those with their phone cameras wishing to get pictures; they would probably sell pretty well. Those people are like the media, who are clamoring to get in themselves. He had to assign a man just to keep them at bay.

He sees the door open and the creature Ahtsag Znuul ducks under the doorjamb followed by the manager of the hotel. They both look fairly happy. In fact, the creature turns to the manager and shakes his hand. Then it hops across the countertop, stepping toward him and his policeman.

It stops about five feet from them.

"I would have my property back now."

The sergeant looks to his men. The one in charge of his swords looks back with so many questions in his eyes.

"You will need to come with us," says the sergeant.

He does not care for the stern look given him. The creature beckons him forward, with a flex of his index finger, so he steps forward, uneasy.

The creature bends down to him and whispers, "I will have my property back. I will not come with you. And I do not wish to harm you or your fine men. Please do not think you have either the strength or established a relationship enough with me to sway my resolve."

The sergeant doesn't break eye contact out of principle, but inside he is worried. This thing cut its way through an army with just swords – what will his men do against it?

"Bring Ahtsag Znuul his swords."

There is a moment of hesitation in the officer, and the sergeant gestures him on. He walks up to the creature and offers the swords. It looks down on him and smiles an inviting smile.

"Why thank you, young man," it says and takes the swords.

It leans back down to the sergeant.

"I am going to leave now. I can imagine your comrades are outside waiting for me. I strongly suggest you tell them not to strike unless struck against. It would be most unpleasant if I had to assert myself as I did against the soldiers of I.I.S."

"Most unfortunate abbreviation," the sergeant says back, with a small smile.

The creature nods back to him with a look of agreement and amusement.

"Please advise the others of my exit. I would take no satisfaction today in having to hurt those just trying to protect their home."

The sergeant considers those words and speaks into his radio, "Do not engage the target. Target is not hostile unless engaged. Please do not unleash the demon's wrath."

"Thank you," Znuul says back to him and heads out the exit doors.

∴

After leaving the sergeant and his men, Znuul is again confronted by the revolving glass door. A chill runs up his spine, envisioning himself trapped in it. No, the valet door it will be again. Already paused, he takes in the outside scene: the lights from numerous police cars bounce about. They have set up a barricade, and it appears some media types are vying for position.

Media? Why did it have to be the media? He dreads the vapid questions, the leading questions, and the just none-of-your business questions. He could easily take to wing and avoid the circus. But all that does is lead to rampant speculation.

And that liar rat-bastard Abu Adan Deir Ezzor has already started enough of that.

He mutters the words and recasts his magical shielding; then he plunges through the door.

The police are pensive and armed. They train their weapons on him. The media are calling out for him. He scans over the top of the assembly and not noting any additional threats other than the police, strides forward to the barricade.

"Ahtsag Znuul! A statement! What do you have to say about your actions in Syria?"

The media pepper him with a sea of questions that collectively sound like little but noise.

He continues his stoic, unemotional demeanor, looking over the top of this small, but noisy crowd. He senses the unease of the officers nearest him. They grip their weapons tightly.

He looks down to the one on his right and says, "Let them come closer. I will make a statement."

The police officer looks at Znuul in disbelief.

"I will make a statement," Znuul booms out.

Microphones and cellphones are thrust at him.

"Powerful and wicked beings are coming for you all. Now is the time for mankind to unite and push back this challenge against the very sovereignty of your home. Put aside your petty disagreements of whose god is better than the other. Put aside your petty arguments of what is the best way to worship the same god. Put aside your petty political and social differences. Because I promise you those that are coming will not care and will show you no mercy. They will not recognize your borders. They will not recognize your right to exist."

He scans over the crowd, making sure not to look in any eyes or cameras.

"I should not be the one warning you of such things. There are protectors of this realm, allegedly. They choose to wait for the coming horde. I would think it better prevented in the first place."

He looks across the crowd again, then takes to wing.

Chapter 45

After five days, I have come to appreciate Sharjeel quite a bit. Obviously, it didn't start off all that great with a gun in my face and all.

I think he won me over when we were discussing the whole Syria/I.I.S. debacle. He said something to the effect that it appears Znuul was singling out his faith.

My reply was something like, "Well, what if they said Ka-La-La-La-La-La, off with his head?"

He told me I was racially insensitive.

I corrected him. I am culturally insensitive.

He actually laughed and agreed with me.

I was sold; this is a good man. Later that same day, we caught Znuul's little escapade and press statement in Turkey.

"This is what I need to know," he shouts at the screen. "He rallies us. But why?"

I can't answer that question. But I do know Znuul threw a shout-out to The Protectorate to wake up and smell the coffee. I shared the observation with him.

"That is supposed to be their job. That is why I make weapons for them," he told me.

Shortly after, I find out he makes all of Greg's more traditional throwing and striking weapons, plus a whole lot more for other factions of The Protectorate.

Today is just another day in the bunker. Sharjeel is asking questions of Sheyliene, hoping to understand where she comes from. Vets and I take some training in the backyard.

And we all wait patiently for the landlord to return. Me, so I can move on. Sharjeel so he can get some direct answers. That's how it is doing the bunker hunker.

So when the red lights start flashing, I have to smile. I flip on the screens and see a large man on a motorcycle pulling up. It looks kind of goofy, like a teenager on a small kid's first bike.

"Well, he returns. Finally," Sharjeel says over my shoulder.

The front door bursts open followed by, "Arthur, we're going to have to get moving."

Znuul stops in his tracks at the sight of Sharjeel and drops the large satchel he is carrying. The smile that was there is gone, replaced by a scowl.

"Did you think I would not recognize my own handiwork?" Sharjeel says before Znuul can utter a word. "I must know, have I created weapons of evil or weapons for the good of man?"

"Neither. You made weapons to serve me."

"We have company, Z," I say as flippantly as I can, stating the obvious and hoping to break the tension.

That gets me a smirk from the large one.

"So what is the truth?" Sharjeel asks "Your words of 'be good, then do good'? The saving of children in Russia? The merciless slaughter in Syria? Or warning of demons coming? I must know."

Znuul picks up the large satchel, walks from the front door to Sharjeel, and pitches it at his feet.

"All of it is true. And for the record, I also said if you would do evil, then be evil also. Do not forget that. To do one and think yourself the other is, at best, self-deception and, at worst, manipulation. There are your swords; good work I must say."

They stand there for what feels like the longest time, saying nothing until Sharjeel breaks the silence.

"Are you good or evil?"

"I am. That is all. Good or evil are the labels put upon me. I do as I see fit to benefit myself."

"He's not as evil as he used to be," comes Sheyliene's voice from the side. "He used to be the worst, real demon scum."

"Well, then I shall rephrase my question," Sharjeel says with a smile. "Do you wish to help or harm mankind?"

"Neither. I would prefer things remain as they are."

I have to pipe up, "What he's trying to say is he doesn't want his homeworld screwing up our world. And they will screw it up, bigtime."

"What I wish to know," Znuul says as he leans to Sharjeel, "is whether or not I have to burn this place to the ground because of your flapping jaws. I have a sizeable investment here. It would displease me greatly to write this home off as a loss."

"Are you threatening me?" Sharjeel asks.

"Not directly. You may feel free to walk right out the door. But should our paths cross again and you have cost me dearly… well, you're a smart man. All I would need is the smallest of excuses to justify your extinction."

"Why not kill me now?"

Znuul smiles, finally.

"Because you haven't cost me yet. A great sorcerer taught me that it's not revenge until someone actually does you wrong."

That would be Grey. Damn, I miss him. I know Znuul does, too.

Sharjeel picks up the large satchel and drags it back to Znuul with both hands. To my surprise, Sharhjeel smiles at me.

Znuul looks down at the large satchel at his feet.

"So, dark one, you abide by a code of honor. That is better than some of us mere men. You give me the opportunity to wrong you, so you do not break this code of honor." He takes a deep breath. "I will say nothing of you or this place or this person that you keep with you."

Nice. I'm a person Znuul keeps with him.

"Well then, we're good," Znuul says flippantly. "Arthur, I have information to get to Percy and Edgar. Would you be so kind to tend to our guest? We have ambassadors to find."

He walks away from us as if we aren't a thought in his mind.

"Well, Sharhj, there you go," I say, shrugging any importance away.

He smiles at my shrug.

"Well, I see I have my work cut out converting him to more godly ways. Luckily, I am patient. He will know Allah. I will show him."

I laugh, not as much at him, but at the fact that Znuul would probably prefer being wronged versus being "taught" godliness on a constant basis.

Chapter 46

We spent little time at the bunker after Znuul's return – just enough time to arrange for a flight back to the USA. And enough time for Sharjeel to shadow Znuul, peppering him with constant questions and observations. All posed very respectfully. I think it drove the big guy to distraction. Not because of the questions, but because of the statements and observations that would potentially come later. None of those statements dropped, but I know Sharjeel is just building up for a good "talk."

I know Z is sensing the same thing, too.

I hope I can be there when that conversation does happen. It's bound to be amusing if not enlightening.

The flight back was pleasant enough. I found out the leader of P.I.S. basically caved in and promised he would never speak ill of Znuul and take responsibility for his actions. The press coverage tells me how much of a man of low character he is. Znuul's take is he's not worth focusing on now, meaning payback comes on Z's terms – later. After a while of being around him, you understand how to interpret Znuul. It's not hard really – screw with him and get screwed back, in spades.

I didn't call my personal chauffeur, Carl Turner, given the hour I got in. A regular taxi will get me home. It's not a terrible fare, and the ride is easy enough. I dismiss Arix and Hjuul, leaving Sheyliene, Vets, and me.

We're dropped off at the front of my building. I take a moment to soak it in. Home again – sort of. We make our way to the back and take the service elevator to the second floor. Once inside, I re-call Arix and Hjuul.

"Thank you, my Wielder," Arix says in such a way I can't be sure that's what he really means.

Hjuul says nothing but goes immediately to the sniffing around routine. Good boy, checking for unwanted visitors.

"It's late, group. I'm packing it in," I share, because, yes, I am that damned tired. I get back to my apartment and promptly collapse on the bed. I look at the clock and see it's 2 a.m. I sit up to take my blazer off and consider that my super-secret Znuul team phone is in it. I put the battery and chip back in and fire it up. A moment or two passes and I get a nice "bonk," meaning I have messages.

Two voicemails and a series of texts – all from her Sil-ness. I scan the texts, and one takes my eye immediately: "I'm no longer a fugitive!"

I have to check that out.

"Paul's been working so hard to get me leniency from The Protectorate. Today we just learned I am no longer on the most-wanted list. I have to report to a parole officer of sorts – same guy Paul reports to – and wear a damned ankle bracelet thing to make sure I don't leave town. But still! Call when you can! XXX OOO XXX."

The time stamp was five days ago. I can imagine some celebration was had.

As I know Sil is a bit of the night owl and figuring a 2 a.m. call couldn't be too out of place, I dial her up. After a few rings, she answers in a hushed tone.

"Hey there. You're back? You get my messages?"

"Just got back, saw the good news, and thought to call."

"I am so glad you did. Hang on."

The phone goes very quiet, and I think I hear muffled voices.

"Sorry about that. When can you come?"

"Soon, very soon, just let me make sure all's good here. Was that Paul, or Jex?"

"No… I'm taking auditions."

"Oh, the feeding thing."

"Yeah. Awkward, eh?"

"And you broke away for me, aww."

That gets a quiet giggle.

"He's spent. I was ready to make an exit. I think the phone woke him."

"Well, sorry about that. Pass on my apologies."

"That's funny. Let's talk more tomorrow, okay?"

"Okay."

"Love you. Miss you."

That actually stops me. "Yeah… love you, too."

We hang up, and I bask in the strangeness of what just happened. She was laying with another man and telling me afterward that she loves me.

And I say it back.

Chapter 47

Sil wasted no time calling me early in the morning, sounding excited as can be. No problem as I am, after all, a morning person, though I was hoping to sleep in past 7 a.m. It was mostly a one-sided phone call where I get to occasionally add a monosyllabic response like "yeah," or "really?"

I'm glad she's so happy to share. I'm not that conversant before my first cup of coffee.

I got to hear all the details of how Paul pushed so hard to get her amnesty and how she hid out at Mr. Jaw-Long Hou's place. Apparently, he's the wizard who Paul has to report to as part of his amnesty program. Now she reports to him, too.

Nothing like hiding out in the last place The Protectorate would think to check, namely with their own guy.

He sounds like a neat, crusty old man who thought his service with The Protectorate came to an end a while back. Being a crusty old guy myself, I can relate. She says he's a wise, kind man, but his wife really doesn't care for her or Jex. No newsflash there. She knows what Sil is. She knows what Sil does.

I get to hear about how she's moved in with Paul and Jxsiga since her "parole." Parole turns into a brief complaint of her ankle bracelet and questions of why she has to wear one and Paul doesn't. That and she can't leave Louisville for two years without advance notice and approval. After that brief interlude, I get to hear that Paul gave her the guest room on the second floor of his condo.

Everything sounds great.

Then she says, "And it's so nice to be living with my own kind. We just get each other. So many things are just understood without having to explain or apologize. It's beautiful."

It's the pause in my monosyllabic responses that tips her off I am seriously considering that statement.

"I didn't mean that you don't understand me. I just meant... it's very nice. None of us are trying to manipulate, or control. It's nothing like where we came from. It's nothing like... It's new to all of us. Even the twins used to play terrible mind games with each other before... Before we all changed. It's hard to explain."

"I'd get it better if I was an incubus, right?"

"Maybe not. I'm talking about love, respect, and consideration. And yes, because I know your mind is going there, touchy-feely, too. I told you things would be strange."

She wasn't kidding. But she's not hiding anything and seems truly happy to share it. I can tell she feels awkward also. I change the topic to another point of strangeness.

"Yeah, you did. So, how go the auditions? Is last night's guy a keeper, or is he getting pitched back?"

"Jury's still out. He might be too clingy. Paul shared his rules for regulars with me. They make sense. Partners have to be able to deal with things casually, you know, a late-night booty call or a regularly scheduled thing. They can't be calling me or following me. Once they start doing that, you have to cut them off. That and you can't see any one person too often; there's that whole addictive aspect we have to be careful of."

"Yeah, good to consider that. Can you do me a favor?"

"I hope so, what?"

"Don't wreck any homes – avoid the married ones, please. There's plenty of unattached."

"I hadn't even thought of that. Yeah, I will for sure. But you know the real rascals aren't going to tell me anyway. Hey, when are you coming up? You can stay with us. It'll be great."

"Well, give me some time here. I'll go online and see if I can buy a house unseen. Maybe you can come live with me."

"Yeah… maybe split my time?"

That says a lot. I shouldn't be surprised. She's with her own kind, and it sounds like nothing I could offer.

"I didn't mean that I wouldn't want to be with you," she says quietly. "I just... We have a very nice thing going on here. I..."

"I get it," I say, cutting her off, really more like letting her off the hook. "It wouldn't hurt to have more property in the portfolio. I'll try to get up as soon as I can. Hell if Z can buy a house in Houston in three days, I think I can find one in a week or so."

"I know you can. Please hurry. I miss you."

"Miss you, too. Let me get going. Coffee is calling, and it sounds like I have a property to buy."

"Okay. Don't forget to take your medicine. You've been doing that – right?"

"Yes. I'm keeping the curse at bay. And I will. We'll talk soon."

We hang up, and I go through my prayer ritual. I move over to Yayne's case, pull him out, and say "good morning."

I get what I perceive to be the mental equivalent of a nod in acknowledgment.

"Talked with Sil; they've given her amnesty. She's moved in with the others of her kind."

"I had wondered. There was conflict in their decision-making. Is there word on the battle for this world?"

"Not yet. Znuul uncovered some information, and others are investigating."

"I am ready when the time comes. And, your guardian is here."

Holy mackerel – Dory is here. I try not to become a stuttering mess. "Where is she?"

"Not fully coalesced. She is literally around us. She says to tell you that you are much loved, and it pleases her that you keep the curse in check."

"I love you, too, Dory. I wish you were here." I cringe at the faux pas. Obviously, she is here. "You know what I mean. I, uh, well you know all about Sil. I mean that she's real and now... Of course, you know. I haven't stopped loving you. Things are just so strange. What should I do?"

"The guardian says to follow your heart," Yayne says in my head. "She says it is a good heart and repeats that you are much loved. Now she transcends."

"She what?"

"She left."

My chest is thrumming. "Thanks, Yayne. I hope we can do that again. It means a lot to me that you could share her thoughts with me. I am blessed by both of you."

"I suspect the guardian knows that you share words of prayer to her after your ritual cleansing and our conversation. Perhaps timing will be fortuitous again. She tells you to trust your heart with the dark-souled life eater. Interesting, don't you think?"

"You could just call her Sil, or Silithes."

Laughter. Laughter from Yayne. Not a mocking laugh, but heartfelt. It's a level of connection we haven't shared before.

"I could, yes. I should, probably. Tell me we are going to smite evil and save the world again, Arthur."

"We are going to smite evil and save the world."

"Then I will follow your heart. Maybe it sees more than mine. Place me by the window, please, for today."

"Of course."

I get up and put him across the small end table and head out for the next important ritual of the day – shower and coffee.

Arix has made the coffee as Pffif is still at the North Dakota bunker. I thought about re-calling him, but to do so without warning is kind of rude. Arix sits down at the dining-area table with a coffee, and I dial up Znuul as none of my summonlings got the special-issue phones.

"Calling early," comes his deep voice. "You miss me that much already?"

"My heart pines for you. Can you get Pffif on the line?"

I think I hear Kitten sighing or something.

"I will in a little bit. He'll be calling you."

Click.

Well, at least he took the call.

I hear a door in the hall close and have to figure it's Vets. After a few moments, I'm not disappointed.

"Train this morning?" she asks, walking to the refrigerator pulling out the eggs. Before I can answer, she asks, "Are these still edible?"

I motion to her to bring the carton over – over a week expired.

"Probably all right. Just smell them before you cook them. If they smell bad, they are bad."

She nods, pulls a glass out, cracks four of them, smelling each one before depositing them in the glass. Then she powers them down.

"Satisfying. I shall be training on the second floor."

That's big girl – she's no chef.

I take in the feeling and relax in it – routine, blessed normalcy.

∴

Five days pass quickly and comfortably. Online house hunting was fun, but fruitless. For the price of a six- to eight-bedroom luxury home, I could about buy a whole apartment building that would offer some income potential, in albeit less-than-swanky areas. But, come on…

I've asked my property managers in Charleston to make the decision between two large multifamily rental properties, with the understanding that I want a whole floor to myself.

The feeling of routine and normality has returned, and it's nice. Pffif is back with us. The Hidden Eye is chugging along, and the kitchen has had no code violations. Part of me is thinking it's going to be a shame to pick up and move to Louisville.

But that's where Sil is. And taking Dory's advice, I'll follow my heart. Our twice-daily calls are now on the up and up on a landline as opposed to our "Team Z" lines. If The Protectorate wants to listen in, we're both smart enough not to talk about anything sensitive – other than our feelings.

Aww, shucks.

Today's activities are going to be highlighted by a healing session with a really nice witch I know that operates a popular store in the quarter. She's not with The Protectorate, but she's well-known, and so is her wife. I made the mistake of taking coffee at Du Monde and got seen. Apparently, there's a daughter of a friend of theirs who has leukemia. I know, and they know, it's a long shot. But it's a little girl, so I have to try. They're going to cover for me being a real healer, with faux ritual and hopefully real potions. We'll do everything we can.

The parents can't know about me. That would break one of the tenets of the healing hands. There's not enough healing to go around, so we heal clandestinely unless one knows of the Hands. Luckily for this little girl, Miss Neferini does. I'll give it my all.

Pffif and I are taking in the morning news with our mugs of coffee. It's good to have the little man back. There's something comforting about his presence. Sheyliene took off for the gardens, wherever that may be. I'm guessing to find her Winx. Given she's been gone a couple of days, I'll bet she found him.

Good for her.

Coffee is good, and Pffif's company is always appreciated, even though he can't get past the fact that "the news shows don't really change."

Then the elevator buzzer rings.

I've had security installed after the vampires sent their emissary, as nice as she was. I figured it shouldn't be as simple as press "three" to see Arthur.

I go to the security console and see that the elevator is full. There's that runt mage that is always hanging on Alistair's coattails. There's another mage type and two obvious Techno-Mage types. I see Gunter and at least one other Paladin. I surmise that based on the sword strapped to his back.

I push the button for the intercom and say, "Come on up, guys."

I figure if Gunter is there, it can't be all bad. After all, he knows everything that's going on.

After waiting a short while, I hear the lift stop and the doors slide open. I open up the door for them and am promptly greeted with a taser.

Chapter 48

Stiffened on the ground, I think I hear the sounds of suppressed weapons fire. I know I am being dragged. Then I have the distinct feeling of my summonlings returning to the white. That's right before I get another dose of taser.

I'm flipped over quickly, and my hands are bound behind my back. I feel myself being picked up gruffly and look into Gunter's eyes, right before he throws a bag of silence over my head. I'm moved around gruffly and put in a chair.

They leave me in darkness for a while. I know the routine. I calm myself. The hood comes off, and there's Runtly, Gunter, and the others.

Right off, Runtly is in my face screaming, "You've betrayed your own kind! Where is Ahtsag Znuul?"

"I can't know exactly," I tell him.

One of the Techno-Mage guys puts a truth stone around my neck.

"Answer me again," Runtly screams, partially spitting in my face.

"I can't know exactly."

Blue is true, and that's what the stone says. Because whereas I may have a good indication of where he may be – I can't say exactly.

Demon word games can work for humans, too.

"I can loosen his tongue," Gunter says, putting on a padded glove. He grabs me under the chin, gives me a look that tells me I'm nobody he cares for, then lets go of my chin and backhands the hell out of me.

That has to be a lead glove. I spit out some blood and try to collect myself. That effort is foiled by the blast to the gut I receive that removes any breath I have.

The next while is a litany of questions by Runtly, followed by punishments from Gunter and the other Paladins. I answer their questions honestly, but in no way that affects Znuul or anyone else that is trying to stop the Dzemond invasion.

Runtly takes my chin in his hand and says, "You think you are smart; you will tell us everything we wish to know. You will bow to my will and the will of the worm."

He turns and pulls out a mortar. He cuts his hand and begins muttering phrases in a language I don't understand. I recognize dark magic when I see it, This is not going to be good. He thinks it's going to be good, though, based on the smile on his face.

That smile is erased by Gunter's large fist.

"Necromancy! Dark magic," he yells, as Runtly collapses to the ground from the blow.

The Techno-Mage guys point their hands at Gunter. The Magerium types point their wands and staves. The other guys from the Order of Light have their swords at the ready.

Gunter just stands over Runtly.

"You would conjure a mind-worm? I heard you did this at the Vatican. That magic is black and prohibited from use. You are no better than the demons we wish to fight."

Runtly is rolling into consciousness.

"You will pay for this, Paladin. Alistair himself will hear of your crime."

Gunter's answer is a boot to his face.

"The order will tend to its own. We will interrogate this man, and afterward release him from his bond to the sword so it may be passed to another. And, yes, we will film everything. No detail will be omitted."

Crapsticks. Crap double sticks. What he means is they are going to torture me, then kill me – so Yayne can go to a new wielder.

Chapter 49

I'm ushered out and, from what I can tell, into a vehicle. I have little concept of time. Truth is, I'm in no hurry either. Only torture and death await me. Crapsticks indeed. Time pushes on, and all I am aware of is that the vehicle is moving. I guess I could have counted or something.

Seems like a waste of effort to me. It's going to be what it will be.

Or if I'm lucky what I can make of it.

The hood comes off, and I see that I'm in the back of a van, with one Paladin next to me, Gunter in front of me, and I sense the other behind me. And, of course, a driver.

"Well, Arthur, this is a fine mess. Is it not?" Gunter says to me just a bit too cheerfully.

I choose not to say anything, instead opting for the stinkeye.

"Oh. I see. You are angry. Imagine if I *really* hit you with that lead glove."

Man, I want to rip a smart-ass reply. I stick with the stinkeye instead.

His smile grows.

"Please. I had to make it look good. We heard about the attempted use of necromancy in Rome by that one. I didn't think he would be arrogant enough to try it again. Much less in front of warriors of The Order… Fool."

"Uh… so this is good cop?"

The van erupts in laughter.

"No, Arthur. This is The Order of Light looking out for its own. We realize The Protectorate has been corrupted, most likely from the top. You are our inside man for the demon Znuul's efforts. As much as it pains me to say, at least that beast seems to act with a sense of honor."

"Oh, okay."

"Release his hands, please."

The block behind my back is opened, and my hands are freed. I look around the van at my captors who are really my liberators.

"Um … Thanks."

"We need to get to a house we have set aside for interrogating you. From there, you will overwhelm us and escape. We will be very angry and disappointed that we could not stop you."

The other Paladins let loose with laments to their inadequacy for not being able to stop me.

"Hey guys," I say. "Be easy on yourselves. You did your best."

∴

We arrive at a nondescript row house and pile out. I am handed Yayne's box and a duffle bag presumably with stuff that they were going to investigate.

"Come in," Gunter booms out. "We have some things to share with you before you go."

I drag my things inside and find an empty house, except for a metal chair in the middle of the living room atop a tarp. Yes, this is a nice site for brutal torture and execution.

"Please feel free to take a seat, Arthur," Gunter says, holding an arm out in invitation.

"Think I'll pass."

Gunter walks over and takes the seat instead. He looks to one of the Paladins.

"Please tell me we have beer."

"I'm sure we do. Let me get you one, sir."

Gunter nods and smiles at the man before he leaves. His eyes turn back to me.

"We have two points of unpleasantry to deal with, Arthur."

"Only two?"

"That is enough. First would be the harm you and yours must inflict upon us to have plausibility for your escape. Yes, you will have your revenge. Surely you understand I had to make it look good, right?"

I laugh. "Yes, but I think you enjoyed it a bit too much."

"Not true. Second is, I have a video I am sworn to show you. It was supposed to help break your will. You understand, I swore to show you this, right?"

My mind swirls. What video would break me? My family at gunpoint? Surely Gunter would never allow for that.

I don't have to think about it for too long as he says, "Summon the fairy and the sorcerer."

"All right." I run my finger along their sigils, and they ripple into existence amongst us.

"Sorcerer," Gunter proclaims to Arix. "You need to singe us with either lightning or light fire, so we can say we were overwhelmed. Please do not seriously harm anyone. If you do, we will return the favor with your wielder's assistance."

"Oh, well, then I best consider my spell choice carefully. Regardless, to leave a mark, you know it will hurt – yes?"

"Of course. We are not averse to pain."

"Speak for yourself," says one of the Paladins.

Gunter just laughs. The other Paladins join in.

"Well, collect yourselves together," Arix says after the laughter subsides. "I'll attempt a minor ball of flame that should do little more than singe your clothes and hair. Please understand, it's easier to make it bigger, than smaller."

"Fair enough, demon. Bring on the fireball."

The Paladin group moves in together tightly. Arix's hands weave, and he mutters quietly. A flaming pebble appears in between his thumb and forefinger.

"Close your eyes, gentlemen," he warns.

Arix pitches the fiery pebble at them, and there's a flash and the smell of burning hair and cloth.

"Well, see, no real lasting harm."

Gunter laughs that laugh of his again. "Indeed! I needed a haircut, this works mostly the same." He slaps the backs of the Paladins around him.

"Now," he continues, "I must take an arrow wound from the fairy. Does anyone else volunteer?"

The Paladins all look amongst themselves and seem to concur that taking an arrow is a bad idea. Gunter laughs again.

"Fairy, make it a flesh wound here," Gunter says, pointing to his chest near his shoulder.

"You sure?" Sheyliene asks.

"Yes."

Sheyliene pulls her bow and draws down on Gunter. "You sure?"

"Yes."

The arrow flies and goes straight through Gunter's chest where he wanted. He looks at the other Paladins.

"Blood must be spilled."

They look at each other and square off. Each one punches the other in the nose, drawing blood. They stand there bleeding on themselves, then they begin with the laying on of hands. One by one they heal each other, Gunter being last.

"Now we have a plausible escape," Gunter exclaims. "Blood and evidence of violent magic. What could be better?"

"Beer?" asks one of the Paladins.

"Yes! Join in drink with us, Arthur?"

"No, thank you, Gunter." Somehow, I think staying clear-headed makes the most sense.

"Ah, yes. But you may wish for a drink, considering the video I must share with you."

"No. Just bring it on."

Gunter smiles and reaches into a duffel, pulling out a tablet. One of the other Paladins comes by and hands him a can of beer. He looks at it in disdain.

"American beer, bah. But better than no beer." He sets the tablet down and pops the beer, taking a healthy gulp. "For the Order."

"For the Order," I say in return to the toast along with the others.

"So you know, Arthur, I am oath-sworn to share this video with you and to play a certain clip of audio. I find this… movie most unpleasant on many levels. The Order insisted we watch it to better understand our foes."

"Gunter, what the heck?"

"How about we start here." He swipes the tablet and turns it to me to hit play.

I see what appears to be a winged female creature all in yellows and red, making the facial details almost impossible. She's astride another figure and… it must be Paul. The other smaller yellow-red-winged humanoid that is apparently kissing and rubbing on him must be Jex.

The smaller figure pops up turns and kisses the larger buxom female figure, then playfully pushes her away, and I hear my first audio clip.

"My turn, greedy!"

No doubt that's Jex. And when Sil replies, "You little minx," there's no doubt it's really them and not some CGI thing. Sil gets up and sidles up to the now-riding Jex, gives her a kiss, then rearranges herself over what must be Paul's face.

There's a manly sounding "Mmmm," and I see one of his hands reach up to take her gently by waist and tail.

I've seen enough. I push the little play button to stop it and hand the tablet back to Gunter.

"So they planted a video camera in their home? That's just wrong."

"I must agree. But they did not put a camera in the home. They used a high-definition camera with a heat-sensing technology. The man stood outside the bedroom wall of the incubus' home." Gunter takes a swig of his lousy American beer. "I do not approve of voyeurism. The cameraman did not have to record over seven hours of their… activity. What real secrets did he think he would find?"

"Over seven hours?"

"Yes, I understand he ran out of memory cards. Their stamina and appetites are unnatural. I was made to watch the whole thing. You know, it appears to this outsider that, when one climaxes, the others do, too. It goes on for quite a while."

I'm looking into his eyes, and he's perfectly serious.

"Surely you're not going to make me watch all of it."

"I'd rather not. Besides, the reality is quite simple. Your demon girlfriend is promiscuous. I think the common term would be a slut. A demon slut."

Arguing the point would be fruitless.

"Yeah, she's kind of that way, Gunter. I think they all are. And yeah, when one goes, they put out this neuromantic pulse thing that makes their partner do the same. She explained it as a self-defense thing. Though, I don't believe they're defending themselves."

Gunter's eyes tell me he's not too amused. He takes a swig of beer and gives me a halfish smile.

"Pays to do a good job then, no?"

I chuckle. I could not imagine a quip like that coming from him. Ever.

"Let me play this clip they insisted you hear, then we can be done with it. It's during one of their lulls."

"They had lulls?"

He hands me the tablet, shaking his head, and presses the play symbol. The three of them are laying lazily on the bed. Jxsiga's yellow-red blob resting comfortably on her back in between his legs, her head resting on his pelvis. Sil's buxom yellow, red blob is next to him, his arm wrapped around her and her hand tracing little circles around his belly.

"Poor, Arthur," comes Jxsiga's voice.

"Yeah, humans," comes Paul's voice.

"It is a shame," says Sil.

"I wish he could, too, but you know… humans," says Paul.

"I don't think Arthur would… be good enough," says Sil.

"Someone has to do a better job of audio editing." I hand him back the tablet. "They pulled that same hack job act on Sil. I'm not going for it. It sounded choppy."

Gunter is staring me down. "I would agree. But still. They prefer their own." He breaks eye contact with me to finish his beer. "No reason they shouldn't. They are built for this purpose, right? Seduce and corrupt?"

"You left out manipulate and control. And life-eating."

Sheyliene's voice breaks the tension.

"What are you all looking at?"

Gunter shares a wicked smile.

"Let me set it back to the beginning, you should see for yourself." He swipes the pad and hands it to Sheyliene who looks at him curiously.

"Cartoons?"

"Not exactly, Shey."

Gunter laughs. "I should get another beer before the others drink them all. Press play, fairy. Enjoy the show."

She presses play, and I see her blink a few times. I see the realization come across her face.

"Wow. That's Silly. And she's going for it. So's Jexubus. And the boy succubus."

Shey looks at me and blinks a few times, her mouth looking like she might say something. This is a first, Shey considering her words.

"Succubusses will play," she says with all seriousness.

"If you're going to watch that, take it somewhere else, please. I don't want to listen."

"Yeah," she says, pressing the play button to stop it. "I should find some earbuds. Then she's off in search of earbuds with the tablet in tow. I can't believe she wants to watch that. But Sheyliene does as Sheyliene does. I go the opposite direction to find Gunter in the kitchen. The small kitchen at the rear of the row house is the place to be. All the Paladins, singed and covered in their own blood, are having a cheery time over beers. All the eyes of the room turn to me. Nothing is said.

"Thanks for the bail-out guys."

More silence. After a few moments, Gunter breaks the silence.

"Your things and some of your group's things are in those duffel bags. Your three phones are in your blazer, over there. I wonder what we may find if we were to turn those over to the Technos?"

"You know damn well what you'd find, smartass. And I meant what I said. Thanks. All of you. I know you think I'm crazy having a succubus girlfriend and for trusting Znuul. But, the girlfriend thing is complicated, and The Protectorate isn't protecting anymore."

"It's not complicated, Arthur," says one of the Paladins with black curly hair. "You're thinking with your little head."

That gets a round of laughter. I'm not going to argue the point and bother them with ideas of true connection, soul touches, or that she passed the judgment of the sword. They wouldn't get it, or care to. Instead, I just nod, smile, and go along.

Besides, I am feeling a little put-off by my glimpse of the video. It is one thing to think something is going on; it's a whole other to have it thrown in your face.

"Yes, we know things aren't right with The Protectorate. And the beast Ahtsag Znuul appears to be working in good faith for our world. Though that mess in Syria was not good PR for him. If I didn't know better, I would say he was trying to send a message."

"He was," I say back to Gunter.

"The armor?"

"No, we got that resolved. I think he's just feeling a little... bullied."

"So he bullies the army of I.I.S. to make himself feel better?"

Everyone snickers at the most unfortunate acronym.

"He told me he wasn't going to start anything. But if they did, he would send a message to the world. Znuul tells me the guy claiming he attacked without provocation is a liar and a man of low character."

"Fair enough. I believe him. I think it is time we part ways. Take our vehicle. Stop by your closest bank and pull out as much cash as you can. The Techno-Mage Guild will be tracking your known banking activity. Keep us informed. The time for action grows near. I can feel it. We will give you an hour and a half before we let The Protectorate know of your most violent escape."

He's right, the time for action is growing near.

Chapter 50

After a quick stop by the bank to pull out as much cash as I can, we are on the road. I haven't bothered calling Znuul yet, figuring I should make some time first. Besides, there's no telling which of his bunkers he's hiding out in.

Sheyliene bummed some earbuds off one of the Paladins. She's in the front seat next to me watching the whole infrared-voyeur video. Occasionally we are subjected to her low "ooohs" or "mmms" that I assume we are not supposed to hear. For the last while, she's been fidgeting and readjusting herself in the seat. I interpret that as my fairy getting worked up.

Why she would want to do that to herself, I have no idea. But there she is.

"Shey," I say, reaching over and tapping her lightly on the thigh.

She jumps and pulls one of the earbuds out. "What?"

"Can I see that tablet?"

"Sure. It's pretty amazing. I haven't seen Silly going at it like that in a long time. We used to… Well, not we, it wasn't really me. You know the old boss made me do things. And when she was in charge, everybody did things for her."

"Well, no I didn't know that exactly."

I hold my hand out for the tablet. She unplugs the earbuds and hands it to me with a smile, squirming a bit to readjust herself again.

I push the passenger window button down and Frisbee the damn thing out the window.

Arix snickers.

"Did I do something wrong?"

"No, Shey. It just probably had tracking devices in it."

"Oh yeah. It probably did… I wish Winx were here."

"Me too, Shey."

"Except he probably knows. I think he saw me disappear."

"You know it, or think it?"

"Think it mostly. Well, know it. I mean we were flying around."

"Hmmm."

I make sure to get a few hours of driving behind us. At some point, I have to let the victims of this voyeuristic intrusion know what's going on. I really don't want to hear Sil tell me, "I told you it would be strange," so I decide to call Jxsiga. She'll make sure any cameramen are dealt with, and she can let Sil know I'm okay.

And there are no hard feelings.

Mostly. It still stings a bit. But she warned me it would be strange, and it's not like I didn't know she was up to things with those two. But still.

I pull over eventually and get out of the vehicle. I use my phone for the Znuul network to look up Jxsiga's and Paul's home number. I call them on my Protectorate phone. I know it's tapped; The Protectorate needs to hear this conversation.

It rings, and eventually I hear Jxsiga's voice pick up.

"Hello?"

"Yeah… it's Arthur. Can't talk long as I'm now on most-wanted status with The Protectorate. Just had to let you know that people are filming you having sex with Sil and Paul."

Dead silence.

"What?"

"Yeah… there's this infrared or heat camera they have, and they shared this whole thing with me of you all going at it. It's yellow-red stuff, but still pretty detailed. I thought you'd want to know they're doing that."

"People are filming us? What?"

Exactly the response I expected.

"Yeah… they had this whole seven-hour video of you guys going at it. I didn't watch it all, but Sheyliene got an eyeful. I figured, since we're friends now, I should let you know. Oh, geez, that is a low thing to do, film y'all like that."

I had to add that for any Protectorate types listening, which I must assume they are.

"Yes, it is."

"Well, that's all I got. Sil warned me it would be weird. It is weird. I'm not angry. It's just strange… and strange."

"Let me get her to call you. You two need to talk."

"We probably do. But I have to burn this phone. And I need to go underground. Just tell her I'm not angry or anything. I'll be in touch when I can. If they're filming you through walls, they're probably bugging other things. And listening to this conversation. If they are, guys you have to know something's not right with all this. You have to."

"Arthur…"

I hang up. Now they know they're being watched. That was the important thing. And knowing Jxsiga, some heads are going to roll. If she finds those heads.

Chapter 51

My next call was to Edgar, using the Znuul network phone. I let him know what was going on and asked for a pickup after pushing on to Little Rock. He told me to push on to Nebraska and call back. I told him I wasn't comfortable driving this car any further.

So we crash in Little Rock. I park the car blocks away, figuring it's tagged somehow. I sent Arix in under disguise to buy our rooms.

You can never be too safe.

After a night's rest, I send Shey out to the vehicle to judge if it's being watched. After a report that it's not, we jump in, gas up, and make the drive to right outside Omaha. I put the battery back in the phone and call Edgar again.

He tells me to find a place to hang tight, and they'll send a ride to me.

So no-tell motel here I come again. I get us two rooms: one for the guys and one for the girls. That works mostly, except Shey is asking about "helping" again. We collectively shut the idea down quickly.

It's a day of fast food and magic fingers until Znuul's team phone rings. I pick it up.

"Hello."

"I'm about five minutes from you," comes a bubbly female voice that I finally recognize as Kitten's.

"Oh, good."

"I've been driving all day; you drive back?"

"Sure."

"Yay! See you soon." Click.

Sure as shootin' in five minutes, there's a knock on the door. I don't even bother with the peephole and open the door.

"Hi!"

"Well, hello to you, Miss Kitten. Please come in."

She says "thanks!" and does. "That was a long drive. Where's Sheyliene?"

"In the other room with Vets."

She wastes no time going to the other room.

I guess little itty-bitty slave girls should have a club.

Arix looks at me, "So, are we leaving this dismal place?"

"We are, sir."

"Now?"

"Working on that, Arix. The recovery team is here."

Kitten comes back out and looks at me in as much seriousness as I can imagine from her.

"I need a friggin' nap. Do you mind if I sleep a bit before we go? It's a huge drive."

"Surely. Whatever you need – remember I offered to drive?"

"Oh yeah. See how tired I am? You want out of here, eh?"

Arix answers before I can.

"Oh, yes please."

∴

Our destination is in the GPS. All I have to do is follow the directions. Kitten is passed out in the front seat, and my crew is in the back of the Hummer. We've been driving for a few hours.

Kitten begins to stir. Her eyes open, and I get the doe-eyed smiley face.

"How far?"

"We have about two-and-a-half hours, Ms. Kitten."

"Nice. I'm ready to get back. I hate being away from Master… and Missus."

"Well, you will be back soon. Anything new going on in the bunker?"

"No. Not really. Well… maybe. I think Greg is hooking up with the evil bitch. I have a sense for these things."

"Really? Greg and Ahzna?"

"Can't be sure, but I kind of think so… I don't know for sure."

"Ewww…" comes Shey from the back. "Who would lay with the evil bitch? She's like… evil."

Arix chuckles at all of us.

"I can't be sure. It just seems like it," Kitten says defensively.

"No worries," I tell her. "Sounds like bunker business as usual."

Chapter 52

About a week of bunker life and I'm already disgruntled with it. Not that the bunkers are so bad, it's just that I really prefer to be living in my own house, puttering around my business and my things.

Unfortunately, life isn't allowing for that.

At least there's routine. Everyone gets up at the crack of dawn, grabs a communal breakfast of sorts, then disappears to either the office or the garage. The garage has been converted to a makeshift "war room" of sorts with office partitions used more for pinning things up than partitioning. The office really belongs to Edgar and Percy more than Znuul now, and while he's been fairly gracious about it, I have the feeling his territorial side is unhappy.

Speaking of routines, Sheyliene offers her "help" regularly – usually right after lunch and right before bedtime. I still don't get how it is "not cheating" – but Sheyliene is Sheyliene.

Tonight she threw me a curve; she wants to snuggle with me. Now snuggling is not a bad thing. Sheyliene and I have snuggled for years. Heck, she loved to snuggle with Dory. The issue is the bunker room: they are equipped with a twin bed which doesn't make for a lot of room. But Shey has some ingenuity and a simple solution to that. In a cascade of silvery dust, she resizes herself to about the size of a Barbie. The issue for me is, with her being latched on my arm, what if I roll over?

I do not wish to smash or smother my fairy.

So, sleep isn't happening – I extricate myself gently, grab my notepad, and head out to the living room. Maybe I can gel some thoughts and be of some service in figuring out where the ambassadors are or where they'll be going. Percy offered me a tablet thing, but for me, paper and pen are better for collecting thoughts and making notes of ideas for business.

I know these ambassadors started with the People's Islamic State, so I guess they're looking for the zealot type. I start to jot down a list of the most likely candidates: North Korea, Russia, Iran, maybe even China. After a little bit of soul-searching, I realize my thoughts are rather parochial, as I left off the United States of America. While I don't think that the American people are necessarily looking to dominate the world, I do believe politicians are politicians, and politicians are more worried about their own personal power than the greater good.

I review the list and get a little frustrated. I'm not breaking any new ground. Perhaps somewhere in this short and very obvious list, a likely candidate exists. So, I think another approach is called for. I start thinking of countries not to expect. First up is the Swiss, more than likely because of Znuul's complaints about Swiss bankers and their refusal to share information.

I hear the sound of a door opening on the upstairs bank of rooms. I glance upstairs and out from Greg's room slinks Ahzna in full Baalig form. She looks down at me sourly and jumps over the balustrade and with an easy "poof" of the wings lands lightly on the floor.

Based on how the Chicago Bears shirt flipped up I can see that's all she's wearing. She pads over to me and stands over me imperiously.

"You saw nothing."

"Actually, I got quite an eyeful when you jumped over the rail."

"You will say nothing."

"Is that you telling me I saw nothing or you telling me not to say that I saw anything that I saw?"

"I am telling you to be silent of this matter, or else."

This is rich. I am being threatened – again.

"Well, let's see. You've already established that you're going to destroy my family person by person, kill my girlfriend, and save me for last so I can truly despair. Exactly what is it you are threatening me with? There's really nothing else is there? So, I say go pound sand, EB."

I look back down to my notebook, pretending to go back to doing what I was. Moments pass, and to my dismay, she hasn't left.

"How may I secure your silence in this matter?"

"Well, if you had walked over here and asked me politely first, I might keep your secret under my hat. But you went with threats and intimidation, so there's nothing you can do, except leave."

I go back to my notebook, hoping she takes the hint and goes.

"Everyone has a price. What is yours? Perhaps you want the pleasuring? You have not experienced life until you have coupled with a fully aroused Baalig female."

I think my poker face actually works to my advantage this time. She understands quickly that I am repulsed by the thought of being with her instead of intrigued.

"Don't judge what you haven't experienced. We are negotiating? Two nights of the pleasuring."

"No nights."

"Do you realize what you are declining?"

"Yes."

"Two nights and my mouth right now, in private," she whispers.

"Go away, EB."

The look is priceless: shock, contempt, and confusion all wrapped in anger. It actually makes me kind of happy.

"You will regret your decision," she says, turning to walk to her first-floor room. "My memory is long."

Her door closes very quietly, and I'm finally left to myself again.

I'm going to have to talk with that boy, Greg. He's definitely thinking with the wrong head.

Chapter 53

I'm joined for morning breakfast by Greg. He slaps me on the shoulder and says, "Let's talk outside. I understand you and Ahz shared a little time last night."

"Very little, Greg. It wasn't exactly a bucket of fun."

"Come on!"

He heads outside, and I guess I have to follow. So I do.

Greg sits at one of the picnic tables, and I sit across from him.

"So you're diddling the evil bitch?"

Greg smiles, "Yeah, I guess I am. More like I'm getting done. I took her to a Chicago football game and next thing I know she's all coming into my room, letting me know that she needs some attention. So I did. She's a freaking trip, let me tell you. It's like she loses her mind or something. Is that how Silithes is?"

"I don't kiss and tell, Greg."

"Fair enough. But man… Anyway, she had a little conversation with me this morning and basically told me I need to go on a walk with you, then kill you, and leave you in a shallow grave."

Well, not what I expected to hear. My face says more than my mouth could.

"I'd never, man. She's just all wanting some of big Z, for whatever that biological thing is that's between them. She's worried he'll think she's weak or something for enjoying her time with me. Personally, I don't think he'd care. Kind of strange doing the deed with her, knowing she would really rather be with someone else. But, that's friends with benefits, right?"

"Sounds demeaning to me, Greg. They call it the biological imperative, an attraction to the closest in blood for some Dzemond species. But if it's good for you, who am I to say – right?"

"I suppose. Anyway, can I count on you to keep this chilled until I deal with it properly? Please?"

The sliding glass door opens and in sashays Ahzna, wearing her jog-bra and athletic shorts. "Oh, I see you two are talking. This is good." She comes to sit down. "So it's a beautiful day; will you two be going for a walk?"

"No," says Greg.

"Why not?"

"Because Arthur agreed to keep our little secret quiet. That and he's my friend."

Ahzna locks her eyes on mine.

"You would…"

"He asked nicely. You didn't."

Ahzna gives me a very demure smile. I don't trust her smile. Not a bit.

"Hey, let's head inside," says Greg. "Everyone else is there."

We do; it seems innocuous enough.

I follow Greg to the large peninsula counter separating the kitchen area from the living room. Karred, Kitten, Z, Edgar, and Vets are there, taking in some morning food.

Greg takes a seat and with a big smile on his face says, "Hey, Z. Got a question for you."

Znuul returns the smile. "I may have an answer for you."

"I've been knocking boots with Ahzna. That's not a problem, is it?"

The reaction across the whole island is immediate and if nothing else, cute. Everyone smiles and looks as if to say, "there it is!"

Karred proclaims, "I told you she's been mellower."

Kitten adds, "I knew it!"

Everyone seems okay with that statement, except Ahzna.

"Why would you say that, you imbecile?"

"Hey, now we don't have to sneak around. It's all out there."

"I would rather sneak around than admit I am so desperate for satisfaction that I take it with an inferior species – even if you are somewhat of an exception. Have you lost your mind? Your peers will chastise you for taking sex with the enemy. And now Ahtsag Znuul will judge me as unworthy for taking pleasure with a lesser species."

"Excuse me, Ahtsag and I did that before I became this," Karred says.

"Hey, me too," Kitten adds.

"Lesser species? What the hell?" says Greg.

Ahzna turns to him with spite in her eyes.

"You are a defective, lesser being. How could you be so stupid to share that? Your kind will spite you for being with me. My kind will look at me as desperate for being with you. I must have been. Your very presence right now offends me. What were you thinking? You could have continued to enjoy this, but no, your stupidity precludes that from ever happening again. You disgust me."

Greg looks at Ahzna with surprise in his eyes.

"I disgust you?"

"Yes. You will never touch me like that again. To think, I took your pathetic human seed."

Greg turns to Znuul, "She's still bound to speak only the truth, right?"

"Yes."

There's no genius required. I could see Greg's face turn to disgust of his own. The realization that Ahzna said everything with the conviction of truth passes over all of us. The room is silent.

Greg takes a second to compose himself. That's admirable. Then he looks around at all of us, passing over Ahzna with his gaze.

"Well, I'm sure The Protectorate is looking for me to do something, somewhere. And for damn sure I don't need to stay here." His gaze turns to Znuul. "No offense, but it's time for me to go. You can find someone else to do human therapy with that evil bitch."

His eyes turn to me.

"You named her right, man."

I guess I did.

"You should go," Ahzna spits at him. "Weak, little human, go away."

Greg turns to her, not very happy.

"Greg," says Znuul quietly. "She is bound to me; please don't kill her."

Greg turns to Znuul, "Yeah. But I need to get out of here."

Then Greg turns to Ahzna, "Lucky for you, evil bitch. I don't even have words other than… goodbye forever."

Ahzna just sneers at him.

Greg storms off.

"May I suggest you go apologize to him and beg him to stay?" Znuul says once Greg is out of earshot.

Ahzna stands and casts her eyes across all of us.

"He is beneath me."

She turns and stalks away.

"Pride," says Znuul. "One of my favorite sins. It always makes for such a humiliating fall."

Chapter 54

Greg bolted the day of Ahzna's rebuke. I barely got to say goodbye. It didn't take long for my itch to leave the bunker to take firm hold. I can't speak to why as much, but I have to get to Sil. I'm pretty sure it's the eyeful I got, messing with me.

Kitten and I are heading up the driveway, back to the bunker after a trip to town. The trip was for my makeover to ensure I'm not recognized as Arthur MacInerny. My hair is now dirty blond, and straight extensions put it in a proper mullet. I got some worn jeans and a bunch of T-shirts I normally wouldn't be caught dead in. To finish out the new me is a nice jean jacket from a second-hand store, complete with patches.

Coming in the mail, hopefully today, will be some off-the-shelf scars and moles that I can apply to my face. That should throw off any facial recognition thingees.

The fact is, I have to pay Silithes a visit. I'm not feeling productive at the bunker. It's a combination of that and the need to hash things out. I think. It just feels urgent. It can't wait.

The smart thing to do is sit on the sidelines and let Sil play. She's been upfront about everything. She said it would be strange. It is. She did tell me she would be affectionate with them. I saw a little more than affection, not that I didn't know what she meant.

It must be jealousy.

We get to the bunker, and Arix is the first to set eyes upon me. He tisk-tisks and shakes his head in disgust. I accept that – after all, I am a redneck, bred in North Carolina. I make a beeline for the office where Edgar and the group always are. When I step in, all eyes are on me.

"Hey guys! Where's Z? I need to talk to him about getting a car."

"Why do you need a car?" Karred asks. "Why do you have a mullet?"

"To go see Sil. I have things that need to be worked out."

"That's the first place they'll be looking for you," she says, getting up.

"She's right, you know," adds Edgar.

"Hey, this fine hairdo with the scars and moles that are coming should be enough to throw most of the facial recognition off track. But yes, you're right, and I'm still going. So I'll need a car. Where's Z?"

"On the back porch most likely," says Edgar.

Karred gets up and takes me by the arm to escort me.

"You aren't going there to break it up, are you?" she asks as soon as we clear the office.

"I don't know. I mean, I don't think so."

We round the corner into the living room area, and I see big Z sitting atop one of the picnic tables gazing out into the distance.

"That's good, Arthur, and there he is. Just be warned, he's been testy lately."

I make my way to the porch area and go through the sliding glass doors.

"Hey, Z," I call out to get his attention.

"That's quite the retro fashion statement you're making there, Mr. MacInerny. Why is that?"

"Well, I plan to head out to see Sil. You know I have the money, but buying a car might be an issue given my wanted status. Was hoping you could help me get one."

Znuul is taking in my right-out-of-the-trailer-park look with some amusement. I head it off at the pass.

"You can take the boy out of the trailer park, but you can't take the trailer park out of the boy, Mr. Ahtsag Znuul."

"Fair enough. You know going there is less than bright. We can't stop you or, should I say, won't. We'll get you your car, but please, don't get in an accident or anything that would trace registration back to us. It looks like I throw money around like water, but I do care. And I would hate to have to abandon any of my properties. I'd hate it even more if anything tracks back to me."

He concentrates for a moment, then looks back at me. "She's coming."

I hear the sliding glass door open and Kitten's voice.

"Yes, master?"

"Why don't you get dressed for town and go buy Arthur a car? He needs to travel."

"But I just got dressed, and we just got back. And it's late. We should do this tomorrow."

What she means is she just put her house uniform back on – a silken tie-down robe and nothing else, except sometimes slippers.

But it is late, and by the time she gets to town, the dealerships would be closed.

"Fair enough. I know you like shopping, Kitten," Znuul says with a smile.

"I like other things better."

"After you get back tomorrow with the car, I promise. I know it's been a while."

I have to chuckle. I know what he means.

"Why not right now?"

He doesn't say a word. Instead, he gives a weary look.

She points at Znuul. "Tomorrow then; you promised!"

Then she turns to me.

"So what kind of car do you want? Judging by the look, I'd say a Camaro or something."

She's so right. But it's not all about image.

"Dependable. Louisville's a long drive. Nothing too flashy."

"Easy-peasy, Arthur. I'll get you a good one. But you'll need to come or send someone who can drive. I can't drive two cars you know."

"I'll get Vets to go with you."

"Cool!" she says, and runs to hug Z. Then she's gone. That's how it goes, I guess, and that's not necessarily a bad thing.

Tomorrow I get my new ride. I wish it were now.

Chapter 55

Forgalon Provence, Helterezen Prime

Ehzig takes a steadying breath before entering the cavernous dining room. He knows his father and family are waiting for him there. He knows it's not going to be good. But, then again, things were never that good when father was involved.

Upon entering the room, he notes immediately that the main dining table has been moved to the side. That means one of two things: either they expect a fight or they expect him to submit in front of all the family.

He's been violated enough. He'd rather make a message of his defiance. He makes sure he shows no apprehension and steps into the room as if he has no care at all. He takes in the room, noting that Zarda, his father and clan leader, stands out in front of the litany of stepbrothers and stepsisters of his clan along with his stepmothers.

While the clan ranks have thinned since their fall from the emperor's graces, there is still more than enough Baalig muscle there to overwhelm Ehzig or any Baalig for that matter.

Ehzig doesn't like that. No, he doesn't like that at all. But he knew what he'd be walking into.

"You have some explaining to do, whelp!" shouts Zarda. "And you took your time getting here. So, how is it that one from this clan fails and is expelled from The College of War? You?"

Ehzig meets Zarda's eyes and refuses to acknowledge any intimidation – or respect.

"I came as quickly as I could. As to the how, it did take some doing – they set the bar rather low at the entry level."

The room ripples with gasps and then silence. To think that one of theirs would deliberately bring such shame upon themselves and the house was unthinkable. Even Zarda is without words, but only to a point.

"You deliberately failed yourself and brought even more shame upon house Arkrenduur?"

"That about covers it. Just a pity mother isn't here to enjoy it the way you are, Father."

"You're of the blood, boy. One of blood hasn't failed the College of War... ever. We dominate the College," Zarda says, stepping into Ehzig's personal space. "What do you have to say for yourself?"

Ehzig smiles, knowing his response will infuriate his father.

"I guess it was about time?"

Zarda reaches back to slap Ehzig and is surprised to find that Ehzig has easily stepped away. Zarda becomes enraged. Ehzig should have taken his punishment. The gasps and laughter from the rest of the clan add to Zarda's anger. He looks at Ehzig coldly.

"Well, whelp, are you ready to step up and take your place as leader of this clan? Do you think you can best me? Do you dare try? I will crush you and humiliate you again in front of all."

Ehzig looks around the room and then focuses on Zarda.

"Well, I guess it wouldn't hurt to try, given you've got the room stacked for a beat-down anyway. Besides if mother could best you so handily, I may stand a good chance, right? Just a question before we start, Father. Why is it you so enjoy raping your own from behind? I never really understood that. Though I had to endure it. Wouldn't it be more productive to take your daughters?"

"Some of his daughters take him," proclaims one of Ehzig's stepsisters, meeting with approval from his other stepsisters.

Zarda takes great glee at the affirmations afforded him. He turns his back to Ehzig and holds his arms out, eliciting cheers from the clan. He turns back to Ehzig.

"Come try to take this clan. Please. Give me more of an excuse to end you, than you already have."

Ehzig wasn't going to take that bait. Father wants him to attack first – mostly so he could claim self-defense. Partly, because he really wasn't that gifted a fighter.

"Not much of a clan to take anymore," Ehzig says, turning to the gathered family. "I blame lack of leadership."

Zarda responds with a cry and a bull rush.

Predictable.

At the last second, Ehzig jumps up and with a flex of the wings, floats over him, landing gracefully on the ground behind Zarda.

Zarda lashes out with his tail, but a single easy step back takes Ehzig out of its range. Zarda wheels around and carefully wades in toward Ehzig, who holds his hands up taking a defensive posture. Once in range, Zarda throws a huge overhand right hoping that sheer strength will overwhelm his somewhat smaller, much younger adversary. Ehzig doesn't back away from the blow, but steps in, meeting the blow with his right forearm, sweeping it to the side along with Zarda himself.

Then Ehzig punches Zarda in the back of the head at the neck. Stunned, Zarda falls, catching himself. He starts to pick himself up, but Ehzig's shin across the side of his head sends him tumbling.

"You couldn't beat my mother. Why do you think you can beat me, Father? I'm no whelp anymore. Oh… maybe you thought I'd fight like you?"

From his knees, hate filling his red eyes, Zarda looks to the room.

"Get him! He disgraces us all!"

Five of Ehzig's stepbrothers and three of his stepsisters mobilize immediately. These are odds no amount of natural ability can offset. Ehzig immediately goes into motion, taking to the air to avoid being circled on the ground. As soon as they take to the air after him, he drops – then drops the brother rushing into him with an elbow followed by a fist.

Spinning, blocking, feinting, Ehzig still finds himself taking more punishment than he's handing out because of the numbers game. Focusing on not being surrounded, he doesn't see the large metal dining chair that Zarda hurls at him. But he sure feels it.

He is stunned and off center from the blow, and his family descends on him. His stepbrothers' and sisters' fists beat him. They pummel him almost to the point of blacking out. Then he feels himself being raised up, strong Baalig hands on his arms, and a foot on his tail. His slumping head is raised up by the horns.

The slap across his face focuses his vision. Zarda stands in front of him.

"You have disgraced this clan and our blood. Failure. Insubordinate."

Zarda's fist didn't miss this time. It couldn't the way Ehzig was being held in place. Ehzig's eyes roll into his head, and he goes totally limp.

"Turn him around and take his pants off. We will take our satisfaction before removing him from this life." Zarda turns to the family that didn't jump into the fray immediately. "That applies to all of you as well. Come enjoy yourself at his expense. You – bring that ceremonial ax, the handle will serve nicely."

Ehzig's eyes roll back down, and he feels himself being repositioned and his pants being cut off. He knows that humiliation is coming.

"I'm not the disgrace," he spits out.

All attention shifts at the sound of the large explosion coming from the entrance to the clan's complex. That sound is followed by the noise of weapons fire and screams.

"To arms," Zarda shouts, but it's too little too late. There are only ceremonial arms in the dining hall. King's guard troops swarm through the door, fully armored and armed – a mix of Baalig and V'dvel troops. A V'dvel with command insignia steps forward.

"Karstil, what is the meaning of this? I am the emperor's prime of the guard."

"Not anymore, Zarda," Karstil replies, shooting Zarda repetitively with the Dzemond equivalent of a stun-gun. Karstil looks about the room.

"Contain those three females. Shackle Zarda, that male, and the bloody one on the floor. No other survivors. This house dies tonight."

The room reverberates with the sounds of panic and weapons fire.

Chapter 56

Kitten sent me photos of two potential candidates. First is a 1994 fire-engine-red Ford Mustang with about 78,000 miles on it. The other is a 2003 Camaro with about 180,000 miles. I know she's going with my new mullet look, but I feel I have to point her in the direction of something more dependable.

But there is something about a Mustang, even a 1994. I might even be able to work on it – a little. Who am I kidding? Not a chance.

"Keep looking?" she texts back.

After a little consideration, I type back "get the Mustang."

No sense quibbling – for its age, it has low miles. That and – Mustang. It does work with the persona I'm putting out, and honestly, I might kind of feel younger for maybe having it.

I take in the fact that I just bought this car and then jump out of my skin as an "ARRRGH," followed by a series of crashes comes from the garage. I turn toward the garage, and the door opens, Znuul ducking through it – obviously not happy. He stalks out through the cavernous living area, notes me, and stops.

"Swiss bankers are without vision or comprehension of what faces them. I cannot cure stupid."

That being said, he stalks on to the hallway leading to his bedroom.

I get up, knowing that Karred was in the garage with him. Once I open the door, I see a broken plastic banquet table, computers, and papers strewn about. Karred is trying to straighten up. She looks at me with a weak smile.

"Can I help?" I ask.

She looks up at me, trying to hold onto that weak smile while picking up papers.

"I don't know, but if you can, I'd sure appreciate it," she says back, brushing a lock of her red hair from her face.

I get to the picking up of stuff. The thick vinyl table was snapped in two, metal supports bent. It reminds me that Znuul is capable of the sudden and violent – the kind that one doesn't return from.

We continue picking up things until it seems there are no other things to pick up.

She flops down in a chair and looks at me like this has been a huge ordeal.

"What happened while you two were gone? Something happened. He hasn't been the same. He's been trying to act like nothing's changed. But something did. Can you tell me, Arthur?"

I'm sure the look in my eyes totally conveys that she's right. I don't try to hide it. Instead, I go with the truth.

"He hasn't told you anything?"

"No."

"I hope you understand, it's not my place to discuss his business. I can confirm some strange stuff happened. But the details are in his head. And I have no right speaking for what's going on in someone else's head. I hope you understand."

"Of course… But what can you share?"

"Not a lot. His armor did something to him. What, I can't say in detail. He turned it around, or so I thought. You really need to speak to him about it. I can only speculate. Speculation does nobody any good."

"Well, that's something, Arthur. God, he's keeping secrets from me now."

What do you say to that? Obviously, there's tension brewing.

"Tell him we spoke, Karred. Ask him for the details. I wasn't asked to hold a secret or zip my lips."

She nods an affirmative at me, but I can sense her heart is somewhere else.

"What's up, Karred? Sure there's this, whatever this is. But something else is weighing on you. You care to share?"

I can tell she really doesn't want to say by the wounded little smile. But to my surprise, she says, "Yes, well, not really. But if I don't, it's going to eat me alive."

I try to give a reassuring smile.

"I'll hold this conversation in the strictest of confidence. So, what's eating you alive?"

"Ahzna."

"She's not worth your worry, Karred. Don't give her that power."

"If it was that easy, Arthur. There's a biological draw, you know. Have you heard of it?"

"I think they call it the imperative or something like that. Yeah."

"It's real. It's subtle at first; then it just kind of builds. It's an annoyance, but you know how much of a creature of satisfaction Ahtsag is? She is constantly throwing herself at him."

"Hey, give Z some credit. He has an iron will when he chooses to use it."

She points at me with an ear-to-ear smile.

"You are so right. But that works the other way also. If he decides he wants a taste, he will."

Karred stands up and starts to pick up the mess that was once on Z's desk area. A nervous response I'm sure – a bit of avoidance. I understand. So I get to moving the broken desk.

"You know what her plan is, Arthur? To get him in the sack and get pregnant. She wants to be the queen of this house. I'll stand confidently against any other magic practitioner or soldier. I've waded into war. I'm just not so confident I can stand against her… in the bedroom. Oh God. I said it."

"Sometimes you have to name the devil before you can exorcise it."

"If only it were that easy, Arthur. She just exudes a sexual aura. I know she has to be well- practiced and confident. Me? I'm just a skinny witch. I mean, I still think of myself that way. God, Arthur, sometimes I look at her and think…"

I don't say a word.

"It's the damn imperative thing. She knows it, too. The other morning, she stopped me in the hallway, pushed me up against the wall, and propositioned me – me? She's working all the angles."

"She did what?"

"She told me, 'It's easier once you give in to it.' Then she tried to kiss me. Well, she did for a brief moment until I broke it off. She touched me inappropriately."

"Please tell me you kicked her ass."

"That wasn't what I was thinking at the time. Arthur…"

"You wanted that?"

"I know it's just that biological thing. I did say no. I did warn her not to do that again, ever. You know what she did? She smiled at me. No, not just smiled at me – she let me know what she knows with that smile. She told me my mouth tasted good. That bitch."

"Evil bitch."

"Yes, you named her quite well. But, if I feel it, imagine the pull on Ahtsag. He's male; she's female. It's just a matter of time. And… she's better than me that way. I'm…"

I've heard enough.

"You're the love of his life. She's at best a piece of ass. Don't forget that. You're selling yourself short, Karen, err Karred. Listen, my girlfriend is a succubus. You want to talk weirdness? I'm nothing more than a human. She's bedding down with others of her kind. How do I compete with that? You're at least in the same genepool. Listen, I know he cares for you. You know he does, too. You know he's not exactly normal. I mean, you know, the demon thing."

"Thank you, Arthur. I can be insecure, believe it or not. It's just … he has been different since coming back. I know you're right. I should ask him what's going on. I just… would you talk to him first? Please? I don't want him thinking he has to coddle me."

I am a sucker for a woman in distress. I should be hard and tell her she needs to work through it on her own. But, no – that's not happening. Arthur comes to the rescue.

"Sure thing, Karred, but if he confides in me, then it stays confidential."

"Of course. And thank you." The smile lets me know it's genuine. "Help me with cleaning the rest of this up?"

∴

Having at least picked things up from the floor, I leave the garage in search of Big Z. First stop is the office Edgar and Percy have taken over. No sign of Z. I make with cordialities and move on.

He's not in the cavernous living area, and I don't see him outside. That leaves either Kitten's room or the master bedroom. As Kitten is getting my new car, I have to assume the master suite. I walk past the kitchen, down the hall to the huge red doors that lead to his room, and knock.

"Come," booms Znuul's voice.

So I do. There he sits on the floor, in front of the huge, custom bed, sitting cross-legged.

"Had to check on you, big man. Sounds like you've got some stress."

"Yes, the bank does not understand the stakes. They're under the impression, because they work with both sides now, that when Helterezen invades, they will be respected the same way. Truth is when homeworld invades, there will be no respect and no neutrality. I'm going to have to pay them a visit. It's an unnecessary waste of time and money."

"Well, you and Karred get to see Switzerland. And you get a break from the evil bitch."

He shares a sneaky smile.

"Ahzna has been consistent in expressing her desire. It is getting old. Maybe I should look at the trip as a good thing. But, we both know the clock is ticking on this world."

"Yeah, maybe it is. But, are you all right? You seem a little more testy than usual. I know that some strangeness happened with your armor and…"

"The armor is no longer an issue."

"Fair enough. So, you're okay?"

"I am all right."

"Nothing you want to talk about? Syria? Switzerland? Amsterdam?"

"I'm good, thank you."

If there's one thing I know, it's that you don't push Z. If he wants to talk, he will. He doesn't lie, but he will dodge. Saying "I am all right" is a non-answer. I recognize that. He probably knows I do, too. There's no reason to push further.

"Well, had to check on you."

"Thank you."

I turn myself around and walk out the way I came. Once the door is closed I pause for a moment. I can tell things are weighing on him. But, if he's not sharing, then there's nothing I can do. I take a deep breath and head back to the living area.

Before I can get there, Ahzna steps out from the kitchen. She's holding no pretense of being human, her purple skin, wings, horns, and tail showing proudly.

"EB," I say chipperly, meaning to pass around her.

But that's not happening. Her hand grabs me by the jaw, and I'm pushed up against the wall. I feel my feet leaving the ground. She's smiling an evil smile.

Crapsticks.

Chapter 57

Zebulon Prime, Helterezen Prime

Ehzig's vision comes slowly into focus. It wasn't as much the beating that his family put on him, but the repeated application of the pain sticks by the troops afterward that caused him to pass out. He realizes he's in prisoner restraints aboard a military transport. He looks to his side and sees Zarda in restraints next to him. It appears Hefiz, Zarda's son by Wearta, is confined on the other side of him.

"Oh, the Baalig of the hour comes awake," says Karstil, looking rather complacent and bored across from him.

"The emperor will have you pay for this insubordination, Karstil," shouts Zarda.

Karstil moves in, looking at Ehzig, not Zarda.

"He's really not that bright, is he? Hard to believe you guys are from the same genetic pool, except that you do look alike."

"You will pay, V'dvel! I will rip your head off!" screams Hefiz.

Karstil reaches over and leisurely pulls out a pain stick. He gets up and walks over to Hefiz and jabs it into his neck, causing Hefiz to gurgle and violently twitch in his restraints.

That makes Ehzig laugh, much to Zarda's chagrin.

Karstil turns to Ehzig.

"You seem reasonable. Listen, I have a question for you."

"Ask."

"Why is it your kind are so into family rape? Us V'dvel, if we have an issue with another, we just shove a knife up the back of their skull or set them up to be killed by another. I mean, I get rough sex, but it's best when consensual."

Ehzig smiles at Karstil.

"No idea. I think it's just a dominance thing. Never really got into it myself, as I never cared for it being done to me. I like your knife approach; that makes sense. Why don't you let me loose, and I can try it on my father, there?"

"It's the only way you could kill me, whelp."

Karstil laughs.

"No, all of you need to appear before the emperor. You don't think for a moment, I would do anything less than my duty, do you? Zarda… you've seen what happens to those that disappoint the emperor. I would not care for that fate."

That gets a silent response. Fear of the emperor is universal.

After a long while of silence, the transport comes to a stop. Karstil stands and looks to the troops around him.

"Hood them, and transport them to the audience chamber."

∴

They pull the hood from Ehzig's head, and he finds himself in a large chamber, next to his father and stepbrother, all still restrained and attached to the trolleys that brought them in.

He says nothing. This isn't the place to be spouting off. He knows that much.

Karstil walks in front of the three of them, saying nothing. He doesn't have to. They are in the emperor's receiving chamber.

The curtain at the rear rustles and two succubi appear. They hold back the curtain, and a cloaked figure walks in.

Ehzig's hearts pound. He is in the presence of the emperor himself.

"Well, if I am not presented with the last remnants of house Arkrenduur," he says pleasantly. "I am sure you have many questions. Please, my first, take off their restraints."

Karstil looks at the emperor with a question in his eye.

"Oh please, Karstil. Do you think I fear a few Baalig?"

"Your Eminence…"

After only a returned look from the emperor, Karstil and his lieutenants begin releasing them.

"Leave us, please."

Karstil again checks the emperor with his eyes and tells his team, "Let's go."

The emperor pulls back the hood of his cloak, revealing a serpentine-like face, with mismatching eyes, the unmistakable sign of his very mixed blood. He is smiling widely as if he is setting eyes upon long-lost friends.

Ehzig doesn't feel the good intentions.

"My Lord, why this persecution?" Zarda asks. "I am not questioning you, but I am seeking understanding."

"You understand the level of betrayal your progenitor has shown me? The fact you would forsake his name pleases me. But, a price must be paid in blood. Surely you understand. His disgrace is… so disgraceful."

"Of course, but we always served you without question."

"Really? What is this about that one failing the College of War, in the first cycle no less."

Ehzig's sphincter clinches.

"He is yours to do with as you wish," replies Zarda. "He disgraces us all."

"You are all to do with as I wish," the emperor says, fixing his eyes on Zarda. "All are to do with as I wish. Is it not?"

Zarda takes to a knee and says, "Yes, my Lord."

The emperor's eyes scan Ehzig and his stepbrother. Ehzig immediately takes to a knee.

"So, young Arkrenduur. Explain how you fail so spectacularly from something that has come so naturally to your blood?"

Ehzig pauses, not looking up at the emperor, but feeling the weight of his gaze. To lie to him would result in an epically painful death, so instead, he goes full-bore with the truth, turning his eyes to meet his inquisitor.

"Hard work, your eminence. Very hard work. The College's standards in the first cycle are less about achievement and more about attendance."

"Oh," the emperor says, giggling at Ehzig who is looking back down at the floor. "Well, I'm surprised you weren't killed. So, you disgrace your already-disgraced lineage – why?"

"Maybe I don't want to be some Baalig stereotype. Maybe I want to be something else."

"Ah," the emperor says, cackling in giddiness.

"Who could imagine such foolishness?" spits out his stepbrother.

The emperor ignores that comment and collects himself for a moment.

"Well, what it is that you are so much better fated for, Ehzig Arkrenduur?"

"I don't know."

The laughter and light clapping of the emperor is contrasted by Zarda's groan.

"This is so delicious. So you know, you remind me of one I knew long, long ago, young Ehzig. Only he knew what he wanted. But you both share a wonderful rebellious streak. You scream 'why can't I?' at the world and fight back when it says 'because I said so.' Now, all of you, please stand."

They do as commanded.

"Zarda, you have been first for some time in my personal guard, as was your father before you, and so on. Surely you know where all this is going and why?"

"Problems with the blood of this clan, my emperor. You are going to kill us all to remove the defect."

Zarda's answer rings true with Ehzig and fear sets in.

"Mostly true, Zarda. But not all need to die. From the ashes of this shame can arise a new clan taking the best and leaving behind the worst."

"Take him, my lord, and we will serve you with renewed commitment," Zarda says proudly.

Ehzig's heart drops as he sees what appears to be black steam beginning to roil about the emperor. He's heard the stories of what happens when he lets the demon inside of him to the outside of him.

"Thank you, Zarda. I think I shall enjoy this," the emperor replies. The cloud of blackness turns to Ehzig.

Ehzig's heart pounds, but he refuses to show that fear. He'll take his fate standing defiantly as he can, having already been beaten down by family and the guard.

The emperor cloud moves suddenly – alarmingly so, but not to Ehzig. The cloud engulfs his half-brother. There is a brief shout of pain, followed by sounds of wheezing and crunching. Ehzig sees Zarda in shock and watches as he steps away from the spectacle of death unfolding next to him.

The black smoke recedes to more of a mist surrounding the emperor. Hefiz lies in a broken dried-out pile at the ground. He sees the pleasure on the emperor's face and Zarda's fear.

"It's not the blood that's wrong with this house, Zarda," the emperor says with a bemused tone. "It's the spirit. I don't need sycophants, I need the ruthless."

The mist suddenly turns to the full-on cloud, and Ehzig sees Zarda engulfed. Screams follow. Ehzig's vision turns to darkness as the emperor's dark aura engulfs him. He feels a gentle hand on his cheek. The smoke returns to a mist and absorbs back into the emperor.

The gentle hand on his cheek lightly slaps him. Ehzig looks to Zarda who is still alive, but not well; his feet and hands are broken and bent in ways they were never meant to be.

"You are alive and well, boy," the emperor says with a smile. "You have work to do. I need you to kill Ahtsag Znuul." The emperor turns his back on the two of them and begins to walk toward his throne. "What, no questions?"

"It is not our place to question your will," says Zarda, pulling himself up painfully to his knees.

"I meant the boy, idiot."

"No, sir," Ehzig sputters.

"Not even why I only maimed your father, rather than devour him, like your dear half-brother?"

"Umm… I guess."

The emperor reaches behind his throne and pulls out a long, black sword.

"Why? So you might. Think of it as practice for when you kill Ahtsag Znuul. You know, there's nothing like the old weapons …"

He twirls the large sword off-handedly.

"Sire. My emperor. I have served you unwaveringly. I…"

"Would you prefer I devour you slowly, Zarda? I thought I was doing you a favor. One cleaving blow versus… me slowly relishing the meal of your life and pain?"

Zarda looks at Ehzig with pure hatred.

"Do something right and strike cleanly and quick. That much I know you can do."

Zarda turns back to the emperor.

"This is insane. We are assets. This clan… I have served you like no other. I…"

"Silence! Full of himself, isn't he?"

The emperor hands Ehzig the sword by the hilt. Ehzig takes it, noting its solidness and excellent balance. He looks at Zarda, broken and kneeling on the floor because his feet won't support his weight.

"Well, Ehzig? We do despise our parents, don't we?" the emperor says. "Come now, don't tell me you also bear hidden feelings just waiting to come out."

The emperor's goading smile tells Ehzig all he needs to know.

"I hate this loaf of excrement, sir."

Ehzig raises the sword and smiles when Zarda closes his eyes.

"Coward," Ehzig says.

The sword comes down, and half buries into Zarda's neck. Zarda's eyes open wide, and he tries to gurgle a word out through his flowing blue blood.

"Sorry, Father, bad swing. Let me try again."

Ehzig takes a step, raises the sword over his other shoulder and drops a backhanded blow that partially cleaves the other side of Zarda's neck. With a twist, he pulls the sword loose and looks into his father's dying eyes.

"I guess I didn't do it right, after all. Shows what you know. Oh, and in case you think I'm weak or incompetent..."

Ehzig raises the sword rapidly and brings it down suddenly, splitting Zarda's head between the horns and continuing down into his chest cavity. He kicks Zarda's torso, to release the sword.

"Rape me now."

"Such malice, young Ehzig. That was a tremendous performance. I truly hope you accomplish your mission and return to us. I sense greatness in you. Now, if you would, please return my property to me.

Ehzig turns back to the emperor and hands him the sword formally by the hilt as it was presented to him. The emperor takes the sword and, with his other hand, traces a finger along the blade to gather a taste of Zarda's blood, then sets the sword down against the throne.

"We're almost done, Ehzig Arkrenduur. Just one final question. Why do you think I'm sending you on this mission?"

"To die at his hands. I mean, you want him to finish off his own bloodline. And if for some reason I am successful, your will is done. You cannot lose. But I have a question, can't he just start up a whole other line?"

The emperor claps giddily at Ehzig's response.

"Oh, yes. You are a bright one, aren't you? In theory, yes, he can. But the truth is, I'll just kill them, too. Delicious isn't it?"

Chapter 58

The last thing I need to do is panic, thrash around, and break my own neck. That is probably what she would like to have happen. While this situation is, at best, uncomfortable and certainly demeaning, Ahzna's not cutting off the blood flow to my brain or my air supply.

She's been willed to do no harm. I guess this display doesn't count as harm in her eyes.

"Put me down, you evil bitch."

"Eventually. For now, I think it's best you understand how easy it will be when the time comes. And that time is coming, pathetic human Arthur. You see, it's just a matter of time before Ahtsag Znuul gives in to the urge. When that happens, I will satisfy him in the ways only the purest of blood can. His satisfaction will meet the egg I release, resulting in a child and my place forever at the head of this clan. He will free me and watch as I follow through on my word to you. All who taste of Ahzna, give all to Ahzna for more."

"Unless you're Greg Inosanto."

When I feel her grip tighten, I realize that was maybe not the wisest time to spout off a one-liner.

"He'll be back. They always come back. And you will watch all you hold dear perish."

She drops me without warning, then pushes me back against the wall.

"I am bound to speak only the truth. These things will come to pass. You will beg for your death to protect those you hold dear. Just wait. You'll see."

She gives me a evil smile and turns to walk away.

The shock clears quickly and pissed-off sets in. Truth? She's about to get an earful of it.

"No. We're not done," I say quietly. "You march your purple-skinned, demon-looking ass back over here and take a listen to the real truth, you evil bitch."

She pauses for a moment as if considering whether to come back.

"Don't make me chase you down."

She turns with a bemused expression, then casually walks back over, right into my personal space.

"You overestimate yourself, EB," I say, moving in even closer. "I know you think you're all that. But truth… real truth? You're just another purebred plaything for Znuul. How many do you think he's had? Judging from the stories, how many do you think he's devoured? What makes you so special? The truth is, absolutely nothing. You're the same thing he's had before and before and before that. You know what you are, right? Basically life support for that cooter of yours."

"Cooter?"

"Your woman parts. The only reason you exist is because he started some pure line thing ages ago so he'd have something to take his jollies with and make babies."

"You make my point."

"No. You see there's more at play here than just a good time. You may be a purebred piece of ass, but I was his brother. Brother in revenge, that is. And you know, we're still close. You think he's just going to stand to the side and let you bring harm to me and mine? I mean something to him as a friend. And don't even get me started on the depth of Karred's relationship with him. You? You're just a womb hoping to be used. All that super-warrior, super-lover shit you think you are? Think again."

She's furious. I stoke the flames by pushing my chest up against hers.

"So, miss can-only-tell-the-truth. Plainly deny any of what I've said."

I'll give her credit for trying to form the words. But none come out. I give her a shove back out of my personal space to throw a little gasoline on the flames I've stoked.

"Let me tell you how it's going to go down. First, because I'm his friend, I'm going to tell him to will you to keep those damn eggs in the ovary. There will be no getting pregnant. Once that command goes down, your plan is up in smoke. Tell me I'm wrong. Come on with the truth; set me straight."

She emits a low growl. Normally that might be a bit intimidating, but I'm not feeling it.

"Arthur MacInerny, I am going to…"

"You're not going to do squat. Let me tell you what's really going to happen. When the time comes for you to be released, I will be there. He will command you to kneel with your head down and that tail of yours between your legs. Then at the moment he unbinds you, I will take your head with my holy sword. Game over. Checkmate. You're not going to hurt anyone."

My eyes are boring into hers, daring a response. She looks away, then back with a different intensity. Fear, I sense it.

"Tell me how I'm wrong, EB. Please, tell me how I'm wrong."

Again, she tries to form the words.

"I can't."

"Didn't think so. Now get to stepping. I've seen enough of you for a lifetime. What? You can't harm me. Don't think for a second I'm fearful of you."

I step in and slap her hard on the face. I immediately regret it. I don't hit ladies. But, then again, she ain't no lady.

The look I get from her is less rage and more realization of her circumstances. I can abuse her, she can't return the favor without permission.

"I've been hit much harder."

"Good news then. For the record, I don't plan to strike you like that again. Next time it will be with a sword, and you'll be on your knees knowing that it's coming. You got anything else for me?"

"No."

I turn away from her and make my way back toward Znuul's chambers. Right before I knock on the door, I hear Ahzna scream in what sounds like frustration. The big red door opens.

"I heard everything," Znuul says. "Well played. I just shut down her ovaries as you suggested. Come in. I seem to feel more like talking now."

Chapter 59

Interdimensional Nexus Port, Helterezen Prime

Ehzig looks out and sees that they are planning the transport at three carriers deep. The three carriers at a configuration of sixteen by ten cubicles can carry a total four-hundred-eighty occupants, unless the unit is used for supplies. Forces are aligned against the walls – a combination of lesser races and various Dzemond races. Basically cannon fodder and their leaders.

He takes a moment to consider his hideous armor. It was assigned to him specifically by the emperor, or so he was told. It's an extremely light nanite armor that is bleach white. The worst part is it only extends to his thighs and across his biceps. The contrast with his dark purple skin makes him stand out like a sore thumb.

That's the idea, he knows.

Ehzig looks at his assignment number that corresponds to his place in the honeycomb of the carriers. Obviously, he's in the second section. He looks for his place in the staging and finds it among the Vetisghar and Hjuulak. There's no sense arguing the point. He walks toward his staging area, trying to ignore the sniggering of the Dzemond around him.

He gets to his area, and at least the Vetisghar and Hjuulak make room for him. He is, after all, their superior. He leans against the wall to take some rest, but that is soon brought to an end by the booming voice across the room: "Ehzig Arkrenduur. Report to Garrison commander Garaung immediately at the command area."

"Great," Ehzig says to himself. He begins trudging to the command area in anticipation of his next degradation.

Once at the command area, he checks in with an insect-like Shaggorat administrator.

"Third office on the left," it says.

Ehzig goes to the office and knocks on the door.

"Come," says a deep, gravelly voice.

Ehzig enters and sets eyes upon the grizzled visage of Garrison Master Garaung and his entourage. Garaung takes a look at Ehzig and gestures to the others in the room to leave. They take their queue and go.

"Nice armor, Arkrenduur," he says to Ehzig. "Could be worse; he could have put a bullseye on your chest. Come over here so I might look into your eyes."

Ehzig does as he's told by his commander and steps over to him.

"Baalig, you know you're expected to die at his hands, right?"

The bluntness of the remark takes Ehzig back.

"I, uh, suppose."

"There's no suppose, whelp. The emperor has sent you to die. Look at your armor, fool. I've seen too many wear that armor of shame. It's a waste. I understand sending lesser races to die, but true Dzemond? Upper Dzemond? Wasteful and I do not agree. But I'm not one to stand against the desires of the emperor."

Ehzig's mind spins. He tries to hold his composure. Garrison master Garaung is a legend in his own right. The fact that, at his age, he's still being given a command and that none have killed him speaks volumes.

"No sir, to defy the emperor is to court death," Ehzig says. "Sir, a question?"

"What?"

"Your reputation is that of one not to be crossed. You've left so many dead in your wake. How is it you disagree with the sacrifice of a nobody like me?"

"First, most of those I've ended were for personal reasons: they challenged me, angered me, or just otherwise assumed they could dominate me. Second, I hold to a high professional code of conduct. I can look past a great deal when it means meeting our objectives until it becomes personal. Are you challenging me personally, Arkrenduur?"

"No sir, just curious."

"You failed in the first season of the College of War. That takes some work. Why would you do that?"

Ehzig smiles at his perceptiveness.

"I guess I'm just rebellious. Mother and father ..."

"Yes, we do hate our parents. That being said, my progeny has control of command off-world. You would do well not to rebel against him. Do you understand?"

"Yes, sir."

"Good. You may live through my progeny's command. It is doubtful you will live through any encounter with Ahtsag Znuul. You are purposed to kill him, correct?"

"Yes, sir. I am to either kill him or die at his hands."

Garaung pulls a device from his hip, grabs Ehzig's hand, and puts it there.

"When he takes you, boy, put that under his chin and engage it. Not against his armor, but on his flesh. It should take the damn thing's head off. He's not Baalig – he's a damned thing of the black pool, like the emperor. Of course, you will be blinded, deaf, and you'll lose your hand, but you will have stopped him.

"When he takes me?"

"He always toys with his prey. He'll look you in your eyes and dare you to stop him. He'll taunt you, make you feel despair. I've never seen anyone stop him. I think he enjoys the pain of those he devours. He says it adds spice. That arrogance is when you'll know to use the device. He won't expect it, and you'll destroy him, probably yourself, too, but you were dead anyway. That is, unless you're so paralyzed you can't.

Ehzig looks at the device and then at Garaung.

"You made this for yourself."

"I did," says Garaung. When you work with that one, you come to realize you are only as valuable as he sees you. If he came for me, I would be ready."

"So he never did?"

"No, but I was ready then, and now it is ready for you. My progeny has one also. Good luck. Now get back in line. It's time for you to go off-world. I got you a space in the second row. Damn engineers are always too aggressive on first entry. The last row almost always gets cut off – a terrible waste. That's why I always make sure that Vetisghar, Hjuulak, Hjuul, and the spiders are in them. Never supplies or true Dzemond."

"Thank you, Garrison Commander."

"Don't thank me, grunt. There are still battle-proven lessers in the first row."

Ehzig nods in accord, saying nothing. There is nothing to say. He moves to take his place in the line. He looks at the rows of cubes, wondering which will be his. He smiles at the realization that it doesn't matter – as long as he's not in the third row.

Chapter 60

The drive to Louisville, Kentucky, was long. We made our way to Znuul's bunker outside the city in Oldham County, making sure to deactivate the alarm at the mailbox. Once at the bunker, we unload, and I read the paper Znuul gave in phonetics while placing my hand on the doorjamb.

I see the runes light up and feel secure that no scrying eyes will fall upon us.

Everyone piles in. Everyone, but Arix. He chose to stay back.

"Grab a room," I shout out. "Sheyliene, you're with me now. We need spy work."

That's an understatement. I'm sure The Protectorate is looking for me. So, it's imperative I find them first. Sheyliene and Pffif are the best at that kind of work. I'm going with Sheyliene because she can cover the greatest amount of area. Mr. Pffiferil shares his disapproval.

"Yer bein'a damn impulsive fool, ye know that right? I mean, ye got one big bug up yer butt about this."

He's right – that I have a big ol' bug up my butt and maybe more. I am acting impulsively. But, no, he's not right about me being a fool.

"I'll try to be careful, Mr. Pffiferil."

"Don't ye 'Mr. Pffiferil' me. What're ya in such a damn hurry for? To get an eyeful first hand? She's a succubus. She's livin' with others of her kind. Ye think they spend their time playin' cards and baking cakes? They do what they do."

"I …"

"And they like it. They like it a lot."

"It's just something I have to do. Heck, I'm not even sure why I'm so hell-bent on this. But I am. I have to go to her. I have to figure it out. It's important."

"I've figured it out. Ye gots a fire down below. The fairy'll give you her hand. Ain't much risk there."

"It's not that. I can't explain."

"If ye can't explain it to yerself, it might not be worth riskin' all our freedoms."

He makes a point. He does that a lot when he's not so drunk you can't understand him.

"You make sense. I hear you. I'm not making sense, and I know it. I'm going with my gut. Sorry. I'll just have to be smarter than the people looking for me."

"Bah!"

We stare at each other, him trying to bend my resolve and me trying to let him know I can't make him happy about it – I'm going to do what I do.

"Well, let me come along then. I can be sneaky. I make a right good spy, so I been told."

"The best."

"Bah. Now yer suckin' up to me," he says, a smile coming across his face. "Let me know when it's time."

"It's time. No rest for the wicked."

∴

The first area to case is outside Paul's place of business – "Hot Stone. Warm Sensual Yoga." It seems like a good cover business for an incubus. It also seems like a good place to stake out looking for me. Sil has taken to doing what she called "secretarial" work for Paul at his business. It's logical I'd stop by.

I cruise the block a few times looking at the nearby buildings and anything that may jump out – nothing. That only means I do not see it. I park us a block away and look at Sheyliene.

"You're up. Get tiny and get flying."

"Okay," she says, reaching up to her hair and in a cascade of silvery dust goes tiny and to wing.

I roll down the window, and out she goes.

"Well, close yer eyes and I'll get goin', too," Mr. Pffiferil says. "Between us both, if there's someone a spyin', we'll find 'em."

I close my eyes and count to five. I open my eyes, and he's invisible. I open the passenger door and sit back. I know he's now on the prowl for our spies.

I just lean back and roll down my window. Maybe I'll get some rest.

∴

"I found them," comes Sheyliene's voice in my sleepy ear.

My eyes pop open, and I sit up.

"Where?"

"Hiding in a van called "Zippo Plumbing." There's two guys in the back.

"And they're using a camera through a hole in the decal on the side," comes Mr. Pffiferil's voice. For the record, I found 'em first."

"We both found them, and now Arthur knows," Sheyliene says.

"So there's a van, with Zippo Plumbing on the side with a couple of guys in it taking video. Good catch. Now – what to do?"

"We could take them down," says Sheyliene with all seriousness.

"Just makin' problems there, fairy," says Pffiferil.

"Yeah. I think I have an idea. You two wait here."

I get out of the car and walk down the street away from Paul's business. Finally, I get to a diner-like place. I step in and ask if they have a payphone. I get a look like I'm from another place and time. I guess I am.

"Payphone? Are you kidding? What kind of call do you need to make?" the hostess asks.

"911, there are some perverts down the street taking pictures of ladies without their permission."

"Here, use our phone."

I dial 911 and put on my best hills of the Carolinas accent.

"There's some guys in a van with Zippo Plumbing on it on Bardstown Road near Tyler taking nasty pictures of girls walking down the street and of the women going in and out of a yoga place. It just ain't right. I think they're takin' pictures of the young'uns, too. You need to do something about that."

I hang up.

With my plan in play, I thank the hostess and leave. I walk down to the car and look in on a now full-size and human-looking Sheyliene and Mr. Pffiferil.

"Come on; we should watch Louisville's finest in action."

They pile out, and we take a short stroll down the street. Once in position, we stop and take a view of the van. We wait, but not for long. Two police cruisers stop in front and back of the van. They get out and pound on the van's doors. Not much later, two men are escorted from the van in handcuffs.

That's one down.

I take us back to the car, and we drive to Paul's place. It's an older-looking condominium complex named Cedar Grove. I find it hard to believe that some studly, well-to-do, more than likely richer-than-rich incubus lives here. But he does.

"Guys, I need you to check the neighbors and neighborhood. They may have bought a unit to spy on them. Be careful and thorough."

Sheyliene tinies up and I close my eyes so Pffiferil can go invisible. Like that – they're gone again, and I try to rest.

"Ain't nuthin' I see," comes Pffif's voice as the passenger-side door opens. "Fairy be checkin' places I can't as well. She'll be comin' soon. If'n there's something, she'll find it."

Smiling, I tell him, "I believe you."

We wait a few minutes, and Sheyliene comes flying in, lands in my lap and says, "Looks clear."

"So you two are sure?"

"Yes," they say in unison.

"All right then, let's head back to the bunker. I'll be dropping in on Sil alone."

"But I want to see Silly, too," Sheyliene says.

"Soon enough, but not now."

I put the key in the ignition and start back toward the bunker.

Chapter 61

I park the car in a street space about half a block from Paul's place. Putting my baseball cap and fake horned-rim glasses on, I make my way to Paul's place. I may be too early at six-pm-ish, but I am not too worried. There's one of those half-sized smart cars in the place set for Paul's unit, so I know someone must be there.

An incubus with possibly one of the most unsexy vehicles ever? No compensation there.

I approach and knock on the door.

It opens, and there is Jxsiga. Her face contorts, and her head cocks to the side. I smile.

"Is Silithes home?"

She straightens up, smiles, and says, "As a matter of fact, she is. Please, come in. But one question: What's up with your hair?"

"Camouflage."

"I see. You're just in time for egg rolls."

She turns around to go back in, and I follow.

"Company," she calls out.

There's a short hallway and kitchen to the side. The hall connects to a larger open area for a dining room and living room. Paul is in the kitchen cutting egg rolls in half. We exchange glances. Not sure of what to say, so I just nod to him distantly.

When we round the corner, I see Silithes, and she sees me.

"Arthur? What are you doing here? I mean, they're looking for you."

She stands up and walks around the table to give me a hug. The hug is cordial at best.

I figure she must be feeding off the air I'm giving. Honestly, I'm not even sure why I'm here, other than the feeling it's very important.

"Yeah, they are looking for me," I say to break the ice.

"If I knew you were coming, I'd have made more," Paul says, bringing a lazy Susan with halved egg rolls and dipping sauces. "It's just a prebowling snack."

"Bowling night," Jxsiga says with rolling eyes, like that explains everything.

Sil grabs an egg roll. Smart move, don't have to talk as much.

There we are at the dining room table. Uncomfortable silence surrounds us.

"This about that video thing," Paul says, his eyes no longer cordial.

"Probably," I say, matching his glare. "Truth is, I'm not sure I'm being very rational about any of this."

I look over at Sil.

"Not smart for me to be here, right?"

"Glad you are," she says back quietly. "Arthur and I will get some dinner since he didn't snack with us." Sil looks back at me with a halfish smile. "We can talk in private about what we need to."

"You're not going to dump her, are you?" Jxsiga asks.

Loud thumping on the door interrupts my potentially poor explanation of why I'm even here. We all look at each other. The doorbell rings three times in rapid succession.

I think it's The Protectorate. By the looks around the table, I may not be alone.

Two more rings of the doorbell.

"I'll get it," Paul says.

He gets up and walks down the hall to the front door. I reach back to check the Smith and Wesson I have tucked away.

"Who are you," a male voice asks.

"I'm Paul. This is my home."

Both Sil and I relax – it's not The Protectorate coming for me.

"Where is she," we hear the voice ask.

"And you are?" Paul responds.

Sil's eyes roll. She knows who it is. Jxsiga giggles.

"I know she's here."

We hear Paul say, "Hey!" and are joined a moment later by a light brown-skinned young man.

"There you are, baby," he says to Sil, a very loving look coming over his face. "I couldn't wait for your call. You know, what we …"

Paul takes him by the arm, and the young man rips it free, turning on him with fists balled. Paul holds his hands up and takes a step back.

"You touch me again, and I'll knock your ass out." He turns his attention to Sil. "Baby, something that special only happens once in a lifetime. I know you felt it. Come on with me. I want to take care of you. Let me be your everything."

Sil gives the young man a dour look and shakes her head in disapproval.

"You broke the rules, Anthony."

"There are no rules in love."

"I told you how it works," Sil says. I call you. I meet you. We … enjoy each other. Now you've embarrassed me in front of my fiancé. We're done."

Anthony turns to Paul, "Sorry about your luck, man. She's found better."

"I'm not her fiancée," Paul says.

"Me either, though I am her lover," Jxsiga says.

His eyes turn to me. His face turns to disbelief.

"This Joe Dirt-looking motherfucker? Really?"

My disguise is good.

"You can take the girl out of the trailer park," I say trying to keep a straight face.

His eyes go wide, and his jaw ever so slightly drops.

"You blew it," Sil says. "It could have been fun. But now I know I can't trust you. You should go."

"I know you felt it, too."

"Come on," says Paul, moving toward Anthony.

But Anthony postures up, causing Paul to take a step back.

"I told you, I'll knock you out. Don't test me, motherfucker."

Jxsiga rolls her eyes and stands up.

"Time to go, Anthony," she says, walking over to him.

"Are you tripping, little girl?"

He gives her no more regard, a big mistake.

"Stephanie, baby. He can't give you what I can. I'll give it all to you. Let me take care of you. Let me … hey, get out my face, little girl."

"You leave on your own, or I'll drag your limp carcass out the door and feed you to the squirrels," Jxsiga says.

"Yeah right," he says, bending down presumably to menace her.

Another big mistake. One of Jxsiga's hands grabs his chin; the other his earlobe. Her foot sweeps his legs out from under him. Now prone, she releases her grasp on his chin and slides her arm under his neck. She begins dragging him to the door, Paul stepping quickly out of the way.

"Well, she works fast, doesn't she?" Paul says. "Good thing, too. Don't want to be late for bowling."

Silithes laughs.

I hear the front door open and Anthony protesting.

"Go. Now," we hear Jxsiga say.

"Bitch, I'll …"

Paul's eyes widen, and he runs for the door.

I look over at Sil, who's sharing a concerned look.

"Did he hit her?" I ask, standing and ready to assist.

"No. I think she acquainted him with the pavement."

Chapter 62

Sil takes me to a restaurant down the street – a Japanese place called Naki Migri. The way there was awkward, mostly silence between us. I guess she is reading off my confusion. I'm here where I so needed to be. I'm just not so sure why I needed to be here.

Once in the restaurant, it becomes obvious Sil is a regular. The hostess recognizes her immediately with a "Miss Sil!" We are brought to a booth immediately.

I scoot into my seat. Sil scoots into her seat.

The person behind Sil turns and says, "Excuuuse me."

"Sorry," Sill says back to her. I guess her moving in disturbed them.

After a small pause, Sil asks me, "So you've never had Sushi?"

"Never had reason to eat bait."

"Right."

We are joined by an older oriental lady.

"Sil! So good to see you again. Where are Paul and Jessica?"

Our hostess turns to me with a huge grin.

"They eat so much. I've never seen anyone eat so much."

"That's because it's so good, Hideko."

"Thank you. So, large sake for you, Sil? And for you?"

"Ice tea, sweet, please."

Sil makes some scribbles on a few pieces of paper and hands them to Hideko.

"Oh," Hideko says after looking at them, "You are going to do the uni? I will prepare it personally."

Sil appears animated at that statement and reaches out to take Hideko's hand.

"Thank you, Hideko. That would be an honor."

Hideko starts to leave, but the lady at the table behind us speaks out.

"Excuuuse me. My water is getting low, can you get our server to actually give us some service. We are paying customers, too."

"Oh, yes ma'am," Hideko says, moving to their table. "I will see to it personally."

She scurries off, and that leaves Sil and me alone. We sit there in silence for a few moments, neither of us sure what to say. Finally, Sil breaks the silence.

"So, are you dumping me?"

Why is everyone asking me that damn question?

I look at her, seriously. My poker face works two ways – in this case, it works the way I need it to – I'm telling the truth.

"I don't think so. Truth is, I'm not sure why I took this risk. Just a feeling … like I'm going to lose you or something."

"Don't think so. So it's on the table?"

Hideko returns with our drinks just in time to bail me out.

"The chefs are working on your order."

She turns to go but is stopped by the loud voice of the lady behind us.

"Excuse me, waitress. We will require our check."

"Yes, ma'am."

Hideko leaves, and I'm back under Sil's cross-examination.

"This is about the sex tape, right? I told you we would be affectionate. So you got an eyeful?"

I did. And now is not the time to go on the offensive or the defensive about it. I look away from her to collect myself more than anything.

"What? Can't look at me now? Do you imagine me with his dick in my mouth?"

I'm going to reply, but the lady behind us beats me to it, swiveling around to confront Sil.

"Excuuuse me. Do you mind? We are at a restaurant."

Sil smiles at her demurely. "Actually, no I don't mind doing that at all. It's rather fun. What I do mind is if some little dribbles get away and stain my blouse. Especially if it's a nice silk one, like the one I'm wearing. Or even worse if he…"

The lady gasps.

"You get the idea. Thanks for asking."

Sil turns away from the lady and back to me.

"No, Sil, I wasn't imagining that, and I didn't get far enough into the tape to even see that. I was just collecting myself so my reply would be more even keel. You might want to consider that approach yourself."

Her eyes are boring holes into me, but not in a bad way. She's thinking, considering in that way she does.

"Crap. I flew off the handle again, didn't I?"

"Maybe a little."

She pours some sake and shoots it down, then gives me a halfish smile.

"Sorry. I just don't want to lose you, or them. And I don't really feel I did anything wrong. We were celebrating like we do. You know."

"I'm learning. Listen …"

A server and Hideko descend upon us with a mountain of various white rice covered roll-looking things. They place the trays on our table, and Hideko presents a small plate with three green tube-like things with a spongy orange substance atop them.

"Uni. Please tell me what you think, Miss Sil."

Sil pulls out some chopsticks, breaks them in two then deftly plucks up the strange roll and eats it whole. Her face lights up.

"That is so fresh. Delicious. Thank you, Hideko."

Hideko turns to me. It's my turn I guess. I look for my chopsticks.

"He's never had sushi. We're going to start him slowly."

"Ahh," says Hideko. "Try this one; it's very good."

Sil's chopsticks go into motion, and she grabs up the roll.

"Open up, Arthur."

I prepare myself for the experience of eating bait and open my mouth. It's not bad. Not bad at all. Not fishy and kind of sweet and crunchy. Maybe I can do this?

"That's the Ohio roll. Fried catfish, snow crab, and cucumber," Sil says.

"You enjoy," Hideko adds, leaving us to ourselves again.

Maybe I will. If not anything else, having a mouthful of these rolls will allow for some time to think about what to say.

After another round of sake, I can tell Sil is ready to get back on topic.

"Again, I'm sorry if I'm a little wound up. But you have been putting out a pretty strange vibe; real prickly. So, I have one very important question."

She's looking at me so intently, I'm sure trying to read me. That's funny. I'm an open book.

"Okay."

"Do you still love me?"

"Yeah. I must, or I wouldn't be here."

"Then we can work through whatever. So how much of the tape did you see? Oh, try this one," she says, pointing to another roll.

"Less than ten seconds' worth, plus a hacked audio thing."

Sil rolls her eyes, and the sneer of hers appears.

"I can't believe I fell for that. You know I was freaking out, right?"

What do you say to that – nothing.

"Only ten seconds? Hope it was one of the good parts."

"It left a mark, Sil. Obviously. Seeing you ride his face, it touched all the wrong nerves."

"Oh. My. God," comes the lady's voice from behind us.

I thought I kept it down; maybe not enough. Sil's eyes roll again.

"Well, when it comes to the riding I am a ..."

Sil's statement is interrupted by the lady behind us getting up and the booth shoving forward. She had to mean to do that. The lady steps over to our table and looks at me with disdain.

"Your girlfriend is a slut and is lacking in moral fiber. You can do better."

She looks us over. She stares at me. "Well, maybe not. You, sir, can at least try to do better. You should."

Her husband moves on, not wanting to be involved.

"Hmmph," she says to us as if that says everything and begins to follow her husband.

Actually, it kind of does.

"What do you consider moral fiber?" Sil says, stopping the lady.

She turns around and says to Sil, "When is the last time you have been in church?"

"When's the last time you've been judged by a holy sword of the Order of Light?"

I chuckle.

"You need help," the lady says, and leaves.

Sil and I look at each other and smile. She pops down another roll. I realize exactly how much she's eaten. Hideko was right.

"We can work through this," Sil says.

∴

We leave the restaurant and walk back to Paul's place, their place, hand in hand. Words are at a minimum. After the discussion over sushi, there wasn't a lot left to be said. We have feelings, and matters are a bit strange for me.

And really good for her.

We make it to the stoop of Paul's unit, and I have no idea if anyone is home. She's looking in my eyes in that expectant way.

"Thanks, Sil."

"Ahh, so this is the awkward moment where the boy isn't sure about giving the girl a kiss goodnight?"

"I should get back to the bunker."
"No, you should come inside."
She takes me by the hand and turns to put her key in the lock.
I could say no. But why?

Chapter 63

There's something majestic about having Sil astride me. She's still in human form, but I can imagine her wings unfurling like they do when she climaxes or is feeling a little dominant. I see her head rock back, and I enjoy it, too, thanks to what she refers to as the succubus self-defense mechanism: a strong neuromantic pulse that encourages the partner to do the same when she climaxes.

She wanted her morning satisfaction, and I'm not going to deny her that.

It is a great way to meet the morning.

She slides off me to my side, her arms still wrapping around me.

"If Jxsiga asks, we had our morning happy. It's like religion here in our house."

The statement, "our house," is not lost on me.

"Would she be checking?"

"Probably not, but she still might decide to share some happiness of her own. If she decides to give me a nice rub, or something more, just know that it's pretty usual. Every morning is greeted with a warm celebration. Just sometimes Jex likes to perform in front of Paul. And maybe she might want to do the same in front of you."

I have no words. This is definitely succubus stuff.

"Oh, don't be that way," she says reading my reaction. "It's not like it's mind control, or manipulation or anything bad, she just … overshares sometimes."

"She overshares? By your definition?"

I am graced with a genuine Silithes smile. She knows I know her.

"Both Paul and I prefer things a little more private, but she just likes to show off sometimes. It's no big thing. It makes her happy, and it's fun to watch. She's quite talented, you know. And if you can believe this, sometimes a little goofy when she really lets her hair down."

I try to summon a smile. I do not see Jex as goofy, but the other parts I can believe.

"So I may have to watch her … and you … you know."

"More like watch her please me. I'll just kick back and enjoy. But hopefully, she'll get that we've already taken care of business, and it will just be hugs and kisses."

"Yeah."

She puts her hand on my cheek.

"You saw the video. You know we share. I'm just trying to prepare you for what might be."

I take a deep breath. I have questions.

"So, with Paul, how serious are you two?"

She smiles at me knowingly.

"You know I am very much closer to Jxsiga, right? But Paul … it started casually… fun and giggles. It's hard not to have feelings for him. He's very open. He cares. He feels."

She stares into my eyes.

"So?"

"I have feelings for him. I think he does for me, too. He is amazing, and I mean that more than just sexually. But his heart belongs to Jex. Mine belongs to you. You're my one."

I smile back, genuinely, because I feel she means what she's saying. And while her admitting she has feelings for him has consequences, it also means she's not just using him just for her gratification. Or he using her; after all, they can tell a lot with just a kiss.

She looks at me seriously.

"Hey, try to be a little nicer with him by the way. You were a little on the prickly side last evening."

That's news to me. But, then again, everyone kept asking me if I was dumping Sil, so maybe I was putting on airs I'm not aware of.

"Sure, sorry if I was … prickly."

∴

"There they are," rings out Jxsiga's happy voice.

She trots across the living room and wraps Sil in a hug. Her eyes move over to me.

"I'm so glad you spent the night. We were worried you were going to dump her last night."

Sil breaks the hug and holds Jxsiga out at arm's distance.

"That's not happening, and we greeted the morning appropriately, before you get any ideas."

Jxsiga's eyes are all on me when she says, "I am always so full of ideas."

Then she turns back to Sil and slides back into a hug. Followed by a kiss that Sil cuts off short. Meaning, they'd still be at it if she didn't.

Paul's voice breaks the moment.

"Ladies. We need doughnuts. Put more clothes on and go get us some."

Jxsiga looks over at Paul.

"Doughnuts?"

The look he returns is deadly serious.

They stand there staring at each other for a moment until Jxsiga replies, "Let's get dressed, Silithes, we need to get doughnuts."

Sil shrugs, leaves Jxsiga, and kisses me on the cheek.

"Remember, don't be prickly" is her passing advice to me as she bounds upstairs to her room.

"You drink coffee?" Paul asks me from the kitchen.

"Yeah."

"There's a fresh pot. Come out to the patio after you get yours."

Jxsiga stops on the way to their bedroom and looks at Paul with a patented "The Lady" glare of intimidation.

"Be nice, please. We don't want to…"

"Jexi, just get the damn doughnuts and leave us to talk."

I'm graced with a raise of the eyebrow from Jxsiga before she disappears into their bedroom. Paul stalks off to the patio area.

Well, apparently, I was a little prickly last night.

Chapter 64

Shenyang, Liaoning Province, China

The disorientation of interdimensional travel behind him, Ehzig notices the sounds of wailing and pain coming from behind him.

Apparently, Garaung was right – the engineers did overpromise their ability to deliver, and the third row got cut off. Now there's nothing to do but listen to the wails of the Vetisghar, Hjuulak, Hjuul, and spiders that were unfortunate enough to have been partially severed during the entry.

Separation of the cubicles and extraction takes time. Ehzig waits patiently for his block to be opened. When it is opened, he scoots out and takes to the floor. He looks around and sees the first cell grid has been emptied and the group of other Upper Dzemond has begun to congregate and check their command tablets for troop assignments.

That makes him think to check his. He has six assigned to him – five Vetisghar and one named Hjuulak, P'Melk.

He's pleased he, at least, has one named in his group. That implies some experience. He knows better than to call them immediately. Most of them were probably in the third row, meaning they're damaged goods unless they knew enough to cram themselves against the front of their cell.

He walks toward the other Baalig, V'dvel, and other races that are obviously there as command or elite troops. But he doesn't get too far before the laughter starts.

They see his armor of shame. He is marked, marked for death by the emperor himself. Regardless of that recognition, he pushes himself ahead, knowing he has some command and, therefore, some status.

A large, fat Baalig takes notice of him and smiles wickedly.

Once Ehzig is near them, the Baalig speaks.

"You. Child with the armor of shame, come polish my boots."

There's only one response that won't lead to humiliation or future shaming.

"Polish your own boots."

The fat Baalig moves forward into Ehzig's personal space.

"Do as you are told," he says, menace dripping from his voice.

But Ehzig knows otherwise. If he gives in now, then he'll set a precedent. That's how it works.

"Clean them yourself. And jerk your own cock, because we both know where this is going. If you don't like it, assert yourself. But don't be surprised if I cripple you."

The statement enrages the fat Baalig.

"You are a child! I will break you and make you my happy point of satisfaction!"

Ehzig, who just stood before his entire family and albeit lost, was not worried about this one Baalig testing him, especially after being healed.

"No, you won't."

The fat Baalig screams and lunges toward him. It was so predictable. Ehzig moves to the side and easily sweeps out his feet with his tail.

The fat Baalig attempts to scramble to his feet, but Ehzig is already flanking him, ready to deliver the blow.

"This will stop now," yells a large human in the Dzemond language.

Ehzig immediately understands this is really no human, and it is most likely the commanding officer, so he steps back.

The fat Baalig scrambles to his feet and turns to the human.

"This is no longer professional. I claim personal differences. He is mine."

"Mevrlid, would you please set your personal issues aside until such time I might issue my commands? Or will you and I have personal differences?"

"Never that, sir. But this whelp does not know his place."

Ehzig says nothing but holds attention.

The human walks toward Ehzig and slaps him.

"He understands the chain of command," the human says. "This one does not fall under your authority. He is under mine."

The human that is not a human locks eyes with Ehzig then turns to those around them.

"My captains, follow me. I have direction for you."

∴

The command brief finished, and Ehzig turns to leave the room and brief his charges. But he is stopped by Commander Garaung's loud words.

"Stay, Arkrenduur."

Ehzig does as told.

The commander walks right up to his face.

"You have the gift boy, don't you? The gift of your blood?"

Ehzig meets the commander's eyes.

"That's more for others to say. But, yes, physical combat comes easily to me."

"Like your mother. Like some others in your line. Not your father, though. Zarda fights like a thug, not a trained warrior."

"You knew him?"

"Knew? He met his fate? You?"

"Yes, he met his fate. I struck the blow, but the emperor put him to his knees."

"We do hate our parents, don't we?"

Ehzig takes in that statement, not sure how to respond.

"True. But you and yours don't seem to hold the same or not as much."

"We made arrangements. Father would abdicate the governance of our house to me, publicly, and I would allow him to live."

"And," Ehzig says back with a smile.

"He would allow me to live. He is old as Helterezen's dirt, but not one to trifle with. We agreed the house would be run by me with him as my advisor. I could ask for no better advisor. Aggressions and humiliations are no more between us. We ... coexist for the betterment of the house. Assuming you have the gift, like your cursed mother, and some before her, I am telling you not to kill Mevrlid. He has singled you out as weak and someone to build his reputation upon."

Ehzig looks at his commander with disbelief.

"You can't be serious?"

He smiles at Ehzig and holds his arms out in the casual capitulation of the statement.

"I bring him to every invasion event. I know what to expect with him – he follows my orders. He is not the brightest, but he is determined and loyal. Again … I know what to expect of him. He will come for you. Hurt him, cripple him, but do not kill him. We can heal his wounds. But we cannot heal dead."

"Yes, sir," Ehzig says, knowing to say anything else would be folly.

"Good. Now, did my father give you one of these?"

He pulls a black cylinder from his side like the one given to Ehzig. Ehzig returns the gesture by showing his.

"You know you have been sent to die?"

Ehzig says nothing, but nods in the affirmative.

"Good. Send him back to the black pool where he spawned."

Chapter 65

Preparing my coffee is easy. I take it black. I still take a moment in the kitchen before heading out to the porch to whatever confrontation awaits me. After all, clearer heads prevail.

Sil and Jex took no time getting ready and are out the door with a "Bye!" in unison.

I leave the sanctity of the kitchen and slide the porch door open. Paul is sitting there, looking serious.

"Are they gone?"

"Yeah, just left."

"Good. You and I need to have a talk. I have an issue – with you."

Reacting to a statement like that is easy. I try to bite my tongue. I don't get a chance to respond.

"I get you and Sil have a thing. Or at least she does with you. I've no issues with that. Makes her happy, makes me happy. Now, what I can't tolerate is being made to feel uncomfortable in my own home. I mean … my home. My refuge. I understand you maybe feel whatever about how Silithes and me... how we enjoy all aspects of our company. But for us, it's natural. It's nice and fun and … so very … you get the idea."

His green eyes are boring a hole in me. I close my eyes and turn away. Not out of fear, not out of acquiescence, but just to collect my response.

"Apparently, I've been putting on airs, unaware."

"Really?"

"Yeah really. Apparently, I've been putting off a prickly vibe. For that, I'm sorry. I did not mean to make you feel uncomfortable in your own house. I wouldn't care for that either. Truth is, I'm not even sure why in the hell I'm here. Yeah, there's the video. Yeah, there's the whole, whatever you call how you guys live, sex all over the place thing. But for whatever reason I truly thought if I didn't get my North Carolina redneck ass down here, right now, I'm losing her. And you know the really funny thing?"

He pauses for a moment, trying to read me.

"No, what?"

"Everyone keeps asking me if I'm going to dump her. Hell, she even asked me."

Silence follows. He's sitting. I'm standing.

"I didn't mean to make you feel uncomfortable in your own house, Paul. That's just wrong. But I do have a question."

"Thanks. Okay. What's the question?"

"Do you care for her? I mean, do you have feelings for her, or is it just another one of those succubus sex things?"

His stone face breaks into a smile.

"For the record, I am considered an incubus. And … yeah, we've grown close. Nothing like her and Jexi, which by the way, I don't see you having as much of an issue with. And not like my bond with Jexi. But yeah, I care for her. Kind of hard not to, once you get to really know her."

I smile; Sil just admitted feelings for him, too.

"Good news. She cares for you, too, Paul."

"I know."

Durned incubi-succubi and their whole "tell a lot by a kiss and a lot more with a lot more" thing. Of course, he knows.

"Well, call me captain oblivious, Paul. Sorry about that."

"Are we going to be able to coexist?"

"Going to have to, for her. Listen, I don't mean to put on airs. But let's face it. You are what you are. You do what you do. She is what she is, and I've heard how great it is. It's kind of humbling, and I feel out of my element."

"Yeah. I bet. Try this, wrap your head around the fact her feelings are not because of what you do to her, or anything like that. She's into you because she knows you're into her, and you two have done that soul-touching thing a freaking ridiculous and reckless amount of times. That in and of itself is just crazy. You two are … just you two now. She doesn't need you to be an incubus or anything like that – just be yourself. And be there for her."

"Yeah, thanks. It's just out of my comfort zone with others involved."

"Life with the Cubati," he says, as if that answers everything.

We let the silence stand for a moment. I take a sip of my coffee, now lukewarm instead of hot. His explanation actually starts to make sense to me.

"Arthur, if you like, I can stop instigating affection. I mean, I'm not … one of those horny- all-the-time types, if you can believe that. But if she comes asking for attention, I'm not inclined to turn her away. That would be rude."

I remember before all the who's doing who stuff started, I liked Paul. The story of his family and their cruel ways – how he cried; it felt human. He really didn't seem at all what I'd think an incubus would be like.

"Don't do that, Paul. I mean, I'm on the run. You two have something, and it doesn't involve running from The Protectorate. Just … I don't know. Just don't stop on my account. It's not fair to her. It ain't about you or me. It's about her."

"Well, I have bad news then, if it's about her."

His face has that "I know something you don't know" look. That can't be good.

"Would you rather I keep my mouth shut, Arthur?"

I have to think about that for a moment. Sometimes ignorance is bliss.

"Lay it on me."

"You know Silithes so much better than I do. So, what's better than taking pleasure with me or you?"

"Jxsiga?"

"No. Think again."

Oh, damn. It's Znuul's joke.

"Better than me or you is you and me – at the same time. She's going to ask, Arthur. Just giving you a heads-up. Come on, you know this. You have to."

Crapsticks. Crap a brick. Crap … he's right.

Paul is laughing out loud at my reaction.

"Oh, come on, Arthur. Don't panic. I won't be making a grab at you."

Oh, crap, crapping pointy sticks.

"Oh, please. Listen, when that time comes – just focus on her. I mean, that's what she'd want anyway. She would just want to lean back and be adored by us. Now, Jexi – she's more of a pleaser. But that's not on the table – yet."

"Yet?"

"Another thing you need to know: Jexi's out to get you, Arthur. She thinks, if we're all sharing, then you won't bail on Silithes out of jealousy. It's kind of like why she hooked Silithes and me up, to get the drama out of the way. There is some validity to her thinking – at least from the Cubati mindset."

"Out to get me?"

"She's a planner. So yeah, she has it worked out in her mind. She's going to come in on you and Silithes and insert herself into your affections. It's not a bad plan."

"Except I can lock the door."

Paul points at me in acknowledgment of my counter and nods in the affirmative.

"Your plan works, too. I'll be quiet about it."

"Really? To Jxsiga? The one who broke your curse? Your one true love?"

"Yeah her. She's not right all the time. No one is. I love reminding her of that. She needs it, unfortunately. She's great, but everything is always on her terms and always right now. Well, not everything. Not me, always. Not you."

I chuckle for a moment.

"Yeah, not you. That's BS."

To his credit, he laughs that off.

"Yeah, most likely true. I am weak to her. And – you know – I love her. So, you and I? We're okay?"

"Yeah, Paul. Just maybe not okay on the let's both pleasure Sil thing."

His turn to chuckle.

"I promise I won't raise the matter, Arthur."

But it's Sil pushing the matter that is the real thing.

"Thanks, Paul."

"I know you don't get this, but I understand where you're coming from. All my friends are human – quite a few of them in committed relationships. How we are, yeah, it's not what you're accustomed to and, really, I understand. But you're not seeing a human girl. Silithes is a succubus and quite a specimen, too. You know what it means. You know what she needs. More than anything, though, you know her. So…"

"So I need to buck up."

"That's putting it harshly, but, yeah."

I look away considering the truth set before me and take a gulp of my now-almost-cold coffee. I hope my smile lends some understanding.

"Paul, I'll do the best I can."

We let the silence stand between us for a while. But it can only stand so long.

"Looks like it's going to be a nice day," Paul offers.

I take it in; he's right.

"Yeah."

The sound of the door opening distracts us.

"Hey, boys! Doughnuts," yells Jxsiga.

Chapter 66

Chocolate cream-filled has always been my favorite. We're all enjoying the fried, sugary goodness as Paul makes more coffee.

"So you two are all good now?" Jxsiga asks.

The look in her eyes as she eats the doughnut suggests I might be next on the menu.

"We're good, Jexi," Paul responds for us.

That gets a big smile from Miss Silithes no one could miss. She even sidles up to me, putting an arm around my waist.

We all take each other in, and I feel peace amongst us. Jex wraps herself around Sil, and we're now officially a unit.

Strange in how it feels almost normal, for a moment.

But the kicking in of the front door removes any feeling of normalcy. We all spin around to see two men in hoodies with strange weapons enter.

"Thoop! Thoop!" is the sound of the weapons followed by their hideous cackling.

Jex holds up the doughnut box, catching one of the projectiles. Sil is struck on the chest and immediately tears off her shirt. Jex throws the box back at them, and Sil follows in kind with her wadded shirt.

I recognize them from Orlando. I hit the deck and hear the crashing of the glass porch sliding doors. I hear more "thoops" and then hear the explosions around me as the doughnut box and shirt, along with other explosives that missed their target, detonate.

Using explosives in a confined area isn't a smart move. I look up to see it's taken our attackers off their feet, too, and stunned them as well as us.

Partially deafened, I reach to Vets' sigil and dismiss her. Then as fast as I can, I call her back. She ripples into appearance and needs no instruction. She turns to our attackers, and I hear another "thoop, thoop."

Two green globs on the breastplate of her armor, Vets dives into the attacker that shot them at her, tackling him to the ground. There's a moment of struggling, followed by the explosions off her chest, throwing her into the air and rendering the attacker still.

I roll over and grab Yayne's box from the corner. Looking up, I see Jxsiga in acrobatic moves keeping herself at a distance from the slicing knives of the hoodie guys. It looks like she's taken a cut on the cheek. I take that moment to re-call Sheyliene.

A bare-chested Silithes, slams one of them with a bludgeoning strike, then spins out of range taking the center of the room, back to back with Jxsiga

I summon Sheyliene. She appears before me.

"Kill these bastards!"

She immediately goes into huntress mode, and the bow unfolds into her hands. Arrows fly immediately, taking two aggressors to the ground. Quickly she's over to Jex now, flanking a standing intruder.

I look over to my left and see Paul leaving the kitchen to engage the fray. Like a blur, Sil slams into him, blocking him from the shot that was intended for him.

She rocks back. I hear the hoodie freak cackle in glee. I see a fist-size hole in Sil's chest as she falls backward rubber-legged to the floor.

My heart stops.

I jump up, Yayne in hand, leaping over the knocked-over dining room table and cleave off the hand that shot Sil. He's not cackling anymore. A silver arrow blows through his head, and I'm pretty sure he's not doing anything anymore.

"Silithes! No," Paul cries out.

His face is sorrow and disbelief. Silithes is going into shock, her mouth moving but nothing coming out because of the hole in her chest. Her eyes are wide in fear.

Paul growls, and I step back. With a little too much ease, he tears a wooden leg off the dining room table and screams, "You!"

Just like that, he's on the dead, missing-hand hoodie guy, beating him into a pulp, growling and spouting out what must be curses in the Dzemond language.

"Oh no. Silithes," Jxsiga says, now recognizing the situation.

Sheyliene is stalking the living room in that eerie focused, calm way of hers when she's in killing mode, using extra arrows to ensure that the hooded freaks stay down.

I slowly turn back to Silithes. The world feels like it's stopped.

The words, "Oh God," slip from my mouth as I look at her.

Her lips are quivering. Her eyes roll back and her head slacks.

The sound of Paul's cursing and continued beating of the hoodie guy seems to mute. Everything feels like it's gone to this eerie slow motion. Then the realization sets in:

Oh my God. I've lost her.

MORE?

As independent authors we don't have the luxury of a big publishing house marketing department. In fact, in the case of this hobbyist writer, there's only me.

And you.

Consider taking some time and leaving a review. It doesn't have to be clever, lengthy, or something that sounds like a college professor's thesis. It's just got to be honest and from you.

Reviews help. They help by showing numbers of readers, they help by informing potential readers of what to expect and they help this writer's motivation.

Because it ain't the money that's keeping this keyboard clicking.

So if you'd like to see more of my work, _or any other independent author_ trying to find their way - give a review.

They make a difference. And so do you.